"So," Ta
"what's the on

Michael looked at her. "In the battle of good and evil," he said, "evil is stronger, and it wins."

She raised an eyebrow. "Interesting. Is your series protagonist likable, sympathetic?"

"He's a brutal, sadistic serial killer," Michael answered. "And you're going to love him."

Taylor pursed her lips, stared down at the manuscript, and let out a long sigh. "That's a tall order, Mr. Schiftmann. Usually the bad guy loses, and that makes people feel good. Affirms their moral view of life."

"This book's going to change their moral view of life."

"Hmm," she said. "Again, tall order."

"Give it a try," he said, motioning toward the manuscript. "It works."

BY BLOOD WRITTEN

By Steven Womack

By Blood Written
Dirty Money
Murder Manual
Chain of Fools
Way Past Dead
Torch Town Boogie
The Software Bomb
Dead Folks' Blues
Smash Cut
Murphy's Fault

STEVEN WOMACK

BY BLOOD WRITTEN

HARPER

An Imprint of HarperCollinsPublishers

By Blood Written was published in a slightly different form in 2005 by Severn House Publishers Ltd, in the United States and England.

This is a work of fiction. Names, characters, places, and incidents are drawn from the author's imagination or are used fictitiously and are not to be construed as real. Any resemblance to actual events, locales, organizations, or persons, living or dead, is entirely coincidental.

HARPER

An Imprint of HarperCollins*Publishers*
10 East 53rd Street
New York, New York 10022-5299

Copyright © 2005 by Steven Womack
ISBN: 978-0-06-113770-9
ISBN-10: 0-06-113770-7

First Harper paperback printing: November 2007

HarperCollins® and Harper® are registered trademarks of HarperCollins Publishers.

Printed in the United States of America

Visit Harper paperbacks on the World Wide Web
at www.harpercollins.com

10 9 8 7 6 5 4 3 2 1

Acknowledgments

Books are rarely written in a vacuum; this one is no exception. Without the help of a number of people, this book could neither have been written nor come to life in published form. With your indulgence, I'd like to thank a few people who were particularly responsible for helping this book see the light of day.

First of all, I'd like to thank Lieutenant (retired) Tommy Jacobs of the Metro Nashville Police Department's Murder Squad, who inspired this novel one afternoon just over a decade ago when he called me at home to tell me I'd been accused of committing a particularly grisly double murder. The thought of a writer committing murder as a form of research grew into this book. I'd also like to thank him for not taking the accusation seriously.

Collier Goodlett, a brilliant and overworked Assistant Public Defender in Tennessee's Nineteenth Judicial District, became my legal guru and advisor for this book. He patiently and graciously fielded dozens of phone calls and provided enormous help. If the legal aspects of this novel and the courtroom scenes ring with any authenticity, it is because of him. If there are any mistakes, they are mine alone.

Otto Penzler, a legend in the mystery world in more aspects than I have room to depict here, was the first person to see any merit in this story after a number of people had passed on it. I'm grateful for his help in getting this novel into print.

Sarah Durand, my editor at Avon, was supportive and insightful and constructive in every way; in short, the ideal editor. As Rick said to Louie, I hope this is the beginning of a beautiful friendship.

Finally, I'm incredibly grateful and appreciative of my wife, Alana, and our two daughters, Isabel and Ava, for their love, support, and endless patience in meeting the challenges of living with a writer.

—SW

BY
BLOOD
WRITTEN

PART I

THE TOUR

CHAPTER 1

Saturday night, Manhattan

She fought the urge to scream; after all, there were people downstairs.

The blaring music—loud, driving retro punk—and the relentless din of party chatter probably would have covered her cries, but some last, long-buried remnant of propriety wouldn't allow her to let loose.

On his back, underneath her straddled legs, gazing up as she shook and trembled, he knew she was barely holding it in. He felt her thighs tighten, the quadriceps hardening, breath quickening. Her eyes closed tightly, the squint deepening into furrows that would, in another decade or so, be crow's feet. Her blond hair—long, straight, expensively coiffed—danced from side to side as the air in her lungs compressed with the constricting of her chest. She leaned forward and dug her fingernails into his chest, the sharp, manicured edges digging through the first layers of skin and stopping just short of bloodletting.

He smiled at the pain and thrust upward into her. She was delicious, exquisite, all the more intense thanks to the lines of coke they'd done a half hour earlier. She'd matched him push for push, rhythm for rhythm, until the energy swept over her like the tides that foretold a hurricane's leading edge. And when the storm finally broke, when the air burst out of her lungs like an explosion, there was only the suppressed yelp of her release and then collapse.

She lay on him, exhausted, sliding against him in their sweat. *Like posting*, he thought. *Like steeplechasing . . .*

He reached behind her, around the small of her back and below, and dug his fingers into the soft flesh of her hips.

It was his turn now.

He pushed her up then pulled her down, arching his back, jamming himself into her rhythmically, in time with the pulsing energy that was growing within him. Despite her enervation, she struggled to match his pace, to help him find his center. She wanted that, realized she wanted that even more than her own release, and she had wanted release more than anything, she thought. She smiled as she felt his muscles tighten below her.

Once he let go and allowed himself to float free, his moment came as it always did.

When he decided it would.

They rested there a full ten minutes without speaking. She felt herself drift in and out, in that sweet, postcoital languorousness that she had so seldom known. The floor beneath them vibrated with the pounding bass and the frenzied dancing of the party downstairs.

"God," she murmured sleepily. "That was great."

He moaned softly in agreement.

"How do you do it?"

"Do what?" he whispered.

"You know," she said, her voice rising shyly. "You know, go so long . . ."

He smiled. "I like to make it last."

She nuzzled into him, her hair draping over his face, tickling his nose. They were still locked together.

"I like it that you like to make it last."

He shifted under her, moved his arm to wipe her hair out of his face. "Should we get back to the party?" he asked. "We don't want to appear unsociable."

She giggled. "What? You think they haven't already noticed?"

"Probably. Why don't we get dressed anyway?" It was not a question, although she didn't realize it at the moment. She pressed her palms into his chest and eased herself back into a sitting position.

"God," she whispered. "I could almost use a shower, I'm so—"

He brought his hand up from between them. The fingertips were wet, red.

"Oh no!" she burst out. "I'm so sorry! I can't believe this! I'm not supposed to start until tomorrow. Goddamn it, this is so embarrassing."

She turned her head, self-conscious and awkward now, and started to jerk away from him. He felt himself sliding out of her and decided this was not the way he wanted to end it. He grabbed her by the waist and locked her down.

"Hey," he said. "It's no big deal. Really. Doesn't bother me at all."

With his right hand, he touched her chin and pushed it softly, until she faced him again. The effort left a red smudge on the side of her face.

"It doesn't matter," he said gently. "Don't worry about it, see?"

He slid his right hand down his belly, to where the two of them were joined. When he pulled the hand back, it was bright red. He drew a coppery, crimson line down the middle of her sternum, between her breasts, the width of two of his fingers, down to her navel. Then he curled his torso toward her and gently, sweetly, ran his tongue up her chest. He nuzzled her breasts, daubing the wet red over them. When he pulled away, there were sanguineous liquid smears on his lips, his chin, the end of his nose.

"See, no big deal," he said softly. "It's natural. Just a part of you."

Her eyes started to fill and she let herself fall forward into his arms, pressing him down onto the bed.

"God," she whispered. "You're so special."

He stared at the ceiling, his arms loosely around her. "I know," he mouthed silently. "I know."

He had almost drifted off when the pounding started. He came up out of the netherworld between slumber and wakefulness to the spraying hiss of water against tile punctuated by the bass of someone slapping a hollow-core door open-palmed.

"Yeah, hold on," he yelled, half asleep. He grabbed a robe and threw it on. How long had he been out?

He cracked the door of the darkened bedroom and stared out sleepily. The woman on the other side of the door was at least six inches shorter and seventy pounds lighter than he, but her irritation seemed to fill the space around her. Her hands were on her hips, petulance on her face.

"Well?" she said. "I'm really annoyed with you."

He looked down, feigning embarrassment. "Taylor, I'm sorry. I didn't mean to—"

"Looks like she wore you out."

"We were just—" he stammered. "Things just got out of—"

"Don't explain. I don't want the details. Your guests are wondering if you're going to be back down this evening. This party is, after all, for you."

He grinned and shook his head, throwing a long shank of hair back off his forehead. "Guess you caught me, babe."

"Michael, who *is* she?"

Michael Schiftmann, in whose honor the party downstairs was being held and over which control was rapidly being lost, shrugged. "I don't know. She told me, but I forgot. At least I think she told me."

"How long is she going to stay in my shower?" Taylor Robinson demanded. "She's not moving in, is she?"

"Calm down, sweetheart, I'll get rid of her. We'll be down in a few minutes."

"See that you do. Jesus, Michael, Audrey Carlisle's downstairs. Give a little thought to your career."

Michael smiled at her, his white, even teeth almost glowing in the dim light. "If I didn't know better," he murmured, "I'd think you were jealous."

Taylor's jaw tensed. "Don't be silly," she snapped. She squinted and stared intently into the shadows that surrounded Michael's face. "What's that on your chin?"

He tucked his chin into his chest and slid behind the door. "Nothing," he said. "Taylor, you'd better, uh—"

"Better what?"

"You might want to bring me a set of sheets."

Taylor sighed. "That bad, huh? Okay, I'll change them."

"No," Michael interjected. "No. I'll do it."

Taylor laughed. "Well, at least you haven't gotten so swell-headed you can't clean up after yourself."

"C'mon, give me a break. I was just having a little fun. Maybe it got out of hand."

Taylor turned toward the linen closet at the end of the hall. "I guess you're entitled to it," she said as she walked away. "After all, it's not every day you finally get a book on the *Times* best-seller list."

"And you know what they say, don't you?" Michael called after her. Behind him, from the bathroom, the water stopped.

Taylor stopped and turned, facing him. "What?"

Michael grinned. "You never forget your first time."

CHAPTER 2

"I never thought I'd say this, but thank God it's so cold," Detective Gary Gilley said as he shivered in the frigid wind of a February night. "Imagine the stink if this was July."

Lieutenant Max Bransford fumbled with his disposable butane lighter, cupped his hands around it, and struggled to light his thirty-eighth Marlboro of the day. Bransford compulsively tracked his daily cigarette intake. Each week, he tried to lower his average in a now months-long attempt to cut down. He braced himself against the wind that had roared out of Canada days earlier from near the Arctic Circle, swept through the Great Plains and Texas, then circled as it always seemed to through the mid-South on its way up the East Coast. Nashville, Tennessee was three degrees colder tonight than Toronto.

Bransford leaned against the side of the building and shielded the lighter. After a few seconds, he managed to get the end of the cigarette lit. He and Gilley were ten feet beyond the yellow crime-scene tape, a safe enough distance not to contaminate the scene with ashes.

"I wish them son of a bitches would get here," Bransford griped. "My wife's going to have my ass if I don't get home soon."

"That's not a problem I have very often," Gilley said. "Given that my wife wants as little of my ass as possible. What the hell . . . Feeling's mutual, I guess."

Bransford looked at his watch. "What time did they leave?"

"Hell, I don't know. I just know what time we called them. They've had time to get here. It ain't but a couple of hours to Chattanooga even if you're not in a hurry."

"Maybe that's it," Bransford said. "Maybe they ain't in a hurry."

"Would you be?" Gilley asked offhandedly. He turned back toward the small building, to the doorway where a uniformed officer stood guard blocking the entrance from the news media and curious onlookers.

Irv Stover, the paunchy, late middle-aged forensic investigator from the medical examiner's office, exited the building. He wore an ill-fitting white shirt, a stained tie, and a down ski parka that made him look like Alfred Hitchcock doing a clumsy imitation of the Michelin tire man. He strained and managed to step clumsily over the crime-scene tape without tearing it, then approached the two detectives and hunched his shoulders against the wind.

"We can tag 'em and bag 'em as soon as those Hamilton County boys get a look. Where the hell are they?"

"Beats the shit out of me," Gilley said.

"Wish they'd get here," Stover said. "There's a movie on Showtime tonight I want to catch."

Behind the three men, the blinking neon sign above the doorway flashed EXOTICA TANS over and over in the deepening night.

"That damn thing's giving me a headache, Gary," Bransford said, turning away from the vibrant hot-pink, blue, and red neon. "Reach in there and turn it off, will you?"

Just then, a white and blue squad car with the markings of the Hamilton County Sheriff's Department pulled into the parking lot. It came to a stop, and a large man in a gray suit, with a blue ski parka as an overcoat, exited the car.

"Hey, Hint," Bransford called.

"Hey, Max," the man called back. "Sorry we're late. There's a helluva wreck on I–24 down around Manchester."

"Howard," Bransford said, motioning, "this is Detective Gary Gilley, Metro Murder Squad. Gary, meet Sergeant Howard Hinton, Chattanooga Homicide."

The two homicide investigators shook hands as Hinton gazed at the crime-scene tape flapping slowly in the icy wind.

"So where's the party?" he asked.

Bransford motioned with his head toward the crime-scene tape.

Hinton sighed. "Let's get it over with."

Irv Stover reached into the large side pocket of his ski parka and extracted a plastic bag. "Here," he said. "You'll need these."

The Hamilton County Sheriff's Department detective opened the small bag and pulled out a pair of slip-on disposable booties and latex gloves. Stover turned, walked back toward the white ME's van as Bransford, Gilley, and Hinton stepped wearily over the crime-scene tape and into the building where the two slaughtered girls lay. They walked through the tiny reception area with the cheap, office furniture warehouse desk and tacky green vinyl sofa, then down a narrow hallway lined with cheap paneling, their gloved hands clasped behind them to avoid inadvertently touching anything. A pasty-faced investigator carrying a large strobe-equipped Nikon and a heavy camera bag backed out of a door to their right. There wasn't enough room in the dimly lit hallway for the men to pass each other. The crime-scene tech took three steps backward to make room for the three detectives.

"You guys about finished?" Bransford asked.

"Yeah," the tech answered. "Just wrapping up here."

Bransford turned to Hinton. "This's the first one you come to. Be careful," he warned. "The floor's still kinda sticky."

"I'll watch it."

The three men stepped single-file into the room, Bransford leading, with Hinton in the middle, and Gilley a couple of steps behind. The room was perhaps twelve by fifteen feet in size, dimly lit and musty. A table with various lotions, oils, and sex toys nestled in one corner. Against the opposite wall, a massage table was covered in a blood-soaked sheet. Sprawled across the sheet was the mangled body of a barely recognizable young woman, her legs spread-eagled over the sides of the table, her ankles bound to the table legs with thick cord. Her arms were splayed out to the sides, her wrists tied to the front two table legs with the same type of cord. Her lips were pulled back over her teeth, frozen in an encrusted, horrific rictus.

Gilley averted his eyes; he'd seen as much of the victim as he needed. Bransford stepped aside, stopping just short of the thickened pool of nearly black blood. Hinton stepped around him and stared.

"She mutilated sexually?" he asked.

"Irv said severe vaginal and anal tearing."

Hinton turned. "Irv?"

Bransford, fatigued, shook his head and rubbed his blood-shot eyes. "Sorry. Irv Stover, the fat guy outside. Forensic investigator from the ME's office."

"He got a probable TOD?"

Bransford nodded. "Eighteen hours at least. Maybe longer."

Hinton turned, squinted. "That means late last night, early this morning. When were the bodies discovered?"

"About five-thirty this afternoon. One of the girls got suspicious when she reported for work and couldn't get in. The lights and the heat had been turned off. She called the manager, who drove over, opened the place up, and found the two girls."

"Hmm, strange," Hinton offered.

"This part of town is pretty deserted late at night. Any potential customers would see the lights off and just keep on going."

"You get a statement from the girl and the manager?"

"Yeah," Gilley answered. "They're clean. We took their statements, sent 'em home."

Hinton turned, gazing at the carnage before them. His thoughts turned briefly to how young the girl was, and how beautiful she must have been. He forced himself back to cop mode, to clear his mind, to observe clinically and record every image.

"Got an ID?"

"One Allison May Matthews, twenty-two years old, student at Middle Tennessee State University. No sheet on her.

Her clothes and purse were in a room down the hall, in a changing room, along with the other girl's stuff. Money still in her purse. Money still in the strongbox up front as well, so it wasn't robbery."

"I could have told you that over the phone," Hinton said. He stared a moment longer at the scene in front of him, remembering the first time he'd ever seen a dead body. There was something about a corpse that just wasn't real, he'd always thought. Maybe it was the strange, skewed angles that lifeless limbs often took; perhaps it was the pallor. Nothing alive ever got that shade of gray. Hinton had depended on that thought to keep him together through some gruesome nights, to disassociate from the horror he'd seen in his life.

"She wasn't a pro," he speculated. "Just picking up a few bucks spending money. Paying her way through school, maybe." Hinton turned and faced Gilley. "Call her family yet?"

"Chaplain's on his way," Gilley answered.

Hinton stared at the wall above the girl. A single block letter—M—was inscribed neatly over the table in a crimson so deep it was nearly black.

Hinton turned. "Let's check out the other one."

Gilley stepped out of the room and down the hall to make room for the other two. "You guys don't mind, I'll take a pass. I've seen enough."

"That bad?" Hinton asked.

"Worse'n the other one," Bransford said, his voice low.

Hinton padded down the hall, the plastic booties sliding on the scuffed linoleum. Bransford followed a few steps behind, then paused as the Chattanooga man stopped at the doorway to the room.

"Jesus," Hinton muttered.

"Yeah," Bransford said. "Looks like the ME's got a head start on the autopsy."

The girl had been gutted like a field-dressed deer, a deep Y-incision down the front of her torso to her navel. The skin was peeled back, her internal organs obviously removed, scrambled, then shoved back in the cavity.

"Guy took souvenirs off this one," Bransford said, staring over Hinton's shoulder into the killing room. "We've searched the whole area, can't find her nipples anywhere."

Hinton gritted his teeth and exhaled sharply through his nostrils to control the waves that he felt rising within him. He forced his eyes to travel up the walls, to where a foot-high letter L had been painted neatly on the wall in blood. He winced slightly, turned to the heavy man blocking his way down the hall, away from the hellish scene.

"The ME'll find 'em," he whispered.

Bransford looked down at the man, confused.

Hinton raised his upper lip in disgust. "They're in her stomach."

The blood seemed to drain from Bransford's face. "You mean—? I mean, how do you know?"

Hinton ignored the question. "You're going to have to leave the two of 'em here," he said, reaching into the pocket of his down ski jacket and pulling out a cell phone.

"For how long?" Bransford demanded.

Hinton extended the short antenna and punched a speed dial code into the phone, which began a series of high-pitched beeps. He turned back to Bransford with the phone to his ear.

"As long as it takes," he said.

"As long as *what* takes?" Bransford asked irritably. "The families are going to want the bodies as soon as the ME finishes with—"

Hinton made a shushing sound and held the cell phone to his ear. "Hank?" he said as a voice on the other end crackled with static.

"Hank, this is Howard Hinton, Hamilton County, Tennessee, Sheriff's Department, Homicide Squad. You need to book a flight to Nashville ASAP. We got two more for you."

CHAPTER 3

Late Saturday night, Manhattan

Taylor Robinson stepped out of the tiny kitchen just off the main room of her renovated SoHo loft and surveyed her guests. Against the exposed brick wall across from Taylor, her boss, Joan Delaney, leaned forward in rapt conversation with Michael Schiftmann's editor, Brett Silverman. Taylor frowned, hoping that Joan wasn't off on another of her diatribes about the sad state of the publishing industry.

Taylor decided a rescue was in order, so began weaving her way through the crowded room. Eighties dance music played at a volume just below the level that would make conversation difficult, but loud enough to keep the party's energy level up. In one corner, a small group of editorial assistant types—the ink on their honors degrees in English and comparative lit still wet—danced away on that thin line between professionally cool and unprofessionally out-of-control.

Taylor slid gracefully around two men engaged in a heated discussion over the upcoming New York senatorial race, smiling and nodding amiably at them but never losing her momentum so as not to get trapped, and made her way over to the wall.

"Frankly, I don't care what happens to the independent booksellers anymore," Joan spouted, her mass of tangled, dyed black hair vibrating in time to her words. She'd propped her glasses up on her head, a move that Taylor knew meant Joan Delaney was itching to get in a good fight with someone, anyone. It was important to stop her before she started talking with her hands. That, Taylor knew, meant the plug had been pulled.

"The world's changing," Joan shouted over the music, "and the independents are dinosaurs who've refused to adapt to an evolving marketplace. If Amazon.com sells more of my clients' books, then they deserve to beat out the mom-and-pop bookstores."

Good God! Taylor thought. *Brett Silverman's father owns a bookstore in Hartford!*

Taylor sidled up to the two women just as the color was rising in Brett Silverman's pale, drawn face. Brett was in her late thirties, a couple of years older than Taylor, and had been around long enough to gain the kind of confidence necessary to deal with the likes of Joan Delaney, but not long enough to let Joan's over-the-top opinions slide off her without leaving skid marks.

"Hello, ladies," Taylor interjected. "Has anyone seen the star of the evening?"

"Yeah, where is he anyway?" Joan demanded, her already shrill voice rising a notch.

"No," Brett said quietly. "He disappeared a while ago."

"Well, he was upstairs powdering his nose earlier," Taylor said, "and said he'd be down in just a few. I wondered if you'd had a chance to ask him how this latest leg of the tour was going."

Brett turned, plainly relieved to steer the conversation in another direction. "I talked to Carol Gee yesterday afternoon. He drew a good crowd at Davis-Kidd. People lined up for hours."

"How about Birmingham and Atlanta?" Taylor asked. "We were speculating on whether the deep South was ready for Michael Schiftmann."

Brett shrugged her shoulders, her sheer silk blouse sliding loosely across her freckled skin. "Not so good. Atlanta, maybe twenty. The Little Professor in Birmingham was a bust, though. Less than ten . . ."

Taylor grimaced. "Jeez, and the *Times* list was already out."

Brett smiled. "Maybe once you get west of the Hudson, the *New York Times* best-seller list doesn't carry as much weight."

"Bite your tongue, girl!" Joan snapped. "We live and die by The List."

Taylor took Brett's left elbow softly in her right hand. "Maybe we need to make some adjustments before the last leg of the tour kicks off. Why don't you and I step into the kitchen for a moment and make some notes."

"Yes," Brett said, her eyes thanking Taylor in advance. "Good idea."

"Would you excuse us, boss?"

"Sure," Joan said, holding up her empty glass. "If you need anything, just call me. I'll be at the bar."

Taylor leaned in close to Brett as the two strode arm-in-arm across the room toward the kitchen.

"You'll have to excuse her," Taylor said soothingly. "You don't get to be head of one of the top half-dozen literary agencies in the city by being a shrinking violet."

"Shrinking violet's one thing," Brett said as they stepped through the swinging door into the kitchen. "Dragon lady's quite another . . ."

"Yes, she's abrasive and in-your-face and loud and vulgar," Taylor said. "And she also fights like a pit bull for her clients and everyone who works for her."

Brett held up a hand, palm-out, toward Taylor. "Hold on, girlfriend. You're preaching to the choir. Remember? I've been up against her."

"Then you understand why her clients are desperately loyal to her, and so are her employees."

"Yourself included, I guess," Brett commented.

Taylor smiled. "Yes. And now that we're away from the crowds and the music, why don't you tell me what's really going on with Michael's tour."

Brett sighed and leaned against the refrigerator. There was barely room for both women in the cramped kitchen at the same time.

"Well, it's kind of weird, really," Brett said slowly. "I can't quite figure it out, and I'm not sure it's anything serious."

Brett paused, crossed her arms, and lifted an eyebrow. "You've seen how women react to him?"

Taylor pursed her lips, thinking of the situation she'd just encountered upstairs. "Yes," she said. "It's kind of hard to miss."

"I mean, the guy's really good-looking!" Brett said. "Am I right or am I right?"

Taylor nodded. "You're right, Brett. When you're right, you're right."

"And he's funny and he's warm and he's sexy and he's personable and he's smart and—" Brett hesitated for a moment. "*God!* Why can't I find a man like that!"

Taylor laughed softly. "Don't forget, he's very close to rich and famous as well."

"Yes!" Brett exclaimed, her arms flapping out to her sides in an exaggerated gesture. "That, too! I want to say the guy's a hunk, but that word doesn't quite fit, does it?"

Taylor thought for a moment. "No, it really doesn't and I'm not sure why."

"Half the time I want to jump his bones and the other half of the time I want to take him home and make him dinner," Brett said. "Forget that he's one of my authors."

"Don't forget that," Taylor warned. "Never forget that. Don't even think of it."

"I can't help but think of it!" Brett placed her hands on her hips and slouched even harder against the refrigerator door. "Besides, I'm only half serious. I'm a lot of things, my friend, but deluded isn't one of them. I haven't got a chance with him . . ."

"Brett," Taylor said, feeling like she was interrupting a reverie that really wasn't much of her business. "What are you trying to tell me? Out there, you sounded like there was some kind of problem."

"I can't figure it out," Brett said. "Given what an attractive, charming, sexy man he is—"

"Yes?" Taylor asked after a moment.

"How come Carol Gee hates him so much?"

* * *

Audrey Carlisle was the first to spot Michael Schiftmann as he carefully made his way down the spiral staircase from the second floor of Taylor's loft. The black wrought iron bent and squeaked as he descended, but the din of party chatter and music covered what would otherwise have been an annoying sound. Audrey, a short, severe woman in her late fifties who'd been the *Times* main reviewer of crime fiction for more than two decades, had managed to solidify a comfortable and safe niche for herself. The more academic and literary critics stayed away from popular fiction, especially mysteries and crime novels, while the less accomplished reviewers of pop culture novels had been beaten into submission.

Crime fiction was Audrey Carlisle's turf, and she guarded it zealously. She'd made careers and she'd torpedoed them. Writers respected her and feared her, the savvy ones anyway. But in all her years of dealing with writers and authors—the distinction between the two being very real, she thought, authors considering themselves officers while writers were enlisted personnel who worked for a living—she had never encountered anyone like Michael Schiftmann.

He was what she considered a workmanlike writer. Audrey had briefly reviewed his first two novels and found them perfectly competent but less than outstanding. She worked in a couple of paragraphs about his first book in a column that reviewed a dozen other first novels as a favor to an editor. Schiftmann's first book had been published as a mass-market paperback, had spent its customary six weeks on the shelves, and then faded quietly into obscurity.

A year later, Audrey found in the basket of review copies that inundated her office every day Michael Schiftmann's second book. It, too, had been designed, published, and marketed in a completely forgettable fashion and, once again, got a cursory two-paragraph mention in Audrey's regular column. When a third book landed on her desk eight months after the second, it wound up in a canvas bag jammed full of other review copies and bound galleys and shipped off to the VA hospital in Queens.

That was the last Audrey Carlisle heard of Michael Schiftmann for several years. She vaguely remembered seeing more paperbacks come across her desk, but in the avalanche of paper that gushed in and out of her office on an annual basis—enough to stretch from Manhattan to Tokyo every year—she couldn't be completely sure.

Audrey continued to eye Michael as he took the last step off the spiral staircase and was immediately sandwiched between two young women in tight sheath dresses, martini glasses in hand. The pouty-lipped brunette to his right leaned in close as she talked to him, wrapping a curl of hair around her left index finger as she spoke in what Audrey knew was classic body-language come-on. Audrey felt her brow tighten as she watched the two young women fawn over Michael, who seemed to be politely enduring the attention. The short blond in the red vinyl said something apparently considered funny. Michael laughed, and the lines of his jaw shifted under his skin. His teeth were white and straight; Audrey wondered if he'd had them bleached.

She felt vaguely uncomfortable, as if she couldn't figure out which was more alluring; the brunette with the sexy, thick lips or the warmth radiating from Michael Schiftmann as he stood next to her pretending—Audrey hoped—to listen.

Audrey felt her face redden and turned away, heading toward the bar with her empty glass. It was always this way for her at parties. Never successfully forcing herself to be comfortable, she often found herself standing alone with an empty glass in hand. No one ever offered to fill it for her. No man ever chatted her up. The small talk others made with her varied, depending on the place the other person occupied on the publishing feeding chain. Writers clawing their way up the ladder were either sycophantic, deferential, and fawning, or they were too intimidated to talk to her at all. The established authors whose careers were already made condescended to her, patronized her, now that she was no longer essential to their success.

In either case, Audrey realized, none of them really knew her or gave a damn about her. As her turn at the bar came, Audrey decided to have one more Scotch and soda, then call it a night. Parties always brought her down. At least, she thought, that dreadful music had stopped momentarily.

"Excuse me," a masculine voice behind her said. The voice was low, a smooth baritone, confident and relaxed. She turned.

"You're Audrey Carlisle, aren't you?" Michael Schiftmann stared over the top of her glass, making direct eye contact and offering her his right hand.

"Yes," Audrey said. She switched the glass from her right hand to her left, then took his outstretched hand before realizing her palms were wet with condensation from the glass.

"Oh, I'm sorry," Audrey said, pulling her hand away and wiping it on the side of her corduroy jacket.

"No problem," Michael said, smiling. Audrey realized, suddenly, that the black-and-white picture that took up the entire back cover of his latest hardcover didn't do him justice. His blue eyes were clear and penetrating, and the deep lines around his eyes seemed to bring an age and maturity to a face that would have otherwise perhaps been too boyish.

"I was hoping we'd get to meet," Michael said, taking her arm and gently escorting her away from the bar. "Taylor told me she'd invited you. I'm so glad you came."

As the two crossed the large room, the music started up again. Audrey winced.

"Wish they wouldn't play that so loud."

"Here," Michael said loudly, motioning toward the far wall, "we can get away from most of it."

A moment later, Audrey noticed the room's acoustics did seem to direct the music away from the corner where she now found herself in intimate conversation with Michael.

Suddenly it seemed as if they were the only two in the room, that he was devoting his entire focus and attention to her. Audrey Carlisle felt warm and hoped she wasn't too visibly flushed.

"This is probably totally inappropriate," Michael said, leaning in close to her, "but I wanted to thank you for the piece that's coming out tomorrow."

Audrey smiled. "Why would that be inappropriate?"

"I don't know," he said, shrugging slightly, "professional

detachment, that sort of thing. Maybe in this business it's just not cool to admit that you're in someone else's debt."

Audrey had convinced her editor to run a full-length piece on Michael's latest book, *The Fifth Letter*, and to time it with the book's first appearance on The List. As was the paper's practice, she'd sent an advance copy of the review to Brett Silverman as a courtesy, and obviously Michael had been given the chance to read it. It had been the first of Michael's new series that she had reviewed personally. After reading the latest, she did something she had rarely done before in her career: She went back and read the first four installments before writing her review.

"I guess I just wanted you to know how grateful I am," Michael offered.

"You know," Audrey said, sipping her drink, "I almost tracked you down to interview you for the piece, but I was up against deadline, and Brett Silverman said you were somewhere down in South Carolina or someplace like that."

"I did three signings in South Carolina," Michael said. "One in Charleston, one in Hilton Head, and the other in—"

He hesitated a moment. "Jeez, I can't remember. Columbia, maybe? I'm two-thirds of the way through a forty-city tour, and they're all starting to run together."

"I'll bet," Audrey said.

"So," Michael asked, lowering his voice, "what would you have asked me if you'd been able to track me down?"

Audrey took another sip of the drink, this one longer and fuller, and felt the bubble of warmth in her stomach pulsate back and forth as the Scotch hit.

"I think the thing I'm most curious about is the disparity," she said after a few moments.

"Disparity?"

"Yes, the disparity. The incongruousness of someone who seems so nice, so pleasant, so normal, writing novels that clearly reflect an imagination so—"

"So what?" Michael asked.

"Deviant," she said after a moment's hesitation.

Michael's forehead seemed to tense, the blue eyes darken. "What do you mean by that, Audrey?"

"Other writers have written books featuring assassins, hit men, as protagonists. Larry Block, Andrew Vachss, Elmore Leonard, for instance. But your books are the only books I've ever read that authentically, realistically capture the mind of a sociopath, a serial killer, a human being totally without conscience or sense of ethics or morality, and do it in such a way that you're so drawn into the story that before you even realize it, you're cheering for evil."

Michael Schiftmann stared at Audrey Carlisle for a few beats, then looked uncomfortably down at his drink.

"Tell me, Mr. Schiftmann," Audrey said, "do you have a moral compass?"

"In this day and age, how does one even know what a moral compass is?"

"Oh, one can know quite precisely what a moral compass is, and whether one has one . . ."

"I believe that all crime fiction is a morality play," Michael said. "Everyone who writes about crime must confront the duality of and the battle between good and evil. I do it in my own way and with my own insights. I look around me every day and I see that in the battle between good and evil, evil is winning."

Michael stopped for a moment, pausing to sip his own drink. "How else can you explain the resurgence of the Republican right wing?"

Audrey smiled. "Okay, you've got me there. Still, no one's ever seen anything quite like this before. At least not with this degree of popular success. How do you do it?"

Michael smiled back at her, then raised his glass as if about to make a toast. "With the same two tools every writer uses: imagination and research."

CHAPTER 4

Max Bransford couldn't remember the last time the entire Murder Squad of the Metro Nashville Police Department had been assembled in one room at one time. The fourteen investigators were a mix of male and female; black, white, and Hispanic. On the surface they appeared diverse, almost a chaotic and random sampling of the population yanked in off the street and cast as homicide detectives in a cop movie.

Bransford knew, however, that each of his homicide investigators shared one common trait: the inability to fit in with any other part of the police department. Homicide detectives were mavericks, independent and contentious. More than a few of them were openly disrespectful of the police hierarchy, local politicians, and authority in general. Many were obsessive-compulsive to the point of burnout. Unable to let go of their work, they often had to be forced to take accumulated vacation time.

Gary Gilley, for instance, hadn't been home in almost thirty hours. He was already beyond his shift end when the call came in on the two murdered girls at Exotica Tans. He could have passed the case along to another detective, but had chosen to stay on as the primary. He'd been at the crime scene most of the night, then at the lab waiting for the autopsy and the results from the dozen or so tests that had been performed on the victims. Now Bransford watched as Gilley wearily sat down in a folding chair, eyes swollen and red from lack of sleep, stale air, and cigarette smoke. Bransford knew that if Gilley's stomach was anything like his, it was already burning from too much charred squad-room coffee and too little decent food. Bransford intended to order Gilley home to sleep as soon as the briefing was over.

Bransford stepped to a worn wooden podium in front of a dusty chalkboard and cleared his throat loudly.

"Let's go, folks," he announced. "Let's take our seats and get rolling on this one."

"This better be good, Lieutenant," Maria Chavez—Music City's first Hispanic female homicide investigator—announced. "You know how my mom hates me to miss Sunday dinner."

"I know," Bransford said, his voice guttural and strained. "I hate to call you all in on a Sunday, but this one's a no-brainer. Had to do it."

To Bransford's left, near the door, a well-dressed, neatly groomed man in a dark suit stood with an almost military bearing. Clasped in his hands was a leather-bound, three-ring portfolio bulging with papers. Seated in a folding chair next to the man was Howard Hinton, the homicide investigator from Chattanooga.

Bransford rapped his knuckles on the wooden podium and cleared his throat again.

"Okay, folks, listen up. As most of you know, we had a double murder last night down on Church Street near Baptist Hospital. Little place tucked away in an old strip mall called Exotica Tans."

Two of the younger investigators in the back row whooped at the mention of the tanning salon.

"As you might have guessed, there was a lot more going on in those tanning booths than the simple nurturing of melanomas."

More hoots followed as Bransford held up his hands, palms out, for silence.

"Yeah, real funny, you clowns, except for the fact that two coeds from MTSU were literally slaughtered and set out on display."

Bransford looked down at his notes. "The first victim was a nineteen-year-old Caucasian female, one Sarah Denise Burnham. No sheet, no warrants, no record. The second was Allison May Matthews, twenty-two years old, also Caucasian female. No file on her, either."

Bransford looked back up, rubbed the bridge of his nose, and forced his eyes to focus on the now silent faces in the squad room. "What we've got here are two young girls who we figure were picking up some extra cash to get through school. We're trying to track down someone from the MTSU registrar's office to get their school records, but this being Sunday, we haven't had much luck.

"Gary's taking primary on this one, and he'll be assigning chores after this briefing is over. The entire Murder Squad is on task force for this one. Even though these two girls were working their way through school at a hand-job joint, they still came from regular families, and believe me, folks, there are some mothers and fathers out there right now demanding to know when we're going to catch the animal that did this. Even the mayor called the chief's office on this one. And you all know what that means."

"Yeah," a voice called out from the back of the room. "Shit flows downhill."

Amid the ensuing laughter, Bransford turned to his left, caught the eye of the man in the dark suit, then nodded to him.

"This is the real reason, though, that we're putting all we got into this one," Bransford announced loudly, "and it's not the mayor's phone call. It appears from the crime scene and the results of the lab investigation that we may have a celebrity at work. Seems that our tanning salon murderer may be a pro. We've got a gentleman in from Washington who's going to tell us what we're in for and who we're looking for. I'm going to turn this discussion over to him now, and after that, Detective Gilley will meet with you briefly.

"Then," Bransford added, stepping away from the podium and moving to one of the folding chairs in the front row, "he's going to go home and go to bed if I have to throw him in the back of a squad car to get him there."

"Oh, poor baby," Jack Murray cooed. Murray was the newest member of the Murder Squad, having just transferred in from Vice a little over six months ago.

"Yeah," chimed in Maria Chavez. "You poor, delicate little rosebud."

Gilley turned, grinning. "How'd you guys like to spend the rest of the day Dumpster diving in the snow?"

"If you kids don't play nice," Bransford intoned, "I'll have to send you to your rooms without supper."

The dark-suited man approached the podium, opened his leather case, and spread it out in front of him.

"Quiet everybody," Bransford growled. "Listen up."

"Thank you, Lieutenant," the man said. "Good morning. I'm Special Agent Henry Powell of the FBI. I'm assigned to VICAP, the Violent Criminal Apprehension Program, and within VICAP, I'm a supervisory agent with CASMIRC."

Powell surveyed his audience and noticed several raised eyebrows.

"I know," he said, smiling, "and I agree. Washington has terminal acronym disease. CASMIRC is the Child Abduction and Serial Murder Investigative Resources Center, which is the rapid response component of CIRG, the Critical Incident Response Group. What this means in plain English is that when a crime is committed and the local authorities decide or suspect that this crime might be the work of someone who has done this before, then I get called. Last night, I was just finishing my dinner when Sergeant Hinton, your colleague down in Chattanooga, examined the crime scene on Church Street and called me at home. It took him about two sentences to convince me I needed to get down here fast."

Maria Chavez raised her hand, and Powell nodded to her.

"How did Sergeant Hinton get called up here from Chattanooga?"

Bransford turned in his seat and faced the group. "Hint and I go back a long way. The Metro crime lab was consulted several years ago when a similar murder occurred in Hamilton County. I called him after Gary called me to the crime scene. Then he called Agent Powell."

"So we leapfrogged from one to the next," Powell continued, "and, as you'll see, for good reason."

Powell stepped out from behind the podium and leaned against it, his right elbow cocked at an angle. "Now without giving you my complete semester-long FBI Academy course called Intro to the Psychopathology of Serial Killers 101, let me just start by telling you that the two victims of last night's murder were, we believe, murdered by the guy whom we've dubbed in-house the 'Alphabet Man.' Any of you ever heard of him?"

Powell's eyes wandered left and right, searching for a response.

"Good," he said, his easygoing smile returning. "That means, for once, we're doing our jobs. We've emphasized with this particular perp more than any other case in my experience the absolute necessity of keeping this guy's signature just between ourselves. For once, the news media hasn't put this together. If they ever do, we're screwed."

Powell paused, and as he did, a hand rose in the back of the room.

"Yes?"

Jack Murray leaned back in his folding chair and cradled his hands behind his head. "The guy leaves a signature?"

"Yes, practically speaking. I've investigated over two hundred cases in which the homicide was considered the likely work of a serial killer. In those two hundred-plus cases, I've seen the work of about two dozen perps and have interviewed fourteen of them after capture. In the case of each one, there was some aspect to the crime that was so unique and repeated so much that it became a signature aspect to the crimes. It was, so to speak, the guy's calling card."

"So what's our guy's calling card?" Murray asked.

Powell stepped away from the podium and over to the wall. "Detective Gilley," he said, flipping the switch to turn off the overhead lights. "Why don't we just show them our guy's signature?"

Gilley nodded, then stood and walked to the small table holding a slide projector at the back of the room. As he turned on the projector—the fan clattering as its ancient motor sputtered to life—Powell slowly lowered the screen from its holder on the wall above the podium. Gilley pressed the control button, and the first slide came into view on the dingy gray screen.

Low moans erupted as the slide came into focus. In the first view, the massage table that served as a butcher's block revealed the bloody corpse of Allison Matthews, her arms and legs still bound, her straining facial muscles still frozen as testament to the nature of her death.

"What we have here," Powell explained, "is the work of what we believe to be a primarily organized killer with some random elements of disorganized behavior."

Powell paused as Gilley moved to the next slide. This was another view of the murder scene, this time from the opposite side of the room, focusing over the young girl's body to the large block M painted in her blood on the opposite wall.

"You'll notice," Powell said, "that even with all the blood and carnage of this scene, everything is relatively neat."

"Relatively . . ." a voice whispered in the dark.

He pointed to one side of the slide. "For instance, you'll notice on this table that none of the bottles of massage oil are knocked over or even out of place. The large battery-operated vibrator in the corner here is still standing up. If our killer bumped the table and knocked it over, he was fussy enough to pick it back up and put it in its place."

Powell stepped into the light and pointed to the middle of the victim's torso. "You can't really tell from this slide because of all the blood, but in autopsy it was discovered that a series of shallow cutting wounds were made throughout the chest, torso, and abdomen of the victim, Allison May Matthews. These wounds were superficial and parallel to the lines of cleavage, which meant the sides of the incisions remained together, in some cases almost closing. The incisions were within a quarter-inch of being uniformly spaced apart all the way down the anterior side of the ventral cavity and were within a half-inch of being the same length."

Powell turned to face the room and stepped out of the light. "What this means is that our killer is anatomically savvy and very precise. He might even have some kind of medical training."

A hand went up in back, from just ahead of the projector. "What's a line of cleavage?" a voice asked from the darkness.

"The ME could explain it better than I can, but essentially muscle tissue in the body runs in groups that continue in certain directions. These directions are called 'lines of cleavage.' If you cut along, or parallel to these lines, then the wounds tend to remain closed, depending on the depth of the incision, of course. If you cut across these lines of cleavage, then the incised wound will be gaping or open and generally much nastier."

"So our boy wasn't trying to chop these girls up?" Bransford asked.

"Quite the opposite," Powell said, turning again to the slide and pointing. "Try to look past the gore. What we've got here is a situation where Allison was tied up and then patiently, carefully—and extremely painfully—bled to death. She also experienced violent sex as well, with both moderate to severe anal and vaginal tearing. However, I'll have more on that aspect of the scene later."

"Was she raped?" Maria Chavez asked.

"There was no evidence of semen found on either body during crime-scene examination and the autopsy," Gilley offered.

Maria turned, faced Gilley. "Kind of a quick determination, isn't it?"

"We took swabs, ran acid phosphatase and microscope examination. We're waiting on the P30," Gilley said, referring to the test for a specific glycoprotein found only in seminal fluid.

"In the past murders, we haven't found semen, either. So we're going to take for granted at this point," Powell said, "that the sexual violations were with foreign objects or by a condom-wrapped penis."

"So the guy goes into what's essentially a massage parlor," Maria Chavez spoke up again, "pays his money, goes to a back room with the girl, where, say, the guy offers her an extra fifty or hundred to let him tie her up. Once she's tied up, the guy takes his time on her."

"Let's hold judgment on that for the time being," Powell said. "For now, just examine the scene. Notice one thing, up here on the wall opposite the table—"

"The letter M," Jack Murray said. "The guy's signature!"

"Yes," Powell answered, "but look at this next set of slides." He motioned for the next slide.

Soft, low moans erupted again as the slide of the second victim flashed on the screen. Exponentially more brutal than the first slide, and more brutal than anything most of the investigators had ever seen, the second slide depicted a victim who must have died in unimaginable agony and terror. Sarah Denise Burnham's last moments of consciousness had to have been as close to hell as any living human could get and still be drawing—even if only for a few moments more—breath.

Behind him, from off his left shoulder, Powell heard retching disguised as coughing. He'd heard this sort of reaction before from even the most hardened veteran homicide investigators. No one could remain unaffected by a scene like this one.

"As you can see," Powell said, "our boy was considerably more thorough with this victim. The ME estimates that he must have spent at least two hours in this room. What you're seeing is essentially the beginning of an autopsy performed on a live human being."

Maria Chavez let loose a sound that was a cross between a gasp and a squeak. "Surely," she croaked, "the poor girl wasn't conscious!"

Powell turned. "Your ME estimates that it's possible the victim could have retained some level of consciousness perhaps even up the point where the thoraco-abdominal incision was complete."

"The what?" a voice asked from the back.

"The Y incision, which in the female begins roughly in the area of the navel and extends upward through the anterior ventral cavity, between the breasts, and then branching out to the shoulders."

Powell turned back to the slide. "However, it's extremely likely that the victim was in a state of severe shock by then and was hopefully rendered insensate. Let's hope so, anyway, for Sarah's sake."

"*Mi Dios*," Maria Chavez whispered, her voice choked.

"If you examine this photograph closely, you'll see that following the completion of the thoraco-abdominal incision and the removal of the breastplate, our killer then manipulated the internal organs of the victim. According to the ME, the muscle tissues of the heart were constricted and bruised in a manner consistent with a kind of strangulation maneuver. This is another signature aspect of the Alphabet Man's murders. In all instances up to the first victim you saw here this morning in the previous set of slides, the killer has performed the beginnings of a surgical-quality autopsy and literally stopped a beating heart with his own hands. Then he has removed and manipulated various interior organs before replacing them back in the body cavity.

"Keep in mind that this is not your typical postmortem evisceration and savage mutilation consistent with the psychotic, disorganized work of a delusional, out-of-control madman. What we have here is the very careful and precise work of an organized, psychopathic sexual sadist. And while I know you're all quite sick of this much detail, there is one other signature aspect of these homicides."

"God," Jack Murray moaned from the back, "we're afraid to ask."

"But you need to know," Powell said calmly. "Before beginning the thoraco-abdominal incision, the Alphabet Man removes the nipples of his victims and forces the victim to consume them."

Maria Chavez, still seated in her chair, bent over at the waist, gagging and retching, then stood up and bolted for the door. Two other male investigators, hands held to mouth, ran after her.

Powell looked down at Bransford. "Don't be too hard on them," he said. "That's not the first time that's happened."

A hand from the back corner went up. "Yes?" Powell asked.

"Do we have any indication of the type of weapon used?"

"Good question," Powell said. "Unfortunately, it's one that we don't have a complete answer for. You're looking for a small, thin-bladed weapon that's surgically sharp. It could be a straight razor, a scalpel, probably not a box opener. Perhaps an X-Acto knife. And our guy knows how to use it."

"Which means what?" Gilley asked. "Is he a doctor or something?"

"Probably not, but he may have some kind of medical training, perhaps a biology background."

"He sure as hell has some dissecting skills," Bransford added.

"Maybe he's a butcher," another voice from the shadows behind the projector suggested.

"Don't think so," Powell noted. "I've reviewed our case files on every murder committed by a butcher going back about thirty years, and in not one have we seen this degree of precision and care. So I'm not ruling it out, but it's not probable."

To Powell's left, the door opened and a shaken Maria Chavez stepped into the room, still swabbing a wet, dark brown paper towel across her face.

"I'm sorry," she said weakly.

"Please, Detective, don't be," Powell offered soothingly. "You're by no means the first."

Chavez forced a smile. "Murray's still in the men's room. I could hear him through the door."

"Why don't we kill the slide projector and bring the lights up," Powell said. "We've seen enough of this for now."

As Gilley stowed the projector and Hank Powell switched the lights back on, the other two ill detectives filed back into the room looking distinctly hangdog and took their chairs. Powell stepped back to the podium and looked briefly at his notes, then up to the group.

"I've got a classified set of photos from the other crime scenes we've investigated that will be available for you to examine until I go back to Washington, which won't be for another day or so. I also have a map of the eleven other cities, all different and apparently random, where the other murders were committed. I recommend that each of you spend extra time examining the Nashville crime-scene photos as well. What you'll find is that there are a couple of things about this particular crime scene that are unique and different from the Alphabet Man's normal routine."

Powell stepped out from behind the podium, once again in the manner of a professor nearing the end of a lecture.

"First of all, this is the Alphabet Man's first double homicide. He's never done a twofer before, and if you examine closely the nature of the two murders, you see some obvious and profound differences. In the first set of slides, the one with the M painted on the wall in the victim's blood, we see a degree of savagery that is in the great scheme of things quite subdued, at least by our guy's standards."

Powell walked over to the table by the far wall and picked up a poster-size blowup of a line drawing of the crime scene and held it out to his side.

"What does this mean?" he asked. "Here's what we think happened. The Alphabet Man enters the business via this door and finds one of the girls . . ." Powell paused and looked down at his notes.

". . . Allison Matthews at the reception desk. We know business is slow on Church Street, even on a Friday night, because of the intense cold. Practically nobody's out, which is a tailor-made evening for our boy. Perhaps he was hoping to find just one girl there, or maybe for whatever reason, this time he didn't care. His MO in the past has been to find women alone in places of business late at night. The D victim, for instance, was working alone in a convenience market. He went in there, subdued the victim, then closed the business and locked up. They found her the next morning in the walk-in cooler."

Max Bransford turned in his seat and faced the detectives. "We interviewed the manager, and he told us Allison had just started at the tanning parlor the week before. He also said that she was just the receptionist. She didn't work in the back."

"Did she know the second girl—" Maria Chavez spoke up, then looked down at her notes. "Sarah Burnham?"

"They were roommates and, apparently, best friends," Bransford answered. "Sarah got Allison the job."

"The job that got her killed," a voice from the back of the room whispered.

Bransford nodded, then turned back in his seat to face the front of the room. "Allison May Matthews was in the wrong place at the wrong time."

Powell turned back to the diagram and pointed. "In any case, our guy somehow gets Allison to go back to this room, which is the first one you come to."

"To coin a phrase . . ." a voice in the back spoke up.

Powell cleared his throat. "Yes, to coin a phrase. So he ties her up, gags her—"

Powell ran his finger down the hallway toward the second room, where the L girl was found.

"Then he scouts out the place and finds Sarah Burnham, the second girl. Maybe he walks in on her, startles her. Maybe he offers her, as we've already speculated, a bondage bonus, and maybe Sarah figures it's been a slow night and she can use the extra, but then decides no, she's not into that. Anyway, it takes a bit more to get Sarah down. It looks like she may have fought him some, but our boy's an expert. She goes down without too much trouble. So he ties her up as well. He checks the place out, figures it's late. The restaurant next door is closed, the block is deserted. So just for grins, he decides not to gag her. And he takes his time."

Powell turns, sets the poster down, and faces his audience grimly. "Meanwhile, Allison in the first room has to listen as her friend is slowly tortured to death. She hears the screaming, the shrieks of agony and fear, the begging and pleading, the crying for momma, and then this awful, terrible, deadly silence . . ."

"And then footsteps coming down the hall for her," Bransford interjects.

"Exactly," Powell said. "And by the time he gets to Allison—the M girl—who will be his thirteenth victim, he's tired and he's spent. So there's just the slow, exquisite mental game of torturing someone to death. It's not the death of a thousand cuts, but it's damn close."

Powell stood there for a few moments in his own terrible, deadly silence. His form seemed to droop as he finished his analysis and suppositions about what had happened sometime early Saturday morning at Exotica Tans on the coldest February night in Nashville, Tennessee, that anyone could remember in a long time.

Sergeant Frank Woessner, the Homicide Squad's senior African-American investigator, a man who'd successfully attended a half-dozen summer courses at the FBI Academy, spoke up from the back row. It was the first time he'd spoken during the meeting. His voice was low and smooth, but coldly serious.

"So," he asked calmly. "How do we catch this motherfucker?"

Powell straightened, reached back for his notebook, and held it out in front of him.

"With this," he said. "With the information we already have on this guy. We already know more about what makes this guy tick than his own momma."

Powell turned, walked back behind the podium, and opened the notebook. "In the past twenty years or so, since the Psychological Profiling Program became a part of what was then called the Behavioral Science Unit in Quantico, we've carried psychological profiling a long way. I can't give you this guy's name and address, but I can give you a very accurate estimate of the type of individual that commits this type of crime. This is a tool for you to use, but it's only one tool. You have to use every other tool and investigative technique in your arsenal to solve this crime. And if you do, you hit the jackpot, guys. You get the grand slam."

"So who the fuck we dealing with?" Gilley asked.

"I've got complete, detailed handouts for all of you, but to quickly summarize, the Alphabet Man is a classic, organized, psychopathic sexual sadist. This means that he is not—I repeat, *not*—a raving maniac who's going to go nuts in the middle of traffic and start slashing people during rush hour. A psychopathic sexual sadist is, above all else, a person who is completely amoral and asocial. He has no capacity for remorse, guilt, or shame. He's a sociopath, without a moral compass or any sense of ethics or responsibility. He's a charming person; if you met him at a party you'd like him, even gravitate to him, especially if you're female. He's intelligent, well-read, perhaps well-educated, although he's more likely to have lots of excuses as to why he's not well-educated.

"The Alphabet Man thinks entirely too much of himself. His particular disorder is what the shrinks call paraphilia; sexual deviations that are marked or characterized by persistent sexual arousal patterns in which unusual or deviant sexual situations are required for the perp's arousal. His fantasies revolve around completely dominating and objectifying his victims. While he's torturing, having sex with, and then slowly killing his victims, he's experiencing a kind of euphoria."

Powell paused, his eyes roaming the room as some of the investigators frantically took notes while others sat staring, almost in awe, at the description of the man they were now hunting. Powell had seen all these reactions in hundreds of faces in his career, and yet it never ceased to fascinate him.

"On a more specific note, ladies and gentlemen, get your pencils out. First of all, he's male and he's Caucasian. He's around thirty-two, give or take a year or two, and he's good-looking, maybe even *GQ* quality. Somewhere around five-eleven, one-seventy-five, maybe one-eighty, with a body that he works hard to keep in shape. He might be married or have a serious girlfriend; in any case, he's sexually competent and may frequently enjoy what we would consider normal heterosexual relationships with a variety of partners. In fact, women may chase him, and those that he doesn't torture, rape, and kill probably have a good time. He's intelligent, maybe extremely intelligent. As I said, he may be well-educated, but—and this is probably an important key—he may have in his academic background a history of disciplinary problems. He was a firstborn child and probably an only child. His mother adored him and his father was present when he wasn't working at his good, stable job. However, if he got any discipline at home as a child, it was inconsistent. He wet the bed until about the age of twelve and probably was torturing cats and puppies before he graduated to college coeds and night-shift clerks. He's spoiled, wants what he wants when he wants it, and he's a thrill seeker. He aspires to fame and glamour and attention. He's probably interested in cops and criminology as well. In fact, if you get any leads or communication about these two murders, I'd take a good look at where the tips are coming from."

Maria Chavez piped up, her voice strained: "How do you guys know this?"

Powell smiled. "Years of interviews, hundreds of hours of conversations, piles of statistics, and great big computers. But keep in mind, this is a profile. Statistically, this is what he should be like, but there may be some variations."

"Amazing," Gary Gilley mumbled.

"We're just getting started," Powell said. "He makes good money. If he drinks Scotch—and we think he does—then he drinks the best Scotch whisky. And he drinks when he kills, but never enough to lose control. He's highly mobile. Either his job allows him to travel a lot or for whatever reason he doesn't have to worry about money. Maybe he's rich; maybe he married well. He plans his crimes well, but handles unexpected circumstances—like finding an extra victim—with some style. He drives a nice car, but probably doesn't drive it when he's on a kill. Maybe a rental, or he's got a kill car stashed away somewhere. He almost certainly has assembled a 'murder kit,' and you should search very hard for it if you find him. If he's ever caught, he'll feign innocence so effectively you'll be tempted to believe him. When he's finally nailed, he'll express remorse, but always remember: He's not sorry for what he did; he's only sorry he got caught."

Woessner's hand shot up again. "Speaking of catching him, what are the chances that he's still around so we can nail his sorry ass?"

"Virtually nil," Powell admitted. "He's already on the move, long gone. But what's left behind is his detritus. He didn't kill those two girls, then take a cab to the airport. As organized and planned as these murders were, they were also damn bloody and messy. He's never left fingerprints, so somewhere in the vicinity of that strip mall are a pair of bloody latex gloves. Probably coveralls and other articles of clothing as well, not to mention a weapon of some kind and perhaps a discarded small bag full of duct tape and rope and perhaps a pair of handcuffs. Find it. Find his garbage. And use it to track his sorry ass down."

Powell stopped, closed his notebook. "And on a personal note, I happen to ascribe to that branch of psychiatry, psychology, philosophy, theology, whatever, which factors in the component of human evil. The murders committed by this person transcend our ability to understand them or in any way rationalize them. This man is not an animal; animals don't rape, torture, sodomize, and kill. He doesn't kill for food or survival. He kills because he's a predator. Remember that, above all else. He kills for one reason and one reason alone."

Powell paused once again, this time plainly and openly for dramatic affect.

"He likes it."

CHAPTER 5

Monday afternoon, Manhattan

Taylor Robinson's office at Delaney & Associates was on the northwest corner of the second floor of the renovated East Fifty-third Street brownstone that Joan Delaney's second husband had left her. Joan's third husband had tried to get a piece of the brownstone in their divorce, but Joan's attorney—who later became her fourth husband—managed to chase him off. After the fourth died two years later, Joan's claim on the house was forever uncontested due to her resolve to never marry again.

The four-story brownstone, located on the north side of East Fifty-third between Second and Third Avenues, was a short two-block walk from Sutton Place, where Taylor often sat on a bench and ate a sack lunch on warm days. She would stare out over the East River, the Queensboro Bridge towering over her left shoulder, and for a few short moments leave Joan Delaney's shrill voice behind her. The screeching of modems and fax tones, the smell of toner and burnt coffee, the background din and chatter of a busy office became just a memory blocked from her mind, at least for a while.

As Taylor sat in her tiny, high-ceilinged office on a Monday that had already seen more than its usual share of crises, she longed for a warm spring day and the benches of Sutton Place that overlooked the blue-gray ribbon glimmering in the sun that was the East River. Unfortunately for her, this was still February. A bitter wind poured down the avenues, its momentum only slightly broken by the concrete and plate-glass forest of Manhattan. The temperature wasn't expected to reach twenty degrees today, and the wind chill/ agony factor was well below zero.

Taylor was frazzled and already weary before her normal one o'clock lunchtime. She felt as if she had been locked in a room full of hungry, yapping Chihuahuas, not one of which could actually bring her down and finish her off, but all of whom together could wear her down and frustrate her nearly to the point of screaming.

Her state of mind and morale weren't helped by having a houseguest all weekend. It wasn't that Michael Schiftmann was such a bother. In fact, he was the most low-maintenance houseguest she'd had in months. But there had been the party she'd thrown for him Saturday night, and on Sunday afternoon she'd accompanied him down to the Village for his signing at a small mystery bookstore. After the book signing, she had taken Michael, the bookstore owner and his wife, and a couple of other hangers-on out for a dinner that lasted until nearly ten. By the time she got home, de-compressed, and got Michael all squared away in the guest room, it had been past midnight before she collapsed into bed herself.

Sundays were almost always sacred to Taylor; a day when she often didn't even bother to get out of her bathrobe un-til dinnertime. It was a day of lounging around reading the Sunday *Times*, catching an old movie on cable, drinking hot herb tea in the middle of the afternoon, and perhaps even taking a nap. Sundays restored Taylor Robinson, centered her, gave her that calm place deep inside herself in which to rest and recharge. She knew that by the end of the week, the loss of a Sunday was going to leave her ready to shut down completely. In essence, she'd already worked eight days without a day off, with at least four more to go.

Even tonight was shot, as Michael's publicist had set up a signing at the Barnes & Noble superstore on the Upper West Side. It never occurred to Taylor not to accompany her star author to the signing; that sort of thing simply wasn't done in Taylor Robinson's way of conducting business.

Taylor heard a knock on the doorjamb of her office. She turned as Neil Macher, the head of contracts for the agency, stuck his head in. A lock of thinning, greasy black hair hung down over his forehead as he stared over the top of his smudged glasses.

"Bad time?"

Taylor looked around her tiny twelve-by-fifteen office, its floor-to-ceiling bookcases, and its one visitor's chair piled high with manuscripts.

"Sorry I can't offer you a seat," she said, shrugging helplessly.

Neil stepped in, a stack of papers in his left hand. "Who's got time to sit, anyway? Is Michael coming in today?"

"Probably not," Taylor answered. "I'm meeting him for drinks and a quick dinner before his signing tonight."

"And then he's flying out tomorrow, right?"

Taylor nodded. "Boston."

"Then you'll have to get him to sign these tonight, okay? Don't let him get away without going over these contracts and getting his signature." Neil leaned over a stack of manuscript boxes and extended his hand to Taylor.

"Have these incorporated the last-minute changes we talked about?" she asked, taking the half-inch-thick stack of papers.

Neil nodded quickly. "I've gone over them, Joan's gone over them, and legal's gone over them. Their legal department signed off on them last night. Everything's cool and ready for signatures."

Taylor smiled. "God, Neil, my first seven-figure deal."

Neil grinned back at her. "Maybe a little celebration's in order tonight."

"I just hope Michael's happy with all this."

Neil backed out of the door frame, waving his hand dismissively. "If he's not, he's crazy." He stopped, looked back at Taylor with a raised eyebrow.

"Then again, he's a writer. By definition, he's crazy."

Neil closed the door as he left, leaving her to make one last review of the contracts. It was, by any sane and reasonable standard, a fantastic deal for the author and the largest book contract Taylor had ever negotiated by a factor of ten. Under the terms of the three-book contract, Michael Schiftmann would receive one-point-five million dollars for the next book in his series, to be called *The Sixth Letter*. For the seventh installment, he would receive an advance of two-point-five million, and for the eighth book in the series, and last in the contract, he would receive four million.

"Eight million for three books," Taylor whispered. "Jeez . . ."

And, she reminded herself, fifteen percent of that eight million went to Delaney & Associates. One-point-two million in commissions, a percentage of which after expenses would go to Taylor in salary and bonuses.

Taylor smiled, but behind the smile was an undercurrent of tension. To her credit, Taylor had managed to negotiate a contract that not only provided a hefty advance for each book, but also built in a number of other provisions to protect her client. The contract was what Hollywood called "pay or play," which meant the advances were nonreturnable. If for any reason—including turning in an unacceptable manuscript—publication of any of the three books was canceled, Michael got to keep the money. If the books exceeded their sales goals, there was a sweet performance bonus built into the deal, but if they failed to meet their targets, Michael incurred no penalty. The publisher retained most subsidiary rights—foreign, paperback, audio, electronic—but had to split all sub rights revenue with Michael. And on top of that, her client had retained all film and television rights to the books and all the characters appearing in the books, which would mean additional revenue down the road.

All in all, Taylor felt, this was the kind of contract that would free up an author from ever having to worry about money again. It meant artistic and financial freedom. It was, Taylor mused, what Humphrey Bogart called "fuck you money."

But Taylor also knew that this kind of book deal held some intrinsic dangers for an author as well. The industry was full of legendary tales of writers who'd received huge, phenomenal, record-breaking contracts and then crashed and burned. Fame and wealth were deadly if one didn't have the psychological underpinnings to handle it. Writers were notoriously fragile, which was why in a profession that gave its top practitioners prestige, money, and freedom from the soul-killing strictures of traditional corporate life, there was so much depression, substance abuse, divorce, insanity, and suicide. The occupational hazards were real and very, very dangerous.

And as far as Taylor could tell, the jury was still out on Michael Schiftmann. Could he handle this? Would his ego explode over his intellect? Would he, in the greatest danger of all, come to believe his own press?

As Taylor's eyes strained to read every word of the fine print, she couldn't help but replay in her own mind that first conversation with Michael Schiftmann when he'd called her office just over five years ago. Taylor had been a literary agent herself for only a short while, having decided after several years as an editorial assistant that spending sixty hours a week for twenty grand a year simply wasn't worth it.

Joan called her that late autumn morning and practically shouted, in her usual manner, that she'd made an appointment with a writer from Ohio or Illinois or some such place out there and now didn't have time to keep it.

"You talk to him!" Joan ordered.

"But who is he?" Taylor asked.

"Shiffman, Pittman, Sheffield, Schmetering, something or other . . . Hell, I don't know, just handle it!" Then Joan slammed the phone down.

"But I don't even know who—" Taylor protested to the now silent phone.

Asking herself if any of this was worth it, Taylor had buzzed the receptionist and at least gotten the writer's accurate name, then asked that she hold him off for a couple of minutes while she cleared a place for him to sit.

Five minutes later, Taylor walked out into the reception area and introduced herself to a man about her age and several inches taller, wearing khaki pants and a worn corduroy jacket. He needed a shave and a haircut, and the briefcase under his arm was scuffed leather with tarnished hardware.

He looked nervous and, Taylor thought, a bit like a frustrated graduate student. There was something about him, though, that Taylor found almost boyish. She invited him back to her office, where she apologized for inconveniencing him and explained that Ms. Delaney had suddenly been tied up in conference and would be unable to see him today.

"But how can I help you?" Taylor asked in as polite and professional a tone as she could muster.

For a moment, he sat there staring at her, his dark eyes darting shyly around the room. Taylor found herself wondering how old he was. Finally, he spoke. And as he began his story, Taylor found herself curiously yet cautiously drawn to him, as if somehow an element of fate or destiny had brought them together.

Michael Schiftmann explained to her that he had already published five novels in five years, all of them paperback mysteries. He went on to explain that as an unpublished writer, he had been turned down by every agent he'd queried with the exception of a man who operated out of his home in Lexington, Kentucky. That agent, as it turned out, was a disbarred lawyer and former concert promoter whose wife was supporting the two of them by working at the local Kmart. The agent had sold his first novel to the paperback imprint division of a major New York trade house for an advance of thirty-five hundred dollars. At the time, after nearly ten years of collecting rejection slips, Michael Schiftmann had been thrilled to finally break into print. His first novel was well-received and reviewed, even winning a nomination for a mystery award. Michael thought that finally his career was on its way.

But then the offer for his next book came back and he was shocked to find that with all the good reviews and the prize nomination, his first novel had failed to sell out its first printing. Michael's editor explained that the best he could do was offer another thirty-five hundred.

Shock turning to disappointment, Michael took his agent's advice and accepted the offer. Over the next four years or so, he went back to contract three more times, for a total of five published books. His latest book had sold for an advance of five thousand dollars. When Michael went back to contract for a sixth book, he told his agent he wanted a hardcover deal and at least a ten-thousand-dollar advance. The agent had laughed over the phone. When the agent came back with an offer of six thousand dollars, still mass-market paperback, Michael fired him on the spot and caught the next bus to Manhattan. Now he was staying in a midtown hotel that catered to budget travelers, eating at hot-dog stands and kiosks, and making the rounds of literary agents all over town.

"So how many have you seen?" Taylor asked.

"You're the third one today," he admitted, "and the seventeenth agent I've talked to since I got to town a week ago."

"Any takers?" Taylor asked.

Michael's face softened. Relaxed now after telling his story, he smiled at her. He had beautiful teeth, she noticed, and a charming smile. "Not so far," he admitted.

He reached into his briefcase and pulled out a stack of paper, a partial manuscript along with a synopsis as a proposal.

"This is something completely new and different," he explained. "I've spent the last five years writing good books that went nowhere. I learned what made a good mystery, a good crime novel, and I used that to write books that got me great reviews, awards, prizes. Everything a writer could want, except one thing: a living. So I'm breaking molds here, Ms. Robinson. What I've got here is the first in a projected series of twenty-six novels, which means if we make this work, we've both got job security for the next couple of decades. This is something nobody's ever seen before. At least not like this . . ."

He handed her the stack of papers. Taylor read the title page: *The First Letter.*

"So," Taylor asked, "what's the one-sentence pitch?"

Michael looked at her. "In the battle between good and evil," he said, "evil wins."

She raised an eyebrow. "Interesting. Is your series protagonist likable, sympathetic?"

"He's a brutal, sadistic serial killer," Michael answered. "And you're going to love him."

Taylor pursed her lips, stared down at the manuscript, and let out a long sigh. "That's a tall order, Mr. Schiftmann. Usually the bad guy loses and that makes people feel good. Affirms their moral view of life."

"This book's going to change their moral view of life."

"Hmm," she said. "Again, tall order."

"Give it a try," he said, motioning toward the manuscript. "It works."

"Maybe," she said. "We'll see."

Taylor felt the manuscript in her hands, thumbed through the first few pages and saw that it was professionally prepared, that it had the feel of a manuscript done by a pro. You could tell a lot, Taylor knew, about the look of a manuscript. When a novel came in typed single-spaced on onion-skin paper with handwritten corrections and hand-drawn illustrations, it was almost always as badly written as it was prepared.

"So tell me, Mr. Schiftmann," she asked casually. "Where do you want to be as a writer?"

"At the top," he said without a moment's hesitation. "On The List."

Neither of them had to elaborate about which list he was referring to. She eyed him for a second. He didn't appear delusional or crazy, just determined. She wondered if he knew what he was in for. She found herself feeling protective toward him, as if she could somehow shelter him from the price one paid for that kind of success.

"Can you get me there?" he asked. "Can we go there together?"

"That depends," Taylor said, looking down at the manuscript. "It all depends on the pages."

"Fair enough," Michael Schiftmann said. "I'm staying at the Midtown Motor Lodge on Eighth Avenue and Fiftysixth. I've got enough money to stay two more days, and then I'm on the dog back home. I'd sure like to know something before I leave, if that's possible."

"And where is home?" Taylor asked.

"Barberton, Ohio," Michael replied.

"Never heard of it," Taylor admitted.

"Nobody has. It's working class, industrial. Close to Cleveland."

"Oh," Taylor said.

"Yeah."

Taylor stood up, offered him her hand. He took it and held it firmly as they shook.

"Mr. Schiftmann, I'll call you."

Perhaps it was that Taylor Robinson had only about a dozen clients on her roster, not one of which was actually making a living as a writer. Perhaps it was something in Michael Schiftmann's eyes or voice or the way he stood or the way he sat that convinced her he was somehow different from the parade of frustrated novelists who moved from agent to agent like hungry wolves roaming an unforgiving landscape. In any case, Taylor spent the rest of the afternoon reading Michael Schiftmann's book proposal, and after that she called a friend who worked at the publishing house that had published his first five books.

Taylor Robinson learned that Michael Schiftmann's agent had never pushed for him, had sold him cheaply into a house that was famed for paying little and promoting even less. His books had languished first in the warehouses, then on the shelves, and finally on the tables containing stacks of remaindered books that were sold practically by the pound in discount stores and buyers' clubs. The ones that were still lying around after that were pulped, ground back into mash, and recycled for another writer's words.

Not one of them was still in print. Michael Schiftmann's career as a writer was history. The nominations and prizes, the reviews and the praise meant nothing. Taylor Robinson was experienced enough to know that there was a lot more to publishing success than writing well and producing good books. But never had she seen a writer more ill-treated.

After reading Michael's manuscript, Taylor Robinson decided to change that. In *The First Letter*, the series debut, Michael introduced his protagonist, known only as Chaney. In Chaney, Michael had created a protagonist who was the personification of true evil, a man for whom murder became an act of artistic and personal liberation. Yet he was also a charming, intelligent, and erudite man, with a sense of style and taste that couldn't help but endear him to readers. As Michael was careful to establish from the beginning, Chaney's victims never exactly deserved their fate, but they weren't entirely innocent, either. It wasn't what Taylor could call a new moral code—just as there are no new stories, there are no new moral codes—but the story, in its unusual approach to style and voice, reflected the ethically ambiguous state of the world today.

More important, the book was a damn good read. Taylor convinced Joan Delaney to let her take him on as a client. That night she phoned Michael at his hotel and told him that if he'd have her, she was willing to take him on. And while she couldn't guarantee him a slot on The List immediately, she could promise him that no matter what, she'd break her back for him if that's what it took.

Taylor sold the first book for ten grand, not much in the pantheon of contemporary book deals, but it was a hardcover deal to a publishing house that took its writers seriously and promoted the hell out of them. *The First Letter* was published just in time to hit the bookstores for Christmas. The first reviews were astounding. The reviewers either loved the book more than anything that had come off the line in years, or they vilified the book so passionately that one couldn't help but go buy a copy to see what all the hubbub was about. What the reviews didn't do for the book, word of mouth—that most powerful of all publishing promotional tools—did. The book earned out its advance in a month and was sold to nine foreign publishers, then into a hefty paperback reprint deal that garnered enough to allow Michael to quit his job as a proofreader for good. The second in the series went for seventy-five thousand, the third for a hundred and a quarter. The fourth book sold for two hundred thousand dollars and missed The List by only a couple of slots. She'd gone back to contract for Michael Schiftmann a year and a half ago and gotten him a neat three hundred thousand for *The Fifth Letter.* By then, momentum alone carried the book onto The List.

Taylor Robinson had worked herself bleary-eyed for Michael, and she had brought him from a third-rate publisher to the top of the heap. They'd worked closely together, with Taylor bringing all her editorial talent and skills to bear on the books. They had become true partners in a life's work. And now, with this contract, she was set to make him rich.

So, Taylor Robinson wondered that icy February afternoon in her overheated office, why was she so uneasy?

CHAPTER 6

Monday afternoon, Nashville

Master Patrol Officer Debbie Greenwood carefully wheeled her blue-on-white Ford Taurus squad car down the exit ramp off I–40 and onto Charlotte Avenue just a few short blocks down the hill from the Tennessee State Capitol. The sun had finally burned off the worst of the gray cloud cover that seemed to hang over Nashville for weeks at a time during the winter months. A dazzling, clear blue sky, accompanied by temperatures in the mid-thirties, had begun to melt off the worst of the black ice that Greenwood knew was waiting to ensnare careless drivers at the foot of the exit ramp. Shaded by the freeway bridge and the traffic passing overhead, the ramp always seemed to be the last place to show pavement again after a thaw. Since the cold front had moved in five days ago, bringing with it the worst ice storm in a decade, Greenwood had already written up a dozen accidents at this very spot.

The light on Charlotte changed to red, and Greenwood lightly tapped the brakes of the Ford. She felt the rear wheels begin to slide and was instinctively beginning her counter-steer when the wheels caught and the car slowed. Four years on the force—and four Februarys patrolling the dangerous winter streets of Nashville—had taught her to stay ahead of the curve, to anticipate the dangers that might lie in front of her. More than once, that instinct had served her well.

The light in front of her changed, and Greenwood slowly

lifted her foot from the brake pedal. True to form, though, a kid in a Toyota to her left raced the yellow and ran through the light just as her squad car began moving.

"Typical," Greenwood groused, briefly considering pulling the car over and issuing a ticket. But it was cold outside, and she was near the end of a long shift. The overtime gods had been good to Debbie Greenwood this winter, but one can have too much of a good thing. Feeling slightly guilty at letting the kid off, in addition to irritated, Greenwood pulled out onto Charlotte Avenue and turned left, heading away from downtown and out toward Centennial Park.

A half mile or so down, Greenwood wheeled her squad car into the parking lot of a convenience store that perched on the edge of a large housing project. The store had been robbed three times this year already, and the desk sergeant had asked that all patrol officers try to do a drive-by at least once a shift. Greenwood didn't mind; the coffee was hot and fresh, and the clerks were always glad to see her.

As she parked the car, she spotted an elderly black man in a ragtag overcoat, torn stocking cap, and dirty, worn Nikes pushing a grocery cart down the sidewalk through the gray slush and onto the parking lot of the convenience store. Greenwood smiled, knowing what was coming next. Like most of the other Central Sector patrol officers, she knew that despite a lifetime in prison, the old man—known only as "Pops"—was completely harmless, if a bit disconcerting at first.

Greenwood parked the squad car and sat there for a few seconds with the motor running. As Pops struggled to push his grocery cart through the slowly melting frozen mud, Greenwood turned the car ignition off and stepped out of the Ford. A bitter wind caught her square in the face, causing her to shiver and pull her jacket tighter around her shoulders.

"Hey, Officah!" Pops called out from the other side of the parking lot.

"Hey, Pops," Greenwood answered. "You keeping warm?"

"Yeah, but I just got me one question."

Greenwood smiled, knowing what was coming. "What is it?"

"You ever let a ol' niggah eat yo' pussy?"

Greenwood cleared her throat, thankful that the parking lot was empty except for the two of them.

"No, Pops, can't say I ever have."

The old man smiled a toothless, pink grin at her. "Well, you evah decide to, you call me, ya hear?"

"Sure thing, Pops. I'll let you know." Greenwood turned toward the front door of the market. "You want a coffee?" she yelled back over her shoulder.

Greenwood knew Pops had been banned from the store years ago. If he wanted anything from inside, somebody else had to get it for him.

"Just like me, baby!" he yelled. "Hot and black!"

Greenwood assumed that was a yes, but truth was, you could never be sure with Pops. She entered the store, nodded to the clerk, made small talk, and walked around the store a couple of times. She was close enough to the end of her shift that if she killed a few more minutes, it would be time to head in and sign out. Just another day at the office.

Greenwood poured two Styrofoam cups full of coffee, added a packet each of sugar and artificial creamer to hers, then capped them both. The clerk—a pretty, young African-American woman—offered her the coffee for free, but Greenwood smiled and made her take a five. The woman made change, thanked Greenwood for coming in, and smiled pleasantly back at her. It felt good that the girl was glad to see her.

Out on the sidewalk, Greenwood dodged the few icy patches left on the concrete and walked around the front of the store to the corner. Pops's grocery cart was pushed up against the cinder-block wall next to a large Dumpster. Hanging out of the Dumpster, she saw the baggy seat of the old man's pants, followed by his bony legs dangling from his two-sizes-too-large trousers and wondered how the hell he ever managed to stay warm.

"Gotcha coffee, Pops," Greenwood announced.

The old man pushed himself out of the Dumpster, his feet sliding as they hit the frozen ground. Suddenly the old man let out a whooping sound as he struggled to regain his balance.

"Man, dey's some nasty shit in deah!" he yelled.

Greenwood held out the cup of coffee toward him. "Be careful, it's slippery out here."

"You gots to see dis," the old man said.

"I don't gots to see nothing," Greenwood said. "It's a Dumpster, Pops. Of course there's some nasty shit in it."

The old man ignored her outstretched hand. "No, lady, you gots to see dis. I ain't seen nothing like dis since dey had da riots in '76."

Her curiosity piqued, Greenwood took a couple of steps closer to the grime- and filth-encrusted Dumpster, thankful that at least with the brutal cold, there was no smell.

"Pops, what the hell are you—"

Greenwood stopped as the old man backed out of the Dumpster gate again, this time unraveling an ice-encrusted, stiff pair of green coveralls splattered with dark, nearly black, coppery stains.

"Look at dis," the old man shouted. "Somebody done got stuck dis time! *Whooo-whee!*"

"Pops," Greenwood said slowly, cautiously, every instinct telling her that this was not your usual convenience-store garbage. "Listen, buddy, I need you to put that back where you got it and move over here away from that thing. You hear me, Pops?"

"But I can wear dese and dey's some cans and shit in deah, too," the old man whined. "I git me some money . . ."

"We'll get the cans out later," Greenwood said. "Come on over here and get your coffee, Pops. C'mon, it's cold out here. You need to drink your coffee."

Pops smiled at her, stepped over and took the coffee out of her hand, and licked his lips.

"Stay close by, Pops. I'm just going to take a look in there, okay?"

Greenwood pulled the Maglite off her utility belt and walked carefully toward the Dumpster. The late-afternoon sun was setting just off the horizon; dusk was barely ninety minutes away, and already this side of the building was heavily in shadow. Greenwood approached the Dumpster carefully, not knowing what to expect, and then sidled up to the door and peeked in, the Maglite's sharp, focused beam playing over the surface of the garbage.

Most of the contents of the Dumpster was the usual rubbish: broken-down cardboard boxes, plastic soda containers, cans, a couple of discarded whiskey bottles, and piles of amber beer bottles. And on top of the trash—a heap of rags, crumpled up, frozen with something that looked enough like dried, frozen blood for Greenwood to realize her shift wasn't as close to being over as she thought it was.

She reached for her Handie-Talkie to call in, then thought better of it. Her instincts were at work again, and her instincts warned her that the news media, freelancers, and a host of private citizens supplemented their dreary lives and endless winter cabin fever by keeping a police scanner going at all times. The city was due for an eight-million-dollar grant to convert over to a high-tech digital communications system that was impervious to the analog scanners, but the money had been held up by a political catfight in the legislature.

Greenwood reached inside her jacket and pulled out her cell phone. She raised the tiny antenna, punched in a number, and held the phone to her ear. She held on while the phone rang twenty times before someone answered.

"Murder Squad," a voice said, "Chavez speaking."

"Detective Chavez, this is MPO Deborah Greenwood, Central Sector."

"Hello, Greenwood, what can I do for you?" The voice sounded young, with a slight Hispanic accent.

"I thought I'd better call on the cell phone rather than go through dispatch. The desk sarge this morning gave us a handout on those two girls that were killed down on Church Street Friday night."

"Early Saturday morning," Chavez said. "What've you got?"

"I'm down at the Mapco Express on Charlotte Avenue just off the I–40 interchange. Got a local Dumpster diver down here who came across a pile of bloody rags and clothes. I just happened to be stopping by for coffee and he led me here. I don't know if it's anything or not, but thought I'd better call."

The voice on the other end was suddenly tense. "Officer—what did you say your name was?"

"Greenwood, Deborah Greenwood."

"Officer Greenwood, I want you to secure the scene, keep the guy who found this nearby, and sit tight till we get there. And nothing goes out over the radio, got it?"

"Got it."

"Good," Chavez said. "Now give me your cell phone number in case I need to get to you before we arrive."

Greenwood gave her the number, then grabbed her pad and scribbled down Chavez's cell phone number.

"And Greenwood," the voice said.

"Yes?"

"You done good."

Greenwood smiled. "Thanks, Detective Chavez."

Special Agent Hank Powell got the call on his cell phone just as he was pulling into the parking lot of Nashville International Airport to catch his flight back to D.C. He had spent the last two days working with the Nashville police reviewing the case history of the Alphabet Man, detailing the other eleven crime scenes, and working to establish the kinds of linkages and clues the homicide detectives should be searching for.

Powell clicked off his cell phone and drove past the entrance to the rental return parking lot, all the way around the outskirts of the massive facility, and back onto the freeway headed downtown. By the time he got to the Mapco Express, the homicide detectives had the entire parking lot cordoned off with yellow crime-scene tape and were holding off a phalanx of media vehicles interspersed with curious onlookers, most of them young and black.

Powell flipped his badge wallet open at the uniformed officer controlling access to the parking lot, signed the crime-scene log-in sheet, and parked his rental next to an unmarked white Crown Victoria. On the other side of the lot, near the corner of the building, he saw Lieutenant Max Bransford and Detective Gilley huddled together, vainly trying to keep the wind off them.

"What've we got?" he asked, approaching the two men and pulling his overcoat tightly around him.

"I think we got lucky," Bransford said. "That uniformed officer over there—" Bransford pointed toward Officer Greenwood, who was leaning against the hood of her Ford Taurus as Maria Chavez stood next to her scribbling in a notepad.

"—just happened to be doing a drive-by of this place when some wacky old guy who makes his living in the entrepreneurial recycling industry came across a pile of bloody clothes inside that thing."

Bransford pointed behind him. Powell took two steps to his left and spied the Dumpster over Gilley's shoulder.

"What've you found?" Powell asked.

Gilley flipped open his notebook and looked down at his notes. "The lab techs are still in there scouring the place out. But so far we've got a bloody, torn jumpsuit, a pair of white socks with bloodstains, a couple of bloody white towels that are consistent with the type of towels we found at the tanning parlor . . ."

Powell felt his heart begin to race. Of the thirteen murders committed by the Alphabet Man, this was the first instance of any of his effects being found. For the first time, the police had found his dump site.

"And, best of all," Gilley said, "two pairs of latex gloves covered in what appears to be blood. One of the four gloves is torn."

"Jesus," Powell said. "That means maybe one of the girls managed to scratch him, tear a piece off one of the gloves, and he had to change."

"Meaning," Bransford said, finishing Powell's thought, "that maybe we've got some of the killer's blood on that glove as well."

Powell looked around, scanning the scene. "It's getting dark out here," Powell said. "Can the lab get some lights up?"

"Already in progress," Gilley said.

Powell turned to Bransford, knowing that he was the ranking officer at the crime scene and not wanting to step on anyone's toes, but also not wanting to mince a single word as to the importance of this discovery.

"Max, we need that Dumpster scraped and swabbed all the way down to the paint. I know it's miserably cold out here and this is rough duty, but this is our first chance to really nail this bastard on some forensic evidence. There may be hair, saliva, fingerprints. Hell, we don't know."

"We're going to get it all, Hank," Bransford said, reassuring him. "But it's going to take time. I think our best bet is to have the Dumpster hauled downtown and have the techs go through it in the garage."

"Works for me," Powell said. "But let's get a thorough search of the area around it before we move it. There might be footprints, tire tracks."

"That'll be a tough one, Agent Powell," Gilley said. "There's a lot of foot traffic here, this being the closest convenience market to a housing project. Some of this ice has melted, which is going to distort any tire tracks. Plus lots of discarded bottles, cigarette butts. Hell, people are just trashy, you know."

"Get what we can, as much as we can, now, before it's too late," Powell said, urgency in his voice. "We can sort it all out later."

"Okay," Gilley said, nodding. "We're also canvassing the neighborhood, and we've got the manager inside going through his time cards to see who was working the cash register late Friday night, early Saturday morning. Maybe this guy dumped his clothes, then came in for a six-pack and a loaf of bread afterward."

"What about surveillance cameras?" Powell asked.

"None on the exterior," Gilley said, waving his hand around the parking lot. "The manager's pulling the tape out of the interior camera."

"Is it a looping tape?" Powell asked, knowing that if it was, the traffic from the night of the homicide would be long erased.

"The manager doesn't know," Gilley said, grinning. "He's new, never had to do this before."

"Great," Powell said. "We'll just have to check the time and date stamps. And, look, I just thought of something. Who touches a Dumpster? I mean, you're gonna throw stuff in there, you try *not* to touch anything. So dust the area around the metal door for prints, then fume it with iodine, ninhydrin, silver nitrate, whatever. You guys got a laser in the lab?"

Bransford nodded. "Yeah."

"Shoot it with that, then. Maybe there won't be as many prints on there as we think. At least we'll have them in the file. This is our chance to nail the bastard. Let's not blow it."

"I called the TBI lab," Bransford said, "I've told them to bump the specimens to the head of the lab. I want a DNA profile ASAP."

"Great," Powell said, "and if they get jammed up, I'll get Washington in on it."

"Super," Bransford said.

Powell looked at Gilley and Bransford, and a smile slowly came to his face.

"You know what this means, don't you?" he asked.

Gilley shook his head. "What?"

"The guy's fucked up," Powell answered. "For the first time, he got sloppy. No matter what happens from now on out, this is the beginning of the end. He's ours now. He's history. I can taste it."

CHAPTER 7

Monday evening, Manhattan

A light dusting of snow had covered the sidewalks as Taylor Robinson pushed open the heavy wooden front door of Joan Delaney's brownstone. Moments earlier, she'd glanced up from the manuscript she was reading and saw the time: six-fifteen. She yelped, bolted out of her chair, threw on her overcoat and wool hat and grabbed her briefcase, then raced down the stairs. She had fifteen minutes to make it all the way across town and up the West Side, a task that on a snowy February evening in Manhattan was a practical impossibility.

She glanced to her left, then right, desperately hoping to spot an available cab. The street was lined with cars moving along at walking speed, but the only cabs she saw had darkened roof-mounted medallion lights. She began walking west the two long blocks to Third Avenue, hoping that by getting to a cross street, she'd have twice the chance of catching a taxi.

The winter gusts seemed to rip through the Manhattan canyons faster and more powerfully than ever as they gathered strength on their way to the East River and Queens. Taylor pulled her coat tightly around her and bent into the wind, forcing herself to move as quickly as she could while still maintaining her balance on the slick streets.

New York was gray in the seemingly endless wintertime. Even then Taylor loved the city, its gloomy days melting into early darkness and frigid evenings. She found the cold invigorating, the nights romantic, even though it had been months since she'd had the chance to share a romantic evening with anyone.

Taylor loved the city; what she hated was being late. She'd been reading a manuscript from the slush pile that actually might have some promise. Maybe, she thought, Michael will understand.

About fifty feet from the intersection and just ahead of her, a yellow Checker Cab pulled off to the right in front of the Hawthorne Building, its door opening and discharging an older woman in an ancient fur coat carrying two large Bloomingdale's bags. Taylor put her fingers to her mouth and whistled, hard, just the way her brother had taught her when they were kids. The shrill, piercing noise easily caught the driver's attention. Seconds later, Taylor slid into the rear seat, pulled her briefcase in behind her, and slammed the door. The driver turned, scowling at her through the dingy bulletproof Plexiglas panel.

"Sorry," she said, "didn't mean to slam it."

The driver's wrinkled face softened a bit. "Where to?"

"Broadway and Seventy-eighth," Taylor answered.

The driver shifted, turning to face the front of the car and grabbing the wheel. "Care which way we go?" he asked.

"Whatever's fastest. Your call."

"Gotcha," the driver said, slapping the handle on the meter and jerking the car forward as the light at Second changed.

Twenty-five minutes later, the driver turned onto Broadway a half block from the restaurant. "There," Taylor instructed, pointing out the right front corner of the cab. She checked the meter and quickly figured a generous tip that could be left without having to wait for change, and pulled two bills out of her wallet.

The driver pushed the slide tray into the passenger compartment. "Thanks," Taylor announced loudly as she stuffed the bills into the plastic bin and reached for the door handle.

"Pleasure was all mine," the cabbie said, his voice a mixture of stress and sarcasm.

Taylor stepped gingerly out onto the slick street and was careful not to slam the door again. She made her way between two parked cars over to the sidewalk and up the front steps of La Caridad, the neighborhood restaurant Michael had requested for dinner. The front of the restaurant was, as usual, packed with locals waiting for a table. She scanned the crowd, looked past it, and spotted Michael at a window table near the middle of the restaurant. She slid past a group of chattering college-age kids and wove her way through the crowd. He glanced up from the menu just as she approached the table.

"Sorry to be late," she huffed, realizing that the dash up the sidewalk had left her short of breath.

"No problem," he said, rising halfway up out of his chair as she pulled her coat off, folded it onto the chair next to her, then sat down. She pushed her briefcase under the seat with her right foot.

"Been here long?"

He shook his head. "About fifteen minutes is all," he answered. "But I just now got a table. I was late, too. This being rush hour, I took the subway. Even it was moving slow today."

"Believe it or not," Taylor said, unfolding a menu, "I got here in about twenty-five minutes."

"From your office?" Michael asked, surprised, as he held up his hand and motioned for the waitress.

The cuisine at La Caridad was Cuban-Chinese-Hispanic, a curious combination of flavors that Taylor could not recall having seen anywhere outside Manhattan. She had eaten here a couple of times before and found it to be cheap and scrumptious, a combination that was getting harder and harder to find in the city.

The waitress approached. "Maybe we'd better go ahead and order," Taylor suggested. "We've only got about an hour."

"Yeah, go ahead."

"No, you," Taylor said, reading the menu as the waitress fidgeted.

"Okay, I'll have the lemon pork chops," Michael said,

closing the menu. "Skip the salad. Oh, and a glass of Chardonnay."

"I've had a hard day," Taylor said. "I want the shrimp paella and a Cuervo Gold margarita."

Michael smiled as the waitress scribbled their orders and turned to walk away. Then his smile faded as he turned back to her.

"Taylor . . ." he said. He looked down at the table, his eyes flicking back and forth nervously.

"Yes." Taylor felt a knot beginning to form in her stomach.

"There's something I want to talk to you about."

Taylor studied his face for a moment. "Okay."

Michael crossed his arms and leaned forward, his elbows on the table, then looked up at her. "About the other night," he said. "I feel really bad about that."

Taylor stared at him a moment, confused. "What?"

"The girl," he said. "The blond."

Taylor sighed. It was her turn to look away. "Yes, the blond," she said.

"I don't usually behave like that," Michael said, his voice low. "It's not something I make a habit of."

"Michael, you don't have to explain—"

"This isn't an explanation," he said. "It's an apology. I'm not making any excuses. I behaved badly, and in the home of someone I happen to respect very much. Someone I owe a lot to."

"Look, we're both adults," Taylor said, looking up at him. "And our relationship is a professional one."

"It's more than that," he snapped. "It's more than that to me. You saved my life, Taylor. I was sinking fast and you rescued me."

Taylor felt her skin flush. "C'mon, Michael. You're a talented guy. You were going to make it no matter what."

"Bull. Lots of talented writers never get anywhere. You know that as well as I do. Talent's about fifth on the list of things you need to have to make it in this business. Number one on the list is the right person to work with. The right person and the right place and the right time. You gave me that and I'm grateful to you. More than grateful . . ."

Okay, Taylor thought, *give it up. Go ahead. Permission to blush granted.*

"You're blushing," Michael said, grinning.

She held up her hands, palms out. "I know. I know."

"I am sorry," he said. "That's all I wanted you to know. And it won't happen again."

"Consider it forgotten," Taylor said as the waitress brought their drinks.

"I think it's just the pressure of the last few months," Michael said. He took a long sip of the wine and closed his eyes. "Being on the road," he continued. "Always moving, then working seven days a week when I'm not on the road."

Taylor felt the Cuervo Gold warm her stomach as she set her glass back down. "I thought you said no excuses."

He smiled. "Touché."

Taylor smiled back and then unsuccessfully tried to stifle a yawn. "Excuse me," she said.

"You are tired. So why the hard day?"

Taylor leaned back in her chair, pulled her hat off, and ran her fingers through her hair, shaking it loose and back over her shoulders. "I swear, prosperity's going to be the death of me yet."

"We should have those kinds of problems," he said.

"I'm serious," she shot back. "I need a vacation."

Michael stared thoughtfully at her. "Maybe you'll get one soon."

She sighed, shook her head. "Not any time soon." Then she leaned across the table and lowered her voice. "Well?" she asked.

"Well what?"

"Don't you want to see them?" She raised an eyebrow.

"You mean you've got them here?"

"Why not? There's no time like the present."

"If I'd known I was going to sign an eight-million-dollar contract over dinner, I'd have taken us someplace nicer."

Michael's large blue eyes were clear, shiny and bright like

those of a boy on Christmas morning. Taylor felt suddenly warm again, flushed all over.

"Want to see?" she asked. He nodded.

She reached down and pulled her briefcase into her lap, extracted a sheaf of papers, and handed them across the table to him.

"There are three sets there," she said. "An original for you, one for my files, and one for their contracts department."

Michael Schiftmann looked down at the bundle of paper in his hand, the stack of contracts that virtually guaranteed him everything he'd always desired: wealth, fame, the freedom to do what he wanted both creatively and personally. For a few moments, he stared at them silently with a blank look on his face.

"I still can't believe it," he murmured.

Taylor leaned across the table and laid her right hand over his left. "Believe it," she said. "It's quite real."

Then she sat up straight and pulled a small rectangular box out of her purse. The box was tied with a red ribbon. She handed it across the table to him.

"A little congratulatory gift," she said. "I thought it might come in handy right about now."

Stunned, Michael took the box, slowly untied the ribbon, then opened it. Inside lay a brand new Montblanc fountain pen.

"My God," he said. "You remembered."

"That first day in my office," she said. "The day we met. You said someday you wanted to be the kind of writer that signed books and contracts with a very expensive fountain pen. Well, buster, now you've got one. Let's see what you can do with it."

He grinned. "Has it got any ink—"

"It's locked and loaded," Taylor said. "Go for it."

Michael pulled the cap off the pen. He folded back the sheets of the contract until he came to the last page, where a blank line awaited his signature. With a flourish, he signed his name to first one contract, then the second, and finally the third.

He lifted up his wineglass and clinked her offered margarita.

"You know," he said. "I think we're going to like being rich."

Taylor smiled and took a long sip of the drink.

We? she thought.

Taylor stood in the back of the packed store and found herself suppressing the urge to shout. She'd done a quick, down-and-dirty head count of the crowd at the Barnes & Noble superstore at Eighty-second and Broadway and figured that Michael had to have drawn upward of two hundred and fifty people to his signing. *And this*, she thought, *on a Monday night in February when it's nasty as hell outside.*

It was all she could do to keep from squealing. Not only were the numbers good, but Michael was as relaxed and as charming and as appealing as she had ever seen him at a book signing. He had bantered playfully with the audience and then, after reading one of the darker, more violent passages from *The Fifth Letter*, had made a wonderfully self-deprecating offhand comment that broke the silence and got them all laughing when the reading was over.

As Taylor stood in the back of the crowd, leaning against a bookshelf with her coat folded over her arm, Michael was wrapping up a question-and-answer session that had now gone on for more than twenty minutes.

"Yes," Michael said from the podium, pointing to a raised hand in the third row. The questioner stood up, a young woman in tight jeans, black turtleneck, long blond hair pulled behind her.

"How far along are you in the next book and when will we see it?"

Michael smiled. "I've just completed the manuscript for *The Sixth Letter* and I'm about halfway through the rewrite. And I've started the research for number seven."

The young blond's hand shot up again. "How do you do research for these books?" she demanded. "How do you bring so much realism to them?"

"Well," Michael said, leaning forward on the podium, "the research, for me, is the fun part. I've read stacks of books on the psychopathology of serial killers, case histories, interviews with both the killers and the relatively few victims who survive these kinds of attacks."

A chorus of murmurs erupted throughout the crowd.

"Okay," Michael said, reacting to the crowd noise, "maybe 'fun' isn't the right word. Some of this stuff is pretty grim. But I find that it's necessary to really get inside Chaney's head. After all, this guy kills people, sometimes for fun, but always for what, to him, is a good reason."

The young girl sat down as the bookstore manager stepped to the podium and announced that the line for signed copies should form to his left. Taylor looked down at her watch; between the introduction, Michael's talk, and the questions, they'd been there nearly an hour. She eyed the crowd of eager buyers lining up for autographs and realized they'd be there at least another hour, maybe longer. She sighed wearily and turned around, searching for a comfortable chair, when she spotted Brett Silverman across the room.

Brett turned, caught Taylor's eye, smiled a thin smile, and nodded. The two women began walking toward each other and met in the center of the large second-floor gallery where the signing had taken place.

"Well," Taylor said, "so much for the reports that he's drawing small crowds."

Brett Silverman was dressed in a dark green business suit with a camel hair overcoat draped across her shoulders. Her eyes were tired, bloodshot, and Taylor guessed the hard-working editor had been in her office up until the signing.

"It's amazing what adding the words '*New York Times* Best-Selling Author' will do for a crowd. I must admit," Brett confessed, "he had 'em wrapped around his little finger tonight."

The two women turned at the sound of laughter across the room. At the signing table, Michael had just said something to a middle-aged woman carrying a sack of books to be signed that had caused her to break out cackling. Several other patrons were laughing and smiling as well, and the broad grin on Michael's face was an indication of just how good a time he was having.

"You know, I think he's learning how to do this," Taylor said. "I was worried. In his own way, he's quite shy, you know."

"He does seem to be in a good mood," Brett offered.

Taylor reached into her briefcase and pulled out the stack of signed contracts. "Maybe it's the things he's been signing lately besides books. Here, consider these hand-delivered."

Brett took the contracts from Taylor. "I guess this would put just about anybody in a good mood."

"Don't worry," Taylor said. "He's worth every penny and you know it."

"I heard him say he's finished the first draft of six. Have you talked to him about it?"

Taylor closed her briefcase. "He'd have it turned in already if you guys hadn't added another twelve cities to the tour," she said teasingly.

"Yeah, well," Brett said, "that was upper management. Personally, I'd rather have him home writing."

"He will be, and soon."

Brett yawned and rubbed her eyes. "I'm beat," she said. "It's been about a fourteen-hour day for me. I was going to stop and chat with him for a while, but I think his legions of adoring fans would lynch me if I broke in line."

"I'll tell him you said hi," Taylor said. "Go on, grab a cab home. Have a glass of wine on me."

"Hah," Brett said wearily, turning toward the staircase. "A hot bath and bedtime is all I want."

"The glamorous life of an editor," Taylor called.

"Hah!" Brett said again, for emphasis.

It was quarter past ten by the time Taylor and Michael stepped out onto the icy sidewalk on Broadway near Eighty-second. The snow had shifted gears and was now a slow, grainy drizzle. Michael stepped out into the street and raised his hand with an index finger pointed up. Almost instantly, a cab appeared and braked to a stop next to him.

"Your karma's incredible tonight," Taylor said as she ran

out from under a canopy over the sidewalk. Michael held the door open for her. "You don't even have to wait for cabs."

Michael slid in next to her and shut the door. "When you're hot, you're hot . . ."

The cab driver—a turbaned Sikh with a ponderous black beard—turned to them. "V'ere to?"

"Let's stop for a drink somewhere," Michael said.

Taylor looked at him. "You have to be at Rockefeller Center in roughly"—she looked at her watch—"seven hours. Remember, that little *Today* show gig?"

"Aw, c'mon," Michael said, mock-begging. "There's no way I can get to sleep now anyway. I'm too pumped. Let's stop, please?"

Taylor shook her head from side to side. "What am I going to do with you? All right, we'll stop at Ñ's," she said. "It's just around the corner from my place. One drink and then it's bedtime, okay?"

"Yes, mommie dearest," Michael answered.

Taylor raised her voice to be heard through the Plexiglas shield. "Crosby Street, down in SoHo, between Grande and Broome."

The driver turned, shrugged.

"Jeez," Taylor whispered, then raised her voice again. "Just stay on Broadway—" She pointed out the windshield. "Down Broadway just before Canal? Okay?"

"Okay," the driver said, smiling and nodding.

The cab jerked out into traffic and began speeding down Broadway as Taylor settled back for the long ride. The trip down Broadway from the Upper West Side to SoHo was a long one by Manhattan standards.

"Brett was there," Taylor said. "She left when you started signing."

"That's too bad," Michael answered. "We could have asked her to join us."

"Not a chance. She was exhausted. Even looked tired, which is not like her."

"She's got a lot going on," Michael said absentmindedly as he stared out the window. Then he turned back to Taylor. "Did you give her the contracts?"

"Yes," Taylor said softly. "It's a done deal."

Michael smiled at her. "Well, it's not a completely done deal until they countersign and we see a check."

"I know," Taylor agreed. "But there's nothing in the way. It's going to happen. I expect the paper back tomorrow afternoon."

"Great," Michael said. So subtle as to be almost imperceptible, he relaxed his body and moved closer to Taylor as the driver slowly negotiated the Broadway traffic tie-up north of Lincoln Center. His left shoulder brushed against her right as he turned to her.

"I can't tell you how grateful I am to you," he said. "It's been a tough few years. I appreciate you hanging in with me."

Taylor met his gaze. "I've enjoyed it," she said. "We've had a good run at it."

"We make a good team," he said, then, looking down at his lap, he seemed to hesitate for a second before speaking again. "I've been thinking about making some changes."

"What kinds of changes?"

The cabbie swerved to avoid a collision with a car that had cut in front of him, swearing loudly and rapidly in a language Taylor didn't recognize. The motion caused her to slide across the seat even farther, pressing against Michael hard. He laid his hand on her arm and made no effort to move or ease the pressure.

"I've lost touch with so many friends over the years," he said. "I've just been so buried in work. I don't know that many people in Cleveland anymore. And I need a change. I'm thinking about moving here, to the city."

Taylor felt the slightest tension high in her chest, nearly in her throat. The sensation surprised her.

"Well," she said cautiously. "That would be nice, Michael."

"I seem to know more people in publishing than anything else these days," he went on. "And I know the city. I love being here. I've always thought that if I could afford it, I'd love to live here."

She smiled. "And now you can afford it."

Michael smiled back at her and squeezed her arm. "Yeah," he said. "Thanks to you, I can afford it."

Michael moved his hand down her arm and touched her hand. "Your hands are cold," he said, his voice low, soft.

"It's cold tonight," Taylor said. He took her hand in both of his. His hands were warm, strong. Almost without realizing it, she leaned over and rested her head against his shoulder.

An hour later, Taylor finished off her third and last brandy of the night as Michael stood up and held her coat open for her. They had stopped off at Ñ's, a warm, cozy bar that was hip and trendy and yet had somehow managed to remain reasonably civilized, which was no small feat in the never-ending struggle for domination in the Manhattan bar scene. It was narrow and dark, with rich leather couches and candles and soft music playing from speakers discreetly hidden in the corners. They sat and talked and held hands and sipped brandy until they relaxed and fatigue caught up with them.

As Taylor stood up, holding her arm out for her coat, she swayed a bit.

"You okay?" Michael asked, smiling.

"Just tired," she answered. Then, as her arm went through the sleeve and she spun to put the other in: "Okay, so I'm a little tipsy."

"Good thing we don't have too far to go," Michael said. He took three twenty-dollar bills out of his pocket and laid them on the table, then picked up Taylor's briefcase.

"I can take that," she said.

"Let me. I'm glad to." He took her arm and led her toward the door. Taylor looked back over her shoulder at the table they'd just left.

"Kind of a big tip, isn't it?"

Michael smiled. "I'm feeling generous tonight. Besides, we can afford it."

He pushed the door open and they walked out onto the sidewalk. The sleet had stopped and the cloud cover had passed on, leaving a clear, dark sky above them. The streets were as deserted as Manhattan streets ever get as they turned north toward Grande Street, then walked the two blocks past

Broadway to Taylor's loft. She fumbled for the keys, then got the front door open. She and Michael took the stairs up to her front door. Taylor yawned as she unlocked the three locks and let them in.

Michael went in behind her, crossed the large main room, and set her briefcase down on a glass table in front of the sofa.

"Can I get you anything?" Taylor asked, relocking the front door.

"I'm fine," he answered, turning to face her in the middle of the room. Taylor tossed her hat and coat on the sofa.

"It's late," she said, suppressing another yawn. "Aren't you sleepy?"

"I guess I'm too . . ." Michael hesitated. "Too excited, I guess. Maybe too happy, for once."

Taylor walked over to him. "That's sweet, Michael."

"I owe it all to you."

"I'm just—" Taylor stopped for a moment, looking into his face. Something she saw there made her abdomen tense up, as if in anticipation of something, but she didn't know what.

Michael brought his arms up and took hold of her arms through her tan silk blouse just below her shoulders. Then he pulled her toward him and kissed her, softly at first, their lips barely brushing, then harder. And he let go of her and wrapped his arms around her whole body, pulling her tightly into him.

Taylor stiffened at first, but as her lips met his and the two began to melt together, she pulled him to her as well, bringing her arms up around him, holding him tightly. Perhaps it was a strange and unpredictable mixture of fatigue, brandy, closeness, and her own loneliness that had caught up with her. Despite herself, her own misgivings and fears, she gave in to an impulse that was sweeter and more powerful than she ever expected it would be.

And when Michael Schiftmann turned, took her hand in his, and began walking toward the black metal spiral staircase leading to the upstairs bedrooms, she followed him.

* * *

Taylor Robinson's head pounded and her ears hurt as she spiraled up out of some dream she was even then losing. There was a blaring in her head as well; she couldn't figure out where it was coming from. Her neck hurt and her mouth felt like it was full of dried grass. She moaned and rolled over in the darkness just as the thin line of light under her bathroom door exploded.

"Damn it!" a voice said, as she struggled to remember where she was. "I thought I turned that off!"

Taylor moaned again and started to sit up, but felt the bunched, tangled sheets dragging across her bare skin and stopped. She felt her torso, pulled the sheets tight, and realized she was nude.

A dark form enshrouded in yellow light from the bathroom behind it leaned down next to her and switched the alarm clock off.

"I am so sorry," the voice said. Taylor squinted and realized it was Michael.

"Wha—" she croaked, startled to find him in her bedroom. *What's he doing here?*

"I thought I turned it off," he said. He leaned down, smoothed her tangled hair back across her head, then softly kissed her on the cheek.

"Didn't mean to wake you up," he said softly. "Go back to sleep."

"What time is it?"

"Five-fifteen."

"In the morning?" she squeaked. "That's the crack of dawn."

Michael laughed. "No, my dear, to be more accurate, it's actually the butt crack of dawn. And the limo'll be here in fifteen minutes. Remember, that little *Today* show gig?"

Taylor groaned again and tried to roll over. "I better get dressed," she said, still not quite sure where she was.

"Don't be silly," he said. "Go back to sleep. Besides, the limo's taking me directly to Newark after the taping. I've got a flight out to Boston, then Minneapolis, remember?"

"Oh, yeah," she murmured. "Boston, Minneapolis. You sure it's okay if I don't go?"

"Of course," Michael whispered. He rubbed her back, running his hands lightly down the sheet, to her hips, and then squeezing her beneath the sheets.

Taylor began to wake up, and with wakefulness came the memory of the previous evening, which had ended only about three hours earlier. She felt herself reddening again.

Damn, she thought, *this man can make you blush.*

"I've got to go," he said. "But I'll call you tonight."

She smiled. "I'll be here. Trying to recover . . ."

"It'll be an early evening for me, too." With his index finger under her chin, he pulled her face toward him and then kissed her, full and long. His mouth tasted fresh, clean, and she was briefly embarrassed that she hadn't had the chance to brush her teeth.

He stood up. "Bye, you."

"Bye, Michael. Be careful."

She drifted there a few moments as he turned off the bathroom light, plunging the room into darkness. Then she heard footsteps on the metal staircase and the front door opening, then closing again as he left.

Taylor fought off sleep long enough to get up, put on her robe, and walk downstairs to the front door to lock the deadbolts. Then she walked into her kitchen and thirstily drank half a small carton of orange juice. When she got back upstairs to bed, she flicked on the table lamp next to her bed.

The sheets were tangled, bunched, the bottom sheet pulled completely off the mattress.

"It was a good fight, Ma," she whispered. "But I think I won."

And as she crawled back into bed, reset the alarm clock, and turned off the lamp, she lay there in the dark a few moments staring at the ceiling.

"Good heavens," she muttered. "What have I gotten myself into?"

CHAPTER 8

Friday evening, Las Vegas

His head still buzzed as Michael Schiftmann snapped the plastic cable tie that had been looped through the latch on his hotel minibar and pulled out a tiny, airline-size bottle of Dewar's. He unscrewed the cap, poured the contents over a tumbler filled with ice, and took the first sip.

That first sip always burned, but it was a good burn to Michael, for it signified the end of another long day. Five days into the second phase of his book tour and he was already starting to have trouble remembering where he was.

Let's see, he thought. *Monday, Manhattan; Tuesday, Boston and Minneapolis; Wednesday, Detroit; Thursday, Denver; Friday, Las Vegas.*

And tomorrow, he left for two days in San Francisco, then on to what felt more like a whistle-stop tour down the coast to L.A. and San Diego. He raised the glass to his lips, downed the rest in one gulp, then grabbed a second bottle from the bar. He crossed the room, sat down on the bed, and picked up the hotel phone. He dialed 9, waited for a second dial tone, then punched in ten numbers from memory.

The phone rang four times—Michael knew the machine would pick up on the next ring—when a rushed feminine voice answered. "Hello."

"Hey you," Michael said, raising the glass to his lips and taking a small sip.

"Hey you right back," Taylor said. "I was hoping you'd call. How are you?"

"Tired. I just finished the signing at Gambling on Murder," he said.

"Great. How'd it go?"

Michael pressed his head deeper into the pillow and sipped again from the drink. "Fine, just fine. About seventy-five, I'd say."

"Michael," Taylor said, her voice rising. "That's wonderful! Do you have any idea how big a crowd that is in Las Vegas?"

"I would've thought with this being one of the most famous mystery bookstores in the world, I'd have had bigger."

"Stop it," she scolded. "I've been in Gambling on Murder. You can't fit any more people than that in the whole store. In fact, my guess is you're lucky the fire marshal didn't show up."

Michael smiled. "You always make me feel better."

"I'm your agent; it's part of my job. How'd the interviews go?"

"That lady on the public radio station did an okay job. She at least had read one of the books. But I did that noontime talk show, with that—oh hell, what's his name? God, I met him seven hours ago and can't remember his name."

"That's life on the road for you," Taylor interjected.

"No kidding," Michael said. "Stress-induced memory loss. Anyway, he was an idiot. Typical daytime talk show blow-dried anchorperson. Hadn't read the book, didn't know who I was. At least he sort of stuck to the prepared questions."

"That means he can read," Taylor said. "In the TV business, he's an overachiever."

"So what's new on your end?" he asked.

"I had dinner tonight with Brett," Taylor answered.

"Oh, so no hot date?" Michael offered.

Taylor hesitated. "No, no hot date. But she did tell me you're climbing to number three on the list Sunday."

"Great!" Michael said.

"And on top of that, *The Fourth Letter* made it onto the paperback list. You'll debut at eleven."

"Oh man, I love it!"

"And the contracts have been processed and I expect a check within the next couple of weeks."

Michael stretched on the bed and finished off the Scotch. "If your job is to make me feel better, you're sure doing it well."

"All part of the package," she teased.

"I wish you were here," he said. "I'm stretched out all alone on this king-size bed with no one to massage the tension out of my tired muscles."

"So get a rubdown," Taylor said.

"That's not the muscle I meant," he teased, then lowered his voice. "I miss you."

Her voice lowered as well. "Well, hmm."

There was a long silence filled only by a faint whisper of static on the line.

"You still there?" Michael asked after a moment.

"Yes."

"Something bothering you?"

Another long pause. "I'm just not quite sure what's going on, that's all," Taylor answered. "I mean, I've never done this before."

"Done what before?" Michael asked. "You mean you were a—"

"No, silly," she snapped, laughing the tension out of her voice. "I've done *that* before! I've just never done it with a client."

Michael rolled over on his side with the phone resting on his right ear. "Okay, so it's a little weird, mixing business with a personal life. But there's something going on here, Taylor. Something powerful. I don't know where it's going, but I'd sure like to find out."

"I just don't want to . . . don't want to make another mistake, that's all."

"Look," Michael said, "this stupid tour is almost over. At least I can see the end. Then I'm going back to New York City and find a place, get moved, and get back to work. That's a tall order. I think I'm going to need a rest before I take that on."

"So—"

"What say we get on a plane and go lie on a beach for a week or so? Just the two of us? Maybe someplace in the Caribbean."

Taylor cleared her throat and was silent again for a few moments. "I don't know, Michael, I—"

"C'mon," he said. "It's wintertime. You need to get away. We need to get away. Please?"

"Let me think about it," she said.

"Fair enough. At least it's not a no. So what are you up to for the rest of the evening?"

She laughed. "It's nearly eleven here," she said. "And I'm pooped. I might finish reading the paper and go to bed. Don't know if I've got that much left in me."

"Me, too," Michael said, raising up on the bed and planting his feet on the floor. "I think it's a phone call to room service and then some free HBO. I'll call you tomorrow from San Francisco. Okay?"

"What time's your plane leave?"

"Not until eleven, which is a real treat. Writers aren't used to being up in time to make seven A.M. flights."

"You and Carol will get a break tomorrow," Taylor said. "By the way, how is she?"

Michael felt the muscles in his jaw knot up and fought to keep the tension out of his voice. "She's Carol," he said. "You know."

"Yeah. I guess so."

"Sleep well," Michael said.

"You, too. Talk to you tomorrow."

"Okay," Taylor said. "And Michael—"

"Yeah?" he asked after a moment.

"I miss you, too."

Michael grinned and rattled the ice around in his glass. "Go to bed," he said. "Think of me."

"Can't help it. Good night."

Michael hung the phone up and stood, stretching his arms high over his head and arching his back. He walked over to the large window that nearly covered the wall opposite him. He pulled the drapes aside, revealing the buzzing, chaotic, hyper light show that was Las Vegas on any night of the year. In the distance, he spotted the beam of light coming out of the apex of the Luxor, a light so bright it was visible from the space shuttle when the sky was clear. Off in another direction, the strip ran twenty-five floors below him, lined with cars bumper-to-bumper.

Michael felt restless. He was in Las Vegas, one of the most exciting cities in the world, on a Friday night in a luxury hotel room someone else was paying for, with a very generous expense budget included. And he was alone.

He reached down and picked up a spiral-bound notebook that described and promoted the various features of the hotel. The room service menu was extensive and available any time, day or night. Just pick up the phone . . . Maybe there was a movie on he hadn't seen.

Then again, maybe there wasn't.

Michael walked into the bathroom, ran water over his face and rubbed his tired eyes, then brushed his teeth and combed his hair. He pulled a navy-blue double-breasted jacket out of the closet and slipped it on, then walked to the door of his hotel room and opened it. He stopped in the doorway, took one last look at the rumpled bed, and pulled the door behind him.

In the two years Carol Gee had been the senior publicist at Accent Press, she thought she'd seen just about every form of schizoid author imaginable. She'd once accompanied a best-selling author on a twelve-city tour in which the famous literary author managed to get himself arrested four times—twice in the same city. A mega-best-selling female author had once called her in the middle of the night from her four-room suite and demanded that Carol clean up the mess where her cat threw up. And she'd been hit on by famous authors so many times, she no longer bothered to record that in her mental diary.

Twenty-eight years old, Yale graduate, second-generation Korean-American, and with an IQ that placed her in the top point-five percent of the world's population, Carol Gee was finally beginning to wonder what the hell she was doing with her life. All her career aspirations, her ambitions, her desire to achieve and succeed had been thrown into jeopardy by the behavior of one man: Michael Schiftmann.

Carol had never seen anyone like him. Charming and affable, even warm, one minute, he could in an instant become an over-controlled, seething cauldron of cold fury. In Detroit two days earlier, at an old Waldenbooks in a decaying strip mall, the two of them had arrived for Michael's book signing only to discover that no advertising had been done, no announcement made, and the only notice of the signing was a handwritten sheet taped to the cash register with the wrong date listed. To add even further insult, the five cases of books Carol had overnighted to the store hadn't even been opened. It took the assistant manager and the sixteen-year-old girl working the night shift five minutes to even find them.

This was not the first time Carol Gee had seen a book signing botched, although it was relatively rare to see one bungled this badly for a *New York Times* best seller. Carol was prepared to deal with it, go on to the next city, and make a note to never schedule a signing at the store again. The usual procedure was to stick around for an hour, chat up the bookstore salespeople, then sign every copy in the store so they could be sold as autographed copies, a practice known in the business as "signing stock."

Carol had grimaced as they walked into the nearly empty bookstore only to have the teenage girl behind the cash register stare blankly and ask if she could help them find anything. Carol started to say something when Michael shot her a look, the coldest, blackest look she'd ever seen in another human being, then turned to the salesgirl.

"Let me see your boss," he said quietly. The young girl gulped, excused herself, and disappeared into the stockroom. The assistant manager came out seconds later, a concerned look already on her face as the enormity of her problem gradually soaked in.

Michael's voice was low and steady as he explained to the poor woman who he was and why he was there, and just how much money and time and energy had been spent in arranging this signing. The woman stammered a barely intelligible reply, then scrambled back into the stockroom and was gone for several minutes.

"Maybe we should just go," Carol suggested.

Michael turned to her. "Not yet."

Moments later, the assistant manager, a thin sheen of sweat on her forehead and a hank of unkempt hair down in her face, returned with a stack of hardcovers, obviously hoping to placate them by offering Michael the chance to sign stock. Michael looked at her, turned to Carol and said, "Wait here." Then he took the assistant manager by the elbow and led her back to her office.

"What's he going to do?" the ashen-faced girl behind the cash register asked.

"I don't know," Carol said quietly.

A minute or so later, Michael emerged from the office, strode quickly across the store, and met Carol at the front.

"We can go now."

"But—" she said. Then she felt his fingers clamp down on her elbow and gently, but firmly, aim her toward the door. The two walked out into the sparse mall crowd. As they exited the store, Carol glanced over her shoulder and saw the assistant manager emerge from her office, tears streaming down her face.

"What did you say to her?" Carol demanded. It occurred to her that she'd never talked to one of her authors like that before.

Michael continued walking quickly, staring straight ahead, with his hand still on Carol's elbow pulling her along. "Let's just say that won't ever happen again," he said. Carol said nothing else until they got back to their hotel.

That had been two nights earlier, and ever since, Carol had wrestled with her feelings from that night. She'd been repulsed by an author's behavior before. She'd been angry at them, frustrated by them, grossed out by them, resentful of them, and each time had managed to suppress all those reactions and emotions and do her work in the most professional manner possible. But this time . . .

This time was different. This time she was frightened by her author, and Carol Gee had never been frightened by an author before.

Denver had gone well, along with the side trip to Boulder, and the day had gone very well in Las Vegas. Still, Carol had kept her distance from Michael. For the first time, she was beginning to think she wasn't cut out for this line of work.

Fatigued and stressed, she had gone straight up to her room after the evening's signing. She was awaiting a FedEx package with the next group of airline tickets, the block of tickets for the last phase of the tour. Several of the signings in Southern California were so close together they would rent a car, and the contract for that was coming as well.

Carol looked down at her watch: nine-thirty. The package was supposed to have been delivered by eight. She'd been unable to get through to the toll-free number to check on the package, and the front desk had been unable to find it if it had been delivered. She was tired, but too restless to eat.

Just as she sat down on the side of the bed and reached for the remote control, the phone rang.

"Yes," she answered.

"Front desk, Ms. Gee," a friendly male voice said. "We found your package. The concierge got busy and forget to let us know it was here. I'm terribly sorry."

Carol felt the muscles just below her rib cage relax. At least she could let go of that worry now. "Good, thanks. I'll be right down."

"I can have it sent up," the clerk offered.

"No, I'd rather come right now. I need the walk anyway."

Carol hung up the phone and left her room. On the elevator, she stared ahead at her own image in the polished brass. Her hair needed trimming, she thought, and in the slight distortion of her reflection on the brass, she saw that she looked even more tired than she felt.

She exited the elevator and wound her way around a group of large men wearing fezzes, smoking cigars, and laughing.

She heard laughter and bells ringing and shouts from the casino. She wondered how people stood it.

The front desk was dark mahogany, polished to a bright luster, with a mirrored tile wall behind it. She walked over to the corner, smiled at the desk clerk, and motioned with her hand. He picked up the package and brought it over to her.

"Ms. Gee, I take it," he said.

"Yes, thanks. We've been waiting on that."

"Great," he said brightly. "I'm glad we were able to locate it. Is there anything else I can help you with?"

"No," Carol said, taking the package.

"Have a pleasant stay."

Carol turned and headed back across the lobby to the bank of elevators. Then, out of the corner of her eye, she spotted two people walking toward the main entrance to the casino from deep inside.

It was Michael Schiftmann, and on his arm was a curvaceous blond nearly as tall as he. She wore a sequined, body-hugging dress, makeup so thick it could have been slathered on with a butter knife, and high heels of the type usually characterized as "do-me pumps."

My God, Carol thought. *Not again . . .*

The two were walking straight toward her. Carol turned quickly and stepped behind a tree that was perhaps fifteen feet tall and in a pot as big around as a tractor tire. She turned her head away from the center of the lobby and peeked out from between the thick branches. Michael and the blond walked arm-in-arm through the lobby, weaving in and out of the throng of people, oblivious to the crowd around them. As they passed by not ten feet away from Carol, she stepped out from behind the potted trees and watched as the two headed toward the main entrance of the hotel. A bellman held the door open as they stepped outside into the arid Las Vegas night.

Carol's eyes tracked them through a bank of windows that ran along the front of the hotel. She strained to see past the blazing reflections of dancing, chaotic, multicolored lights in the massive plate-glass windows.

But she could see well enough to follow Michael and the

blond as a taxi pulled up next to them and they climbed into the backseat together.

Carol Gee watched as the cab pulled away, then shook her head slowly and turned back toward the elevator bank.

How does he do it? she wondered. *Night after night . . .*

This will all be over soon, she reminded herself, as she went for the safety of her own double-locked hotel room.

CHAPTER 9

Monday morning, Nashville

Andy Parks hit the pedal on his rust-streaked, ancient Datsun 280Z and prayed the brakes would hold one last time. He meant to have the car serviced before leaving Chattanooga, but he'd gotten too busy—as usual—and simply hadn't gotten around to it. The pedal had been soft for weeks, and now with the wet cold of the last few days, they'd begun squealing terribly each time he touched them.

The construction on I–24 around Nashville wasn't helping. The traffic was bumper-to-bumper and a light mist was falling that Andy hoped wouldn't turn to snow anytime soon. He knew he couldn't afford to spend the night in Nashville. His boss at the newspaper had told him yesterday afternoon in no uncertain terms that he was about to max out his meager expense account. The *Chattanooga News–Free Press* wasn't known for hard-hitting reporting or for spending tons of money in pursuit of the news. This was different, though. This was the kind of story that was guaranteed to get attention, maybe even a Pulitzer nomination, and in any event a ticket out of Chattanooga and away from that sorry excuse for a newspaper. And at twenty-seven years of age, with five years of dues paying already behind him, Andy Parks was ready for a bigger market.

The brakes screeched as the traffic came to a stop just before the Davidson County line. The outlying counties of Nashville, especially Rutherford and Williamson, were some of the fastest-growing counties in America and they each had the traffic to prove it. Andy came to a stop behind a tractor-trailer rig and tapped his fingers nervously on the steering wheel. He looked to his left, where a blond behind the wheel of a bronze Lexus smoked a cigarette and stared straight ahead. Behind him, the massive grille of a tractor-trailer rig loomed in his back windshield.

Forty minutes of stop-and-go traffic later, Andy parked his car in the garage across from the Justice Center and walked out into the icy sleet falling steadily on the city. He strode quickly toward the James Robertson Parkway, then cut right across the plaza and through the revolving door into the main lobby. A bulletproof kiosk blocked the way into the heart of the building, with a heavy sheriff's department deputy—shaved head, regulation brown uniform—ensconced inside. It reminded Andy of the entrance to a prison.

"Yeah?" the guard asked through the small, slotted metal vent.

Andy reached into his back pocket, pulled out his wallet, and held his Hamilton County press pass up to the glass.

"Andy Parks," he said. "*Chattanooga News–Free Press*. I'd like to see Detective Gary Gilley."

The guard stared at the pass for a moment, then slid a clipboard out through a small slot in the glass.

"Sign in," he said, "and I'll need to see a driver's license."

"But my press pass—" Andy insisted.

"I'll need to see a driver's license." The guy didn't even look up at him again.

Andy pulled out his license, signed the visitors' log, then slid the clipboard and his license back through the slot. It sat there for maybe fifteen seconds while the guard completed filling out some other form. Andy cleared his throat, which had no visible effect on the guard. Finally the guard reached up, took the clipboard, examined it, checked the license, then slid them off to one side of his desk. He reached into a drawer and pulled out a yellow tag that read VISITOR and slid it through the window.

"Attach this badge to your coat lapel," the guard recited

without looking at Andy again. "Keep it visible at all times. Stand over there. Someone will come and get you."

Andy took the badge and wished he'd stopped for a cup of coffee before parking the car. He was sleepy, fatigue like a brittle cap jammed too tightly on his head. He crossed the large lobby and only then noticed there was no place to sit.

Not exactly user friendly, he thought.

He leaned against a column and rolled his neck around on his shoulders, trying to work some of the tension out. Then he stretched and arched his back, trying not to look too odd, but needing to loosen up. He wasn't used to being up this early, and the drive in from Chattanooga, over an icy and nearly closed Monteagle Mountain, had taken a lot out of him.

Andy Parks paced the lobby for fifteen minutes, with little to break the monotony. Arriving police officers, city officials, or friends of the guard's were ushered past without question. Visitors were uniformly hassled and made to wait.

Andy was about to say something to the guard when the door opened and a young woman about his age walked through and into the lobby. She was perhaps two inches shorter than he, with dark eyes, skin only slightly paler than a café au lait, and jet-black hair.

"Mr. Parks," she said, walking up to him.

"Yes," he said. "Andy Parks, *Chattanooga News–Free Press*. Detective Gilley?"

"No, I'm Detective Maria Chavez. Gilley's out in the field this morning. Did you have an appointment?"

"No, I came up here kind of on a spur-of-the-moment deal—"

"You should have gotten an appointment," Chavez said. "We're really busy."

"I know," Andy said, smiling at her. She was pretty, he thought, and if it took being nice to a cop to get what he needed, he was willing to make the sacrifice. "That's why I'm here."

Maria Chavez looked at him without speaking, a question on her face.

"I came to talk to Detective Gilley about the murders of those two girls over on Church Street."

"Oh, that," she snapped. "We can't say anything to anyone about that. That investigation is at a critical point right now, and we aren't speaking to the press or anyone else."

Maria reached into the back pocket of her black wool slacks and extracted a business card. "If you'll loan me a pen, I'll give you the name of the press adjutant for the department. When we have an announcement, he'll put you on the call list."

Andy took the ballpoint out of his shirt pocket, clicked it, and handed it to her.

"When might that be?" he asked as Chavez scribbled on the back of her card.

She looked up. "Not anytime soon, I'm afraid. I wouldn't expect to hear anything soon." Maria Chavez handed Andy the card.

"Sorry you made the trip for nothing," she said. "Now if you'll excuse me, I've got a lot of work to do."

Maria Chavez turned and took two steps toward the door when Andy said, loud enough for anyone in the lobby to hear: "So, Detective Chavez, what are your chances of catching the Alphabet Man?"

Maria Chavez stopped in her tracks and froze. Andy could swear he saw goose bumps on the back of her neck. After a moment, she turned and walked back to him.

"What did you say?" she asked, her voice low.

Andy smiled at her. "J was two years ago in Chattanooga, then K was last year in Dallas. And you guys had L and M early Saturday morning. Don't you think it's kind of creepy that the guy pulled a double for the first time?"

Maria Chavez's eyes widened, and for a moment it seemed she was trying to say something and nothing would come out.

"Look," Andy continued. "I'm exhausted, it's freezing outside, and it's pretty darn cold in here. Can I buy you a cup of coffee somewhere?"

Maria stared at him. "Do you know the city?" she whispered after a few seconds. "West End Avenue?"

Andy nodded.

"Centennial Park?" she went on, her voice barely audible in the cavernous lobby. Andy nodded again.

"There's a McDonald's next to it," she instructed. "Meet me there in half an hour."

Andy checked his watch and smiled at her again. She really was quite pretty. "Great," he said. "We'll be there in time for an Egg McMuffin."

"How the bloody, goddamn hell did he find out?" Max Bransford yelled, slamming his fist down so hard on his heavy wooden desk that the ashtray bounced twice before settling down. The ashtray was clean; the Justice Center had been smoke-free for years, but Bransford kept the ashtray around as a souvenir.

"Max, he ain't going to tell us that," Gary Gilley said, holding his hands out in front of him.

"It's my fault," Maria Chavez said, standing next to her colleague. "I'm not even sure he knew for sure that the guy painted the letters, but when he saw the look on my face, that confirmed it."

"It's not your fault, Maria," Gilley said.

"Why did you talk to the guy in the first place?" Bransford demanded, his face reddening. He shook his head from side to side. "You know, I don't need this shit. I really don't need this shit, guys. I'm too old for this."

"Lieutenant, I was the only one here," Chavez explained. She was trying hard not to beg, but she feared her voice was giving her away. "You weren't here, Gary wasn't here. And this guy was 'Alphabet Man this,' 'Alphabet Man that . . .' No telling who heard him. It was a judgment call and I had to make it. I had to get him out of here and talk to him to shut him up!"

Gilley leaned forward and placed his hands, palms down, on Bransford's desk. "Max, we were never going to keep this quiet forever. It's too big. I'm surprised they've been able to keep it under wraps this long. I mean, hell, Max, this guy's a stone-cold serial killer who's been working all over the damn country for years!"

Bransford sighed, then reached up with his beefy right hand, and with his thumb and forefinger began massaging either side of his neck just under his jawbone. He'd read somewhere that massaging in that place would bring down a heart rate, and right now Max Bransford needed that bad.

"You guys have been watching too many cop shows," Bransford said. "This is a violation of procedure, it's going to make us look like idiots, and when the shit starts flowing downhill, I'll try to stop it at my desk, but I can't guarantee a goddamn thing."

"Lieutenant," Chavez said, "I'm sorry."

Bransford looked at her. She wasn't stupid, but she had been on homicide only a few months, and this was the first big case she'd ever seen. The first one of national scope that had come down the pike in a long time . . .

"When's the story going to break?" Bransford asked.

Chavez winced. "Ten days," she said. "Two weeks at the most."

"One thing we've got going for us," Gilley said. "At least it's the Chattanooga paper. Nobody reads that rag unless they're looking to find a coupon for toilet paper."

"You're fooling yourself, my friend," Bransford said. "We're up to our nether regions in amphibious reptiles. The only thing you can do now is get out there and find this fuck. Meantime, something tells me I better get on the horn to Hank Powell up at Quantico."

Gilley looked across the desk at his boss and for a brief moment almost felt sorry for him.

"Want me to do it, Max?" he asked.

Bransford shook his head. "Nope, this's what they pay me the big bucks for."

CHAPTER 10

Friday evening, two weeks later, Manhattan

Taylor Robinson stepped out of the cab in front of Brett Silverman's brownstone on Twenty-fourth Street, between Ninth and Tenth Avenues, across the street from the massive London Terrace apartments. She paid the driver and opened the wrought-iron gate that led into the tiny courtyard in front of the brownstone. Her coat was draped loosely around her shoulders; it had been a beautiful, almost warm February day in New York. The temperature had climbed into the early forties. Taylor smiled; it had been nearly three weeks since she'd seen the woman who had over the past months become her best friend. Only in New York could she ever remember going three weeks without even speaking to someone she was so close to.

She climbed the flight of wide brick and concrete steps up to the heavy wooden double doors and rang the bell. A few moments later, the tarnished brass doorknob turned and Brett Silverman pulled the door open.

"Hey girl!" Brett called, reaching out and taking Taylor's arm. "C'mon in."

"Hi," Taylor said, stepping into the entrance foyer. Taylor set down her briefcase, shrugged off her overcoat, and handed it to Brett. Brett hung the coat on the hook of a large, ornately carved antique oak hall tree, then turned and opened her arms. Brett and Taylor hugged briefly, then Brett led the way into the large living room of the three-story brownstone.

"C'mon, let's have a quick glass of wine, then we'll walk down the street to the restaurant. It won't get crowded for another hour so anyway."

Brett Silverman had decorated her home in the style of a turn-of-the-century New York matron. Red velvet drapes covered the front window; thick Oriental rugs covered polished oak floors. Her furniture was Victorian and heavy. It didn't suit Taylor's tastes, but it was a welcome change from her recent surroundings. The past couple of weeks, Taylor had shuttled between her apartment and office and seen little else.

Taylor followed Brett through the house and into a large kitchen that was as modern as the rest of the house was Victorian. A large Garland stove dominated one wall, with an institutional-size stainless-steel refrigerator across from it on the other wall. Brett stepped over, opened one of the two large doors on the refrigerator, and pulled out a bottle of Chardonnay.

"This okay?" she asked.

"Perfect," Taylor answered. She pulled a stool over and sat down behind a counter.

"So how's it going?" Brett asked. "I feel like I haven't seen you in a month of Sundays."

"Been kind of crazy," Taylor offered. "Prosperity's going to be the death of us all."

"Where've I heard that before?" Brett joked as she pulled two wineglasses out of the cabinet next to the refrigerator and poured each of them a full glass of the buttery, cold white wine. She handed one to Taylor across the counter, and the two women clinked glasses.

"So tell me, what's the word from our favorite best-selling author on the end of his tour?"

"Well," Taylor said, pausing to take another sip of the wine. "He's bushed, but I think he's happy. The end of the tour went really well. I think he's real tired of being cooped up in a car with Carol Gee. I don't think they're getting along together very well."

Brett Silverman leaned down on the counter and placed both her elbows on the ceramic surface. "I can back you up there," she said. "Carol said they're about to drive each other crazy. I don't really know what's been going on, but apparently it hasn't been very pleasant. In fact, I think Carol's probably going to ask for a transfer when she gets back."

"Oh my God," Taylor said. "I had no idea it was that bad. Michael doesn't talk about it much. It's just that whenever her name comes up, I can hear his teeth clench over the phone."

"When she called last night, she was so upset I told her to take a week off. The tour ends tomorrow in San Diego, she's got friends in L.A. What the hell, take some time off, lie in the sun, decompress, let go of it all."

"Good idea," Taylor said. "At least give her a chance to think things over."

Brett turned, opened the cabinet door behind her, and took out a box of gourmet crackers. She spread some on a plate, then slid the plate across the counter to Taylor. "Here, something to munch on."

Taylor bit into one of the crackers, realizing that she was getting hungry. It had been a long day, and at that moment she couldn't remember if she ever ate lunch.

Three sips of wine, she thought, *and it's going to my head.*

"Thanks," she said.

Brett stared across the counter at her friend, studying her face intently for a few moments. Taylor looked up from the plate she'd been staring at.

"What?"

"Nothing," Brett said.

Taylor frowned. "What? What are you looking at?"

Brett straightened from where she'd been leaning over the counter and fingered the stem of her wineglass. "It's none of my business, but you really do look tired. What's going on? You can't be working that hard."

Taylor paused a moment before answering, as if trying to decide how much to say. "I'm not sleeping well. I've got a lot on my mind," she admitted.

"Anything you want to talk about?"

Taylor turned away, uncomfortable. "Not really."

"You know, when you called today I got the feeling something was the matter. I also figured it was kind of weird your being willing to come to my house. You almost always want to meet somewhere in the midtown area close to your office."

Taylor sighed, took another long sip of wine, and set the glass down on the counter. "Well, there is something . . ."

Brett nervously pulled her long hair over her shoulders into a ponytail and grasped it with her right hand. Her left hand drummed on the countertop. "I think I'm beginning to understand. Something tells me there's a man involved in this story somewhere."

"There is," Taylor confessed. "And if I don't talk to somebody soon, I'm going to go nuts. One thing though . . ."

Brett let go of her hair. "Yeah?"

"You've got to swear," Taylor said, her voice somber. "I mean it, Brett, this can't go any further than this kitchen."

"Whoa, girl," Brett said. "This does sound serious. What is he? Some famous actor or, let me see, the head of a major publishing house? Is that it? You're afraid of being accused of sleeping your way into book deals, right?"

Taylor wearily rubbed her eyes, then squinted and focused on the woman across from her. "Worse than that, I'm afraid."

Brett's forehead wrinkled. "Good heavens, Robinson, who the hell is it?"

"You've got to promise," Taylor insisted. "This is top secret. For your ears only."

"You got it," Brett said. "I swear. No further. But who is it?"

Taylor hesitated a few more moments, still agonizing over whether to say anything. But then, she realized, she had to talk to somebody or she was going to go crazy.

"It's a certain best-selling author we both know," Taylor said softly.

Brett focused on a midair space halfway between her nose and Taylor's. "Best-selling author," she mumbled. And then, as if a burst of light had gone off inside her head like an explosion, her mouth opened and her eyes seemed to quiver in their sockets.

"No!" she gasped.

Taylor nodded her head.

"It can't be," Brett whispered.

"It is, dear heart. Believe it."

"You're sleeping with a client?" Brett asked, aghast.

Taylor leaned forward, rested her forehead on the counter, and moaned.

"Oh my God, is it serious?"

Taylor raised her head. "He's moving here after the tour. And he wants to go on vacation together. The Caribbean . . ."

Brett walked around the counter and sat on a stool next to Taylor, then put an arm around her shoulder.

"I mean, Taylor—" she stammered. "How did it happen?"

Taylor wearily let her head fall onto Brett's shoulder. "Oh, God, he was staying at my apartment. We'd been working so closely together for so long and we went out to celebrate the night he signed the contract and had that great signing at the Barnes & Noble. There was a lot of brandy and hand-holding, and then we went back to my place and one thing just kind of led to another."

"But sweetie, that night of the party he had that blond bimbo up in the guest bedroom."

Taylor sat up straight, reached for her wineglass. "I know," she said defensively. "I know. He apologized. Profusely . . . He was so damn charming about it all." She took another long sip of the wine, polishing off all but a few drops at the bottom. Then she turned and smiled weakly at Brett.

"At least we did the safe-sex thing."

Brett smiled back at her sympathetically. "Well, thank God for small favors." She got up, retrieved the wine bottle, and filled both their glasses.

"I've got to ask this, babe," Brett said as she stuffed the cork back in the wine bottle. "I mean, do you like this guy? Are you in love with him? Is this going anywhere?"

"I don't know," Taylor said, trying not to sound whiny and not at all sure she was succeeding. "But it's been so long since I've been with anyone. I work a gazillion hours a week. You know how hard it is to meet anybody in Manhattan if you don't do the bar scene?"

Brett shrugged. "I don't know. I've never not done the bar scene."

"It's damn hard. And the men I work with are either disaffected grungemeisters or incredibly attractive, perfect men who also happen to be gay."

"Okay," Brett snapped. "You're lonely, you're horny, blah blah blah. *But Michael Schiftmann?*"

"Why not?" Taylor demanded. "I mean, he's a good-looking guy, he's intelligent—"

Brett turned, held up her index finger. "And he is rich."

"Okay, that too. So what's wrong with it?"

"Have you ever read his books?" Brett asked. "The guy's a perv! Trust me, I edit him!"

"Of course I've read his books. His books aren't him," Taylor insisted.

"Okay, grant you that. The main question is, do you like him?"

Taylor thought for a moment. "I like him. Yes, I like him. Could I love him? I don't know."

Brett leaned down on the counter again, smiling, and lowering her voice to a conspiratorial level. "And there is one other thing . . . Is he any good?"

Taylor looked directly into her friend's eyes and stared for a moment, then: "Un-fucking-believable. The best ever, Brett. I mean it, the Earth shook and I was fogged up the rest of the day."

Brett straightened up quickly. "Whoa, girl! Okay, as your friend and spiritual advisor in matters of the heart, I recommend you go for it, ASAP. Ride that wave as far as it'll go."

Taylor smiled. "You think so?"

"Hey, what's the downside? The worst that can happen is it doesn't work out, then you have to suffer with great sex from a rich guy until he dumps you or you dump him."

"It could be worse than that," Taylor said. "I could lose him as a client."

Brett took her hands in hers and squeezed them. "He's a smart guy, Taylor. He knows who got him where he is. Business is business, no matter what."

Taylor thought about that for a moment. "Yeah, I guess you're right. At least I hope you are."

"C'mon, the Empire Diner awaits. Let's get down there before it gets too crowded."

Brett Silverman always considered Saturdays her quiet time in the office; a chance to go through the mountain of paper in her in-box, stack up the phone calls that hadn't yet been returned so she'd be ready to go first thing Monday morning, go through the e-mail messages she hadn't had time to deal with.

Pull together the stack of rejected submissions for Marcie, her assistant, to get started on . . .

Brett had slept late this Saturday after a huge meal at the Empire Diner with Taylor the night before, followed by several more glasses of wine before bedtime after her friend grabbed a cab back to SoHo. She'd watched an old movie on cable, gotten more than a little drunk, then stayed under the covers until almost noon. She drank a pot of coffee and scrambled some eggs and read the *Times* before grabbing a cab to her office around three. There was no particular reason to move quickly on this Saturday afternoon; this was only the latest in a string of dateless Saturday nights she'd endured. She was beginning to wonder how long her dry spell was going to last.

Manhattan had chilled overnight; the afternoon temperatures back down into the low thirties. In line with the latest cost-saving measures, the heat in her building had been cut back. Brett threw off her parka but left her ski sweater on as she sat down at her desk.

At least, she thought, she was here alone: no meetings, no frantic phone calls, no juggling six projects at once.

An hour into her work, Brett Silverman began to get sleepy

and to wonder if she shouldn't just bag it and head back to her brownstone for a long nap before her solo dinner. She leaned back in her chair and rubbed her eyes, fighting the urge to indulge in self-pity at the prospect of eating dinner alone. She wondered if perhaps Taylor might be free again tonight. What the hell, with her new boyfriend thousands of miles away in Southern California, she was probably facing a dateless Saturday night as well.

Brett relaxed and put her feet up on her desk, contemplating Michael Schiftmann and Taylor Robinson as an item. She wanted her friend to be happy, but still there was something that made her profoundly uneasy at the news. She tried to put it out of her mind and leaned forward to grab another stack of correspondence to answer when her phone suddenly went off.

Brett fumbled for the phone, jolted out of what she realized had become a quite serious reverie. She also wondered who would be calling in on her direct line on a Saturday afternoon.

"Hello," she said.

"Brett? Carol."

Brett smiled. "Hello, Carol Gee! Welcome to your last day on the road for a long while."

"Thank God," Carol said. "I quite literally couldn't take another day of this."

Brett felt her grip on the handset tighten. "Has something happened?" She heard Carol Gee sigh loudly into the phone and then groan.

"Oh, I just can't take any more," Carol said.

"What did he do now?"

"Nothing. I shouldn't say anything. I just wanted to call and blow off some steam. You're the only person I can talk to at the office about this."

"Look, it's almost over," Brett said. "I know this has been a rough trip. But after tonight, hey, you're on vacation for a week."

"About time," Carol said. "I just hope a week's long **enough**."

"Go hide out, lie on a beach, forget there are such things as telephones, fax machines, e-mail . . ."

"Best-selling authors," Carol interjected.

"C'mon, it can't be that bad," Brett countered. "After all, his fans like him, his mother likes him—"

"God knows why," Carol said, exasperated. "You know, last night he went out—"

"He's even got a girlfriend," Brett said.

"What?" Carol asked, her voice shocked.

"Oh, I'm not supposed to say anything, but these kinds of things never stay hidden very long. Truth is, he and Taylor have got a little thing going on."

"What? What did you say?"

"He and Taylor."

"Taylor Robinson, his agent?" Carol Gee sounded surprised beyond belief.

"Yeah, it was a shock to me, too," Brett agreed. "But apparently this may be pretty serious."

"My God," Carol whispered, her voice sounding far off.

"Yeah," Brett said, then added, "Hey, you all right?"

For a few moments, Brett heard only the hissing of transcontinental static. "Carol, you there?"

"Oh, yeah. I'm here. Just surprised. That's all."

"The whole world's going to be surprised," Brett said, chatting on. "I expect this is the kind of thing that'll even make the scandal sheets, maybe even *Hard Copy* or *Entertainment Tonight*. But you know what they say, there's no such thing as bad publicity. It'll sell the hell out of his books. Maybe it'll even—"

"Brett, I gotta run," Carol interrupted. "I'll call you the next day or so, okay?"

"Don't you dare," Brett said, her voice mock-stern. "After tonight's signing, you're on mandatory R&R for the next seven days. I don't want to hear your voice until you're back in the office a week from Monday. Okay?"

"Sure," Carol said. Brett thought she still sounded distracted, far away. "Sure."

The two women hung up, and Brett went back to the stacks

of paper on her desk. As she thumbed through the addenda to a contract that had to go out by next Wednesday, she suddenly remembered her pledge of secrecy to Taylor the night before and briefly felt a surge of guilt.

"What difference does it make?" she whispered to herself as she turned to page six. "These things always go public sooner or later."

CHAPTER 11

Saturday afternoon, San Diego

Carol Gee hung up the phone and stared out the twenty-fifth-story window of the Hyatt Regency San Diego. Her room overlooked the harbor and the glimmering deep blue of the Pacific Ocean. The sun was high overhead, the day brilliantly clear. Far below her, in the distance, the Coronado ferry chugged slowly southwest.

Right now, she would have given anything to be on that ferry, sailing away to anywhere but here. Ten stories above her—on the Gold Passport floor, of course—Michael Schiftmann was settling into his room and planning God knew what for his last evening on book tour. Carol had almost five hours to herself, time that she would need if she intended to regroup and steel herself for the signing tonight after what she had just learned.

Carol stood there for a long time, leaning against the heavy plate glass and staring out at the sea. She tried to find a calm place inside herself, someplace where she could sort out all the conflicts, all the noise in her head. She wished, honestly wished, that Brett Silverman had never said a thing to her about Michael Schiftmann and Taylor Robinson's involvement. If she'd never been told, she'd never have been faced with the kind of dilemma now forced upon her.

It wasn't that Carol Gee and Taylor were even that close. They knew each other casually, as professionals, in a business that, as large as it was, was still based on personal relationships. And Carol Gee had also been in the publishing business long enough to know that, to paraphrase the cliché, no good deed goes unpunished. The smart thing to do would be to keep her mouth shut, spend one more night babysitting, then go hang out on a beach for a week to rebuild her diminished reserves and forget the past couple of months.

Carol Gee, however, had one problem: a nagging conscience. She wasn't a prude or moral right-wing zealot; she'd had her share of lovers. And while the number of lovers she'd had in her twenty-eight years would have shocked her parents and probably killed her grandparents, the truth was she was just about average for a woman in her late twenties. So the fact that Michael Schiftmann had been picking up women on the book tour virtually from day one wasn't so much a moral issue for Carol as it was one of trust. If she were in Taylor's position—a thought that momentarily repulsed her—would she want to know the man she was seriously involved with had been bedding the literary equivalent of groupies all across the continent? What about health issues, AIDS and all that? Carol had already seen more than one friend felled by the disease, not all of them gay men.

Carol absentmindedly raised her left thumb to her lips and chewed the nail. Should she tell Taylor what she knew? Should she call Brett back and let her know, or perhaps ask her advice on how to handle it?

And again, the question came back to her: If it were she, would she want to know?

"Damn it," she whispered. She looked down, checked the clock: one-thirty. She and Michael planned to meet in the lobby just before six-thirty to drive to the last signing, at the Barnes & Noble on Rosecrans. They would either get dinner together afterward or, as Carol was now extremely inclined to do, each order in from room service and eat alone.

Carol sighed. "I can't imagine eating another meal with that man," she said out loud.

She went into the bathroom and washed her face, then brushed her shoulder-length, bone-straight black hair. As she stared into the mirror, she saw for the first time how tired she looked.

"You need a break," she whispered to her reflection.

Carol walked back into the room and sat on the edge of the bed. She picked up a stack of brochures she'd gotten out of the lobby. As always, she'd read them, then return the ones she didn't need to the rack downstairs. She looked through the brochure for the San Diego Zoo, then the one for Sea-World. She'd asked at the front desk earlier which was the best attraction and quickly learned that San Diegans split into two camps: Either you're a zoo fanatic or you're a Sea-World fanatic. There didn't seem to be much in between.

Maybe, she thought, a walk on the beach would do just as well.

Then Carol Gee, exhausted, pulled her draperies closed, peeled off her slacks, took off her blouse and put on a T-shirt, and slid between the covers. In a matter of moments, she was fast asleep.

Carol shook her head, trying to focus, to wake completely up, as the polished chrome doors of the elevator opened in the Hyatt Regency lobby. Behind her, the glass walls of the elevator revealed a panorama that Carol, slightly acrophobic, had been unable to stomach.

She bolted out of the elevator, turned to her immediate left, and pushed her way past a crowd of retirees in golf caps and nearly identical plaid shorts.

"I'm sorry," she puffed, out of breath, as she walked up to Michael Schiftmann. He stood in the center of the lobby, tapping his foot, his eyes dark.

"Where have you been?" he demanded, his voice low, controlled.

"I'm sorry," Carol said again before she could stop herself. "I fell asleep and forgot to set the clock."

Michael raised his jacket sleeve and checked his watch. "We're going to be late."

"We won't be late," Carol said defensively. "The bookstore's only ten minutes away."

"We'd better not be," Michael said, turning from her and marching through the lobby toward the back entrance to the parking garage.

Once in the rental car, Carol maneuvered around the hotel until she got her bearings, then headed north on Pacific Highway. They briefly slowed at a tie-up in front of the Amtrak station, but the traffic soon loosened and began to flow freely. In minutes, they were passing the airport on their left, then leaving it behind. Carol checked her directions one last time, then turned left on Barnet, right on Midway, and in two more minutes was parking the car in front of the Barnes & Noble with fifteen minutes to spare. Michael hadn't said a word the entire trip. As she braked the car, he was already unbuckling his seat belt.

"See," Carol said, trying to placate him. "I told you we'd make it."

Carol's intentions failed miserably; Michael turned to her. "Good for you, although let's not forget that the issue wouldn't have come up if you'd gotten out of bed on time and done your job right."

Carol flared. *God, I feel like I'm married to this guy*, she thought.

Michael reached for the door handle as she killed the engine.

"Wait," she said as he lifted the handle on the door. He turned. "What?"

"I want to talk to you," she said. The sentence came out of her mouth without her even thinking, as if it had to, as if she were just the delivery person.

Michael settled back on the brown leather. "So talk," he said calmly.

Carol looked down and stared at the hub of the steering wheel. "This is the last time we have to do this, and I suspect we'll both be well rid of each other. If it were anybody else in the world, I'd just keep my mouth shut and go on with my life. But I can't, not this time."

Michael turned to face her. "So you're going to tell me off," he said. "Okay, get it over with. You won't be the first."

She shook her head. "No, that's not what this is about."

Michael glanced at his watch. "Then what is this about?" he demanded. "We don't have a lot of time here."

"It's about Taylor," she said. "About you and Taylor."

There was a stillness in the car, a silence that filled the interior like a dam bursting.

"What about me and Taylor?" Michael asked softly, seconds later.

"I know about you and Taylor," she said. "And I've watched you these past few weeks while we've been traveling together."

"You've been spying on me," Michael said. It was a statement of fact, not a question.

"No," Carol answered sternly. "Not spying. But you've been so blatant about it, anyone with open eyes is going to see everything."

Neither of them had mentioned what "it" was. They didn't have to.

"How dare you," he said, his voice too calm.

Carol turned to him, her voice imploring. "Don't you know how dangerous that kind of behavior is? In this day and age? You could catch *anything*. The medical risks alone ought to keep you from doing it, let alone relationship and trust issues."

Michael's face reddened slightly, and for a moment Carol was afraid he was going to explode. *At least*, she thought, *we're in a public place*. But then he took a few slow, deep breaths, and the redness went away. He was silent for a few more moments before looking up, directly into her face.

"So what are you going to do with all this?" he asked.

Carol gripped the steering wheel until her knuckles whitened. The interior of the car was beginning to get stuffy, and she wished she'd never brought this up.

"I don't know," she said.

"Are you going to tell her?"

"I don't know."

"If you do, you'll only hurt her," Michael said softly. "And I care for her very much. I don't want to see her hurt."

"Hah," Carol said, her voice low. "Yeah, right."

"What if I told you our little talk here has been a wake-up call, that my behavior is at least partly related to the stress I'm under, and now that the tour's over, so is the stress?"

Carol looked at him. "I want to believe that."

"You can believe that."

"If I thought you were telling the truth, then there would be nothing to protect her from."

"There isn't anything to protect her from."

"You're sure of that," Carol said.

"Absolutely."

"So you've been taking precautions, practicing safe sex." It was the first time either of them had uttered the word.

"Completely," Michael said. "There's nothing to worry about on that account."

Carol sighed. "For the time being, I'll try to believe that. But I want you to know that if I see any evidence that you aren't telling me the truth, then—" Her voice tightened and she seemed unable to get the words out.

Michael smiled at her, a soft, endearing smile that seemed to melt around the edges of his lips. "I understand, Carol. Really, I do. Look, why don't we go in, get this last one over with. Then I can buy you a nice dinner somewhere to celebrate."

"I'm tired. I'm not feeling very well," Carol said, reaching for the door handle. "I think I'd just rather go back and order room service."

The signing went well. Carol counted eighty people in the crowd, which wasn't bad in the sixth largest city in America on a balmy Saturday night in February when there were lots of other things to do. Michael handled the crowd well, she thought. She had to give him this much; he was a great public speaker, relaxed and comfortable with a crowd. He controlled them, using alternating patterns of humor and warm earnestness. He came across as intelligent, passionate about his work, and eloquent. His book sales were rising steadily as he learned the art of warming up to bookstore clerks and salespeople as well as readers. He signed books for more than an hour after the reading, then signed stock for another forty-five minutes. Carol hung back on the edges of the crowd, too tired and bored to be completely present but always staying just close enough to be on call if needed.

After Michael signed stock, he huddled in the corner for a couple of minutes with the assistant manager on duty that Saturday night. The young man's nose was pierced, he needed a shave, and his dirty khakis were riding low enough on his hips to expose the band of his underwear. If he hadn't been wearing a plastic nameplate identifying himself, no one would ever guess he worked here or anywhere else. He seemed to enjoy having a private moment with a *New York Times* best-selling author, and the two talked in hushed tones broken only by a casual just-between-us-guys laugh. Carol was about to start seriously eavesdropping when the conversation broke up. Michael smiled broadly as he said good-bye to the manager and a couple of other people on the way out.

It was almost nine-thirty when Carol followed him out to the parking lot, neither of them speaking. The bright yellow sulfurous lights of the parking lot aggravated Carol's growing headache. Even though the temperature was in the high fifties, there seemed to be a chill in the air. Carol wished she'd brought a jacket or at least a heavier sweater. When they got to the car, Michael crossed to the driver's side and held out his hand.

"Here, let me drive," he said.

It was the first time in forty-something cities he'd ever offered to drive. "No," she answered, "that's okay."

"Look, you said you were tired and don't feel well. Please, Carol, let me at least do this much for you." There was almost a remorseful quality to his voice, as if he had changed, really changed, and was now trying to make up to her.

"C'mon, it's our last night," he said.

And she was so tired.

Carol Gee reached into her handbag and fished out the keys to the rental. They would never be friends, she knew, but perhaps they could at least end this tour on an up note.

"Okay, Michael, if you insist."

He smiled and pointed the tiny black box at the car and pressed a button. The electronic door locks thunked as they opened. Carol, secretly relieved to be a passenger, climbed in on the right side of the red Buick. As soon as she reached for the seat belt, she heard another thunk as the doors locked.

Michael started the car and pulled out onto Rosecrans. The traffic had thinned; the February chill seemed to have settled the city down a bit. Carol looked around, confused. Hadn't they made the wrong turn out of the lot?

"Weren't we supposed to—" Carol said, turning and pointing the other way down Rosecrans Street.

Michael smiled. "I've got a little surprise for you," he said. "I was talking to Jack, you know, the assistant manager?"

Carol nodded.

"And I told him this was our last stop on a very hard tour and that I hadn't always been the easiest person in the world to get along with, blah blah blah—and that I wanted to take you out to someplace really special as a way of thanking you."

"That's not necessary, Michael," Carol said. "Let's just go back to the hotel."

"Oh, we can't do that!" he said. "It's our last night on what was, even with our little difficulties, a very successful tour."

"Look, you don't have to—"

"C'mon, next week we'll all be back in the grind, so let's just have one last blowout. I'll even pick up the tab."

Michael drove on down Rosecrans Street as he continued talking. They were hitting the lights just right. They crossed Nimitz Boulevard and then the smaller side streets off to the right—Keats, Jarvis, one she couldn't catch, then Garrison, Fenelon, Emerson—seemed to buzz by.

"I'm not going back to the grind," Carol said almost offhandedly. "I'm taking a week off. Won't be back in the city until a week from Monday."

Michael turned to her and smiled. "So much the better," he said. "How nice for you. I'm jealous."

"So where is this restaurant," Carol asked, her resolve for room service weakening.

"Not far," Michael answered. "On the point."

"The point?"

"Yeah, down toward Point Loma."

"What are you talking about?" Carol asked. "There's nothing down there."

"Oh yeah, Jack told me all about it. Trust me. It's going to be wonderful."

Carol suddenly felt exhausted, as if the whole of the last two months had caught up with her all at once. She was hungry as well, she realized, and thought that maybe that was where her headache was coming from.

"All right," she said. "We'll get dinner. But let's make it an early evening. You've got a seven A.M. flight out tomorrow."

"You know, it's funny," Michael said. "But I don't really need that much sleep. Too much to do, I guess. What's the joke? *I'll sleep when I'm dead.*"

"I can't wait that long," Carol said. "I'm exhausted."

"Okay," Michael said. "We'll make it an early evening."

Rosecrans Street turned south, into a less densely populated area. There was little traffic now, and the houses were farther apart. Another mile or so on and there were no more traffic lights, then no more streetlights. The terrain was hillier now, or perhaps the rolling was exaggerated by the darkness. The lights of San Diego were off to their left, across North San Diego Bay, and the city seemed much farther away. Carol felt her stomach heave slightly as the car went up and down, which only added to her discomfort from her headache.

"I'm kind of hungry," she said. "Maybe a little nauseous from blood sugar. Will we get there soon?"

"Very soon," Michael said, his eyes never leaving the road. "Very soon."

A couple of minutes later, a sign loomed on their left and Carol caught just enough to read it—BALLAST POINT—as they went by.

"This place must not get very much business," she said. "To be so far out."

To be so far out . . . Suddenly, something caught in Carol Gee's throat.

"Where are we?" she demanded.

"It's not far," Michael said. A sign up ahead read CABRILLO NATIONAL MONUMENT—.5 MILES.

"What's the name of this place?" Carol said, fighting to keep her voice calm.

Michael stepped harder on the gas. The car accelerated. Carol looked down at the speedometer; they were doing sixty on this narrow, curving road.

"Slow down," Carol said.

"I hate it when people tell me how to drive."

"Damn it, where are you taking me?"

"We're going to celebrate," Michael said. "It's the end of our tour."

"Stop the car," Carol said, as they drifted to the right. She could barely see the road in the beam cast by the head-lights.

"Stop the car, I want out," she said again. "Now."

"C'mon, Carol," Michael said. "Whaddaya want out here for? What, you're going to call a cab out here? Just sit still. We'll be there soon."

Think, damn it! Carol felt her forehead flush and her breath coming in shorter bursts, as if she were gulping for air. *Think!*

Not once in twenty-eight years had her superb mind failed her. There had to be a way out of this. If she jerked the door open and jumped, she'd be killed by the fall. If she tried to wrestle the wheel away from him . . .

No, he's too big. It'll never work. The crash'll kill both of us.

"What are you going to do?" Carol said, her voice breaking.

"Carol," Michael said. "You're beginning to bore me."

Carol gripped the armrest on the door with her right hand, feeling the leather beneath her hand, kneading it back and forth, the sweat from her palm rubbing into the material.

He's got to stop sooner or later. I'll jerk the door open, run like crazy. I'm fast. I'm younger than he is.

The car went past a sign so fast it was just a blur. "Welcome to the Cabrillo National Forest," Michael said. "Isn't it pretty?"

She looked outside, through the glass clouded with re-flected light from the instrument panel. All she saw was black.

Fatigue and hunger settled in on her like weight, a weight that forced her outside herself, and she saw herself sitting frozen on the seat next to him, her eyes large and blank. Carol Gee had minored in psychology at Yale; she knew the phenomenon of disassociation, had studied it in a class called Abnormal Criminal Psychology. As if there was such a thing as normal . . .

Fight this! a voice inside her head screamed.

Damn it! Fight!

The car slowed as it made a long, lazy turn to the right. Carol looked up through the windshield and saw that they were at an intersection. Michael turned the car left, to the south, toward the ocean.

Carol reached down and pressed the unlock button on the armrest, while with her left hand she pressed the release button on her seat belt. At the instant the door-lock stem shot up from the door, she grabbed the handle and yanked as hard as she could.

"Bitch!" Michael yelled, grabbing her by the hair as the door flew open. Carol screamed, grabbed at his hands behind her, flailing helplessly, her legs partway out the door.

Michael slammed on the brake, and the car slid to a stop. Carol slammed into the dashboard, her knees exploding in bursts of sharp, focused pain. He yanked her hair again, hard, hard enough to get another yelp out of her.

"No, please!" Carol yelled as she felt herself being pulled back into the car. She fought, scraped, jumped, flailed as she felt him pulling her closer. Then he had her with both hands, cradling her head, pulling her face down onto his lap. She tried to think, but panic swept over her. Her arms fluttered like the wings of a bird caught in a trap, with about as much effect.

She thought of the tiny canister of pepper spray she carried hooked to her key chain, the one she'd left at home because they were going through so many airport security checkpoints.

Then she felt his right arm around her neck, the crook of his elbow right at the hollow of her throat. And pressure. Tightening pressure . . .

Her eyes bulged as she realized for the first time what was happening. She tried to kick, but in the tight confines of the front seat of the Buick, there was nothing to kick, nothing that would help her. She opened her mouth to scream; nothing came out. She felt his forearm against her throat, his right hand locked in the crook of his left arm, his left arm bent around the back of her head. She felt his palm on the top of her head, pushing down into his curled right arm. She opened her mouth, tried to push her face into his crotch where she could bite him, but he held her too tightly to move.

Her eyes watered, the pressure behind them causing them to bulge.

And then . . .

From the corners of her field of vision, tiny sparkles. Red ones and gold ones and blue ones, like glitter. Sparkling and dancing.

Her chest was about to explode.

Please . . .

Her grandmother. She saw her grandmother's face in front of her.

Please . . .

She felt her legs kicking, her arms shaking, as if they were no longer part of her, as if they had minds and wills of their own.

She heard a voice, a soft voice, a low, masculine voice above her, behind her head: "Let go, Carol. Let go. It's easier this way."

Where had she heard it before?

The sparkles were larger now, like a cascade of colored gemstones spilling in on both sides of her, filling her vision.

And as the dark shapes in front of her became more and more dim, the twinkling colored lights got larger and more vibrant.

"That's it, baby," the voice said again, soothing, almost sweet. Michael's voice. "Let it go. Go to sleep, my sweet baby. It's time for you to go to sleep."

Like a vet putting a dog to sleep . . .

So tired, she thought. *So tired.*

Her cheeks tingled red, felt full, the skin stretched almost to breaking. Carol Gee felt an overwhelming sadness that welled up inside her, and as the dancing brilliant blues and reds and greens and purples and yellows ran together and through each other and into each other until they became one pulsating, blood-red globe surrounding her, she felt the sadness drift away and the lights shift from painfully bright to soft white, and there was a humming in her head, like the bowing of a violin string, and then she let go. Carol Gee let go of everything.

And found her peace.

Michael stared down at her as she went limp. He let go slowly, ready to clamp on again if she had somehow managed to fake it better than anybody had ever faked death in the history of the species. He patted her back, felt the bra strap beneath the fabric of her blouse.

No, he thought. *Not now. This is business.*

He shifted her over on the seat, off his lap, then reached down and pulled her legs inside the car. He snatched the door to, killing the dome light inside the car. He listened carefully and looked all around. There was no one. No traffic, no nearby homes, no intruders. He shifted the car back into gear and eased forward down the narrow road.

He drove slowly this time. No need to hurry. Still, it took only a minute or so to get to the end of the road. He parked the car, got out, listened carefully for any unexpected noises. All was silent, except for the wind and the crashing of the waves at the base of the cliff that was the blunt end of Point Loma.

He opened the passenger door and lifted her out. She

couldn't weigh more than one-ten, he thought. During a break in the signing, after the last idiotic inscription had been written and the last sycophant rushed through and out, he had wandered over and picked up a local paper. The tide had crested at nine forty-five, not quite an hour ago. He lifted her up and threw her over his shoulder, grateful that neither her bladder nor her bowels had let go. He'd done his research and verified it in practice: It was a myth that the body always emptied itself at the moment of death.

He walked the fifty yards or so from the end of the road to the edge of the cliff and set Carol down in the grass. He removed her ring and necklace and checked the pockets on her slacks. They were empty; there was nothing on Carol Gee to identify her.

He looked over the edge of the cliff. There was only a thin sliver of moon to illuminate the ocean floor below, but it was enough to see that the waves were still lapping at the base of the cliff.

He closed his eyes and inhaled deeply through his nostrils, savoring the fresh, salty air. The hairs on his arm stood up, tingling and dancing on his skin. The sound of the waves below intensified, grew louder and sharper, more focused.

Like a needle being dragged across a record . . .

Every nerve in his body alive to every sense, Michael Schiftmann grinned broadly and lifted the lifeless body of Carol Gee over his shoulder, holding her by the collar of her blouse and the belt buckle of her slacks. Already she was beginning to stiffen. He backed up a few steps, held her high in the military press position, then ran forward and flung her out as far as he could over the edge of the cliff, barely missing going over with her.

He froze, a clump of dirt under his foot breaking loose and falling, and listened. Perhaps two seconds later, he heard a crystalline, full splash, clear and sharp like the breaking of glass.

The tide would carry her out, out into the vast, endless Pacific. If she was ever found, there most likely wouldn't be enough left to autopsy. And there were a thousand Dumpsters between here and downtown San Diego. Carol Gee's purse and the contents inside, along with her jewelry, would be spread out through a dozen of them.

Michael Schiftmann had never felt more alive than at this moment. It was a sensation beyond sexual, beyond any physical thrill he'd ever felt or experienced.

Michael Schiftmann felt . . .

Liberated.

He sauntered back to the car, relishing the feel of the soft earth beneath his feet, the smell of living grass, breathing plants and trees. He felt the clean air fill his lungs.

Despite the chill, he was warm all over, and in very good appetite.

CHAPTER 12

Sunday morning, Arlington, Virginia

Sundays were always the toughest to get through. The other days of the week he could work, even Saturday. Hank Powell had become a Saturday fixture, in fact, at his office at the FBI Academy in Quantico.

It hadn't always been like that. When Anne was still alive, he had religiously saved Saturdays for working around the house, in the yard, or for simply spending family time with her and their daughter, Jackie. But that had all ended two years ago, when he lost her.

How had it happened so fast? It seemed in his memory that literally one day Anne was playing tennis at the country club and gardening their modest acre-and-a-half lot and then the very next moment she was withering away, her weight visibly dropping from one day to the next, her hair falling out, her eyes settling deeper and deeper into her head until the light in them faded to nothing. She had been only thirty-eight when the doctors made the diagnosis: ovarian cancer. And from the moment they identified the cancer as a particularly virulent and aggressive form of the disease, everything happened far too quickly. A matter of months, they predicted, was all they had together. From a passionate, intelligent, active woman who loved parties and cooking and good wine and everything about life to deathly ill in a matter of weeks . . .

But the doctors hadn't counted on Anne's willingness to

fight, her ability to hang on to every second and to live every moment as hard and as fully as she was capable. The doctors had told them it would be a matter of months; Anne had beaten their odds, beaten their gloomy prognosis, beaten everything except death itself. In the end, she took two long, agonizing years to die. Anne had missed her fortieth birthday by three weeks. By then, Hank—six months older than his wife—had turned forty and felt eighty.

It had been especially hard on Jackie, who had been twelve when her mother became ill and who had turned fourteen two months after she died. It had been Anne's dream that Jackie attend the same boarding school she had gone to, the Butler School in upstate Vermont, and Jackie had insisted on fulfilling her mother's dream. That was two years ago, and now Hank and Anne's daughter was sixteen, a sophomore at Butler. And Hank lived alone in their four-bedroom house, a house he had been intending to sell ever since Anne's death. Somehow he'd never gotten around to putting it on the market. Just too busy, he told himself.

He worked. That's all he did, work. Hank Powell was putting in twelve hours a day, six days a week. In the two years since his wife's death, he hadn't dated a single time. Not once. It was as if with Anne's death, something inside him died as well.

Now he hated Sundays, hated them with a passion. The only saving grace was his weekly phone call from Jackie, which was due in another hour or so. They spoke like clockwork, every Sunday after chapel at the school and just before lunch. Occasionally they would speak during the week, but as Jackie had learned, her father was easier to catch at the office than at home and sometimes you couldn't catch him there.

Hank had taken to having a couple of drinks at night, just to take an edge off the stress buzz and make it a little easier to sleep. Hank and Anne had never been big drinkers, and he wasn't one now. But lately he'd needed a single vodka martini upon arriving at home and then a snifter of brandy at bedtime.

It wasn't just missing Anne that kept him awake at night.

Hank had taken the maximum amount of leave possible during his wife's illness, and was truly, genuinely grateful to the Bureau for granting him that. After her funeral, Hank Powell did the only thing he knew to do: go back to work.

Ever since, the main focus of his life had been finding the man who had so brutally killed at least thirteen young women. Even in the post–9/11 era, when the politicians were trying to remake the FBI into a counterterrorism agency, he had fought to stay on the Alphabet Man case.

Hank woke up particularly early this Sunday morning, and had come to consciousness with an ever-widening sense of dread. He'd been warned and had seen the article in the Chattanooga paper last Wednesday, had been disheartened to see it picked up by the wire services and then the Friday edition of *USA Today*. But the real test was this morning. Whatever rested in the snow on the sidewalk leading out from his front door would determine whether the next few weeks of Hank Powell's life would be manageable, or chaotic and stressful on a scale he'd never experienced.

He brushed his teeth and combed his hair, threw on a flannel shirt and a pair of jeans, then went downstairs and put on the coffee to brew. He pulled the living-room drapery back and looked outside. Two more inches of snow had fallen on the Virginia countryside overnight, but the two plastic-wrapped bundles were on top of a shallow drift with just a dusting on top.

Hank pulled on his galoshes over his bare feet and pushed the front door open. The sharp, icy dry air stung his face as he stepped out onto the porch. The cold shot through the rubber soles of the boots and immediately began to deaden his feet. He jumped off the porch and trotted down the walk, the boots crunching on the dry snow. He reached over to one side of the walk and picked the Sunday *New York Times* off the snowdrift, then leaned down on the other side of the walk and plucked the *Washington Post* off the top of a wind-blown mound of powder.

Seconds later, he was kicking off his boots and wondering whether he should start a fire in the den fireplace. The smell of coffee caught him first, though, and he decided to sit at the kitchen table. He tossed the two papers, which between them weighed several pounds, onto the kitchen table, then poured a large mug of coffee. He pulled the chair away at the head of the table and then sat down in the large kitchen Anne had loved so much.

"Well," he whispered, "let's see what you've got for me."

He pulled the plastic cover off the *Post* first, then removed all the inserts: the slicks and the advertisements, the Sunday magazine and the television guide, then thumbed quickly through the sections, separating the possibles from the not-likelies.

Hank Powell found the article on page six of Section A, above the fold, with about a thirty-point headline that read:

FEDS STYMIED IN MULTI-YEAR HUNT FOR "ALPHABET MAN"

Hank's spirits sunk as he read the article. The reporter had clearly taken the local article from Chattanooga and run with it. The reporter at the Tennessee paper had not done a bad job of writing up what little he had, but the *Post* reporter had considerably more resources to draw upon. As Hank read the article, which covered at least three-quarters of the page, complete with a clouded, out-of-focus crime-scene picture and another photo of Max Bransford in Nashville, he realized that the *Post* reporter had to have a source within the Bureau. When he read some of the details of the Milwaukee killing—the one in which the letter E had been left at the crime scene—he knew that somebody with access to the FBI case files had leaked.

Hank felt his face flush. He knew the press had a job to do, but the one thing he hated more than anything was a press leak. If Hank had gone the other way in life, if he'd become a criminal himself rather than an FBI agent, he'd have hated a snitch just as much. That's what he considered guys who leaked confidential information that threatened the very success of an investigation: snitches who just happened to be on the same side as the good guys.

The *Times* article, on page two of the first section, was

about as bad, only that the reporter had chosen to go after interviews with local cops. He'd focused on establishing a trail and had even discovered something that the *Post* reporter had slipped up on: The eighth murder—H—had taken place in Vancouver, just across the border in Canada. For the first time, the world would learn that the Alphabet Man was a killer for whom boundaries of every type meant little.

"Damn it," Hank muttered. He sat back in his chair, his eyes focusing on the wall opposite him and then gradually losing focus as his mind shifted into an analysis of everything he'd read. A minute or so later, the process was finished, and he reached what he felt was a proper evaluation of the situation: It could be worse, but it was hard to imagine how.

Hank was so lost in thought, it took until the third ring for the phone to break his concentration. He looked at the kitchen clock and smiled. Jackie.

He stood up, grabbed the handset off the wall phone next to the kitchen sink.

"Hello, sweetheart," he said pleasantly.

"Good morning, darling." The voice was heavy-set, masculine, definitely not his daughter's.

Hank reddened, recognizing the voice of Lawrence Dunlap, an FBI deputy assistant director and his immediate supervisor. "I'm sorry, sir," he said quickly. "I thought you were my daughter. She calls every Sunday about this time."

"Then I won't take long," Dunlap said. Over the years, Hank and Larry Dunlap had had their differences, but Hank respected him for being an all-business, by-the-book career agent who had learned to play the game over the years without losing quite all of his integrity.

"Have you seen the papers?" Dunlap asked.

"I just finished them," Hank admitted.

"Pretty bad," Dunlap said. "Any idea who the leak is?"

"No, but when I find out I'm going to ruin his day."

"I've scheduled a meeting for nine A.M. tomorrow," Dunlap said, "in my office at the Hoover Building. The director himself will be there. I went out on a limb to keep you on this case, Hank, and now the pressure's on. He'll want a complete update on the progress of the investigation and how we plan to deal with the media on this one. It's a whole new ball game now and we've got to get our ducks in a row."

Hank ignored both the clichéd mixed metaphor and the burning sensation in the middle of his stomach. "I understand, sir. I'll be ready for any questions."

"Is there anything you need to update me on since we last talked?"

"I'm sorry to say, sir, there isn't. I wish I had better news."

"So do I," Dunlap said sternly. "The squeeze's on with this one, Hank. The old man'll want to know how we're going to nail this. We don't need another strikeout."

"I know that, sir," Hank said, understanding the reference to published reports that the FBI's success rate was the worst of all the various federal law enforcement agencies. Even the BATFucks were outscoring them these days.

There was a slight break in the connection, and Hank realized it was an incoming call, probably Jackie. There was no way he could put Dunlap on hold to check a call waiting cue.

"All right. I'll see you tomorrow morning. Show me something good on this one, Hank."

"I'll do my best, sir."

Dunlap hung up without saying another word. Hank reached up and quickly clicked the telephone button. "Hello," he said.

"Daddy?"

"Hi, precious, how are you?"

"I didn't know if you were going to answer or not," Jackie said. Her voice was soft and sweet to his ears. Another year or two and she would sound just like her mother.

"I'm sorry, baby, I had another call. It was business and I couldn't break away. You know how it is."

"Unfortunately, these days I do," Jackie said, scolding him. "Don't you ever take a complete day off?"

"I'm off today," Hank said. "It was just a phone call."

"Yeah, just a phone call. Are you going into the office today?"

Hank hesitated. A nine o'clock meeting in Washington meant he'd have to spend most of the afternoon in Quantico getting ready. He didn't want to admit what he was up against, yet couldn't bring himself to lie to his daughter either.

"For a little while," he confessed after a few moments. "No big deal."

"Daddy, you've got to quit this," Jackie said, real concern in her voice. "I'm worried about you."

"You're worried about me?" Hank asked. "Who was it that last weekend spent Saturday night working on a term paper until three in the morning?"

"It's winter term up here, Dads," she said. "We're snowed in. There's nothing else to do."

"You could sleep, you know," Hank offered.

"I do plenty of that. Look, Dads, I've been thinking about spring vacation. It's only six weeks away."

"I know," Hank said. He'd been thinking about spring vacation, too, and trying to figure a way to take some time off and travel with Jackie. A beach, maybe, or perhaps even a trip overseas. But with everything going on, it wasn't looking good.

"I think I know what I want to do, if it's okay with you," she said.

"Okay, shoot."

"I talked to Miss Appling yesterday. She wants me to go down to Florida with the soccer team for spring break. It might mean being a varsity starter next year if I do okay."

Jackie had just missed making the starting lineup for varsity soccer last fall and had been terribly disappointed. He knew she wanted to take another shot at it. Anne had been captain of the soccer team her senior year in boarding school.

"Where will you go?" Hank asked, hiding his disappointment at not seeing his daughter over spring vacation.

"Tallahassee," she answered. "We'll stay in dorms at FSU, eat in the cafeteria."

"Tallahassee," Hank sighed. *Tallahassee.* Despite himself, Hank couldn't help but think of Tallahassee, Florida, as the site of Ted Bundy's last murderous rampage at the Florida State University Chi Omega house. He thought of the two girls in the Nashville killing, L and M in the Alphabet Man's lexicon, who were only a few years older than his own daughter.

"Yes, Tallahassee," Jackie said. "Is there something wrong?"

"No, sweetheart, no, it's just that . . . Well, will there be lots of adult supervision, chaperones?"

"Daddy, please," Jackie said, exasperated.

"I just worry about you," he said.

"That's sweet, but I'm a big girl now," Jackie said. "I go off to college in a couple of years."

"Don't remind me."

"Well, it's true. And I can take care of myself."

Hank started to tell her that there were things in life no one could take care against, but held his tongue. There was no need to dump his own baggage off on his daughter. She wouldn't understand anyway.

"I just hope you'll be careful," he said. "I love you, precious. I can't help but worry."

"Daddy, I'll be okay," Jackie said, trying to placate him.

"Okay, you can go. On one condition . . ."

"Yes?"

"You won't be embarrassed if I take off a couple of days and fly down to see you."

Jackie giggled. "I'd love it. Can you?"

"I'll start working on it tomorrow."

"Great," she said, excited. "There's some forms and stuff you'll have to fill out, and it's going to cost a little bit. Not too much, though."

"I think we can handle it," Hank said. "Just promise me you'll be careful."

"Oh, Daddy, stop it," she said.

But Hank knew, as they said good-bye and hung up, that he couldn't stop, could never stop worrying about her, not in this world.

Not ever.

CHAPTER 13

Sunday morning, Nashville

Priscilla Janovich loved Sundays. After thirty-five years teaching high school English in the Metro Nashville public school system, she had never quite gotten used to retirement, even though she was now in her fourth year of it. She had too little to do during the week, and that often made her feel guilty or restless and sometimes both. But resting on Sunday, enjoying her newspapers and her mystery novel and a drink in the middle of the afternoon before a long nap, had been a lifelong habit for her. She savored Sundays like some people savor a fine steak or a glass of wine.

Priscilla pulled back the yellowed sheer curtain over the window in her tiny kitchen and looked out over the parking lot in the back of her apartment building. That damn Mr. Berriman was supposed to have shoveled the snow and salted the walks yesterday afternoon, but of course he'd not taken care of it, and when Priscilla stepped outside last night for a breath of fresh air, she'd been nearly upended by the icy concrete. Now, she noticed, the walks were clean.

An overfed tabby cat jumped from the breakfast table to the counter and rubbed his face along Priscilla's forearm.

"Well, Doodles," she cooed, gently scratching the cat's ears as she looked outside. "It looks like that awful man might actually have done his job for once."

She leaned down into the furry face, rubbing noses with

him as the cat purred happily. "Yes, Doodles, we can go get our paper now."

Behind her, another cat at least twice the size it should be rubbed her shoulders against the doorframe. Her yellow hair was so long it draped on the linoleum and was equally thick and well-combed. Priscilla turned.

"Hello, Prissy," she said. Priscilla picked up her cup of herbal tea and downed the last inch of it, then set the cup in the sink. She pulled her overcoat off an enameled cup hook she'd screwed into the plaster at a skewed angle. At the door to her apartment, she leaned down and gingerly pulled on a pair of rubber boots over her thick wool socks. Then she hooked her purse over her shoulder and walked down the two flights of stairs and out into a freezing late February Sunday in Nashville.

She walked to the corner of Cherokee and West End Avenues, then waited cautiously for the light to change so she could cross the five-lane street. Like many Nashvillians, Priscilla was terrified of driving in the snow, so much so that at the slightest hint of frozen precipitation, she bolted to the grocery store, stocked up on enough food to last a month, then fought her way back to her apartment and locked her car for the duration.

The temperatures had risen into the high thirties, and with the Sunday church traffic jam, much of the ice on the road had turned to dirty yellow-gray slush. Her boots alternated a plopping sound with a sucking noise as she trudged across the street and up onto the sidewalk. It was another three blocks to her favorite bookstore, which occupied a building that had once been a grand, Art Deco movie palace that had fallen on hard times. If the Bookstar hadn't moved in, the building would have faced demolition and, no doubt, been replaced by another twenty-four-hour Walgreens or Eckerd drugstore.

It felt good to be out of the apartment. Priscilla hadn't had a walk since the latest snow had started falling the previous Friday. She was in her third day of hibernation and starting to get a touch of cabin fever. At seventy, Priscilla still considered herself in good shape, and she liked to walk.

Ten minutes later, she crossed the barely passable parking lot of the Bookstar and stepped into the lobby. The architects who supervised the conversion from movie palace to bookstore had done a wonderful job of preserving the look and feel of the building. A grand staircase curved to the right up to what had once been the balcony, but was now the children's books section. To her left, Priscilla stopped and glanced—as was her habit—at the framed pictures and autographs of the stars who had once visited the theater. Her favorite was Errol Flynn, although the photograph of Johnny Weissmuller in a business suit was also very appealing. And next to the framed pictures of movie stars was a white stone tablet mounted on the wall in a clear Plexiglas box covered with the autographs of famous authors who had visited the building since it became a bookstore. Priscilla's favorites, as always, were the mystery writers, especially the women: Sue Grafton, Marcia Muller, Sharyn McCrumb, Deborah Crombie. She loved mysteries; they were her life. She read eight to ten a week.

"Hello, Miss Janovich," the young, pretty girl behind the cash register said as Priscilla passed the counter.

Priscilla turned, smiled. "Hello, Karen," she said.

"The new Grafton just came out in paperback," the clerk offered. "I pulled a copy for you, just in case."

"Bless you, my dear," Priscilla said. "And did you save me a copy of the Sunday *Times*?"

"Didn't have to." The girl walked around from behind the checkout counter and stepped over to the pile of newspapers in a rack by the wall. "With the weather like this, we haven't had much of a run this morning."

"You know, I have to have my Sunday *Times*," Priscilla warned. "If that stack ever gets low, you pull one out for me."

"I will," the clerk said, picking up a copy of the newspaper with both hands so as not to spill any of the inside sections. As she handed the newspaper to Priscilla, she suppressed a giggle. Her boss had told her how Priscilla Janovich had made a single three-day trip to New York City once in her entire life, back in 1965, and ever since had considered herself both an authority on and a native of the city.

"Thank you, dear," Priscilla said, handing the exact change for the newspaper across the counter.

"See you Wednesday, Miss Janovich," the girl said.

"You be careful in this weather, dear," Priscilla warned as she walked away.

Twenty minutes later, Priscilla Janovich carefully measured a pony of vodka into her steaming cup of chamomile tea. The vodka cooled it off just enough to swallow and enhanced the already relaxing effect of the herb.

The fat yellow longhair padded into the living room just as Priscilla sat down on the couch and put her cup on the end table to her right.

"Hello, Prissy," she said. "Where's Doodles? Where's Doodles, baby? We're all going to sit together and read now."

In a gesture of Pavlovian feline behavior, the obese cat managed to hop up onto the couch with only a minimum of panting. Priscilla leaned over and rubbed her hand across the top of the cat's head. The cat purred like a tiny motorboat.

Priscilla unfolded the first section of the *Times* and settled in for a long afternoon. She sipped the tea, the first wash of vodka over her tongue burning ever so slightly, and began reading. She read the lead story—an article on the upcoming New York City senatorial campaign—carefully, along with two sidebars that interviewed the opposing candidates. She read thoroughly, thinking over each issue, each statement, and painstakingly formed an opinion in an election in which she would never be allowed to vote.

She finished the jumps to that article, then turned back to the front page. There was an in-depth story on the latest unfolding Israeli peace initiative, followed by an interview with a senator who had unleashed yet another scathing attack on the president.

"Don't they ever get tired of it?" Priscilla asked Prissy out loud. "You'd think they'd leave the poor man alone."

Prissy raised her head and purred loudly.

"Yes, Prissums, that's right," Priscilla agreed. She finished the front-page lead story, then turned to page two of the first section. Most of that page was covered with a long feature story headlined:

SERIAL KILLER, DUBBED "ALPHABET MAN" BY FEDS, ELUDES CAPTURE FOR SEVEN YEARS

Priscilla smiled. She was particularly fond of serial killer stories. Was it Mary Higgins Clark who'd written that wonderful novel about the serial killer, or was it that Patricia Cornwell?

"No matter," she whispered. After a while, they all began to run together.

Priscilla read on:

CINCINNATI, OHIO: On a blustery June Monday in 1995, nineteen-year-old Susan McCrory left her home in a suburban Cincinnati neighborhood and climbed into her Ford Escort station wagon en route to her summer job at a nearby McDonald's. She never made it.

Priscilla Janovich read the news account as if it were a novel, creating visual images in her mind as the story unfolded of a young woman home from college on summer vacation who worked the morning shift at a local fast-food restaurant. The young woman disappeared, and for several days there was no trace of her. Then two teenage boys who'd rented a storage unit to store their fledgling garage band's instruments opened the door and found the young woman's body on the cold concrete floor. She'd been horribly murdered, tortured slowly and for a long time before death mercifully released her. On the cinder-block wall behind the drum set, a letter had been painted on the wall in blood: the letter A.

Priscilla shuddered. What a horrible story, she thought, and continued reading. Nine months later, the *Times* reporter wrote, a second body was found in Macon, Georgia, in a rest stop just off the junction of I–75 and I–17. The twenty-year-old blond was a clerk at the rest stop's welcome desk, a job she'd taken to make extra money to help pay for her own wedding. The only clue in that murder: the letter B painted in blood on the back wall of the men's room stall where the poor girl had been found.

The next murder took place out West, this time in Scottsdale, Arizona. A young girl who worked as a gas station attendant had been strangled, raped, tortured just like the first two, and stuffed into a metal locker used for storing tools. On the inside lid of the locker, again neatly painted in blood, was the letter C.

Priscilla read on, as the reporter described several more of the murders in great detail, others in less. When she got to the part about the two girls at Exotica Tans in Nashville, she let out a sharp gasp that was loud enough to startle Prissy, who leaped off the couch and disappeared into the kitchen.

Horrified, Priscilla read the end of the story, which summarized how little the police had on this killer, and how the FBI had proven itself especially inept at moving the investigation forward. The *Times* reporter noted that considerable pressure was on at the J. Edgar Hoover Building and that heads were expected to roll if something didn't break soon.

"My, my," Priscilla muttered, polishing off the last of her vodka-laced tea. "What a world."

She turned the page and went on with the newspaper, her senses lulled by the drink and the quiet of the day. She hadn't slept well last night; hadn't slept well in years, to be truthful, and she was finding that the older she got, the more she needed the occasional cat nap. She smiled at the thought, *cat nap*, and wondered where Doodles had gone.

She drifted off after a few more minutes, dozing in a sitting position on the old sofa she'd inherited from her mother. She was almost completely asleep when her meandering, lazy thoughts returned to the *Times* article she'd just read. This serial killer thing, she mused, was becoming so common they were beginning to imitate each other. Yes, she remembered, she'd heard that story before, the story of a wandering serial killer who tortured his victims and left only one clue: a letter painted in blood. In fact, there was—

Priscilla Janovich's eyes snapped open and she was suddenly wide awake.

A letter . . . In blood . . .

"No," she mumbled. "You're going crazy in your old age."

She looked around the room. Where was that damn Doodles?

Priscilla stretched and rubbed the back of her neck to loosen it up. She pulled herself up off the couch and carried her cup into the kitchen to boil more water. She turned on the tap, didn't like the sound of water coming out of the pipe, so decided to skip the tea and just have the two fingers of vodka. She poured the clear liquid into the cup and stood staring out the window at the wintry landscape outside.

"No," she muttered. "It can't be."

Still, she thought, it was an intriguing notion. She carried her cup back into the living room and reread the article a second time, then a third. Always the methodical teacher, she fished a yellow highlighter out of the kitchen drawer and highlighted the key points of each murder. Then she sat at the kitchen table, poured another two fingers of vodka just to ward off the cold, and began thinking.

I'm sure I've heard it before. But where?

She sipped the vodka.

Where?

She went back into the living room. Priscilla Janovich couldn't bear to throw away books, even the tattered old paperbacks her mother had given her before she died. The walls of both her living room and bedroom were lined with cheap lumber and cinder-block bookshelves she'd made to accommodate them. Most of the shelves were layered two deep with books, and still there were stacks of books gathering dust in the corners of each room. Priscilla knew the place was a fire hazard, but figured without her books, she wouldn't want to live anyway.

"Where was it?" she said. Doodles, hearing her speak in the next room, aroused himself from a snooze on the bed and padded softly into the living room. Priscilla was down on her knees, her skirt pulled up to her thighs and her wool socks tracing paths through the dust, leaning over and scanning the spines of row after row of books. The cat watched as Priscilla slid slowly across the floor, moving from one set of shelves to another.

Then Priscilla Janovich came to a row of worn paperbacks and stopped. She squinted to focus on the titles and the author's name and then sat back on her haunches. She pulled one of the paperbacks out of its slot on the shelf and thumbed it open, straining to read it in the low light. She read the first few paragraphs of the first page, then looked over at Doodles.

"Yes," she said blankly. "Yes, I believe this is it."

CHAPTER 14

Maria Chavez shivered as she walked into the Murder Squad break room and wrinkled her nose. An acrid, burnt smell hung in the air. She crossed the room to a counter next to a dingy refrigerator covered in bumper stickers and pulled the brown glass pot off the coffeemaker. The carafe had once been clear and new, but that was before endless pots of coffee with no one ever bothering to wash it out. Lately, someone had developed the habit of not turning it off at the end of the night shift. Maria only wished she knew who it was. She flicked the switch on the coffeemaker and turned the burner off.

"It's too early for this," she whispered. She rummaged through a cabinet and found a mug that could almost pass for clean, then rinsed it out in hot water. She refilled it with cold and popped it in the microwave, then turned the plastic dial to set the timer for four minutes. The break-room microwave was so old you could almost boil water faster on the stove, only they didn't have one.

Still shivering and crossing her arms back and forth, Maria Chavez stopped at the thermostat by the doorway and fiddled with it until she was convinced she'd have no effect on anything, then crossed the hall and into a long, narrow room jammed with gray metal government surplus-type desks. The entire squad shared this one room, with several filing cabinets jammed in at the end partially blocking the only window. The room was cramped, dusty, and claustrophobic when in full use, which was why Maria often came in early, so that she would at least have a little quiet time to go through her files.

Things had been quiet in the last twenty-four hours or so. Metro Nashville was approaching its third day in a row without a homicide. Maria attributed it to the cold weather and, despite the shivering, welcomed the quiet time. Yet even though it was momentarily peaceful, she still had at last count six unsolved homicides on her plate since January 1.

Maria opened the top drawer of one of the filing cabinets and extracted a three-ring notebook containing the file for complaint number 99–87432, which was the case of Althea Grant, a twenty-four-year-old African-American woman who had been found raped and strangled a week ago in her apartment out near the airport, just off Murfreesboro Road. The young woman had completed two years of college, was studying to be a paralegal, and by all accounts didn't hang out in bars, do drugs, run around with the wrong crowd, or any other of the number of things a human being could do to increase his or her chances of being murdered. It didn't take assignment to the Murder Squad for Maria Chavez to figure out that the vast majority of murder victims were doing something they shouldn't be doing at a place they shouldn't be with people they shouldn't be with. She learned that early growing up in the slums of Laredo, Texas.

That was why this case had kept her up most of the night. She'd studied the crime-scene photos, read the reports, most of which as the primary investigator she had filed herself. She'd gone back over her own notes, reexamined the crime-scene photos, rerun the interviews in her head, and still nothing. The only thing she could do was start over.

Maria turned to the first page of the binder, a Form 104 "Supplement Report" filed by the first officer on the scene. The officer had arrived even before Med Com personnel, and had handled the crime scene like a capable, experienced street cop. He'd done everything right and recorded it in that curiously detached manner taught to all recruits in their intensive report-writing classes at the academy. Maria picked up his narrative in the middle of the second page:

> Also revealed was the victim's head and upper torso. The victim was laying on her back with her face toward her right shoulder. Her eyes were open and her mouth appared unusually agap, very wide. Between the victim's chin and her left arm that was drawn across her body tied to the bedpost . . .

Maria smiled at the misspellings. *Okay,* she thought, *so they're not English teachers.*

From behind her, the microwave chimed and Maria crossed the hall to make her tea. As she entered the break room, the telephone on one of the other desks began ringing. Maria looked up at the wall clock: five-fifty. This early in the morning in the dead of winter, she figured it was probably a wrong number.

But the phone kept ringing, even as Maria opened a tea bag and plopped it into the not-quite-boiling water. She dipped it a couple of times and then with mounting irritation crossed back into the squad room and picked up the phone.

"Homicide, Chavez," she snapped.

"Detective Chavez, this is Corporal Rogers in the lobby."

"Yeah, Rogers, whatcha got?"

"Well, Detective, I know it's kind of early," Rogers said. "But I got a lady up here who says she knows who killed those two girls over on Church Street."

Chavez paused for a moment before speaking. "She for real?"

The front desk corporal lowered his voice as if turning away from the visitor. "Kinda hard to tell. She's like this old lady, you know. Looks a little, I don't know . . . Maybe odd."

"*Maybe* odd," Chavez repeated. "Great. You know what

time it is, Rogers? It's six in the freakin' A.M. in the dead of freakin' winter. Make her go away."

"Tried that already, Detective. She says she ain't going anywhere until she talks to somebody."

Maria gripped the phone so hard her hand began to cramp. "Damn it, I shoulda stayed in bed. Who was I to think I could get some quiet time around here?"

"I can't answer that, Detective Chavez. Sorry."

"All right," Maria said, sighing. "I'm on my way."

She hung up the phone, crossed the hall back into the break room, and picked up her teacup. She pulled the bag out and dropped it into a garbage can, then sipped the tea. She winced; it was way too strong now. Maria forced down one more sip, then, disgusted, poured the rest in the sink and started down the long hallway. This was, she conjectured, not going to be a good day.

Maria pushed the heavy door open out into the main lobby and crossed behind the brick staircase over to the command center. Corporal Rogers spied her approaching and motioned with his head to the front of the lobby. Maria stepped past Rogers and through the metal detector.

An elderly, thin woman of medium height stood looking out the front window, her back at an angle to Chavez. Maria stopped for a moment and watched her. She had a brown leather purse slung over her right shoulder, and over her left hung a faded white canvas tote bag with the words MALICE DOMESTIC printed on the front. There was something in the tote bag, something that seemed to put a strain on the woman's shoulders. She wore a heavy checked overcoat and a pair of hiking boots with thick gray socks all the way up to her knees. Her straight gray hair was pulled behind with a red wool beret perched at an angle on her head.

Maria cleared her throat. "Excuse me," she said. The woman turned. Her face was lined and pale; she wore no makeup and her eyebrows were almost completely plucked. But her blue eyes were clear and bright.

"Oh, yes," the woman said. "I'm sorry, I was staring out the window. I guess I'm kind of tired. I've been up all night."

Maria stepped toward her. "I'm Priscilla Janovich," the old woman said, extending her hand. The tote bag slipped down her forearm, causing her arm to jerk.

"I'm Detective Chavez. May I help you?"

"Yes," she said, and as she did so, Maria caught a whiff of the old woman's breath. Maria's nose wrinkled for the second time that morning. *Drinking? This early?*

The shifting tote bag seemed to unbalance the woman, and Maria began to wonder just how drunk she was.

"Yes, you can help me. Or maybe it's the other way around. Maybe I can help you."

"Perhaps you should tell me what's on your mind," Maria suggested.

"Didn't that young man tell you?"

"Well," Maria said, shrugging. "Why don't you tell me again?"

"Of course," the woman said. "I know who killed those two girls over on Church Street. And all the others."

Maria felt her brow knit. "Others?"

"Yes," the woman said. "The Alphabet Man, I know who he is."

Maria felt her stomach jump just above her belt line. This was the second time in two weeks someone had tossed out that name to her in the lobby.

"What did you say your name was?"

"Priscilla. Priscilla Janovich."

"Well, Mrs. Janovich—"

"Miss, please."

"*Miss* Janovich." Maria corrected herself. "Why don't we go back to my office and talk."

"Oh, yes, I think we should," Priscilla said, as Maria stepped aside and motioned for her to go first.

Maria escorted her past the guard cage and over to the heavy metal doors that barred the way into the interior of police headquarters. She slipped her ID out of her front blouse pocket and slid it through the card reader.

"This way," she instructed.

She led Priscilla down the hall until they got to an interview room. "Would you like something?" Maria asked.

"There's no coffee on right now, but a glass of water, a Coke perhaps?"

Shot of Jack Daniel's? she thought.

"No, I'm fine. I think we should get to this." The interview room was small, with a mirror on one wall and a small table with two metal chairs. Priscilla Janovich sat down in a metal chair behind the table as Maria sat opposite her.

"Is there anyone on the other side of that mirror?" Priscilla Janovich asked.

Maria smiled. "You obviously watch a lot of television, Miss Janovich."

"Oh no, only a few shows. But I read a lot. Almost all mysteries."

"Ah," Maria said. "So you're a big mystery fan . . ."

"Yes, that's how I figured out who the Alphabet Man was. After I read that article in the Sunday *Times* yesterday."

"So that's how you heard the term 'Alphabet Man,'" Maria chimed. "For a minute there, I thought everybody'd read our case files."

"So you are investigating the murder," Priscilla said, her voice excited. "You know, I'm so glad they put a woman on that case, it's just—"

"Miss Janovich, there are a lot of detectives working those murders, and we've had a lot of people tell us they know who did it. A few have even confessed. Not one's been straight with us, though."

"Oh, well, I am," Priscilla said. "I know."

"Okay," Maria said. "I'll bite. Who is the Alphabet Man?"

Priscilla Janovich leaned down and pulled the canvas tote bag up into her lap, then upended it onto the table. Four paperbacks tumbled out.

"Him," Priscilla said, pointing at one of the books. "He did it."

Maria stared at the pile of battered paperbacks. "Who?" she asked blankly. "Who did it?"

"Him!" Priscilla said, pointing. "Michael Schiftmann! The man who wrote these books!"

* * *

A half hour later, Priscilla Janovich had finished her synopsis of each one of the four paperback editions of Michael Schiftmann's novels. She explained that she'd read the latest book, *The Fifth Letter*, but hadn't bought it yet since it wasn't out in paperback. Priscilla went on to say in a moment of supreme irrelevancy that she was such a mystery fanatic she read her favorite writers in hardcover on loan from the library, then when the paperback was issued—usually a year or so later—she bought the cheaper edition and read the book again.

"And yesterday, when I read the article in the *New York Times*, I realized I'd heard all this before!" Priscilla said, her eyes beaming.

Maria looked up from the yellow legal pad where she'd been taking notes. "So you're saying this guy commits murders, then writes books about them."

"Yes," Priscilla said excitedly. "He bases the plots of his novels on murders he commits. Oh, he changes the locations around and some of the details, but the substance is there. You can't change that."

"Okay, so—"

"And the books are really good!" Priscilla continued. "I mean, I sat down yesterday afternoon and started rereading them again from the first and wound up reading all four in a row."

Priscilla rearranged the books in order of publication. "I was up all night," she said proudly.

It shows . . . Maria thought.

"And I'm sure that if I got the fifth one and reread it, it would only back up what I already know."

Maria leaned forward on the small table, her elbows perched on the edge. "Miss Janovich, I don't mean to doubt your word here, but can you understand how tenuous this is? Do you see how little this is to go on? I mean, how little sense this makes? I don't know this guy"—Maria looked down at the paperbacks—"Michael Schiftmann, but he's obviously, like, a famous writer and stuff. If the guy's on the best-seller list, why would he go around committing these murders."

"If you read the books, my dear," Priscilla Janovich said, slipping into teacher mode, "you'd know the answer to that question already. He kills because it's the right thing for him and because he *likes* it!"

The old woman's words echoed in Maria's mind. She remembered the first briefing she'd been given by the FBI agent, whose name she couldn't remember because it was too early in the morning and she still hadn't had her tea yet. Even though Priscilla's choice of words made the hair on the back of her neck prickle, it still didn't overcome her common sense, every bit of which told her this old lady was crazy and her story was ridiculous.

"Look, Miss Janovich, I've made notes on what you've told me and I'll enter it in the record," Maria said. "But we can't pursue something like this when—"

"You don't believe me, do you?" Priscilla demanded sternly.

"Well, it's not that, it's just that we have to have more substantive evidence to go on. Sheer speculation isn't enough."

"Why don't you read the books?" Priscilla asked. "See if it doesn't make sense to you."

"I'm very busy, Miss Janovich," Maria said defensively. "We've all got a lot to do around—"

"That's no excuse!" Priscilla snapped.

"Ma'am, I'm sorry, but I just don't think I can do anything on what is obviously speculation. I mean, we don't even know this guy. And anyway, these murders you're talking about that were allegedly recorded in this guy's books, they're outside our jurisdiction. We can't do anything about that."

"What about those two girls on Church Street?"

Maria nodded her head. "See, there you go. Good point. We don't have anything to connect him to those murders. Nothing."

"Oh yes you do!" Priscilla exclaimed.

Maria felt her blood pressure rising. She had to extricate

herself from this as quickly as possible. There was too much work to do.

"What?" Maria asked. "What have we got to connect him to these murders?"

"Well," Priscilla Janovich said in a huff. "How about the night those two girls were killed he was in Nashville?"

Maria stopped cold. "How—how do you know that?"

"I met him," Priscilla announced in triumph.

Maria thought the old lady really had gone off the deep end now. "Oh," she said, patronizingly, "and where did you meet him?"

"At the Davis-Kidd bookstore in Green Hills," Priscilla said, smiling. "He was doing a book signing. Just check the newspaper. Better yet, call them."

An aggravated Lieutenant Max Bransford hung up the phone, pulled his massive bulk out of the worn desk chair, and went to the open doorway of his office.

"Bea, you seen Chavez anywhere?"

Bransford's longtime secretary looked up from her computer screen. "No, sir, not all day."

"Damn it," he muttered, walking past her and out into the hall. He walked twenty feet or so down the hallway and stuck his head in the squad room. Four detectives sat behind desks, each with his head buried in a folder.

"Hey, any you guys seen Chavez?" No one looked up.

"Chavez, guys. Remember her? Short, brunette, slight Hispanic accent, carries a gun. I just got a call from Hershel over at the ME's office. She was supposed to be there an hour ago to pick up the tox screen reports on the Grant murder."

Jack Murray looked up. "I saw her this morning, Loot. Had to run upstairs to Print Division. Passed by the break room up there."

"The break room?" Bransford asked.

Murray hesitated. "Yeah, Loot, the break room. She was laying on the couch."

Bransford felt the pressure from his jaw grinding his teeth together. "She sick?"

Murray shook his head. "Didn't look like it."

"What was she doing then, son?"

"Uh, she was reading a book, sir."

"Reading a book . . ." Bransford said slowly. Murray nodded. Bransford turned and headed down the hall to the lobby.

Reading . . . Lying on a couch . . . In the middle of the day . . .

This was just weird enough to arouse Bransford's curiosity. He walked down to the main lobby, then climbed the staircase to the second story. He ran his ID through the card reader outside the second-floor main entrance, then opened the heavy metal doors. He went down one hallway, turned left, then went down another hallway past the Fingerprint Division. He stopped at an open door, his bulk filling the doorway.

Inside the small room, on a couch against the far wall, Maria Chavez reclined with her head on the armrest facing away from the door. She held a paperback book open between her hands. On the floor next to her was a stack of file folders, a legal pad covered in scribbles, and an open felt-tipped pen.

Bransford cleared his throat loudly, which elicited no response at all from Chavez. Bransford cleared his throat again and took two steps toward the couch. Chavez bent her head while still lying down and looked over her shoulder. She spied Bransford, quickly raised up on her hips, and put both feet on the floor.

"Oh, hi, Lieutenant," she said. Maria still held the book open on her knees. Bransford looked at the spine of the book and read the words: *The Third Letter*. Bransford thought she looked a little zoned out, almost in a trance.

"Hello, Maria," Bransford said calmly. "You want to tell me what's going on here?"

Maria Chavez stared ahead for a second, as if still someplace far away. Then she looked back up, directly into Max Bransford's eyes, and he saw an intensity and a clarity that he'd seen in another person's eyes only a few times in his life. It was the look of epiphany.

"What was that FBI agent's name?" she asked.

Bransford studied her for a few moments. "Powell," he said finally. "Hank Powell."

She looked away. "Yes, Powell . . ." Then she turned and looked back at Bransford. "We have to call him. Now."

"But why?" Bransford asked.

"Sit down, Max," Maria said, motioning with her head to the chair next to her. "You're not gonna believe this."

PART II

THE INVESTIGATION

CHAPTER 15

Monday afternoon, Washington, D.C.

Hank Powell stepped out of the director's office, strode quickly past the receptionist without speaking and through the doors into the outer office, then through that room and out into the hallway. His face was set in stone, which belied the churning in his gut. His temples throbbed. The back of his neck burned as if he'd been too long in the sun. His right hand clenched the black leather portfolio like someone was without warning going to mug him for it. His left fist was a knot of muscle and bone.

Once out in the main hallway, he took a deep breath as he walked to the elevators, trying to center himself, trying not to give anything away to the other starched and suited robots passing him in the opposite direction. All he wanted was out of there, back to the safety and relative quiet of his office at Quantico.

Behind him, a voice called out: "Hank! Wait."

Damn it, he thought. He recognized the voice, though, and turned.

A flushed and winded Lawrence Dunlap burst past the doors of the director's office and almost trotted to catch up with him.

"Wait," he said, puffing as he stopped next to Hank. The air in the Hoover Building, Hank thought, suddenly felt even more stale and suffocating.

"Yes, sir?" Hank asked.

Deputy Assistant Director Dunlap stopped a moment, catching his breath, then reached out and touched Hank gently on his left elbow.

"C'mon," he said, "let's step over here, out of the way of all this traffic."

The wall across from the bank of elevators had an alcove to one side, which led to a door where janitorial supplies and equipment were kept. Dunlap walked over, Hank following, then stopped in the shadows and turned to him.

"Look, for what it's worth, I think the old man was a little out of line in there," Dunlap said.

"I don't appreciate being talked to like that," Hank said after a moment. "But I've been around long enough not to let it get to me."

"Yeah, well," Dunlap said, slowly shaking his head as if trying to figure something out, "go ahead and let it get to you. He was wrong. But you know how he hates this kind of publicity."

"And I don't?" Hank demanded. "You think this makes my job any easier? I've got to worry about not only this son of a bitch going around slicing up girls practically my own daughter's age, but now I've got the director of the FBI crawling up my ass screaming about a press leak."

"Hank, don't lose your detachment here. You've always been a pro. I need you to hold on to that for me."

Hank took a deep breath and let it out slowly. "I know," he said after a moment. "He's under a lot of pressure."

"We all are on this one," Dunlap said. "We've gotten a lot of bad publicity the last few years. The old man wants it stopped. We find this guy and nail his ass, people might forget some of the other cluster fucks that have gone around here."

Hank was silent for a few seconds, then looked up directly into his superior's eyes. "Is he going to pull me off this?" Hank asked. "If he's going to yank me, I want to know. I've got my twenty. The old man relieves me, I'm putting in for early retirement. I mean it. I won't fall on my sword for him. Not when I've done my job as well as anyone could."

Dunlap stared at Hank Powell and realized he meant every word of what he'd just said. "No," he answered. "There's no talk of relieving you. You're still the SAC of this investigation."

Hank's jaw relaxed just enough for him to feel it, but not enough for Dunlap to see it. "Yes, sir," he said. "Thank you, sir. Now if that's all, I have a lot of work to do."

Dunlap nodded.

The thirty-five miles that separated the FBI main headquarters at the J. Edgar Hoover Building on Pennsylvania Avenue NW in Washington, D.C., from the three hundred and eighty-five acres that contained the FBI Academy in Quantico, Virginia, might as well have been the distance between two planets at opposite ends of the solar system.

The back of Hank's neck still burned on the long ride back. As he left I–395 South and merged onto I–95, he saw that the traffic was even thicker than usual. Normally the drive would take between forty-five minutes and an hour, but it had already taken him nearly that long just to hit the freeway. It didn't matter; he barely noticed. In his long career at the Bureau, no one had ever talked to him like he'd just been spoken to. It was all he could do to keep himself under control.

Hank kept a stack of books on tape in his car for long drives and had popped in a tape as soon as he pulled out into traffic. He soon realized, though, that there was no way he could focus on the reading and flicked off the tape player.

Hank Powell also felt bad for the way he had talked to Dunlap back at FBI headquarters. Threatening to resign was no way to gain the support of your superiors, he knew, but in this case he had to do and say something strong enough to let Dunlap know they had pushed him about as far as he was willing to be pushed.

So Hank felt bad for being dressed down in the director's office and for copping an attitude with Dunlap, but what he felt worst of all about was his inability to make any progress on this case at all. The material that had been found in Nashville had yielded a DNA profile, but whose? And nothing else of any use had been gleaned from the Alphabet Man's garbage.

This guy's got to screw up somewhere, he thought over and over again. *But when? Where?*

Hank couldn't remember the last time he felt so low. Even when Anne got sick, it hadn't been quite like this. He'd been saddened, grieving, had felt frustrated and helpless as she became sicker and sicker. But he'd never questioned his own actions, his own worth. He knew he'd done his best for her, had done everything possible.

And, he realized, it was different now because he was so alone. If this had happened years earlier, before he lost her, he'd have gone home at the end of the day and talked to her—never in specifics, but enough to let her know how troubled he was. She would have listened, as she always did, and been savvy enough not to tell him what to do or to meddle in his business. She was his sounding board, and by processing his thoughts with her and through her, he would find something he hadn't seen before, some insight he'd missed, some element that had bypassed him.

Now there was no one.

Almost an hour later, Hank barely nodded to the Marine guard at the gated entrance to Quantico. He wound his way around until he found his parking space outside an office building behind Hogan's Alley, the mock small town made up entirely of façades that was used in training. In the distance, he heard rhythmic gunfire snapping from one of the outdoor ranges.

The air was cold and dry, the sun beginning its slide toward the horizon in a cloudless, blue winter sky. Hank pulled his overcoat tightly around him as the cutting wind from the east chilled him.

Sallie Richardson, the division's longtime administrative assistant, looked up from her desk as Hank entered. She tried to smile, but as soon as she saw the look on his face, her smile disappeared.

"That bad?" she asked.

Hank stopped at her desk and nodded his head. "Hasn't been my best day."

"Sorry, Hank," she offered. "It'll get better."

He shrugged. "Sure." He walked down the hall to his office.

"Oh," Sallie called to him. "Check your voice mail. Max Bransford in Nashville called."

"Thanks."

Hank opened the door to his small office, with the one window that looked out onto the woods that surrounded the academy. He hung up his coat, sat down at his desk, and punched the buttons to retrieve his voice mail. There were four other messages ahead of Bransford's, but none had the urgency that was in Bransford's voice.

"Agent Powell," the recording began. "This is Lieutenant Bransford with the Nashville Murder Squad. I need to talk to you ASAP. Can you give me a call at 615 . . ."

Hank scribbled down the number, then punched the buttons to leave voice mail and get an outside line. Within ten seconds, the phone in Max Bransford's office was ringing. A female voice with a deep Southern accent answered.

"Lieutenant Bransford's office," she piped. "May I help you?"

"This is Agent Powell at the FBI, returning Lieutenant Bransford's call."

"Oh, hi, Agent Powell. This is Bea Shuster. Good to hear from you. The lieutenant's been waiting for your call. Just hold on a second."

Hank smiled. *How can these people be so damn friendly?*

Bransford came on the line before the thought could completely leave his head. "Hank?"

"Yes, Max, how are you?"

"Up to my nether regions in amphibious reptiles. Listen, I won't take up too much of your time but I had to call. You got a minute?"

"Sure." Hank opened a notebook and grabbed a pen. "Talk to me."

The voice on the other end of the line hesitated. "I'm going to ask you to reserve judgment on this one until I finish, okay? This is going to sound kind of crazy at first."

Hank felt his brow furrow. Curious . . .

"I'm listening," he said.

"You remember Maria Chavez?"

"Yes, of course. The young Hispanic woman. Quite sharp, if I recall."

"Very," Bransford said. "Top-notch. Smart as a whip. If this had come from anyone else, I'd have blown 'em off. But she's convinced and I thought it was worth a call to you."

"Okay," Hank said. "My curiosity's running wild. Let me have it."

"About the butt crack of dawn this morning, Maria Chavez comes in to catch up on some paperwork and have a little quiet time. Only she gets a call that there's this old lady out front who claims to know who the Alphabet Man is. Maria figures she's a nutcase. We get a few of those from time to time, you know."

"Like every other day," Hank interrupted.

"Yeah. So anyway, Maria offers to give her five minutes, and the old lady says she knows who our guy is. He's this famous writer, right? The old lady reads all his books and claims he bases the plots to his novels on murders he's committing himself."

"What?" Hank asked. "That's crazy."

"But she's brought in the *New York Times* article and a stack of paperbacks by the guy and she starts spouting off details of the books that sound an awful lot like some of the shit our killer's doing. She convinces Maria to at least take a look at the books. So Maria ushers the old lady out and disappears for a few hours to look over the novels."

The line went silent for a few moments. "And?" Hank asked.

Hank heard Bransford sigh on the other end of the line, the long, weary sigh of a longtime cop who's close enough to retirement to taste and smell it.

"And I find Chavez curled up on a couch in the break

room practically in a fetal position. She's read the books and is convinced the old lady's right."

Hank leaned back in his chair and stared out the window for a moment. For that moment, his mind seemed more still than it had been all day, as if it had settled into a sweet, sublime, and welcome silence.

"You there?" Bransford asked.

"Yeah," Hank said, forcing himself back to reality. "Max, this is crazy."

"I know, it's insane. Completely loony tunes. But what if it's true?"

"Who's the writer? I mean, who the hell is this guy?" Hank felt his own voice rise from the tension.

Hank heard some paper shuffle in the background as Bransford flipped through some notes. "His name's Michael Schiftmann—"

Hank scribbled down the name as Bransford spelled it for him.

"The guy's apparently famous. On the *New York Times* best-seller list, big bucks, movie deals, all that celebrity crap. Personally, I never heard of him, but I get too much of the real thing to go home and read about murder."

"Me, too," Hank agreed. "Who's got time? And what books are these?"

"Chavez made me a list, although it's pretty easy to remember. The first one's called *The First Letter*, the second one's *The Second Letter*, then *The Third Letter*, and so on."

The mention of letters caused the already tense muscles in Hank's neck to contract even further. "Letters?" he asked.

"Yeah. Fuckin' creepy, you ask me. And the hero, protagonist, whatever the hell you call him of the novels is like this crusader, vigilante type who goes around killing bad girls in cold blood, like an executioner or something."

"Or a serial killer," Hank offered.

"Yeah, like that."

"This is crazy," Hank said again. "What do we do with this?"

"Well, I've given Chavez twenty-four hours to write this

up as a full report and make her case. Knowing her, I'll have it tomorrow morning. I'll fax it to your office."

"Okay, thanks."

"Beyond that, we're just going to sit tight. But there is one other thing that's kind of a raise-the-hair-on-the-back-of-your-neck thing . . ."

"Yeah?"

"That night those two girls were murdered over on Church Street, that night Howard Hinton from Hamilton County called you?"

"Sure, I remember."

"This famous author guy was in Nashville," Bransford said. "He did a book signing at the Davis-Kidd bookstore over in Green Hills. Something like three hundred people showed up."

"Three hundred? It was snowing like hell that night. Must've been about twenty degrees."

"Yeah," Bransford answered. "Like I said, the guy's real popular."

Hank finished the call by promising to hook back up with Bransford as soon as he'd had a chance to read Maria Chavez's report. Then he walked out of his office and back down the hall to Sallie Richardson's desk.

"You know where I live in Arlington, right?" he asked.

"Well, I know about where," she answered, looking up from her computer screen.

"Is there a bookstore on the way home? A pretty good one?"

Sallie gazed up at Hank, questioning. "Hmm, let me think. Yeah, you know where Army-Navy Drive is, where it crosses—what is it?—Hayes, I think?"

"Oh yeah, over near that huge, obnoxious mall."

"The Fashion Center at Pentagon City," Sallie said. "And it's no more obnoxious than any other mall. There's a Borders Books across the street."

"Great, the traffic should be wonderful right about now," Hank muttered.

Sallie crossed her legs and planted her elbows on her desk. "Okay," she said, "what's going on?"

Hank checked his watch. It was nearly four. "I think I'm going to cut out a little early today. I'll have my cell phone if anything comes up."

The first fifteen minutes after arriving home from work were always the worst. The house was so quiet, the undisturbed air within so heavy and still. Hank had considered getting a dog, but he wasn't home enough to take care of one. Ordinarily, silence didn't bother Hank. In fact, when Jackie was a baby, he'd often wished for a little silence.

Now, with Anne gone, it seemed that was all he had.

He set the plastic bag full of books down on the coffee table in the living room, then hung up his overcoat in the hall closet. With Hank getting home early, the computerized thermostat hadn't had a chance to warm the house up. He walked over to the keypad and overrode the programming, the gas heater in the basement clicking on as he did so. Within seconds, he felt warm air wafting up out of the vents.

He went upstairs to the master bedroom and changed into a pair of jeans and a sweater, then made up the bed and folded some laundry from the night before. There was a time when Hank's bed was made as soon as he got out of it and the clothes folded and hung up as soon as they came out of the dryer, but that was before the seventy-hour weeks and the sleepless nights the Alphabet Man had brought into his life.

He finished his chores and went back downstairs. It was almost six, and Hank decided, with a twinge of guilt, to go ahead and have his dry vodka martini. He wasn't hungry; it was too early to eat, anyway. He went through the martini ritual and walked back into the living room, settling into an overstuffed chair next to the sofa. He decided it was too quiet and reached over for the remote. He turned on the local CBS affiliate and sat staring for a few seconds at the local news broadcast. Apparently it had been a slow news day because the coiffed blond anchorperson with the Hollywood white teeth was blathering on about a dog show over in Shawsburg that had been disrupted by a group of PETA protesters.

Bored and tired, he took his first sip of the icy martini and, as always, marveled at the shock of the cold combined with the searing of the alcohol. Hank had never been a daily drinker before and sometimes wondered if he was on his way to having a problem. Then he decided to cut himself some slack; given what he'd been through the past four or five years, it was a wonder he wasn't a falling-down drunk screaming obscenities on a street corner.

He surfed around for a few moments and found that there was nothing on that caught his attention. Even his favorite classic movie station didn't offer anything of interest.

Hank took another sip of the martini, then set it down on the end table. He reached over and pulled the plastic bag with the Borders Books logo on it over to him and dropped it on the floor at his feet. He reached in, shuffled through the five books—four paperbacks and one hardcover—and pulled out a copy of *The First Letter*.

The book was expensively printed for a paperback, the large letters on the cover embossed, the ink brightly colored in a kind of neon red. The author's name, Michael Schiftmann, appeared above the title in letters nearly an inch high.

Hank turned the book over and gazed at the author's picture. The photo was that of a handsome man, still young, but with the beginnings of age lines in the corners of his mouth and around his eyes. His face could be called rugged, his eyes a deep and piercing blue. His nose was not unduly sharp and narrow, and his cheekbones were prominent and high. He wore a double-breasted navy-blue jacket, white dress shirt, and tie.

He was, Hank concluded, a poster boy for Handsome Best-Selling Authors Month.

He opened the book and read the first few lines. It was not as if Hank read much in the way of any fiction, let alone murder mysteries. It was as Bransford had said: A homicide investigator or an FBI agent passing his spare time reading murder mysteries made about as much sense as a fry cook coming home and reading a novel set in a fast-food restaurant.

Hank forced himself to read the first few paragraphs. The

first book opened with a murder, a brutal, sadistic murder told from the killer's point of view. The writing was simple and well-crafted, but evocative and powerful. But as Hank Powell read the first few paragraphs and then the first few pages, he found himself being drawn further and further into the story. There was a plot there, he realized, but it wasn't the plot that pulled you into the story; it was the voice, the voice of the protagonist, a stone-cold killer utterly without conscience.

As he read past the first few chapters, the forgotten vodka martini on the table next to him gradually warming to room temperature, Hank began to lose himself in the story. This guy Schiftmann, he realized, knew how to hook a reader. At the end of every chapter, something happened that made it impossible to put the book down. You *had* to keep reading. Hank read on, despite himself, his blood going colder with each scene. How could someone write this stuff? he wondered.

Then he remembered the young salesgirl in the Borders who'd looked at him strangely when he piled five books by the same author on the counter in front of her. He'd asked her if she read Schiftmann, if he was any good.

"Oh yeah," she'd said tensely. "He's good. But I can't read him. This stuff creeps me out."

"But people seem to like it," Hank had countered.

"Yeah," the young girl had said. "We sell a ton of his stuff. Go figure."

Go figure. The young girl's words came back to him as he neared the climactic end of the book, when the protagonist/serial killer, called Chaney in the book, was cornered by the corrupt female homicide investigator in the basement of an abandoned porno theater. Chaney managed to break free of her, to turn the tables, and now he had her. In a scene that was as shocking as it was graphic, Chaney had slowly, exquisitely murdered the woman in a way that turned Hank's stomach and at the same time kept him reading.

Hank turned the last page of the book and closed it. He looked up; it was dark outside. Hank looked over at the clock. It was almost ten.

"Jesus," he muttered. He stood up, rolling his head around on his shoulders to loosen the tension in his neck, and walked over to the front window to close the shutters. Then he walked into the kitchen in a kind of daze and pulled out a microwave meal. He felt drained, pummeled after reading the book, and wondered what it was in the makeup of the human psyche that was attracted to such pure, unadulterated evil. This Schiftmann guy, Hank concluded, had gotten rich by appealing to the very worst, the most ignoble and bottom-feeding instincts in all of us.

He popped his frozen Salisbury steak dinner into the microwave and punched some numbers into the keypad. The microwave began humming as Hank walked back into the living room and picked up his drink. The glass had been sitting there so long, the condensation on the side had dried. Hank took a small sip and winced.

As he took the glass into the kitchen, he realized that something else was bothering him about the book. It was gruesome and graphic, hard to read yet impossible to put down. But there was something else.

Something else . . .

Something about the description of the murder. Some element of the scene, something that stuck, buried, deep in his mind. But what?

What was it?

Frustrated, Hank picked up the book, opened it to the first page, and began rereading chapter one. The first murder took place in a small town in Ohio, a place called Middletown. The victim was a young girl, a college student, working at a fast-food place over the summer. She worked the breakfast shift and arrived early one day, before the manager got there to unlock the doors.

Chaney was sitting in the parking lot, waiting for the place to open. As he stared out the windshield, an elderly man with the air of homelessness about him approached the young girl and spare-changed her. Chaney watched as the girl went off on the homeless man, finally swatting at him with her heavy handbag, almost knocking him over.

As the man stumbled away, Chaney got out of his car and walked up to the girl. Sad state of affairs, he said to her, when a young girl working an honest job can't wait outside her place of employment without being accosted by bums. The girl smiled, agreed, and the conversation continued.

When the manager arrived twenty minutes later, there was no sign of the girl. A week later, she was found in a rental storage unit—raped, tortured, and set out on display. On the wall above her body, the block letter "A" had been painted in her own blood.

"Middletown," he said out loud. "Where the hell is Middletown?"

Hank walked into his study and pulled an atlas off the bookshelf. He turned to Ohio and began scanning. Then, in the southern part of the state, near the Kentucky border, he found Middletown, Ohio, which was close enough to Cincinnati to be a suburb.

Cincinnati.

Hank felt his heart catch in his chest. The Alphabet Man's first murder had been in Cincinnati, and the victim had worked at a fast-food place.

"No," he said out loud. "It can't be. It's crazy."

In the background, the microwave timer dinged. Hank walked into the kitchen, grabbing the second installment of the Chaney series off the coffee table and taking it with him. He carefully pulled the lid off his steaming microwaved dinner and sat down at the kitchen table. For the next hour, he halfheartedly picked at his meal as he read *The Second Letter.*

When he finished that book just after one in the morning, the grease on his uneaten Salisbury steak dinner had congealed into a whitish-gray paste. He threw the box into the garbage, poured himself a snifter of brandy, then turned off all the lights downstairs. He took *The Third Letter* to bed with him. He shaved and showered, put on a pair of running shorts and a T-shirt and slid into bed, the drink on the nightstand, the book next to him.

The night slipped by effortlessly as Hank, almost beyond

exhausted, read on and on. When he closed *The Third Letter* and dropped it on the floor next to the bed, it was just past three-thirty in the morning.

And like Maria Chavez, Hank Powell now knew who the Alphabet Man was. As crazy as it seemed, as insane a theory as this would appear to most people who heard it, Hank knew. He was as sure as he was that the sun would rise in another two hours. Only one question remained.

How the hell was he going to prove it?

CHAPTER 16

Tuesday afternoon, Manhattan

Taylor Robinson was so engrossed in her reading she almost didn't hear the phone in her office buzz. On the third ring, she lifted the handset.

"Yes," she said blankly, still staring at the contract in front of her.

Jennifer, the new receptionist, laughed. "Did I wake you up?"

"No," Taylor said, smiling. "I was just off in the zone."

"Well, come back to Earth. I've got Mr. Schiftmann holding for you on line three."

"Oh, great," Taylor said, punching the blinking button for line three. "Hello," she continued.

"Hi, you," Michael answered. "How are you?"

"Fine. I was just going over the last of the foreign contracts. Did you know you're going to be published in Portuguese?"

Michael sounded surprised. "Really? Where?"

"Brazil. It's not much money, only twenty-five thousand a book, but it's a lot of money for foreign."

"I can remember when I'd kill for a twenty-five-grand contract. Now it's just side money. I think I see a Rio de Janeiro book tour in my future. What do you think?"

"I think that's quite doable. And I think you'll need a competent guide."

"You've been to Rio?"

"Couple of times. One of my favorites. So where are you?"

"Cleveland," Michael answered.

"Ah, Cleveland. Not one of my favorites."

"Well, I won't be here much longer. I closed on the condo today. The movers are coming first thing in the morning, and then I'm out of here."

Taylor frowned, grateful that Michael couldn't see the look on her face. "Are you sure this is what you want?" she asked. "Moving to Manhattan is a pretty big step."

"Of course I'm sure," he said. "Look, it's a long way from the slums of Barberton to the Cleveland lakefront. And when I bought this place a year ago, I thought I'd use it as a base for the rest of my life. But things change. We've changed. I want to be with you, and I certainly don't expect you to move to Cleveland."

There was a moment's silence as Taylor tried once again to take all this in. "Okay, if you're sure. I want us to have a chance, too, and I guess we need to at least be in the same zip code if we're going to give it a go."

"And that's what we're going to give it," Michael said brightly. "Besides, I sold out just at the right time. I made a tidy little bundle off that condo."

Taylor laughed. "Does everything you touch turn to money?"

"Everything I touch since I met you turns into money."

"That's sweet."

"No, Taylor, I mean it. When I walked into your office that day, I had enough cash to my name for one more night's stay in a fleabag hotel and a Greyhound bus ticket back home. Meeting you turned everything around."

Taylor smiled now and held the phone tightly to her ear. "It's pretty well rocked my world too, buster. So when're you coming home?"

"I'm flying out tomorrow night after the movers leave. I'll be at LaGuardia about ten. I'll just take a cab in, if it's okay for me to stay with you awhile longer."

"I'd be heartbroken if you stayed anywhere else," she teased.

"I've got an appointment with a broker Thursday morning. She's got about six places for me to look at, including a house on Hudson Street."

"Hudson Street?" Taylor asked, surprised. Hudson Street was prime Greenwich Village real estate. Very few co-ops ever came up for sale in that area, let alone a whole house. "Great location. Very pricey, though."

"More than I ever thought I'd be able to spend. But hey, who's counting?"

"Wow, the Village. You'll love living there, but it's going to be an adjust—"

"I want you," Michael interrupted.

"What?"

"I want you. Right now, this minute. I want to be inside you, as far as I can be. I want my mouth on you, my hands on you."

Taylor felt her skin flush as a wave of energy went through her. "Yeah?" she whispered. "And then what would you do?"

"I'd roll you over onto your back and hold your legs up in the air and I'd pull almost all the way out of you, almost, and just stay there for a few seconds. And then I'd pull you onto me as hard as I could."

Taylor moaned. "I miss you," she said quietly, hoping no one else was listening in on line three.

"I miss you, too," he said. "This's driving me nuts. Will you wait up for me?"

"I think I can stay awake that long."

"And when I get there, can we have a glass of wine and snuggle up on the couch for just a bit, just enough time to decompress, maybe? Talk, catch up . . ."

"Sure, I'd like that."

"And then can we just go to bed and fuck our brains out?"

Taylor gasped. She'd never before been with a man who so freely and spontaneously and so naturally used the F-word. Most of her other lovers, if they referred to the sex act by name at all, talked about "making love" and "being together" or some other new-age, sensitive-guy euphemism.

She had never talked about sex this way before with a lover. There was something deliciously naughty about it.

"Only," she whispered, "if you do me really hard."

"Oh," Michael laughed, "you keep talking like that, we might not make it to the bed."

"And that would be a problem?"

"Not for me," he said. There was a moment's silence. "I really do miss you."

"Me, too."

"What's the weather like over there?"

"Oh, God," Taylor snapped. "Now we're going to switch to the weather?"

"No, I'm asking for a reason."

"Okay, you got it. It's dark and gray and cold and icy. The wind's picked up. They say it might snow. And how about Cleveland?"

"This is the Lake Erie snow belt in early March, baby. Use your imagination."

"I'd prefer to save my imagination for other things. So why were you asking?"

"You packed?"

"Oh, that. Haven't even started. But we don't leave until Saturday morning."

"Well, you just walk outside in the sleet and the cold and imagine yourself on a beach, the two of us alone, lying on the hot sand practically naked."

"I won't spend too much time on that one, as I have a lot more work to do today."

"Clear everything with Joan?"

"Well," Taylor answered, drawing the word out, "I don't think she was real happy with my being gone for the whole week. But now that I'm representing a guy who's probably going to have five books on The List at one time before it's all over, I've got a little more juice than I used to."

"That's right," Michael said. "You just tell her your star client insists on taking you to Bonaire for an entire seven days of sun, diving, and incredible sex, not necessarily in that order."

Taylor groaned. She had never before thought of herself

as—she could barely bring herself to say the word—*horny*, but ever since she and Michael got together, she thought about sex and needs and drives more than she ever had.

"You've got to stop talking that way," she said breathily. "You know how much I miss you."

"If it's anywhere near as much as I miss you, then we're going to fry the entire northeastern power grid. It'll be the next great blackout."

"Will you please, please, *please* hurry home?"

"As fast as I can, my darling. I'll see you tomorrow night."

"Yeah," Taylor said. "Yeah, you will."

Michael hung up, and Taylor sat there for a moment holding the phone. She stared out the grimy window of her office to the top floor of the discount camera store across the street. Below her, the Manhattan street noises—taxis honking, brakes squealing, loud voices yelling in a hundred different languages, the squall of far-off sirens—seemed muted now, as if there were a fog between her and the rest of the world.

She had never felt this way before. She had been in love and she had been in lust, but never both at the same time. Her stomach knotted and her face flushed as she relived some of the past times in bed with Michael. She tightened her hips as she felt herself getting wet. He was the best lover she'd ever had, by far, and he had brought out something in her that she didn't even know was there. Something deep within her had been freed, and she wondered just how wild and scary and crazy this was all going to get before it was over.

Four days later almost to the hour, Taylor gripped the armrest of her window seat on the starboard side of the ancient twin-engine DeHavilland Otter and squeezed until her knuckles turned white. Next to her, in the aisle seat, Michael sat calmly reading a book as the plane went into what felt like about an eighty-degree bank. Their side of the plane was on the downside of the turn, and Taylor, her throat tight and dry, squatted down to look out the tiny window.

All she saw was blue, the deepest blue she'd ever seen before. *Water*, she thought, wondering what it would feel like to drown.

And then it came into view, the green and browns of Bonaire, the next island over from Aruba just off the coast of Venezuela. The flight from JFK to Aruba had been on board a 757, a huge, comfortable, and what felt like rock-solid safe jet. When they had disembarked at the Aruba airport and the male flight attendant had smiled and pointed toward the DeHavilland Otter, Taylor had felt the blood drain out of her face.

"Oh no," she whispered, grabbing Michael's arm. "Not that. They're not actually going to fly over water in that thing."

Michael smiled, patted her arm. "It'll be fine. It's only about a twenty-minute flight."

"Can that stay up for twenty minutes?"

But it had, and as the pilot lowered the flaps and set the plane up for final approach, Taylor felt herself relaxing even as her stomach rolled with the rapid loss of altitude. The plane was coming in awfully fast, she thought, but then before she knew it, the plane bumped the runway and began slowing. As they slowed to a stop in front of the single building that served as the Bonaire airport terminal, Taylor read the sign that said, WELCOME TO FLAMINGO AIRPORT.

"Okay," she muttered. "Anyplace that calls its airport the Flamingo is going to be all right."

The twenty or so tourists, most of them clearly divers, climbed down off the plane and were whisked through customs. The Bonaire economy was built on tourism, and everywhere, it seemed, the island was geared to make visitors comfortable. Taylor and Michael stood in line for a cab, and barely a half hour later were checked into their bungalow at the Divi Flamingo, staring out a window arm-in-arm as the sun fell slowly into the Caribbean.

"It's stunning," she said.

"Seven hours ago, we were freezing our asses off trying to get a cab in a snowstorm," Michael offered.

"Hard to believe. It really is a different world, isn't it?"

Michael turned and pointed toward the bottle of iced-down Roederer Cristal he'd arranged to be in their room when they arrived. "Thirsty?"

Taylor smiled. "Kind of early, isn't it? It's barely five."

Michael walked over to the ice bucket and pulled the bottle out. "Hey, we're on vacation. Besides, we've got a couple of hours before our dinner reservation."

"Where are we eating tonight, kind sir?"

"Ah," Michael said, gently pulling the foil off the top of the champagne bottle, then carefully unwinding the wire around the cork. "That's a secret. But I will tell you this: this tiny li'l ol' island here has over fifty restaurants on it, many of them world-class. And over the next seven days, we're going to hit as many of them as we can."

The champagne was wonderful, the sex afterward as powerful and as intense as anything Taylor had ever experienced in her life, and the dinner exquisite. The first few hours had taken them from a stressed-out midwinter Manhattan frame of mind and put them firmly on island time. It was nearly eleven by the time they left the restaurant, and just before midnight, they found themselves walking alone on a beach with their third bottle of wine of the evening and a couple of glasses. The Caribbean moon was nearly full and low off the horizon, throwing out bursts of silver onto the ocean's surface that seemed to light up the whole sky.

Taylor slipped off her shoes and felt the warm sand under her feet. She was sleepy, exhausted, sated, but didn't yet want to let go to sleep. Next to her, Michael walked silently, shuffling his feet in the sand. She took his free hand in hers and gently guided him toward the water's edge. The tide was coming in, the water lapping softly against the sand. Taylor dipped her feet in the water and found it surprisingly warm. She leaned over and put her head against his shoulders as they walked.

"Want to sit down and open this guy up?"

"Sure," Taylor answered, smiling. "Although I'm not sure how much wine I'm up for. I'm a little tipsy now."

Michael eased her over to a small mound of sand just ahead of the water and held her hand as she settled onto the ground. He eased down next to her and set the two glasses in the sand, then reached into his shirt pocket and extracted a corkscrew.

"It's amazing," Taylor said softly as Michael twisted the corkscrew into the neck of the bottle.

"What's amazing?"

The cork came loose with a slight pop, and Michael poured two glasses of red wine.

"This, all of it. How can it get any better? I mean, this is perfect."

Michael lifted a glass in each hand and handed one to her. Taylor took it and stared at him over the top of the glass.

"I don't know," he answered after a moment. "I don't know that it has to get any better. When you've reached perfection, that's as good as it ever has to get."

"Great," she chided. "That means we've got no way to go but down."

He reached over, clinked her glass gently. "No," he said seriously. "Never. Never say that. It's just going to get better in different ways."

She lifted the glass and took small sip. The wine was as perfect as the evening had been.

"How'd I get so lucky?" she asked.

"I was just asking myself the same question."

Michael leaned over and kissed her softly, sweetly, as a cool wind from the sea blew quietly over them.

The next morning, Taylor and Michael climbed out of bed about a half day earlier than she wanted, but they had an appointment with the dive master. At Michael's urging, Taylor had signed up for scuba lessons in Manhattan, but had held off on taking her check dive until they got to Bonaire. She went through the procedures, the equipment, and a test dive off the beach, followed by a quick quiz with the blond, sunburned Australian who ran the dive operation. The next thing she knew, she was standing in front of a passport camera having her picture taken for her "C" card, which certified her as an open-water diver.

"Congratulations, love," he said. "Now let's do the real thing."

She, Michael, and a dozen other divers hauled BCDs—the buoyancy-compensation devices that enabled divers to control the rate by which they ascended or descended—goggles, fins, regulators, and the heavy air tanks on board a thirty-foot dive boat. Taylor had eaten a light breakfast with a little juice and coffee, so was able to hold off the worst of the impending seasickness as the boat pushed through the swells toward open sea.

An hour later, they were farther north on the leeward side of the island, where the reefs were pristine and untouched, the water barely sixty feet deep and crystal clear. Michael had warned her that the first time she dived in open water, she might feel just a touch of anxiety, of drowning panic.

"Remember," he told her as they sat on the side of the boat, preparing to roll backward into the ocean, "don't forget to breathe, slowly and steadily. When we go in, let's just float for a couple of minutes until we get adjusted."

Taylor already had the regulator clenched firmly in her mouth. She nodded, pulled her goggles down over her eyes, held the regulator with her left hand and the mask with her right. Then she let go.

It was only a couple of feet from the gunwale to the water, but she felt as if she were falling forever. She hit the water, which suddenly seemed colder, and went completely under. Her eyes widened, and for a moment she felt the surge of panic. She bit down hard on the regulator, trying to calm herself, to fight the urge to start paddling and fighting to the surface.

Then the BCD brought her to the surface and she bobbed there like a cork, her neck and face well out of the water, the heavy metal tank on her back now weightless. She looked around, and Michael was next to her a couple of feet away. He brought his hands up like a referee calling a touchdown and then bent his arms into circles and tapped the top of his head with both hands. It was the universal scuba sign language for "I'm okay, how about you?"

Taylor forced herself to let go of the regulator, then brought her arms out of the water and mimicked his arm motion. She tried to loosen the muscles in her neck and to let her legs go

limp beneath her. She looked down and realized it was almost like being suspended in air, sixty or seventy feet above
the ocean floor. The water was warming now, her body ad-
justing, and she felt almost as if she were inside a womb.

The two floated there for what felt like at least a full minute, then Michael slowly paddled over to her and took the
regulator out of his mouth and held it up out of the water.

"You ready to dive, lady?"

"I guess so," Taylor tried to say, but she didn't take the
regulator out of her mouth and it came out as muffled gob-
bledygook.

"I'll take that at as a yes," Michael said, slipping the regulator back into his mouth. Then he held up the dump tube off
the BCD in his right hand, his thumb on the valve to release
the air inside. He nodded. Taylor held her own tube up, her
fingers tight, and nodded back. She watched as he pressed
the button and his BCD began to hiss softly. As it deflated,
Michael's body sank slowly beneath the surface.

Taylor anxiously pressed her own valve and felt the BCD
around her begin to deflate. There was a hissing sound for
her as well, and within, it seemed, half a second, her head
was slipping beneath the surface into a silent, warm, thick
world of blue.

As her head went under, she realized she'd closed her eyes
tightly. Once under water, she forced herself to open them.
A small puddle of water had formed at the bottom of her
mask. She tried to remember the procedure to clear it.

A few feet way, Michael had let go of his tube and was
hovering just below her. He waved at her slowly, his hand
fanning back and forth in the water. She waved back, forced
a little more air out of her vest, and descended to his level.
He swam up to her, looked into her eyes through their
masks, and reached out for her. He took her two hands in
his, squeezed them slowly yet firmly, and she felt herself
relax. She was with Michael; she could trust him and she
was safe.

He reached for his relief valve again, held it over his head,
held her hand with his free hand, then waited for her to lift
her tube. He nodded. They both pushed the button and be-

gan sinking. Taylor felt the pressure rise in her ears, then let go of Michael's hand, held her nose through the mask, and blew air into her ears to equalize the pressure.

She smiled; it worked. That was the first time she'd ever equalized perfectly the first time. She snaked her hand around and grabbed the lines that held her gauges. She held them up to her mask. They were descending through forty feet. She smiled behind the regulator and held it out to Michael. He looked at it and gave her a thumbs-up.

Taylor looked down and was surprised to find the coral-encrusted ocean floor coming up toward her. She and Michael put a small burst of air into their vests to keep them off the coral, a few feet above. Michael shifted himself into a prone position, hovering above the ocean floor in a Superman pose. She felt herself smile again, her lips hard on the regulator, trying to remember to breathe slowly and rhythmically. She swam up to him and flattened herself out, then reached over and took his hand. The two began slowly kicking their fins in a scissorlike motion, quietly moving over the seabed plants and coral. A school of bright yellow fish that Taylor didn't recognize swarmed around them. In the distance, she caught a glimpse of the other divers and remembered that they weren't alone.

They swam slowly along, alternating that movement with a still, relaxed drift. They swam in circles, never too far away from the anchor chain. Taylor relaxed, trusting Michael to take care of her, to watch over her. She was glad she'd done this, glad she'd met him, glad she'd taken the biggest chance of her life.

Taylor realized that at this moment, sixty feet below the surface of the Caribbean just off the coast of Venezuela, in the early part of March, with a man she'd been with barely a month, she was happier than she'd ever been in her life. For perhaps the first time in her life, she was completely happy.

The last night in Bonaire, Taylor and Michael went to a local place called the Island Café for dinner. Michael had done some research into where the locals went when they wanted to celebrate something away from the tourists. They took a cab into Kralendijk, the only real town on the island, and found themselves in a narrow alleyway near the town center. The alleyway was dimly lit, crowded with locals, and had a different feel than anyplace else they'd been.

Michael held her hand and walked ahead of her down the winding alley, taking one wrong turn, backing up, then taking another. The Island Café was tiny compared to the other restaurants they'd been to, but the smells coming from the kitchen were exquisite. With all the diving and exploring, not to mention the staying up half the night locked in each other's arms, they had both lost a couple of pounds. Taylor was ravenously hungry.

They drank the local beer and ate pastechis, the plump little pastries full of spicy shrimp and meat. They ordered giambo, the thick, spicy okra soup that was sort of like gumbo, only with a twist. They ordered steaks and fish and wine and ate like starved, caged animals for the next hour, almost without talking. When they finished, Taylor leaned back in her chair and stared across the table at Michael.

"I don't want to go," she said simply.

"I don't, either. But we have to. We have to get back to the real world."

"Why?" she complained. "Why can't this be the real world?"

"Because it isn't," he said. "I have a book to write and I'm on deadline. You have clients that need you. Joan needs you."

"She can't need me that much. I haven't had a single call from her."

"That could have something to do with the fact that you didn't tell her where you were going," Michael said, smiling.

"Maybe. But she has ways of finding out."

"You know she's champing at the bit for you to get back."

"Maybe."

Michael leaned forward on the table and took her hands in his, then pulled her toward him.

"There is one thing we can take with us from the island. Something that will make this an even more important week than it's already been."

Taylor looked at him, questioning. "What?"

Michael squeezed her hands and they suddenly felt cold. Taylor looked down at their hands and realized his palms were sweating.

"What? What's the matter?"

"Oh," he said slowly, "nothing's the matter. I guess I'm just a little new at this."

"New at what?" she said, almost exasperated.

He let go of her right hand with his left and reached into his pocket. When his hand came back up to the table, it held a small, velvet-covered cube.

Taylor stared at his hand, stunned. "Wha—"

Michael let go of her left hand and raised his right index finger to his lips. "Ssshh," he said.

"What are you—"

"Let me," he said hurriedly. "Please."

She was silent for a moment, uncomprehending. "Ever since I met you, Taylor, it's been like my life has come together. The day I met you is the day I turned the corner. It was the day when everything started to make sense. Suddenly, I know what I want with my life, and I know who I want to spend it with."

"Michael, I—"

Michael's voice rose just a notch, and he looked directly into her eyes. "Now that you're in my life, I don't ever want to take a chance that something might happen and you won't be. I love you, and I want to be with you and nobody else, ever. I'm through with everything I used to do and used to want. I know what's important to me now, and now that it's here, right next to me, I don't want to ever let it slip away.

"Taylor, will you marry me?"

He opened the small ring box and held it toward her. Shocked beyond recognition, she stared at it a second before realizing what it was—a beautiful European cut diamond that had to be pushing three carats. It was the largest diamond she'd ever seen up close, even larger than her grandmother's.

"My God," she whispered. And as she finally got what he was saying and asking, her eyes began to fill. She looked up from the box, into Michael's eyes, and looked at him through a film of tears.

"Are you sure?" she whispered, her voice barely audible.

He nodded. "More sure than I can even begin to tell you."

She laughed. "A writer at a loss for words. When's the last time we saw that?"

She laughed again, louder this time. "Yes, Michael," she said after a moment, taking the box from him and setting it on the table between them. She took his hands and squeezed them, hard.

"Yes, I'll marry you."

All around them, the other restaurant patrons began clapping and cheering.

CHAPTER 17

Friday afternoon, Nashville

Hank Powell slipped his rented Mitsubishi Gallant into the first available space in the public parking garage across from the Nashville Criminal Justice Center and jerked the gearshift into park with a loud crunch. Next to him, Special Agent Fred Cowan, the resident agent who worked out of Nashville under the supervision of the Memphis Field Office, bounced forward and caught himself with his palm on the dashboard.

"Easy, Hank," Cowan said. "We'll make it."

"We're late," Powell muttered. "I hate being late."

"We've got a couple of minutes," Cowan said, climbing slowly out of the car in a manner far too relaxed to suit Powell. "This is Nashville. Everybody gets hosed up in traffic sooner or later."

"Doesn't matter," Powell said, slamming the door and turning for the exit at a near-trot.

"Wait up!" Cowan called, racing to catch up.

The two agents crossed the side street and walked hurriedly up to the main entrance. Powell already had his badge and credentials out when they got to the main reception desk. He fidgeted nervously as the desk officer phoned upstairs. Less than a minute later, the metal entrance door to the police offices buzzed and Maria Chavez stepped out.

She waved Hank and Cowan past security and held the door for them as they entered the long hallway.

"Sorry we're late," Hank said.

"Don't worry, we haven't started yet. C'mon, this way."

Maria Chavez wore jeans and boots, with a long-sleeved white cotton shirt. She looked like a clean, freshly scrubbed farmhand, with the exception of the nine-millimeter Glock Model 19 attached to her belt.

"Maria, I've got to tell you," Hank said as the three walked quickly down the hallway, "that report you did was sensational. I can't believe you put all this together."

Maria turned, smiling broadly, her white teeth glistening in the harsh fluorescent light. "Thanks, Agent Powell. I appreciate it. But it was really that daffy old lady who convinced me."

"Please, Maria, it's Hank."

"Thanks, Hank."

Maria came to a bank of three elevators and pushed the up button. Hank leaned down and glanced at his watch, which read one-twelve. Twelve minutes late . . .

As if reading his mind, Maria chimed in. "Don't worry, Howard Hinton just got here, too. There's road construction all the way down I–24 to Smyrna. Took him an hour and a half to make the last twenty miles."

Cowan grinned. "I hear the legislature's thinking about making the orange traffic barrel the state bird."

Chavez chuckled. "Good one."

Hank secretly wished Cowan would shut the hell up. He was a bit too relaxed and jovial for the circumstances, or maybe it was just that Hank was unable to be relaxed or jovial about any of this. If this meeting went the way he thought it would, then Maria Chavez's theory was the break in this case they'd been needing for years.

Hank had spent the entire week reading the rest of Michael Schiftmann's work and analyzing Maria's report. He now believed that Maria was right, but he also knew that if she was right, this was going to be the biggest media firestorm since the O. J. case. Hank wasn't even ready to begin thinking about the consequences of charging a celebrity like Michael Schiftmann with being a serial murderer, with the corroborating theory being that he was basing the plots of his own best-selling novels on murders he committed himself.

As Maria Chavez led Hank and Cowan into the small conference room that was already crowded with Murder Squad investigators, the voice in his head was still warning that even though he believed it, no one else was going to.

Max Bransford sat at the head of a long table and rose when Hank entered the room. He looked like he'd gained ten pounds and lost a year's sleep since that cold February night of the Exotica Tans murders. In fact, Hank noticed, looking around the room, they all looked tired.

"Hello, Hank," Bransford said, extending a hand as Hank approached him. "It's good to see you again. Thanks for coming down."

"Thanks for inviting me," Hank said.

"Here," Bransford motioned, "sit next to me."

Hank took a seat to Bransford's left, then nodded and leaned across the table to shake hands with Howard Hinton of the Chattanooga Police Department's Homicide Squad. The two exchanged comments about the terrible Nashville traffic as the rest of the investigators took seats in an informal, but recognizable, seating by rank. Fred Cowan took a side chair near the end of the table where Gary Gilley, lead investigator on the case, sat anchoring the group.

"Let's get to work, ladies and gentlemen," Bransford intoned, as people began shifting in their chairs, shuffling paperwork, and opening notebooks in front of them. "We've got a lot to cover today, a lot of thinking to do. Has everyone had a chance to read Maria's report?"

All heads nodded with the exception of Cowan, who held up an index finger. "I'm sorry. I just got it this morning. Haven't had a chance to get to it."

Hank clenched his jaw. If Cowan had mentioned that to him, he would have brought him up to speed on the long drive down West End Avenue. Instead, the two made tense chitchat as Hank maneuvered his way downtown.

"Don't worry," Bransford said. "Just hang with us. You'll catch up."

There was a moment's silence as all the investigators

turned to Bransford. "I guess the first thing we should do is have a show of hands. Is there anyone in this room who actually believes this cockamamie theory of Detective Chavez's that a famous, rich, best-selling writer comes into town for a book signing and, just for shits and grins, decides to butcher two young girls?"

A few hands went up, including Maria Chavez's and Hank's, with Gary Gilley at the other end of the table holding his hand out over the table, palm down, wiggling it back and forth.

"Okay, Gary, what's that mean?"

"It means Maria put together a helluva report that reads like it oughta be on the best-seller list itself—"

A couple of investigators laughed as Gilley paused for effect. "—but the question is can we prove it to anyone's satisfaction, especially a jury. Personally, I think the DA's gonna laugh us out of town."

"What other theories have you got, Detective Gilley?" Hank asked.

Gilley shook his head. "Not much. We've gone all through these two girls' backgrounds. Deep stuff. There's nothing there. The closest is that the Burnham girl was dating a soldier out of Fort Campbell, a paratrooper with the 101st Airborne. These guys are trained in close combat, especially with knives, bayonets, machetes, shit like that. Also, this guy supposedly had a real temper. Maybe he didn't know his girlfriend was working in a massage parlor and went apeshit when he found out. That was our best bet, but we went up this guy's ass with a very bright light and we didn't see anything up there that shouldn't have been there. He had an alibi for that weekend. And he just got shipped out to downtown Baghdad."

Hank turned to Max Bransford. "What about the forensic evidence from the Dumpster?"

"Yeah, that," Gilley answered. "The soldier boyfriend voluntarily gave us a swab and we typed him against the DNA on the overalls and the rags. Nothing."

"So he's clear," Maria said.

"Anything else from the Dumpster?" Hank asked.

"Oh, yeah, we got blood and tissue matches to both girls. The stuff definitely came from the murder scene. And we got a bunch of stuff we were able to profile, but were unable to match."

Hank nodded to Gilley. "That means we've probably got blood, saliva, scrapings, something from the killer."

Jack Murray, near the end of the table across from Cowan, raised his hand. "So why can't we just get this famous guy to give us a DNA sample and type it."

"Because," Bransford said, "if this guy's got a brain in his head, he'll tell us to go fuck ourselves. And I wouldn't blame him."

"That's putting the cart ahead of the horse," Hank agreed. "We'd have to build a case for subpoenaing the sample and we're not there yet."

Bransford turned to Howard Hinton, the homicide investigator who had raised his hand. "So you buy into this craziness, Howard? Wanta tell us why?"

Hinton, who had been silent before now, leaned his heavy bulk over the table and planted his elbows on the hard wood. He rested his chin on his right palm and sat there for a moment.

"At first, I thought it was crazy, too. Then I went back and did a little checking. The night he did the two murders, the L and the M killings, he was in Nashville at a book signing."

"Yeah?" Bransford said after a moment.

"Almost two years ago, when Laurie Metzger, the twenty-two-year-old blond who worked out of that strip club, Déjà View, became the J murder?"

Hank felt his neck tighten.

"Yes?" Bransford said again, his voice tense.

"Michael Schiftmann was in Chattanooga as the keynote speaker at the Chattanooga Mountain Writers' Conference. Schiftmann arrived on a Thursday afternoon. She was murdered Friday night. Schiftmann didn't leave until Sunday morning."

Hank wondered how Bransford could deliver a bombshell

like this in such an offhanded manner. For a few moments, there was complete silence in the room. Then, from down the table to Hank's left, a voice muttered: "Holy shit . . ."

Bransford turned to Hank. "Did you know this?"

"No, but I would have eventually. I've e-mailed every field office where the Alphabet Man has hit and asked them to cross-check against Schiftmann's book signings and travel."

"This is insane! Do you guys have any idea how crazy this sounds?" Gilley, his voice shrill with tension, shouted.

"Of course it's insane," Chavez said loudly. "But it's insane to butcher two MTSU coeds, too! That's the whole thing with serial killers, Gary, they're nuts! Get it? Serial killer—"

Chavez held her hand out and drew an equal sign in the air.

"—nuts! It comes with the territory."

"But he's not nuts," Hank interrupted. "We have to remember that, he's not crazy. He's a sociopath, he's ruthless and relentless, and he's evil, but he's not crazy. And so far he's gotten away with this, so he's careful and he's smart. And we have to be just as careful and just as smart or we blow this."

Again, there was a tense silence in the room. After a few moments, Max Bransford spoke up. "So, let's strategize. How do we reel this guy in and nail him?"

Hank looked around the room, scanning the face of each one of the investigators. "A couple of observations. If we've learned anything about high-profile celebrity murder cases in the past dozen years or so, it's that the police and the prosecutors usually lose by shooting off their mouths. The first thing we have to do is lock this thing down, tight. If that reporter down in Chattanooga—"

Hank looked over at Howard Hinton, questioning.

"Yeah," Hinton said, "Andy Parks."

"Andy Parks gets this and then it goes to the *New York Times* and the *Washington Post* like that last story did, then we're in deep trouble."

"Everybody got that?" Bransford asked. "If this leaks, we know it came from this room."

"And we don't have to even begin to discuss the world of shit the leaker will be in when I find out who he or she is," Gilley added.

"The second thing is," Hank added, "we've got to coordinate and work together. You guys have to treat this as a local homicide, but I have to deal with it on a much larger scale, even an international scale. Once word gets out that we've got a suspect in these killings, I've got police departments from Macon, Georgia, to Vancouver, Canada, who are going to want everything we've got."

Gary Gilley shook his head wearily. "Jesus, this is going to be one huge cluster fuck if we're not careful."

"That's putting it mildly," Hank answered.

"So where do we start?" Maria Chavez asked.

Max Bransford eased back in his chair and laced his fingers together behind his head. "To a certain extent, we treat it like any other homicide. We have to establish method, put the guy at the scene, look for witnesses . . ."

"And prove a motive," Gary Gilley said from the other end of the table. "That's going to be a tough one. We know why this sicko did what he did, but making it real for a jury might be a bitch."

"Will be," Bransford said. "But let's get started. Gary, you'll coordinate. Get the search warrants and subpoenas under way. I want this guy's credit card records, travel records, hotel registrations. I want the bookstore people interviewed, the hotel people. If this guy rented a car, I want to know which car and what he left behind in it."

"In the meantime," Hank added, "I've got a complete, full-blown background check going on this guy. We've already run his name through NCIC and came up with squat. As far as I can tell, he's never even spit on the sidewalk before. But we're still digging. And later on down the road, if we have to, we'll dive under the Patriot Act umbrella and pull a sneak 'n peek."

"Okay," Gilley said. "Maria and Jack, you'll work with me

on assigning areas. We'll split everything up and everybody into teams. After this meeting, we'll huddle in the bullpen and get going right now."

"You know the weirdest thing about all this?" Maria Chavez asked.

"What?" Bransford answered.

"This whole thing broke because some silly old lady stays up all night reading paperback mysteries."

"If she were here right now," Hank offered, "I'd kiss her on the mouth and give her a medal."

CHAPTER 18

Special Agent David Kelly smiled as he took the exit ramp off I–76 West and turned south toward Barberton, Ohio, one of the dozens of small towns that cluster around the Cleveland/Akron hub. Kelly, at twenty-eight, was the youngest agent in the Cleveland Field Office of the FBI. He'd been with the Bureau less than two years and still approached each assignment with the kind of eagerness and excitement that the older agents seldom exhibited.

Agent Kelly didn't know why he'd been sent to Barberton, Ohio, in pursuit of a deep background check on Michael Schiftmann. He knew who Schiftmann was, being a regular reader of the Sunday *New York Times Book Review*. But he'd never read one of his novels. And when the e-mail came through from Quantico to start digging, he took his orders like the good soldier he was and went out into the field armed with his file folder full of report pages.

He already knew that Michael Schiftmann had been born in Barberton, Ohio, in 1969, during the height of the Vietnam war. Just over a year after Schiftmann's birth, four students would be shot down by the Ohio National Guard just up the road in Kent. Michael's father, a burned-out Vietnam combat veteran with an ever-growing and intrusive drug problem, would desert the infant and his mother and never be heard from again.

And, Kelly discovered from a check of the Summit County

public assistance database, Michael's mother, Virginia, still lived in the same two-bedroom project house in South Barberton that she'd raised him in.

Kelly looked down at his notes, then turned left into Fourth Street South, a narrow street clogged with parked cars—mostly run-down—on both sides of the curb. Even though the street was two-way, it would have been tough for two oncoming cars to maneuver around each other. He leaned over the steering wheel, looking out the windshield for house numbers. Most of the houses looked to be from the thirties, he thought, maybe early forties. They were identical shotgun duplexes, two narrow houses jammed together into one, with a narrow driveway between it and the house next door. Most needed a coat of paint. Random shutters hung askew, dotted by the occasional cracked window. There seemed to be no one around, not even kids or stray dogs. One empty lot was marked by a rusted fifty-five-gallon oil drum set up as a stove and a couple of ratty sofas next to it.

Kind of like his old neighborhood, Kelly thought. Depressing.

He passed the Schiftmann house, but there was nowhere to park. He cruised most of the block before he found an empty slot, then pulled his government-issue Ford Taurus over and cut the engine. He sat there a moment, organizing his thoughts, then opened the car door. The dry, cold Ohio wind hit him hard in the face. He tucked his chin into his neck, slammed the car door behind him, and pulled his overcoat tighter as he walked up the street against the wind.

Virginia Schiftmann lived six houses up on the left, number 232-B. He turned off the cracked sidewalk onto another cracked walk that led up to the house. There was a doorbell button, but when he pushed it, Kelly heard nothing. He tried again, then knocked. From somewhere in the house, he heard the faint sound of a television. He knocked again, louder. His hands were so cold, it hurt to rap them against the wood. He wished he'd brought gloves, but the use of gloves was discouraged because it made the rapid drawing of a weapon difficult.

He raised his hand to knock again when the door opened

a crack. An older woman, heavy, with ruddy red cheeks, wearing a gray housecoat, looked suspiciously out the door.

"What?" she said, her voice a monotone.

"Mrs. Schiftmann," Kelly said, pulling his credentials out of his coat pocket, "I'm Special Agent Kelly of the FBI. I work out of the Cleveland Field Office. I'd like to ask you a few questions."

The old lady peered out through the crack in the door, the light dim behind her, the flickering of an old, seventies-era color television in the background. She examined his ID and his badge, then looked up into his face. Then, slowly, she opened the door wider.

Kelly stepped in, the casual smile on his face designed to be as nonthreatening as possible. He stepped into the small entrance alcove and was hit by a wave of hot, musty air. Michael Schiftmann's mother kept the furnace going full blast.

"I won't take up much of your time," he offered as she closed the door behind him. She motioned toward the living room and he turned to walk.

"I got nothing but time," she muttered.

As they entered the living room, the light got better and Kelly was able to examine the surroundings. Genteel poverty was a stretch, he realized. The carpet was worn and threadbare, with the faint odor of pet urine wafting up in the heat. The furniture was old, and even when new was pretty basic and bare. A framed photo of the pope hung on one wall over the television, partially hidden by a green vase full of ragged, dusty silk flowers.

"Have a seat," she said, walking slowly over to the television and turning down the soap opera she'd been watching.

"Thank you," Kelly said, pulling off his overcoat and draping it over the back of an overstuffed, tired chair. Tufts of white stuffing poked through the material in the corners of the seat pillow.

He pulled out his notebook and a ballpoint pen from his coat pocket. "Mrs. Schiftmann, this is nothing more than a routine background check, and it's standard procedure to go back to a subject's home neighborhood and just ask some questions. It's nothing to be alarmed about."

Kelly looked at the woman and waited for some kind of response from her. As she eased onto the sofa, he realized that she was even heavier than he first thought. The skin of her face was stretched tight, and as the housecoat draped open from her knees down, he saw that the skin on her lower legs was stretched until shiny and broken in several places by networks of spidery red veins.

Then he saw, on the end table next to her, a blood sugar tester and one of those cheap, battery-operated sphygmo-manometers that were available in any drugstore or grocery nowadays. A row of amber plastic pill bottles was lined up next to the machines, stretching from one end of the table to the other.

Type 2 diabetes, Kelly thought, high blood pressure. *All the earmarks of American poverty . . .*

"Yes, well," Kelly said after a moment, clearing his throat. He opened his notebook and pulled out the more-or-less standard form used in these kinds of checks. "The person we're doing the background check on, Mrs. Schiftmann, is actually your son, Michael."

From across the room, Kelly felt the old woman stiffen. Her eyes narrowed, and she seemed to straighten her back on the couch. He watched as her right hand gripped the arm-rest and her knuckles grew white.

"What's he done?" she asked.

Wow, Kelly thought, *that's not what I expected.*

"Uh, actually, Mrs. Schiftmann, I don't think he's done anything. This is a standard background check."

"Why?"

"Why what?"

"Why is he getting a background check?"

"I'm not actually at liberty to discuss that," Kelly answered, thinking that even if he were, he didn't know the answer. "But I assure you, it's just standard procedure, all perfectly above board. These things are very routine these days."

She eyed him nervously and relaxed her grip on the arm-rest. Then she looked down at the floor, her eyes darting back and forth.

"I don't really like to talk about him," she said softly.

"It's just a few questions," Kelly said. "Like, for instance, we know your son was born in 1969. Did you live here then?"

Mrs. Schiftmann shook her head. "No, my husband and I had an apartment in Portage. I moved in here with Michael after he left."

"Which was?"

"I don't know," she said wearily. "It was kind of a blur. I was working in the extrusions factory, worked the night shift. Slept during the day; it was hard."

"Who kept the baby?"

"There was a teenage girl who lived down the way. She was thirteen."

"So a thirteen-year-old was keeping your baby?" Kelly asked.

"I had to work."

"And where did Michael go to elementary school?"

The old woman was silent for a few moments. "O. C. Barber Memorial," she answered. "It was down the street just a mile or so. He could walk."

"And how did he do in school? Was he a good student, did he enjoy school?"

Her head seemed to be shaking nervously, side to side, in a jerky, continuous motion now. "Michael is very smart. He always made good grades, especially in English and spelling. But he didn't like school. The other children were mean to him."

"Mean to him?"

"Because he didn't have a father, because we were poor, because I worked in a factory . . . Who knows why? Kids are just mean."

"Did he have any friends there, anyone he was close to?"

"Not really. That was a long time ago. I don't really know."

Kelly stared at the old lady for a moment. He wondered if she didn't have Parkinson's disease or something on top of everything else. He cleared his throat again.

"How about junior high and high school?"

"He got a scholarship in the ninth grade," she said, with a hint of pride in her voice. The first he'd heard, Kelly noted. "Went away to that expensive, private school."

"What was the name of the school?"

"Benton School, Benton Academy . . . something like that. I have trouble remembering."

"And how did he do there?"

"It was harder than public school," she answered, her voice lowering. "It was hard on him, being away from home, away from me. But he made it, he graduated. Barely."

"Did he have any girlfriends, any close friends at all?"

"I don't know. He was away. He always liked girls, but he was shy when he was younger. We didn't go out much."

"Mrs. Schiftmann, did your son ever get in any kind of trouble at school or anything? Were there ever any kinds of disciplinary problems, difficulties like that?"

The old woman coughed, hard, her whole body shaking as the rumble echoed through her chest. She cleared her lungs after a few hard coughs, then settled back on the sofa and panted a few times.

"No," she said. "Never. My Michael was never in any trouble at all. He was a good boy."

Kelly leaned back in the chair and studied her for a moment. "Mrs. Schiftmann, if you don't mind my saying so, it seems like you and Michael had a lot of obstacles to overcome. A tough time . . . But my question, I guess, is how did Michael go from being apparently a lonely but bright kid to being a famous, wealthy writer? I mean, this guy's on magazine covers now. How did that happen?"

When Michael Schiftmann's mother finally looked back up at Kelly, he could see a shiny film of tears in her eyes. Her hands shook as she raised a finger and pointed at him.

"Because Michael was willing to do what it takes to get what he wants. Once he wanted something, nobody in heaven or hell could stop him."

Kelly made a couple of notes on his legal pad and looked at the form. There were a few other questions he could ask, but they probably didn't apply here. He could tell Mrs.

Schiftmann was starting to get upset. So, on impulse, he closed his notebook and stuck his pen in his pocket.

"Thank you, Mrs. Schiftmann. I think I've got just about everything I need. If there's anything else, I'll give you a call. And while there's certainly no legal requirement for you to do so, we always ask that you keep this just between us. If you don't mind, there's no need to say anything to Michael about this."

Kelly stood and reached for his coat. The old lady looked up at him, her eyes filling even more. "Don't worry," she said. "We haven't spoken in years."

Kelly looked around at the tattered living room, the peeling wallpaper, the general sense of decay, deterioration. He almost said something about that explaining why, even though her son was rich and famous, she still lived this way, but then he held his tongue. He stood, threw his overcoat over his arm, and closed his notebook.

Mrs. Schiftmann struggled to pull herself up off the couch. "Please, don't bother," Kelly said. "I can find my way out."

He took two steps toward the door, then stopped. He turned, faced the old woman as she sat there staring at him.

"Mrs. Schiftmann, this really isn't part of the check, but I'm curious. If you don't mind my asking, how did you and your son become estranged?"

She stared at him through rheumy, bloodshot eyes for a few moments without answering. The silence continued, and Kelly realized he wasn't going to get an answer. He turned and walked toward the door.

Outside, the sky had abruptly clouded over in the short few minutes he'd been in the Schiftmann home. He walked to the sidewalk, pulling his coat around him as the wind picked up. The air felt heavy, as if snow were imminent. After a few years around the Great Lakes, one learned to feel the weather as much as observe it.

He stopped on the sidewalk, thinking. The interview with Michael Schiftmann's mother had been frustrating. He didn't know if she was withholding or if she was just unable to focus. He wondered if he should knock on a few doors, but his supervisor in the Cleveland Field Office had told him not to take any more time than he had to. There were other things on his plate.

Kelly stood there for a few moments, appearing to be almost in a kind of trance. Behind him, at the end of the block, a car drove past with a bad muffler. A siren wailed in the distance. He was about to turn and head back to his car when the front door of the house next door to Mrs. Schiftmann's opened.

An elderly, thin man, gaunt and balding, wearing a pair of dirty khakis and a large sweatshirt, stepped out onto his porch. Kelly looked up and noticed the man's right sleeve was empty, folded in the middle and pinned at the shoulder. His left hand held a cane that looked carved from a thick tree limb.

"Can I help you?" the man said suspiciously. Well-dressed strangers standing on the sidewalk were not common in this part of town.

Kelly looked at the man, then decided to take a chance. He strode over to the sidewalk and smiled at the man. "Yes sir, maybe you can. Have you lived here a long time?"

The man looked at him for a moment before answering. "About thirty years," he said.

"So you've known the Schiftmanns for a while."

The man scowled. "Who are you?"

Kelly smiled. "I'm sorry. Forgot my manners." He pulled out his badge case and ID and held it out to the man. "I'm Special Agent Kelly, FBI. I'm doing a routine background check and I'm trying to get some information on a Michael Schiftmann. Could I ask you a few questions?"

The old man nodded toward the Schiftmann house. "She help you?"

Kelly smiled. "Little. Not much."

The man snorted. "I'm not surprised. She's as crazy as he is."

"Crazy?" Kelly asked.

"Kid was the craziest little psycho bastard I ever seen. Good thing he moved away. I'd have probably had to shoot him, one way or another."

Kelly smiled even more broadly. "Would it be okay if I came in and we talked a bit?"

The old man shrugged, then pivoted on one foot and turned for the door, leaning heavily on the cane with his one good arm.

"Sure," he said. "C'mon in."

CHAPTER 19

Saturday afternoon, Manhattan

The flight from Bonaire to JFK was so uneventful as to be tedious. The sky was gray, overcast, threatening a late winter snow as Taylor and Michael emerged from the plane and walked down the Jetway in a kind of shock. Six hours earlier they'd been in paradise; now they were back in the city.

That said it all.

The two were quiet during the long taxi ride to Taylor's loft on Grande Street. They dragged their suitcases and mesh bags full of scuba equipment upstairs, began unpacking, and then found themselves once more in bed. They made love yet again, perhaps a bit more subdued now that they were out of paradise and a bit more tired, then fell into a deep, silent sleep that went on for hours.

Taylor felt herself coming to and rolled over. The glowing orange numerals of the alarm clock read 8:47. She moaned, unable to believe that they'd been asleep nearly four hours. She shook herself awake and sat up on the side of the bed. Next to her, Michael was breathing deeply and rhythmically, still sound asleep.

She picked up her underwear off the floor and slipped into it, then quietly lifted her sweatshirt from the chair next to her bed. She crept out of the bedroom into the hallway and down the stairs to the main floor of her loft. The cavernous room, as high as two stories, was cold and drafty this time of year. Taylor shivered as she pulled the sweatshirt on, the rough material scraping her nipples. She crossed her arms across her chest, rubbing herself, as she walked into the kitchen.

She hadn't bothered to look at the stack of mail she'd brought up after digging it out of her jammed mailbox. And she noticed the message light on her answering machine was blinking madly. Not completely awake yet, she pushed the mail stack aside and opened the refrigerator. She pulled out a container of orange juice and poured a glass, then casually hit the button on the answering machine.

The computerized voice came on and announced that she had sixteen messages. Taylor shook her head wearily and reached for a pad of paper and one of the pencils from a jammed coffee mug full of pens, pencils, markers, and anything else she could cram in.

The first message was from Brett Silverman, delivered in her usual upbeat, high-energy, in-your-face fashion: "Hey girl! So you're off to the Caribe, eh? You gotta drink some of those frou-frou drinks with the paper umbrellas for me, and for Chrissakes, have lots of sex!"

"God," Taylor whispered, "if you only knew."

The second message was a frantic one from Joan Delaney, something about a lost contract. The third, fourth, and fifth messages were from Joan as well, the last one announcing that the contracts had been located and she could ignore the other messages. There was the usual depressing message from her mother, followed by one from her floor leader on the co-op board about the next monthly meeting, and a few other dreary, routine business messages. Taylor made notes of any message that actually required something of her, and either mentally filed away or dumped the others.

Then the next-to-last message, time-stamped Friday morning at nine-thirty, was Brett Silverman again. "I hear you're going to be in Saturday afternoon. You get your ass out of that apartment and buy the Sunday *Times* the second it hits the newsstand!"

Taylor perked up. There was nothing else to the message but a moment of silence followed by a beep, then another time stamp for Friday morning, nine thirty-four, and Joan's voice again:

"We did it!" she screamed. "He's number one! And the other four are all on the paperback list at the same time!"

Taylor's heart leaped into her throat. Could it be? She dropped the pencil on the counter, grinning broadly, then ran out of the kitchen, her bare feet pounding on the hardwood floors, then breathlessly up the stairs. She flung open the bedroom door and swiped the wall to hit the light switch.

"Wake up!" she yelled.

Michael shot up out of bed like a tiger who'd just taken the first bullet. He was halfway on his feet, furious, something dark, almost murderous in his face. He raised a fist, a wild look in his eye, and took a step toward her.

"Wait!" Taylor barked, startled. "It's me! It's me, baby, just me."

He stood there a moment, stunned, staring at her as if she were a stranger. Taylor looked into his face and saw something she'd never seen before, something that frightened her terribly. She took a step backward, into the doorframe.

"I didn't mean to startle you," she said softly.

Michael stood there at the edge of the bed for a moment, his nude body tight and tense as if poised to leap. Then he seemed to relax, the breath rushing out of his chest, and dropped onto the mattress still sitting up, stunned.

"I'm sorry," he gasped. "I was sound asleep."

Taylor rushed over to the edge of the bed and dropped to her knees in front of him. She put her arms around his waist. "I'm so sorry," she said. "I didn't mean to do that. I was just excited."

He ran his hands through her hair and pulled her to him, his torso bending down over her head. He was still breathing hard. Against his chest, Taylor felt his heart beating like a hammer. Michael hugged her to him.

"I'm sorry, too. I didn't mean to look like a crazy person."

She pulled away from him and looked up into his eyes, smiling once again. "My father always told me to never wake a sleeping dog."

Michael laughed, reached down, and pulled her up off her knees, then fell back on the bed, pulling her on top of him. She leaned down and kissed him softly, as he held her there. She felt him getting hard once again and found herself rubbing against him, feeling him through the silk of her underwear. She moaned softly.

"Oh, wait," she said suddenly. "I almost forgot."

"What?"

"Brett Silverman and Joan both left frantic messages yesterday morning. We've got to go pick up the Sunday *Times*."

His eyes widened. "You mean?"

She nodded. "Yep. You made it."

Michael jerked upright, carrying her with him. She almost bounced off him and landed on the balls of her feet.

"When's it come out?" he yelped.

"There's a newsstand over on Houston that gets them in around nine."

Michael stood, a look of incredulity on his face. "I can't believe it. I can't believe it."

"Believe it," Taylor said. "It's real. It's happened."

"Number one on the *New York Times* best-seller list," he said in wonder, as if it were a dream, an illusion.

The look on his face almost made her want to cry. "I'm so happy for you," she said.

Michael bit his lower lip. "I wish my mother were alive to see this," he said. "She would have been proud."

Taylor nodded. "I know she would have. I'm proud of you."

Michael stepped toward her and threw his arms around her waist, then lifted her up in the air and twirled her. They shouted and giggled and yelled.

Then they got dressed as fast as they could and headed out into the bitterly cold Manhattan night.

Sunday morning they slept in late, partially out of fatigue, partially to recover from the hangovers they were shouldering after the previous night's celebration. Michael had bought twenty copies of the Sunday *New York Times*, which turned out to be a load of newspaper to carry in the wet weather. They'd found a cab and gone to Ñ's, the trendy Manhattan bar where they'd had their first date. The place was packed and they had to wedge into a corner table, made all the more difficult by the nearly four-foot-high stack of newspapers. Michael ordered a bottle of champagne, and while waiting for it, opened the book review and simply stared at the page for a long time. Then he turned the page to the paperback best sellers and held it there in front of him.

Michael Schiftmann, Taylor thought, had done it. It was the culmination of a life's dream. *The Fifth Letter* was the number one book on the *New York Times* hardcover bestseller list, and four of the fifteen slots on the paperback list were Michael's as well.

Taylor wondered what lay in front of him. But then the champagne came, and the thought left her head.

One bottle of champagne was followed by another, and part of a third. By the end of the evening, Michael and Taylor had hooked up with the people at another couple of tables, and soon there was a party going on. They laughed and drank and danced and, in the end, went home with one copy of the complete Sunday *Times* and nineteen copies of the book review, the rest of the newspapers dumped in a wire litter basket on the sidewalk.

Taylor realized as they got to her co-op that she was dizzy from a combination of fatigue, excitement, and champagne. Michael was still wired, still animated. All she wanted was sleep.

And now, at nearly noon on Sunday, she rolled over in bed, faced a sleeping Michael, and smiled at the thought of what he had wanted. The act of smiling, though, made her head hurt even more. She hadn't had a pounding head like this in years.

"You're insatiable," she whispered. He stirred, moaned, and shifted beneath the sheets. She eased herself out of bed, slipped into the bathroom, peed, and swallowed three Advils. She threw on her thick bathrobe and slippers and padded downstairs without waking Michael.

She started a pot of coffee and, while waiting, managed to down half a glass of cranberry juice. She didn't drink much, ordinarily, but if there was ever a reason to celebrate, this was it. She opened the Sunday *Times* book review and turned to the best-seller page again. She stared down at it, almost wistfully, and realized that this was as big a day for her as it was for Michael. That night in Bonaire, the night he proposed, he said that finding her had been the thing that turned everything around in his life. Taylor realized, as she stood there staring down at the pages, finding him had been the biggest break she'd ever had as well. She was already the star agent at Joan Delaney's agency. Now this would elevate her several notches further.

Maybe, she mused, it was time to open her own agency, hang out her own shingle. Maybe she could use this as a stepping stone to lure even more heavy hitters to her own shop. At this moment, standing in her chilly New York kitchen on a cold day in March, it seemed to Taylor as if her options were unlimited.

The world had opened for her.

The shrill chirp of the cordless phone brought her out of her reverie. She picked the phone up quickly and hit the talk button.

"Hello."

"Hey, beautiful! You're back!"

Taylor smiled. "Good morning, Brett."

"Morning, hell, there's precisely ten minutes of morning left."

Taylor glanced over at the clock on the microwave, which read eleven fifty-three.

"Not even that much," Taylor said. "And I'm just getting out of bed. I should be ashamed."

Brett Silverman laughed. "That depends on what you were doing in bed."

"You're terrible," Taylor teased. "So what's up?"

"I just wanted to make sure you got my message and picked up the *Times*."

"Twenty copies," Taylor said. "I thought we were going to have to hire a car to bring them home."

"You could buy the car now," Brett said. "A whole fleet of them. So tell me, girl, how was the Caribbean?"

"Unbelievable. Incredible. It was warm, balmy, sunny, romantic. We scuba dived—or is it scuba dove?—and ate and drank and slept late."

"Either one, I think. Dived or dove. And what else did you do?"

Taylor hesitated. "What?"

"You know . . . Lots of?"

Taylor felt herself blushing. "Yes, plenty of that as well. In fact, I've got a little surprise for you. Word's going to get around anyway, so you may as well be the first. We're engaged."

Taylor jerked the phone away from her ear as Brett shrieked on the other end. The screeching went on for a full five seconds, and then evolved into an almost maniacal laugh.

"I don't believe it!" she squealed after returning to the English language. "That's awesome! Incredible!"

"Yeah, that was kind of the way I took it. It's crazy, but I think we're going to go through with it."

"Where is he now?"

"Upstairs," Taylor answered, cradling the phone in the crook of her neck so she could pour a mug of coffee. "Still knocked out."

"That's unbelievable," Brett said again. "Have you set a date?"

"Haven't gotten that far."

"I'm really happy for you, Taylor," Brett said, her voice suddenly serious. "I wish you nothing but happiness. Always."

"I appreciate that. Really." Taylor raised the mug to her lips and took a sip of the coffee without even adding her usual sugar and cream. The coffee was hot, strong, and she needed it now.

"So is this a big secret? Can I tell?"

"Sure. I'll make the announcement at the office tomorrow."

"Awesome . . . I mean, I can't even find the words. But I do wish you luck. Marriage is hard, you know. I've been there three times."

"Three?" Taylor asked. "I thought it was two."

"Nope, there's another one back there somewhere. I forget exactly where. I was young. It didn't last long."

"Wow," Taylor said softly. "The truth is, I'm scared. I never saw myself getting married. Just didn't think it was in the cards."

"This was pretty sudden, wasn't it?"

Taylor was silent for a moment, thinking. "Yeah, maybe a bit too sudden. But we'll take it slow from here on out."

"Good move, good thinking. Now, you got time for a little business?"

"Sure, shoot."

"Okay," Brett said. "First, Jack Hamlett from ICM called last week trying to find you. They've got the option terms worked out. They're ready to go to contract."

"I hope that means the higher figure we were talking about. You know my motto: 'No cheap options.'"

"Got you covered there," Brett agreed. "We're not giving these guys shit. They're paying top dollar. And he's got a package he wants to present to you and Michael. He didn't give me all the details, but he's got George Melford set to produce and Jack Holt to star as Chaney."

"Jack Holt," Taylor said, impressed. "Damn, he's good. Sexy, too."

"He'll draw the chick demographic, that's for sure."

"So this is all looking good," Taylor offered. "I can let Michael know."

"Tell him to get his signing pen ready."

"He'll be locked and loaded, I'm sure."

"And there's one other thing, Taylor. This one's a little weird. But have you heard anything from Carol Gee?"

Taylor frowned, set the coffee mug down on the counter. "The publicist?"

"Yeah, have you heard anything from her?"

"No, nothing. Why should I?"

"Just wondered," Brett said, pausing. "She's sort of disappeared."

"Disappeared?" Taylor asked, surprised.

"Yeah. Out of nowhere. She was set to take some vacation

after the last tour ended. She was flying from San Diego to somewhere. Hell, I forget where. But apparently she never showed up. And when her vacation was over, she never came back to work."

"Well, has anyone gone by her apartment or tried to call?"

"Kim over in publicity tracked down her roommates. She lives with three other girls in a two-bedroom apartment over in Woodside. They haven't heard from her, either. Big mystery."

"She got a boyfriend?"

"I don't know. Nobody exactly knows how to handle this. Human resources is taking the point on this, but they sent around an e-mail asking all of us who knew her to keep an eye out."

Taylor shrugged. "I haven't heard a word. But if I do hear anything, I'll let you know. When's the last time anyone saw her?"

"The last person we've been able to track down is the bookstore manager at Michael's San Diego signing. The next morning, she did the automatic checkout from the hotel and no one's seen her since."

Taylor glanced upstairs in the direction of her bedroom. "I'll ask Michael when he wakes up. Maybe he knows something."

"Yeah, do that. And are we still on for lunch Tuesday?"

"Wouldn't miss it," Taylor answered. "See you at one."

The two exchanged good-byes, then hung up. Taylor poured herself another cup of coffee and sat down with the rest of the Sunday *Times*. She drank the coffee and scanned the front page, but in the back of her mind, she kept wondering what had happened to Carol Gee.

CHAPTER 20

Tuesday morning, two weeks later
FBI Academy, Quantico, Virginia

Hank Powell closed the door to his office, set a fresh cup of coffee on his desk, and opened the window blinds. Outside, the trees that had been so tired and barren all winter were beginning to bud. Another few weeks and the view outside his window would be a palette of bursting greens, whites, and reds as spring broke through and brought everything back to life.

This was one winter Hank Powell was not sorry to see go. It had been a rough one.

But, he thought, smiling, things were looking up. He turned his back on the window and sat down at his desk. In front of him was a stack of file folders that had come in from all over the U.S. and Canada. Eleven FBI field offices, twelve police departments, nine sheriff's departments, and the Forensic Laboratory Services Directorate of the Royal Canadian Mounted Police had all contributed to what had evolved into an extraordinary effort to stop the Alphabet Man.

Everything had come together, and now Hank Powell's job was to sift through several pounds of paper and try to make sense of it all. If he could do that, then the slow, cumbersome, but unstoppable machinery of justice would go to work. The parents, friends, and families of the thirteen murdered girls they knew about could—if not find peace—at least begin to put this behind them. No one knew how many young women who might have been future victims would now be spared.

And no one knew if there were other victims, other murdered girls who just hadn't been found, who hadn't been part of the pattern.

Hank felt weighed down by the responsibility, but somehow elated at the same time. He'd been living with this so long that to finally see an end in sight made the weight somehow more bearable.

He set a legal pad and pen on his desk to the right of the folders, then opened the first one. He had stacked the folders by order of the murders; the A murder had been committed in Cincinnati, so the reports from the Cincinnati Police Department's Homicide Squad and the Cincinnati FBI Field Office were first in the pile. Hank began reading and making notes.

Then he worked his way, over the next five hours, through the reports from Macon, Georgia, then Scottsdale, Arizona, followed by Seattle, Milwaukee, Philadelphia, New York City, Vancouver, Omaha, Chattanooga, Dallas, and finally, Nashville.

Twelve cities: thirteen brutal, senseless murders.

He took a quick break for a late lunch, then went back to work on the files, this time going over the extensive background material on Michael Schiftmann. The agent out of the Cleveland Field Office, a young guy named Kelly, had done an outstanding job of compiling a biography of Michael Schiftmann. Hank read the interview with Schiftmann's mother and got about as much out of it as Kelly did, but it was the interview with the neighbor that caught his attention.

Schiftmann's mother had painted a portrait of a lonely, mistreated kid who was smarter than the other children, worked harder, was fiercely devoted to books and his studies, and was ashamed of his impoverished background.

"Okay," Hank muttered out loud. "Lots of lonely, weird, nerdy kids don't grow up to be serial killers, though."

But the interview with the neighbor, an eighty-one-year-old disabled WWII veteran named Stan Walonsky, painted an entirely different picture. Walonsky had used terms like "psycho" and "bastard" in describing Schiftmann. This, in and of itself, would have very little credibility. Sometimes people simply dislike each other. But Walonsky had specific examples to back up his claims.

When Michael Schiftmann was eleven, for instance, Walonsky caught him in an outbuilding that he used for a workshop and for storage, masturbating to a pornographic magazine. Walonsky told on the boy, and apparently his mother administered a pretty severe whipping.

"I really didn't mean for the boy to take a beating like that," Kelly quoted Walonsky as saying. "I just thought maybe the kid needed some help."

In any case, Walonsky added, two days later the building burned down in the middle of the night. As the firemen were fighting the fire, trying to keep it from spreading to the nearby houses, Walonsky caught a glimpse of Michael Schiftmann in an upstairs bedroom window, looking down on the scene and smiling.

Walonsky had told the arson investigators about the kid, but his mother had covered for him, insisting he'd never been out of his bedroom that night.

A year later, Walonsky's wife's cat was found dead, the body horribly mutilated. Somebody had obviously tortured the cat to death. Hank grimaced as he read the details. But he also knew that in the details lay the truth.

Hank had twenty years in with the FBI, but he'd come to VICAP in the mid-nineties, long after the pioneer FBI profiler Robert Ressler had retired. He'd never met Ressler, but he'd read all his books and studied his work intensely. Ressler discovered that serial killers often, in fact commonly, shared three traits from childhood. They enjoyed torturing animals, enjoyed setting fires, and were chronic bed wetters.

If Walonsky was telling the truth, Hank mused, Michael Schiftmann was batting .666.

But as he read on, he realized that there were even other indicators. Michael Schiftmann's academic records were revealing. In ninth grade, he tested out on the Wechsler Adult Intelligence Survey as having an IQ of 156—genius level and then some. A sympathetic guidance counselor apparently became interested in the young boy and helped him get a scholarship to the Benton Academy, an exclusive private school on the lakeshore near Oberlin. There, Hank read, Schiftmann apparently learned the art of getting in trouble without getting caught with his hand too far in the cookie jar. His file from the Benton Academy indicated that he was constantly in and out of minor scrapes. He got caught smoking a few times, but always cigarettes, never pot. He got caught drinking beer in his senior year, but not hard liquor. And in every instance, it seemed, he had an explanation. It was always somebody else's booze, somebody else brought the cigarettes, it was somebody else's idea to take that sneak Saturday night.

Schiftmann, Hank noted, did graduate from the academy. But his grades were chronically low—skating along in the low C, high D range—and he actually attended graduation under disciplinary probation. With his brains, he could've aced every course in school without cracking a book. But he was, one teacher noted, "a chronic underachiever."

There were also notes in his Benton file from guidance counselors and teachers who struggled to get a handle on this kid. He had problems with authority, with women, with appropriate social behavior. Of course, Hank realized, he'd just read descriptions of the majority of adolescent males in the country. But this was different. The tone of the guidance counselor reports was serious, foreboding, as if the counselors could see there was something at work here besides adolescent rebellion.

After private school, Schiftmann actually managed to put in two semesters at the University of Virginia, paying with a combination of scholarships and student loans. But his grades here were equally dismal and there were numerous disciplinary problems as well, including one incident when Michael got in a fight at a drunken frat party and actually broke a guy's arm. He left college at the end of his freshman year.

After that, Michael Schiftmann's life became a blur. He apparently worked menial jobs and switched them often. His social security records revealed he rarely made over ten grand a year for a decade-long stretch. He was living in a one-bedroom apartment in a run-down complex in a down-scale section of Cleveland, paying less than four hundred a month in rent and probably barely scraping that up.

Somewhere along the way, and God only knew how, Michael Schiftmann switched from being an inveterate reader to an aspiring writer. The first publication anyone could find was a science-fiction short story in an obscure fanzine published out of Cleveland. Then, a few years later, he published his first novel, a mystery that was brought out in paperback by a small house and was nominated for a couple of awards, but went nowhere. Some copies of reviews were included in the file. Hank read them and was surprised to find them overwhelmingly glowing. Words and phrases like "literate," "compelling," "involving and complex" were used to describe his work.

By then, Michael Schiftmann had gotten a job as a proofreader with a small publisher of religious and archaeological texts. And according to the report, he kept the job from his mid-twenties until he was thirty-four.

Hank scanned the field office report, which listed his next four books as well. Again, good reviews, a couple of nominations, one small award, the name of which Hank didn't recognize . . .

Yet, Hank thought, he couldn't afford to give up his day job. Five books, reviews, awards, and can't afford to quit the day job.

Hank was glad he had no impulse whatsoever to be a writer.

There was almost a four-year lapse in Schiftmann's publishing history. During that time, he held his job, but published nothing. Was this a long dry spell, Hank wondered, or was there something else going on?

Then, five years ago, he'd published *The First Letter*. Six months later, *The Second Letter* was released. Two months after that, Schiftmann quit his day job, this time for good.

After four years of wandering in the desert, Michael Schift-mann had suddenly become a publishing dynamo.

And, he thought, a cash cow for everyone involved.

Hank looked up from his desk and stared out the window. Outside, it was dark. He looked at his watch and was surprised to find it was almost seven. He'd been at this twelve hours almost nonstop. Somehow, the time seemed to go by quickly.

To the untrained eye, Hank thought, there was nothing in Michael Schiftmann's past that would jump out and shout "murderer." To the outside onlooker, Schiftmann looked more like a troubled kid from a troubled background who triumphed over every obstacle to succeed beyond his most impossible-to-imagine dreams. He wasn't an ice-cold socio-path, a stone killer; he was the American dream personified. He was a literary Horatio Alger.

But, little by little, the circumstantial evidence was piling up. Hank Powell looked at his scribbled notes. In every city where the Alphabet Man took a victim, Michael Schiftmann was close by at the time, usually at book signings on public-ity tours, but sometimes at book fairs, writers' conferences, and the like.

And as Maria Chavez had discovered, the order and basic descriptions of the murders in the first five installments of Schiftmann's best-selling series were exactly the same as the real murders, even though some of the details and places had changed.

And finally, Hank realized, everything about Michael Schiftmann—the freedom and lack of structure in his life, his living on the edge of society for so many years, his intel-ligence and his resources, his history in work and school, his egomaniacal drive and lust for fame, recognition, and wealth—fit the psychological profile of a highly intelligent, organized serial killer.

In other words, the Alphabet Man . . .

But was this enough? The key, of course, was Nashville. That's where they had the best forensic evidence. That's where they had the blood and tissue samples, the samples that could be DNA-typed to Schiftmann's blood. If there was a match, he'd go down, hard.

Which meant that without a grand jury indictment, the chance of getting a search warrant to collect the samples was thin. It was possible, of course. Hank realized they were lucky in getting the best forensic evidence in a Southern, conservative town, rather than, say, Vancouver or New York City, where people were commonly less sympathetic to police. Schiftmann, though, had the resources to put up a good fight—primarily the money, but also the fame, and as the American public had learned over the past years, fame is a powerful weapon to a good defense attorney.

So many variables, so many things to consider. Powell and Max Bransford had talked several times in the past few days alone, and the one thing they agreed on was that there was no way they were going to the DA and the grand jury until they had a case that was solid enough to withstand the inevitable hurricane that would follow.

Hank walked over to the window and stared out into the darkening woods. To his left, in the distance, the faint sulfurous glow of the lights over the west parking lot intruded on the darkness. He realized that at this moment, he probably knew more about Michael Schiftmann than anyone alive except Schiftmann himself. But that was the problem: He knew more *about* him rather than really knowing him.

"There's got to be something else," he whispered. "There's got to be more out there."

He went back to his desk and dug out the background file on Michael Schiftmann. The Manhattan Field Office had done a thorough, professional job of bringing Schiftmann's current situation up to speed. He'd sold his condo in Cleveland, made almost six figures on it, then moved to Manhattan, where he'd been house hunting. Hank had everything on Schiftmann's recent moves, up to and including the Northwest flight number he'd taken from Cleveland to LaGuardia.

Then Hank saw a note appended to the report almost as an afterthought, that Schiftmann had been staying with his literary agent, a woman named Taylor Robinson.

Staying with her? Hank suddenly thought. *What? This guy can't afford a hotel?*

It was one of two things, he realized. Either Taylor Robinson took really good care of her clients, or these two were an item.

"Wonder what it would take to find out?" he whispered.

Hank turned to his computer and double-clicked the Internet Explorer icon. He went to Google.com and typed in Taylor's name. In a few hundredths of a second, he found more than forty-seven thousand hits for Taylor Robinson.

The first was her home page at the Delaney & Associates Web site. He scanned her biography and noted she was a summa cum laude graduate of Smith College, that she had been an editor for several years before joining the agency, and that in a few short years, she had become one of the most powerful agents in the business.

Hyperbole aside, he thought, this was an impressive woman. He stared at her picture for a few seconds. She was, he realized, quite lovely as well. The picture was black-and-white, so it was hard to tell colors, but she had dark hair swept down onto her shoulders, dark piercing eyes, and high cheekbones.

She looked, he thought, patrician.

He read a few more pages, learned a little more about her, and generated some assumptions that he would later test.

Because Hank Powell had decided to pay a visit to Taylor Robinson.

CHAPTER 21

Thursday morning, Manhattan

Hank Powell stepped out of the cab on East Fifty-third Street, leaned in, handed the driver a twenty, and stepped back as he drove away. He pulled his overcoat around him as a stiff wind pounded down the street from the East River. Even in late March, the cold concrete canyons of Manhattan could chill a man to his bones.

He looked across the street at the row of brownstones, then drew a small spiral-bound notebook out of his pocket and glanced at the address. He looked back up, scanned the buildings again, and spotted his destination.

In every investigator's professional life, there comes a time when he has to take chances. Sometimes it's a matter of trusting someone you shouldn't; other times it's learning to distrust someone you thought was stand-up. But when you get stuck, when you hit that wall that stands between you and whatever it is it's keeping you from the truth, you have to think differently, move differently, shake things up, and see what happens.

Hank Powell was about to shake things up.

He crossed the street and walked halfway down the block toward Second Avenue. On the north side, a couple of buildings from the corner, sat a four-story brownstone with a bronze engraved plate mounted on the wall next to the front door, which read: DELANEY & ASSOCIATES.

Hank climbed the stairs to the front door, then reached out and pressed the white button just below the plaque. A loud buzz erupted from the speaker next to the button, and a moment later, a female voice fuzzed over by static spoke: "Yes?"

"I'm here to see Ms. Robinson," Hank said into the speaker. "Taylor Robinson."

The buzzer went off again, and Hank heard a relay behind the door trip, unlocking it. He grabbed the door handle and pulled, then stepped into what had once been the entrance foyer of the brownstone a hundred years ago when it was a family residence. Now it was the lobby of one of the most powerful literary agencies in New York.

A harried receptionist with dyed purple hair, a pierced eyebrow, and a petite tattoo of a rose on her right arm just at her shoulder, sat behind a desk to his left, looking like she was in multitasking hell. Behind her, and it seemed on every square inch of available wall space, were framed book covers, photographs of authors, awards. To Hank's right, on the wall next to a polished wooden staircase, was a section of the wall devoted entirely to Michael Schiftmann. An elaborately matted and framed eight-by-ten photograph of Schiftmann was surrounded by framed book covers of the five published installments in the Chaney series.

"May I help you?" the young woman asked between phone calls.

Hank stepped forward. "Yes, I'm here to see Taylor Robinson."

The receptionist eyed him, if not quite suspiciously, at least with a question on her face. "Do you have an appointment?"

"No," Hank said, reaching into the inside pocket of his suit coat for his credentials, "but I think—"

"I'm sorry," the woman snapped. "But you have to have an appointment. Ms. Robinson is far too busy—"

It was Hank's turn to interrupt as he flashed open his ID case, revealing his FBI identity card and badge. "I won't take up much of her time."

The receptionist cleared her throat and looked at the badge

and ID. Her eyes got larger for a second. "Wow," she muttered. "I've never seen one of those before."

Hank gave her his most charming smile. "Wanta see my pistol?"

"You've got a gun?" the girl asked, incredulous.

"And handcuffs," Hank answered. "They make me."

"Bitchin'," she said.

"Ms. Robinson?" Hank asked after a moment.

"Oh, yeah," the girl stammered, as if suddenly coming out of a trance. Hank wondered where her mind had gone, what fantasy had played itself out in that second and a half of silence.

She picked up the phone, punched a few numbers, and spoke low. Then she nodded, hung up the phone, and pointed toward the staircase. "Ms. Robinson's office is upstairs, far corner. Her assistant will be waiting for you."

Hank nodded, smiled. "Thanks."

Hank climbed the curving, polished mahogany staircase that he imagined some Victorian, gilded-aged, robber baron's wife making a grand entrance on a century ago. On the second floor of the house, the rooms had been turned into offices, the once large rooms subdivided by renovation walls, partitions, and a narrow hallway that ran down the middle of the floor. Another young, hip, but this time somewhat bookish woman met him at the head of the stairs.

"Mr. Powell?" she asked.

"Agent Powell," he corrected, knowing from years of experience how much more weight Agent Powell carried than Mr. Powell, even though they were the same person.

"Yes, Agent Powell, this way." The woman turned and led him down the hallway, speaking in a cool, detached, professional manner as she walked. "Ms. Robinson was on a conference call a few minutes ago, but I believe she's off now."

They got to the end of the hallway, which let out into a common area with a sofa and a couple of leather wing chairs. Surrounding the common area were the doors to four offices, each with a desk close by for the requisite assistant. The young woman led Hank over to the far right office and stopped at a closed door.

"I'll see if Ms. Robinson's available," she explained, knocking lightly on the door. Then she opened it and stepped inside, closing it firmly behind her. Hank was alone. He took off his overcoat and folded it over his arm and stood there a few moments, looking around at another collection of framed book covers, these obviously from the agency's less-stellar writers.

As he stood there, a rush of fatigue came over him. He hadn't slept well the night before, had been up since four A.M. in order to make the train to New York. He tried to sleep on the Metroliner, but couldn't turn his brain off. Maybe it was the anticipation of meeting Taylor Robinson; maybe it was dread.

Taylor Robinson's assistant stepped back through the door and held it open. "Ms. Robinson can see you now. May I take your coat for you?"

"Thanks," Hank said, handing her the coat.

"Would you like some coffee? A soda?"

Hank shook his head. "No, I'm fine."

His stomach tightening, Hank stepped through the doorway of Taylor Robinson's office and looked around. The office was much smaller than he expected, not what one would think would be the inner sanctum of a high-powered New York agent. The room was full of clutter as well: manuscripts piled high on the floors in haphazard stacks, books stacked against the walls over a worn carpet, cheap bookcases overflowing with books and more manuscripts. Taylor's desk was piled high with magazines, correspondence, stacks of paper laid on top of one another in layered pyramids. A window badly in need of cleaning looked out onto East Fifty-third.

Taylor Robinson stood up from her desk and motioned to the cheap visitor's chair on the other side. "Please," she said. "Sit down."

Her picture didn't do her justice. She was elegant, he thought, wearing a sheer silk tan blouse over a camisole, a pair of dark designer pants with a thin, narrow belt, and a simple string of small pearls around her neck. She looked educated, well-bred, and well-tended, with almost a Kennedyesque air about her.

Hank sat down, crossed his legs at the knee. "I appreciate you seeing me without an appointment. I know you're busy."

"I'm confused, Agent Powell. It is 'agent,' right? Not 'officer' or something else?"

Hank smiled. "Technically, it's Special Agent Powell. But we don't have to stand on ceremony."

She leaned back in her office chair and watched him for a moment. She was cool, he thought, completely professional. "So I'm confused, Special Agent Powell. Why would you want to see me? What can I do for you?"

Hank tried to choose his words carefully. "Ms. Robinson, I'm going to ask you for some help in an investigation that we have under way. For some time now, the FBI and a number of other local law enforcement agencies of different types all over the country have been looking into the background of one of your clients. We've hit a wall and we need your help."

If Taylor Robinson's face gave away anything, it wasn't much. She shuffled slightly in her chair, but never took her gaze off him.

"Is one of my clients in trouble?" she asked.

"That's what we're trying to determine. Several weeks ago, the *New York Times* published a series of articles—two or three, I think—on a serial killer who has killed at least thirteen women we know of. All across the country and one in Canada. He's been dubbed the 'Alphabet Man.'"

She shook her head. "No, I didn't read them. I often don't have time for newspapers."

"I'm with a division of the FBI called VICAP, the Violent Criminal Apprehension Program, and I work out of an office at the FBI Academy in Quantico. I've been coordinating our investigation into this person's activities and I've been working with police departments in places like Seattle, Milwaukee, Scottsdale, Vancouver, and two places in Tennessee, Nashville and Chattanooga. That's among other places, you know. Is any of this resonating with you?"

Taylor Robinson's brow seemed to tighten just a bit, but again, Hank thought, she kept a good game face. *She's probably a shark sitting across a negotiation table.*

"No, none of this means anything to me. Why should it?"

Hank leaned forward almost imperceptibly in his chair and looked her directly in the eye. "Ms. Robinson, virtually every serial killer does something to set his murders apart from everyone else's. A common weapon, a motif, a sign, something . . . You look at a David Berkowitz killing and compare it to, say, a Ted Bundy scene or a Henry Lee Lucas scene; there's no mistaking the differences. And while every murder scene is different, there seem to be common threads."

Taylor Robinson's face darkened and she seemed almost weighted down. "What has this got to do with me? I still don't understand—"

"The guy we're after has a very distinct signature that he's left behind at every murder scene. In the victim's blood, he paints a neat, almost artistic block letter somewhere in the scene. The first one was A, back in 1995 in Cincinnati. The latest two were L and M, and they occurred in Nashville just this past February. That's how we know there've been thirteen."

This time, Taylor Robinson's face almost certainly gave away more than she intended. Hank sensed that she was beginning to get the message. Her eyes almost went into a squint.

"But wait, what're you saying is that—"

"Letters, Ms. Robinson. The Alphabet Man. Get it?"

Her mouth opened slightly, her jaw muscles quivering. "Just what in the hell are you trying to say?"

Hank let her hang there a moment, the silence between them growing heavier with each breath. Taylor Robinson stared at him, her jaw and chest tight, her hands on the desk, knotted into tight fists.

"What I'm trying to say, Ms. Robinson," Hank said softly, breaking the terrible silence, "is that we think the Alphabet Man is your client, Michael Schiftmann."

Hank Powell knew the next words out of her mouth would tell him what she knew.

The explosion came a moment later. "You're crazy!"

she yelled, slapping the desk hard. Hank wondered what the young honors graduate English major assistant outside thought of that. "That's ridiculous! You're out of your mind! And I'm here to tell you, *Special Agent* Powell, that if anything of this gets out to the media and you either libel or slander my client in any way whatsoever, I'm going to sue you from one end of the Earth to another!"

"Ms. Robinson, if I could just acquaint you—"

"You can't acquaint me with anything, mister, unless the U.S. Constitution has been finally done away with in the past twenty-four hours and I missed it on the TV news. We're still presumed innocent until proven guilty, right?"

"Yes, of course, Ms. Robinson." Hank felt himself slipping into a defensive mode. This was not what he expected. Protest was one thing, but this woman was ready to go straight to war. "But if you'd just let me explain."

Taylor Robinson jerked herself up out of her chair and glared down at him. "You have wasted enough of my time. I don't have to sit here and listen to this insanity and I'm not going to."

Hank scooted forward in the chair. "Ms. Robinson, if you'd just let me lay out some of the facts for you."

"The last time I checked, the FBI manual didn't have a swastika on it. You're not the Gestapo and this is still sort of a free country and you are in my private space. I'll thank you to leave now."

Hank stood up. "Ms. Robinson, you're making a mistake here."

"Now," she commanded, her voice lowering and stone cold. "If you don't leave my office immediately, I'm going to call my attorney, and if he approves, I'm going to call the New York City police and have you arrested for trespassing."

Hank stood there a second, helpless. He held out his hands, palms toward her in supplication, and pushed the chair backward with the backs of his knees.

"Good day, Ms. Robinson," he said as he turned for the door. "Thanks for your time."

Once outside, Hank Powell walked down Fifty-third Street

toward Third Avenue. He couldn't make any sense of this. He was stunned, confused. Here was this obviously well-educated, intelligent, sophisticated, high-powered woman who turned on him like a cornered badger. It was almost as if Taylor Robinson hated cops.

What Hank Powell did not know, and could not possibly have known, was that Taylor Robinson did hate police. Hated them to the core of her soul . . .

CHAPTER 22

Thursday morning, Manhattan

Taylor Robinson stood in the silence of her office, staring at the closed door. From the outside, she appeared calm, almost serenely so. But in her chest, she felt a pounding that, for a moment, genuinely frightened her. She fought to control her breathing, to loosen her neck and jaw muscles.

To stay in control.

She turned and walked to the window. Through the film of dust and grime, she watched as, to her right, the FBI agent exited the building and walked down the stoop onto the sidewalk. He paused, standing still, then shook his head and walked off in the direction of Third Avenue.

She stayed like that for what felt like a long time. Her mind went blank, as if the encounter with the FBI agent—what was his name?—had caused something inside her to empty.

How long had he been here? She had, for the moment, lost perception of time. She gazed out the window to the traffic below on East Fifty-third. Behind her, she heard a door open.

"Taylor?"

Taylor turned. Her assistant, Anne, was in the doorway, a concerned look on her face.

"Yes?" she answered blankly.

"Are you okay?"

Taylor turned and looked back out the window. The sun

was breaking through a layer of gray overcast, throwing random beams of bright yellow light on the street below. She turned back and faced the young woman.

"I'm going out for a while," she said.

She had spent her entire life since that day trying to forget.

It had been her fault, her fault, and she had carried that weight around inside her over half her life.

Over half her life. Twenty years. Twenty years that Jack never got. And many more in front of her that he would never have.

It was supposed to have been the best summer ever. Her brother, three years her senior, was home from VMI. John Prentice Robinson was his full name, but no one ever seemed able to call him that with a straight face. He was too playful, too spontaneous, too reckless, to be a John Prentice Robinson. He was the family prankster, the practical joke master, the puncturer of pretense, the outrageous smart ass that everyone loved. He would always, in everyone's perception, be a Jack. And she adored him.

Handsome, rugged, a born athlete . . . He had captained the soccer team and track team in private school, then gone onto the Virginia Military Institute, where he was soon captain of the varsity shooting team. He came home that summer as a prime candidate for the Olympics.

Her brother, Jack, on the U.S. Olympic Shooting Team.

He was home for just a week, only a week, before heading out to Colorado Springs to spend the rest of the summer training. The days had been buoyant, happy. Her father— one of Greenwich, Connecticut's most prominent cardiologists—had even taken time off from his rounds. They played tennis at the country club, hosted a grand summer party, danced and swam and sang and drank.

Taylor felt as if it would go on forever. That they would always be young and energetic and happy, that life would always be a banquet.

That day, that day it all ended, her father woke early, left in his Mercedes to make his hospital rounds. Her mother slept late, as did Taylor and Jack, and then went out for a tennis date at the club.

Jack climbed into his Jeep and drove off to meet friends for lunch.

Taylor relaxed, hanging around the house, debating what to do with the rest of the day. She had chores to do, had promised her mother to do some laundry and clean up her room. Her senior year would begin in a few weeks as well. So maybe it was time she started going through the stack of college catalogs that had been coming in the mail for months.

Then the phone rang. Her best friend, Dori, invited her over to spend the afternoon swimming, sunbathing, listening to music, talking about boys. The usual . . .

Just guilty enough at neglecting her chores to feel it, but not guilty enough to say no to Dori, Taylor rushed into her bedroom and changed into her bikini, then threw on a T-shirt and a pair of cutoffs just as Dori pulled up in her convertible Mustang. Taylor grabbed her purse and bag, then ran for the back door. Dori honked the horn and yelled to her. As Taylor went out the back door, she slapped her hand across the burglar alarm panel.

And hit the wrong button. The burglar alarm system her father had installed a few years earlier had a silent mode. No one ever used it.

She didn't mean to do it.

God, she didn't mean to do it.

They would later stitch together from bits and pieces how it all happened.

At two-twelve that afternoon, an automated call came into the Greenwich Police Department reporting a break-in at the Robinson home. Dispatch sent a prowl car to investigate. Riding alone that shift was a young, rookie patrolman barely older than Jack. In fact, he had just a week earlier finished his probationary period, which required him to ride along with an older, more experienced officer.

When the officer arrives, a Jeep is in the driveway behind the house.

The officer exits the squad car carefully. There's no sign of a break-in. The officer stands there a moment.

Suddenly, the sliding glass door to the patio courtyard opens up and a young blond man in a pair of jeans, a T-shirt, and running shoes steps out.

With his hands in his pockets . . .

The officer unsnaps his weapon.

Jack, smiling, gregarious as always, never met a fellow he didn't like, walks toward the officer.

With his hands in his pockets . . .

"Stop right there," the officer commands, holding his left palm out, his right hand on the butt of his pistol.

Jack grins, keeps walking: "What's up, Barney Fife?"

"Stop," the officer yells.

Jack suddenly pulls his hand out, cocked, his index finger pointing like the barrel of a gun, his thumb like the hammer, like a seven-year-old boy playing cowboys and Indians. He points it at the officer.

Who draws his weapon and fires.

John Prentice Robinson, star athlete, captain of the varsity shooting team, prankster and naively stupid young man, came home that afternoon and didn't realize he'd set off the burglar alarm when he came in. And as a result, he died that afternoon on the warm clay tiles of the courtyard patio of his parents' two-million-dollar home, of a single gunshot wound to the chest.

They buried him three days later next to his grandparents.

Devastation is too tepid a word, too mild a description, for what happened to Taylor, her parents, her family.

The city settles for one-point-five million. Taylor refuses any part of it.

Her father shuts down, buries himself in his work.

Her mother begins drinking heavily, becomes a recluse, goes on about a dozen different medications for anxiety, depression, insomnia.

Her parents begin fighting, worse than ever. Her father spends more and more time at the hospital.

Taylor spends her last year at home in a haze, retreats

into her schoolwork, graduates with honors and goes on to Smith College. At the time she chose Smith, she had no idea why she chose it, other than it was away from home.

Her parents sell the house, divorce. Her father relocates to Miami and eventually marries a woman Taylor cannot stand. Her mother goes into rehab, comes out clean and sober, but depressed and miserable. The sound of her voice gives Taylor a headache.

The weight never completely goes away. That corner of her heart is locked away, leaden.

And filled with hatred for macho cowboy cops and their guns. Their stupid, goddamn fucking guns.

"Excuse me, ma'am," the voice said. "Are you okay?"

The voice was young, feminine. A woman's voice. Taylor looked up. It was a young woman in a dark blue ski parka and jeans.

Taylor looked around. She was sitting on a concrete bench, so cold she couldn't feel her hips, the backs of her legs. The bench was on a walk overlooking the East River. To her left and above, the Queensboro Bridge towered over it like the drawbridge to a castle.

Sutton Place. She'd walked up to Sutton Place. But when? How long had she been there?

"Ma'am?" the voice asked again.

"What?" Taylor said, finally.

"You've been sitting there staring for a long time. I walked my dog like an hour and a half ago and you were sitting there staring out at the river. I saw you from my apartment. I thought I'd just make sure you were okay."

"Thanks," Taylor said, standing up. Her legs tingled as the circulation was restored. "I'm sorry, I didn't mean—"

"You don't have to apologize. It's a public bench. I just thought I'd make sure you were okay."

Taylor looked into the young woman's face. It was round, pale, with an aquiline nose and large blue eyes. *It's a myth,* Taylor thought, *that New Yorkers are cold and unfriendly.*

"I appreciate that," she said. "I've got to get back to work. I don't know where my mind was at."

The young girl smiled. "Okay, have a good day. I'm glad you're all right."

"Yes," Taylor said, lying. "I'm fine."

Taylor realized she was cold, chilled almost completely through. As she walked the blocks back to her office, the movement began to warm her, and as it did, she started thinking in a more organized, focused fashion.

Powell, that was his name. Special Agent Powell of the FBI. He had come into her office and announced that the man she loved, the man she was going to marry, the man upon whom her fortune and reputation were built, was a psycho, a killer.

She had to think this through. She had to remember as much of the conversation as possible, everything that had happened in the short couple of minutes he was in her office. What he had said stunned her, caught her off guard. But now she had her footing back, and, as always, she knew it was better to act, to do something, even if it was wrong.

She had looked at his badge, his credentials. They looked real enough, but fake ID cards could be purchased anywhere. And as far as she knew, that badge could have come from a war surplus store. She wouldn't know a real FBI badge from a fake if it ran up behind her and bit her on the ankles.

But why would a fake FBI agent concoct such a story? What good would it do anyone?

Why?

As she walked, one scenario after another played in her head. This was a conspiracy by a rival publishing house. Maybe Michael had made enemies somewhere in the past who now sought to cause him harm. Maybe *she* had enemies who wanted to hurt her and were using Michael to do it.

She turned left on Second Avenue and headed south toward East Fifty-third and her office, oblivious to the crowds around her on the sidewalk. There had to be a way to handle this. This had to be taken care of as quickly and as quietly as possible. This would be a public relations disaster if she made a single misstep.

* * *

Hank Powell reached over the front seat and handed cash to the painfully skinny, dark-skinned driver and climbed out of the cab at Federal Plaza. Five minutes later, he'd worked his way through the tight security and was on his way to the FBI New York City Field Office.

Once inside, he tracked down SAC Joyce Parelli in her office and threw his overcoat onto the chair across from her desk.

"You're not going to believe the morning I've had," he said.

Joyce Parelli, a third-generation Italian—three generations in America, three generations in law enforcement—who sounded like she'd rarely set foot out of her native Brooklyn, grinned. She was amused to see Hank Powell, normally so composed one could almost call him smug, exasperated.

"Ah, my poor delicate little rosebud," she said. "Sit down and tell me all about it."

Too agitated to sit, Powell paced back and forth, his arms in constant motion. "I just got thrown out of somebody's office! You believe that? I'm an employee and a representative of the *United States government* and I got tossed out like a door-to-door vacuum cleaner salesman!"

Parelli laughed out loud this time. "And who threw you out, boobala?"

"Michael Schiftmann's literary agent, that's who! And if it won't be a violation of the sex-discrimination statutes, would it be all right if I described her as a first-class *bitch*?"

Joyce Parelli sat up. "Wait a minute!"

Hank stopped pacing. "What?"

Parelli leaned down behind her desk and pulled out a standard, government-issue black plastic wastebasket. She shuffled around in the garbage for a moment and extracted a crumpled roll of newspaper.

"What?" Hank repeated.

"Shush, it's here somewhere." Parelli spread the paper out on her desk and started thumbing through it. "I know I saw it here."

Hank stood at her desk, leaning over slightly, as she scanned page after page.

"Damn it," she muttered. "I know it's— There! Found it."

She spun the paper around on her desk, facing Hank, and jabbed at an item with the bright red fingernail of her index finger.

Hank looked down. "Liz Smith? Who the hell is—?"

"Gossip column," Parelli answered. "Read."

Hank bent down and focused. "'Who's the hot new power couple in the N.Y. literary scene?'" he read aloud. "'Word around the publishing campfire is that superstar novelist and tall, dark, handsome hunk Michael Schiftmann has popped the question to his glitterati literary agent, Taylor Robinson. When you're making the kind of moolah these two are bringing in, you may as well keep it in the family.'"

Hank stood up, shocked. "May as well keep it in the family . . ." he muttered. "Serves me right for not reading the tabloids."

Parelli nodded. "That would certainly explain why you weren't a welcome guest in her office this morning."

Hank nodded, thinking. "Yes, it certainly would, wouldn't it?"

CHAPTER 23

Friday morning, FBI Academy, Quantico, Virginia

Hank Powell was at his desk early the next morning, re-examining the stack of files in front of him and trying to figure out what to do next. He couldn't get his mind off the interview with Taylor Robinson. It festered inside him like a wound gone septic. He was angry, but more than that, he was embarrassed.

He kept trying to figure out what could possibly have triggered her outbursts. There were only two options he could come up with. First, Taylor Robinson was so far in love with this guy that she was simply unable to grasp the concept that he might not be what she thought he was. Either that, or she knew what he was and was part of it.

But could that really be an option? What were the chances that Taylor Robinson was as psycho as her fiancé? What were the chances that two such completely evil people could find each other in this world and glom on to each other?

"Probably better than you think," he whispered to himself.

He reached for his third cup of coffee just as the phone rang. "I've got Max Bransford on line one," Sallie said.

"Thanks," Hank answered, pressing the blinking button on his desk set.

"Good morning, Max," Hank said brightly. "How's tricks?"

"Hank, I gotta talk to you," Bransford said, his voice serious.

Hank felt his neck stiffen. "What's up?"

"Yesterday morning, I got called into Major Katz's office. He's my division commander and immediate supervisor. He reports directly to the assistant chief."

"Okay," Hank said. "And?"

"It was a come-to-Jesus meeting on the Exotica Tans murders."

Hank sat there for a moment, holding the phone, waiting for Bransford to continue.

"Anyway, he wanted the case summarized right then and there. Apparently there's some political pressure on this one. Either that or somebody leaked to the chief that we had a possible suspect. So I didn't have any choice. I laid it all out for him."

Hank had a bad feeling about where this was going. "And?"

"And," Bransford continued, "he called the DA's office then and there and arranged a meeting. We were in there for four hours yesterday."

"So what happened?"

Bransford sighed heavily, almost wearily, into the phone. "Bottom line, Hank, is the DA's going to the grand jury. The shit's gonna hit the fan down here."

"No!" Hank said. "You can't do that, Max. It's too early. We don't have enough."

"The DA is talking about getting one of the judges to sign off on a search warrant. He's gonna try and get hair and tissue samples from Schiftmann."

"No judge is going to issue that kind of warrant without an indictment."

"In the state of Tennessee, if there's enough there to justify a probable cause search, then a sympathetic judge can do it. And it can be done in secret, as part of the grand jury hearing."

Hank's head throbbed. This was a big, major, earth-shaking screwup. "Yeah, and how long will it stay secret, Max? You know what this is going to do when it hits the media. We're going to have a circus on our hands."

"I know that, Hank," Bransford said. "That's what I told the major. This is the kind of cluster fuck that can cause us to lose our amateur standing. You gotta be a pro to fuck up this bad."

"Can you put this back in the bottle? Get them to hold off maybe even a few days?"

"Too late," Bransford said. "The DA red-balled this one right into the grand jury. I finished testifying an hour ago."

Hank Powell moaned. "Okay," he said. "If they think they're good to go and ready to launch, who am I to get in the way? I'm going to get on the horn and call my boss and tell him to hunker down."

"Hang in there, buddy. We're both gonna have to keep our heads down."

Hank felt the coffee churning away in his gut. "Mine already is."

Taylor stood at the kitchen counter, her eyes burning from lack of sleep, her neck stiff. She poured another cup of coffee, took a small sip, and grimaced. The coffee made the already foul taste of bile in her mouth even worse. She poured the coffee into the sink.

She sat down at the counter and stared at the clock for a few moments. It was almost eleven-thirty in the morning and she was still in her bathrobe. Ordinarily, she'd have put in three or four hours in the office by now. But that was after nights when she actually slept.

Not like last night . . .

Michael was still upstairs asleep. Lately, he'd been staying up even later than usual, watching old movies on television or reading, and usually with a drink in his hand. He'd been at her apartment for almost two and a half weeks continuously now. For the first few days it was like a honeymoon, but lately they'd not even been going to bed at the same time. Taylor just couldn't stay up half the night, then get up at seven to be at work by eight. And Michael couldn't go to bed before about two at the earliest.

Last night, she pretended to be asleep when he finally came to bed at three-thirty. He nuzzled her neck, kissed her shoulders. After a few moments of no response, he'd rolled over and was soon snoring.

And she lay there the rest of the night, staring up into the darkness, unable to turn her brain off, unable to let go.

At five in the morning, shortly before the sun came up, she found herself wondering if it was even possible that the FBI agent could be telling the truth, but she pushed that thought out of her mind as quickly as it came in.

She'd gotten out of bed as quietly as possible, then gone downstairs and sat in an easy chair, her feet up on the coffee table, staring into the darkened spaces of her loft. At some point, she might have dozed off for a short time, but it wasn't the good, hard sleep she needed. It was like skating over the surface of a pond when what you needed was to dive in.

She heard a shuffling upstairs and water running. She pulled her bathrobe tighter around her as, a few seconds later, Michael came down the stairs in a T-shirt and a pair of running shorts. He walked over to where she was sitting, leaned down, and kissed her on the top of the head.

"Hi, gorgeous," he said cheerily.

"Morning."

"You're not going to work today?" He opened the cabinet door and took out a large coffee mug.

"Later," she answered. "I wasn't feeling all that well when I woke up. Didn't sleep well."

"You were sleeping pretty good when I came up," Michael offered, pouring a cup. "I tried to wake you up, see if you wanted something to sweeten your dreams. But, alas."

"What time was that?" Taylor asked.

"I don't know. Sometime around three, three-thirty."

"Kind of late, wasn't it?"

"Well," he said, pausing to take a sip of the hot coffee, "I decided to stay up until eight London time so I could call the agent."

Taylor looked up. "And?"

"Looks like it's a done deal, my darling. That two-bedroom flat in Earl's Court is where you and I can stay on our honeymoon if you want. I have to fly over in a couple of weeks for the closing. Maybe you'll come with me?"

"Michael," she said cautiously, "are you sure this is such

a good idea? You bought the condo in Palm Beach and now a flat in London?"

He sat on a barstool across the counter from her and leaned in toward her, smiling. "Look, until you got me a decent book deal, I'd never even been to London. I fell in love with it! And now we've got the money. Let's enjoy it. I've got a lot of time to make up."

"You have the money," she said. "Not us."

He reached over and took her hand in his. "Soon it'll be us. And we have to decide about the house, too. You haven't even seen it."

"I know," Taylor answered. "I've just been too busy. Besides, I'm not sure I'm ready to give this place up. I worked so hard for it, and I've made it so much mine."

"So I'll let the house go and we'll live here. Whatever makes you happy."

Taylor's face went blank for a moment, as if she'd left the room for now but would be back later to claim her body.

"This is all happening so fast," she murmured.

Michael's forehead knitted up into hard wrinkles. "Hey," he said softly. "Something the matter?"

Taylor abruptly stood, almost jumped, out of the chair and walked over toward the sofa. She stopped in the middle of the room, turned and faced him, and looked at him hard.

"We have to talk," she said.

Michael stared back at her for a moment. "Sounds serious."

She nodded. "Yesterday, in my office, this man came to see me. He was from the FBI."

Michael's eyes narrowed. "FBI? You sure?"

Taylor nodded again. "I saw his badge, his credentials. He's an FBI agent in charge of an investigation. And he was asking me questions."

"Questions? What kind of questions?"

"About you, Michael." Taylor's voice dropped off, silence hanging uncomfortably between them.

"What about me?" Michael asked, his voice a low monotone.

Taylor's eyes started burning again, whether from lack of sleep or stress or a combination of both, she couldn't tell. But she felt herself tearing up and made herself fight the welling up behind her eyes. She turned away from Michael for a moment.

"I don't even know how to say it," she said.

Michael got off the chair and started toward her. She held out a hand, palm toward him. He stopped.

"Just say it," he said.

She turned back to him, shaking her head. "This is crazy. I almost want to laugh, but I also want to scream. I just want to scream my goddamn head off. Michael, he says you're a murderer. He says you've been traipsing around the country killing women."

Michael Schiftmann stood there, stock-still, for what seemed like a long time, his hands at his side, his face expressionless.

"The Alphabet Man," he whispered.

Taylor sucked in a huge gulp of air and almost started to choke. "You? How did you— How did you know?"

Michael sighed, a long, weary release of air and tension that seemed to fill the room. "Where do you think I get the plots for the Chaney novels?"

Taylor squinted at him, her arms wrapped around herself now, clenching and holding herself tightly. "What? What did you say?"

"I said," Michael spoke louder, "that the plots to the Chaney novels are based on the Alphabet Man murders. I've been following this guy for years. I'm fascinated by him. Hell, I'm obsessed by him. I have a book carton full of clippings and research I've done on the guy. This FBI moron has got it exactly one hundred and eighty degrees back-asswards. I'm not the Alphabet Man. I just rip him off to sell books."

Taylor's jaw dropped. "You mean that you—?"

"I'm embarrassed," Michael said. "I'm not the creative genius, the artist, the guy with the original story. I'm just a hack writer who takes real life, embellishes it, and throws it out there to the public, who gets suckered into buying it."

Taylor dropped her arms to her side and started laughing. "Oh my God," she said. "You're not a killer."

"No, I'm just a hack."

She came to him, arms outstretched. He took her in his arms and held her tight as she laughed almost hysterically. "I've never been happier in my life to be with a hack."

"Oh, great," Michael said, laughing now. "Thanks for being so agreeable."

She put her hands on his chest and pushed herself away. "Don't be ridiculous. You're not a hack and you know it. Every great writer, up to and including Shakespeare, has based fiction on actual events."

Suddenly Taylor's face went stern, dark. "But that makes me even crazier, that that stupid bastard from the FBI would come around here slinging that kind of crap around. We ought to sue him! Sue 'em right now!"

Michael, grinning, shook his head. "No, that'd be the worst thing we could do. Why draw attention to this and give them the satisfaction? They can't prove a damn thing. They're just desperate. Like I said, I've been following this case for years, and I've managed to dig up some insider stuff through contacts here and there. This is a political hot potato for these guys. It's making them look real bad."

"Yeah," Taylor agreed. "They're just desperate."

Relieved, she came to him again and settled into his arms. He held her tightly, his arms around her, the two of them rocking gently back and forth.

"If we do nothing," Taylor whispered. "This will just go away."

Michael Schiftmann pulled her even tighter. As he held her, he stared at the exposed brick wall that made up one whole side of Taylor's loft.

"Yes," he whispered back. "This will all go away. Don't you worry."

CHAPTER 24

Monday afternoon, Nashville

T. Robert Collier, now serving his seventh term as the District Attorney General for Davidson County, the Twentieth Judicial District of the State of Tennessee, could always tell when a situation was starting to get to him: The prescription medication he took to control his chronic gastro-esophageal reflux disease quit working. Even the blandest of foods, let alone the things he loved, like pizza, coffee, and martinis, would erupt without notice into the back of his throat like a volcano spewing lava.

As he stood in front of Judge Marvin Sandlin in the quiet solitude of the judge's private office, he felt his diaphragm start to convulse in that wavelike pattern that usually meant an attack was imminent. He wished that he'd ordered something else besides the lasagna for lunch.

"Bob, you can't be serious," Sandlin intoned. "I've been an attorney for almost thirty years and in the judiciary for half that time, and this is without a doubt the most outlandish story I've ever heard in my life."

Collier nodded. "Yes, Your Honor, I agree. It's a corker. But I think we're pretty solid on this one, at least solid enough to present you with the request."

Sandlin, who had run unopposed for judge of the General Sessions Court, Seventh Division, a record four times in a row, leaned back in his high-backed leather chair and gazed across his desk almost in a kind of wonder.

"I've read two of the man's books," he said. "And my wife, who's a bigger reader than I am, has read them all. She stood in line for two hours the last time he was in town to get an autograph."

"And it's our contention that after that book signing where your wife stood in line, Schiftmann returned to his hotel room, changed clothes, went back out later that night, and drove about twelve blocks to Exotica Tans, where he brutally murdered two young women."

"My God," Sandlin said, his voice low. "The man's famous. He's rich. He's a celebrity. For God's sake, he's been on the *Today* show!"

Collier nodded. "I know all that. But he's also a murderer and we're just one step away from proving it. If you'll just sign on the dotted line, Your Honor."

Sandlin looked down at the paper lying before him on his broad, polished mahogany desk. It was a search warrant, demanding that Michael Schiftmann provide samples of hair, saliva, and blood for DNA analysis. Sandlin studied it for a moment, then looked back up at Collier, his eyes narrowing.

"And what has the grand jury said about all this?"

Collier felt his stomach rumble, and a heartbeat later, the acid taste of bile in the back of his throat. "We presented the case to them this morning."

"And?"

Collier tried not to squirm. "The matter is still under consideration, but so far they've done nothing."

Sandlin nodded, understanding. "I get it. You took your best shot with the grand jury and it went nowhere. So now you're back fishing. I hate to disappoint you, Bob, but this case has all the earmarks of a first-class disaster. This is all supposition, hypothesis. You've got no witnesses to place the suspect at the scene of the crime, no fingerprints, no forensic evidence, no motive, no chain of evidence. All you've got is theory, and a theory that's about as plausible as the plot to one of this guy's novels."

"But that's it, Your Honor," Collier said, his voice rising. "It is the plot of a novel, *his novel*! This guy's doing his own firsthand research into murder. He's basing the plots of his books on murders he's committed himself!"

Sandlin shook his head. "That may very well be true. I read the article in the *Times* on this serial killer, this Alphabet Man. But you can't use the supposition and circumstantial evidence from one murder as evidence in another."

Collier started to say something, but Sandlin held up a hand. "I'm sorry, Bob. But you've got no probable cause. Say I issue this search warrant and you get a DNA sample that matches the sample at the murder scene. What happens if his attorneys, who by the way will fear no evil because they will undoubtedly be the meanest sons of bitches in the valley, challenge the validity of the search warrant in the first place? Then you've poisoned the well, and the only thing that can tie him to the murders is thrown out, disqualified. What happens then?"

Collier let out a weary sigh. "The guy walks."

"Exactly," Sandlin said, sliding the search warrant across the desk to Collier. "I'm doing you a favor. You know I want to work with you, and if this was just a quiet little everyday homicide, I might let it slide a little. But this case is going to be high-profile. We're talking Court TV, Larry King shit here. You better get yourself right with God, my friend, because you're going to be in the middle of a hurricane if you decide to run with this."

"Yes, Your Honor," Collier said, picking up the paper. "I understand that. Believe me."

"So," Sandlin asked, shifting gears, "how's your gut doing?"

Collier slipped the warrant back into his briefcase. "So-so. The over-the-counter stuff quit working and I had to go back on prescription."

Sandlin leaned back in his chair, smiled, and rubbed his right hand in a circular motion around his paunch. "You should've had the surgery, Bob. I had my Nissen six months ago and haven't had an attack since. You know they do it with a laparoscope now. Three tiny little pinpricks. Two days, you're in and out."

"I've been thinking about it," Collier admitted. "I've just been too busy. Besides, I hate surgery."

Sandlin smiled broadly. "You know, after the surgery, you can never throw up again."

"Great," Collier said, trying to hide the dejection in his voice, "something to look forward to."

Since his first story on the Alphabet Man had been picked up by the AP, the *New York Times*, the *Washington Post*, and about a dozen other newspapers and television stations, Andy Parks found himself occupying a place several rungs higher on the local journalistic feeding chain. He'd parlayed the story into a transfer to the Nashville office, where the *News–Free Press* kept an office in Legislative Plaza. He could walk to the capitol or, if he was feeling especially energetic, all the way to the courthouse.

This afternoon, he was feeling especially energetic. As so often happened in this part of the country, the transition from a long, gray, dreary winter into a glorious, warm spring had happened overnight. Andy had gotten lucky and found a decent parking place in the lot on Capitol Hill. Rather than lose it, he decided to enjoy the walk.

Halfway to the courthouse, just past the Tennessee Performing Arts Center, his cell phone rang. He fished it out of his jacket pocket and flipped it open.

"Yeah," he said, dodging an old lady on the sidewalk.

"I've got something for you," a sweet, feminine voice said. Andy smiled.

"Wow," Andy said, grinning. "I'll bet it's something I've been wanting for a long, long time."

"Silly," the voice chided. "You have a dirty mind. I appreciate that in a man, but it's not what I was referring to."

"Damn."

"But it is something you've been wanting for a long, long time."

Andy held the phone tighter to his ear as a loud garbage truck went roaring by, belching black smoke. "Well, I'll say this much. You've got my interest piqued."

"Guess what the DA took to the grand jury today?"

Andy stopped, ducked into the entrance alcove of a gray granite building. "What? What've you got?"

"The Exotica Tans murders," the voice said. "The DA had a meeting with the head of the Murder Squad on Friday and they went to the grand jury this morning."

"Holy shit," Andy muttered. "Who're they charging?"

"Well, there hasn't been an indictment issued yet, but the DA wants them to charge . . . Are ya ready for this?"

Andy gritted his teeth. "C'mon, don't tease me."

"Ever heard of a best-selling author named Michael Schiftmann?"

Andy felt his forehead scrunching up involuntarily. "Uh, yeah, I think so. Never read his books, but—wait? Are you telling me—?"

Andy shook his head, hard, as if trying to clear out the cobwebs.

"He's got a series of books that are all, like, letters and stuff, you know? Like *The First Letter*, *The Second Letter*, and so on, right? And the guys over in the Murder Squad think this best-selling writer guy is, like, killing chicks and then writing about it. Freaky, huh?"

Andy leaned against the cold granite of the building and pressed his back into it. "Can you get me details?"

"I've got a CD with the transcript," the voice said, in an almost singsong fashion.

Andy's head whirled. He hadn't read any of Michael Schiftmann's books, but he'd read reviews, scanned the best-seller lists, had heard of the guy. He was famous. He was rich.

And he was a murderer.

Not only that, a serial killer.

If Andy could break this story, he'd be so out of Chattanooga, they wouldn't even see his dust. He could see himself on MSNBC, CNN, Fox, maybe even one of the majors.

"Lydia, you are so yummy. I just want to put you in my mouth and let you melt."

"That could be arranged, you know."

"When can we get together?"

"How about eight tonight? The Blue Moon?"

The Blue Moon Café was a wonderful, yet out-of-the-way restaurant where Andy often went when he didn't want to be seen with someone. It was on the river, the restaurant actually built on a dock in the water. You could eat outside, at dimly lit tables, and never be noticed by anyone except the person bringing your drinks and food.

"I'll be there. Probably an hour early."

"Oh, and Andy?"

"Yeah?"

"This one's going to cost you," the voice said. "Five hundred, cash."

Andy smiled. It was cheap at the price. He'd have paid ten times that. *Dumb bitch*, he thought.

"Sure, baby," he said sweetly. "Cash."

Max Bransford was trying to get his desk in order before leaving for home, even though he felt that making sense of the piles of paper in his office was a bit like rearranging the deck chairs on the *Titanic*. Suddenly the door to his outer office slammed open and Gary Gilley burst past the secretary and into his office.

"They found it!" Gilley announced.

"What?"

"The rental. Schiftmann's rental car. It was turned in by a client at the New Orleans airport. NOPD's impounded the car."

Max stood up. "Their forensic guys had a look at it?"

Gilley nodded. "They found some staining in the trunk carpet. They took a Hemident swab. It showed positive."

"Hemident," Bransford said.

"I know, I know, it's just a field test. Doesn't even distinguish between human and animal blood, but unless some guy carried his groceries home in the trunk and his pot roast leaked all over the place, there was something bloody in the back of that car."

Bransford stood there for a moment, and then a broad grin spread across his face. "Get on the horn to NOPD and tell 'em to keep the car. We're on our way to get it. I'll call Collier and let him know. And then I'll call the TBI lab and tell them to get ready. Oh, and I'll call Hank Powell at Quantico and Howard Hinton down in Chattanooga."

Gilley grinned back, then lifted his hand in the air. Max shook his head. "No high-fives, Gary. We'll high-five when we find out the car Michael Schiftmann rented in February has bloodstains in the trunk that match what we found in the Mapco Express Dumpster and that it all came from those two girls."

Gilley nodded. "Okay, Loot. If I'm gonna head to New Orleans, I guess I need to haul some ass."

CHAPTER 25

Thursday afternoon, Nashville

Andy Parks went over his notes one last time before making the call. He got up, locked the door to the press room in Legislative Plaza, then made the call from his cell phone. As far as he knew, he was the only reporter in town who had an inkling of the story that was about to break out of the Metro courthouse.

He intended to keep it that way.

"You've reached the office of the District Attorney General," the computerized voice announced. "If you know your party's three-digit extension, you may dial it at any time."

Andy pulled the phone away from his ear and pressed the 0 key.

"Please hold," the voice announced. A few moments of silence followed that soon stretched into almost a minute. Finally, a human voice came on.

"District Attorney's office. How may I direct your call?"

"General Collier's office, please."

"Please hold."

This had been easier than he expected. Only two gatekeepers, with one to go.

"General Collier's office," a second female voice said.

"Yes, this is Andy Parks of the *Chattanooga News–Free Press*. I'd like to speak to General Collier, please."

"I'll see if he's available. Please hold."

Please hold, he thought. *Like I have any choice.*

These sorts of calls always made Andy just a bit anxious. Even though he had the requisite amount of self-assurance, ego, and arrogance required of most journalists, there was something in his personality that dreaded confronting people in high places with things he knew they would not want to talk about.

"I'm sorry," the female voice said. "General Collier is very busy right now. If you need any information, he says feel free to contact the DA press liaison at extension 7436."

"Great," Andy said. "Would you mind asking General Collier if the press liaison can give me some information about the impending indictment of a *New York Times* best-selling author in the Exotica Tans murders? Because if he can't, I'm going to run with what I've got in tomorrow's paper."

A long, leaden silence followed from the other end. Andy sat there, waiting for the next move. The voice on the other end was the first to flinch.

"Could you hold a moment, Mr. Parks?"

Andy smiled. "Glad to."

Andy looked down at his watch and counted the seconds before Collier came on the line. It took just under fifteen.

"Goddamn it!" Collier's voice was barely under control. "Parks, are you aware that grand jury proceedings are by law secret and protected. It's illegal for you to even know what they're discussing, let alone the details!"

"You can take that up with my anonymous source," Andy said evenly. "In the meantime, I've got more than enough to run with this. It'll be in tomorrow's edition, and all I want from you is comment and reaction."

"I'll file charges," Collier sputtered. "I'll seek an injunction . . ."

"Remember the First Amendment?" Andy asked. "Last time I checked, it was still in force."

"Who's your source?" Collier demanded. "You have to tell me."

Andy laughed.

"I'll go before a judge. I'll have you held in contempt."

"Go ahead," Andy said. "I can't imagine better publicity."

Collier made a noise on the other end of the phone. Andy could swear he was growling.

"Would you be willing to deal?" Collier asked finally, his voice softer.

"What've you got?" Andy asked.

"This is off the record, okay?"

"Wait a minute, you can't sucker me into—"

"I'm not trying to sucker you into anything. I'm just trying to see what it'll take to convince you to hold off for just a little while."

Andy thought for a few moments, letting Collier sweat. "Okay," he offered. "Off the record."

"And in return, you hold off on the story for forty-eight hours. Two days, that's all I want. You hold off publishing the story until Saturday morning at the earliest. By then, we'll know if there's even anything worth publishing."

"Intriguing," Andy said. "Deal."

"We found his car."

"What?"

"The rental car. Schiftmann was in town for a book signing at Davis-Kidd the night of the Exotica Tans murders."

"I knew that," Andy said. "I've already confirmed that."

"And he rented a car, or rather the publisher rented a car for him."

"Okay."

"We found it. Tracked it down."

"All right. And?"

"There was blood in the trunk."

Andy felt a knot in his gut. "What?"

"The car was found in New Orleans. We impounded it, brought it back to Nashville. It's out at the TBI lab right now. They're typing and cross-matching the bloodstain in the car with the blood we found at Exotica Tans and on some other evidence that I really can't talk about right now."

"How long's that going to take?"

"They got the car to the lab about ten last night. We're waiting for preliminary tests now. DNA tests will take a few days, maybe a week, but we can get a type fairly quickly."

"So if the blood in Michael Schiftmann's rental car matches the blood found at the murder scene, then—"

"The grand jury will issue an indictment no later than Monday. If you hold off, I'll let you know the lab results in time for you to break the story over the weekend."

"What if the blood in the trunk doesn't match the scene?"

"Then," Collier said, his voice somber, "you have no story and we have no case."

"When do you expect the results?" Andy asked, scribbling on his notepad.

"They moved this one to the front of the line. I expect to hear something no later than noon tomorrow. Maybe even today."

"Okay, we've got a deal. I do nothing on this until I hear from you. But I expect to hear something from you one way or the other by five o'clock Friday. Grab a pencil and I'll give you my cell phone number. I'll have it with me. Call anytime."

The news that Schiftmann's rental car had been found in New Orleans pushed Hank Powell into high gear. He sent out an e-mail to each lead investigator in every town where the Alphabet Man had hit, suggesting that they track down Michael Schiftmann's rental car records and attempt to recover the cars. He had a meeting with Deputy Assistant Director Dunlap and got him up to speed. The fact that the case seemed finally to be breaking seemed to lessen some of the pressure coming from above. Hank had pushed the limit with his bosses. Their patience was wearing thin. He was glad to be able to go to them with something good.

That Friday morning, the call he'd been waiting for finally came in.

"Agent Powell?" the gruff voice said.

"Hello, Max. I've been waiting for your call."

"I've got good news and bad news," Bransford offered. "Which do you want first?"

Hank felt his chest weigh down. *Damn*, he thought.

"Okay," he said after a moment. "Let's go with the good."

"I'll fax you the whole report, but the bottom line is we got a match. The blood in the trunk positively matches that of Allison May Matthews. It's going to take a couple of weeks to get a full DNA workup, but right now it looks like the same blood was at the murder scene, on the coveralls we found in the Dumpster, and in the trunk of the rental Schiftmann had when he was in Nashville."

"That's it," Hank said, the heaviness in his chest lifting. Not lifting, but releasing, exploding, like a fireworks display that, for a brief moment, let him drop his professional detachment. "Max, we've got him! We've got the son of a bitch! He's toast."

"I know, Hank. We did it. All of us. The DA is taking the case to the grand jury after their lunch break. They've already heard all of the evidence except the blood match-up. After they get that, the DA will get the indictment processed, issue a warrant for Schiftmann's arrest, and start extradition proceedings."

Hank gripped the phone tightly and realized he was smiling so hard his jaw hurt. "Fantastic! This is incredible. But wait? You said there was bad news."

"The bad news is somebody leaked the story to the press. Andy Parks from the Chattanooga paper—"

"The same guy who wrote the other story," Hank interrupted.

"Yeah, that's him. He went to the DA with everything that had gone on in the grand jury room."

"Jesus, how'd he get that?"

"I don't know, but when the DA finds out, I wouldn't want to be in their moccasins. He's loaded for bear. But Collier made him a deal, if he'd hold off on printing the story . . ."

"He'd give him a heads-up on the indictment."

"That's it," Bransford said.

"When's the story supposed to break?" Hank asked.

"Sometime this weekend."

"That means Schiftmann will have advance warning."

"Maybe not," Bransford said. "It's just the Chattanooga paper."

Hank shook his head. "No, not this story. This one'll be all over. Probably be the lead story on the networks Sunday night. Schiftmann's going to find out for sure. No telling what he'll do."

"Think he might rabbit?"

Hank shrugged. "Who knows? He's got money, resources. He's smart."

"Yeah, and he's famous. His picture was in *Entertainment Weekly* and *People* magazine last week. How's he going to hide?"

Hank sat silently for a moment, thinking.

"You there?" Bransford asked.

"Yeah, yeah, I'm here. Max, we already know how smart this guy is. He's killed at least thirteen people we know of. He's bound to know that sooner or later, something like this could happen."

"What are you thinking?"

"I'm thinking this guy's already got an escape route. He's got a Plan B in place, and if we've got a chance of actually seeing him in court, then we better not let the SOB out of our sight between now and the time the New York City police take him into custody."

"So what are you suggesting?"

"I'm suggesting," Hank offered, "that I call the NYC Field Office and have this guy put under twenty-four-hour surveillance. I don't want him to go into a public bathroom without one of my guys standing outside the stall waiting for him."

"All right," Max Bransford said. "Let's nail this bastard."

Hank smiled. "It'll be a pleasure."

Andy Parks woke up early that Sunday morning, dressed quickly, and left his apartment at the Metro Manor. He drove his rusting Datsun 280Z out of the basement garage and turned left onto the James Robertson Parkway. At seven A.M. on a Sunday morning, there was practically no traffic. The day held promise of warm spring sunshine and clear skies. Andy's stomach churned in anticipation. This was the biggest story he'd ever covered in his life. If this story broke like he hoped, a little résumé dusting-off would be in order.

He had worked like a demon these past four or five days. He'd researched Schiftmann's life and work, read three of his books, checked and cross-checked every element of the story. He had kept his word to the district attorney, and Collier had done right by him.

Andy sped up to make the light at Broadway, then turned right and headed toward Vanderbilt University. There was a small coffee and bagel place on Twenty-first Avenue across from the law school that got the Chattanooga paper every day. Five minutes later, he pulled the 280Z into a parking space out front and almost jumped out of the car.

He opened the door, nodded to Gretchen behind the counter, and went straight to the long rack of newspapers against the far wall. The wooden bins held the *New York Times*, the *Washington Post*, and papers from Birmingham, Atlanta, Miami, and, at the far end of the bins, Chattanooga.

"The usual, Andy?" Gretchen called.

"Yeah," Andy nodded, preoccupied. He grabbed the top copy of the *News–Free Press* and smiled. There, in sixty-point bold block type, over the lead story for the Sunday edition, was the headline that Andy had suggested the afternoon before:

BEST-SELLING AUTHOR TO BE INDICTED IN BRUTAL DOUBLE MURDER

Andy laughed out loud and flapped the paper open, scanning his lead to see if the editor had changed it.

NASHVILLE, March 27—The Davidson County Grand Jury will indict *New York Times* best-selling author Michael Schiftmann on two counts of first-degree murder tomorrow in the brutal February slaying of two MTSU coeds. District Attorney T. Robert Collier will make the announcement at a press conference scheduled for 10 A.M. Monday.

Andy folded the paper under his arm and stepped between the empty tables over to the counter, where his double latte with an extra shot of espresso was already waiting for him. Gretchen, the thin, dark-haired Vanderbilt sophomore with an eyebrow ring, gave him a look as he approached.

"What's going on with you?" she asked. "You look like the cat that swallowed the canary. What, did you get lucky last night or what?"

"Yeah, yeah, that's it," he said. "I got lucky." He reached into his wallet and pulled out a five-dollar bill. "Keep it," he said.

"Wow, you did get lucky last night," Gretchen said.

Andy started to walk away, then turned back to her, grinning again. "Gretchen, you ever hit a home run before? I mean, really hit one out of the park?"

CHAPTER 26

Sunday afternoon, Manhattan

Taylor Robinson's violent retching echoed down the hallway of her empty office building.

Inside the women's restroom, she was on her knees in a stall, her hands wrapped around the cold porcelain, not even bothering to hold her hair back. A ferocious wave of nausea swept over her once more, carrying her torso forward as she vomited again. This time, there was little left inside her. A thin trail of slime hung out of her mouth, into the putrid water.

She'd never felt so ill in her life. Her chest hurt; her ribs ached. Her eyes felt like they were going to pop out of her head. Her face and neck had broken out in a frigid sweat. She struggled to get her breath, to try and relax before her heart exploded in her chest.

Then it hit again, a rolling, convulsive paroxysm that began deep in her gut and echoed throughout her abdomen and up into her throat. Her belly was empty, wrung completely out. Nothing came out this time, but the spasm rolled through the top half of her body. As she leaned over the toilet, the almost inhuman noise that came out of her sounded like a disembodied, continuous, agonizing wail.

Inside her head, she backed away from it all, as if she were watching someone else from the outside. The pain in her body seemed to lessen. She wondered if it was possible to die from retching.

And then it seemed to pass, at least for a moment.

Taylor leaned back, her hips on the floor, her back against the metal partition, her legs folded up, her knees against her chest. She tried to loosen her chest, to breathe slowly and deeply, to stop the panicked, shallow panting.

She stared at the scratched gray paint in front of her. This seemed suddenly like a dream, as if this couldn't really be happening.

No, she thought, the voice in her head shouting. *This is happening! This is real!*

The only thing she could be grateful for at this moment was that at least she was alone. She had time to gather her wits, to try and get her head around this.

Brett Silverman, Michael's editor, had called her, tracked her down on the cell phone. Brett had a friend down the street from her brownstone in Chelsea, a gay clothing designer who lived in the London Towers, who had moved to Manhattan from Cleveland, Tennessee, in Hamilton County just north of Chattanooga. He never missed home—Cleveland, Tennessee, being less than hospitable to openly gay clothing designers—but for some reason or other, he compulsively read the hometown paper.

He had been the first to call.

Brett, panicked, had called Taylor's apartment. Michael answered the phone. Brett, thinking perhaps faster on her feet than she ever had before, simply asked for Taylor. She'd gone into the office, Michael said. Something about having some quiet time to clear up some paperwork.

Seconds later, Taylor's cell phone went off. She answered it, and a few short sentences later, was running down the darkened hallway for the restroom.

Taylor reached up and tore off a couple of feet of toilet paper, wadded it up and blew her nose into it. She folded the wad in half and wiped off her forehead.

Then she crossed her arms over her bent knees and rested her head wearily on her forearms. The day that Jack died, she threw up that hard as well, for what seemed like hours, until her body simply gave in to exhaustion.

"This can't be happening," she whispered.

She put her hands flat on the cold, dirty tile and pushed herself up a few inches, then cocked her legs and stood up slowly, unsteadily. She was dizzy, off kilter, wondering if the retching was about to start again. The acid taste of bile backed up in her mouth from her throat, which would, she feared, be raw and sore for days.

Taylor held on to the door as she slowly walked out of the stall. It was dark in the restroom, the only light coming from a translucent window honeycombed with chicken wire. She flipped the light switch on. The harsh fluorescent light flickered painfully. She quickly snapped it back off.

She walked over in the dim light and stared at herself in the grimy mirror. Her hair was wet on the ends, matted, a tangled mess. Even in the low light, she could see that she looked pale, washed out. She'd have to pull herself together before she left.

She turned on the cold water, leaned over, and splashed some in her face. It felt good. A shiver went up and down her back, and she realized she'd been sweating all over. She drank a small sip of the cold water. It tasted wonderful, made her throat instantly feel better.

And it stayed down.

She blotted her face with a paper towel, then walked back to her office almost in a daze. She was grateful that no one else had come in. As she pulled out her keys and opened the front door of the office, the phone started ringing.

Taylor walked over to the receptionist's desk and reached for the phone, but at the last minute held back. She heard the answering machine inside the desk answer with the standard greeting, then a beep, followed by a muffled voice.

"Yes, this is Harry Greene of the *New York Post*. I'm trying to reach Taylor Robinson. It's very important. Please call me back at—"

My God, she thought, walking away from the desk, *it's already started.*

Taylor went back to her office and shut, then locked, the door behind her. She sat down at her computer, brought up her Internet browser, then Googled "Chattanooga newspapers." A couple of clicks later, she was at the Web site.

She felt a spasm in her chest as Michael's picture appeared line by line on her screen. She saw the headline and thought for a moment that she was about to vomit again.

"Oh, Jesus," she whispered. Her forehead broke out in sweat again.

She forced herself to read the story, all of it, including the sidebar on Michael's seemingly meteoric rise to fame and fortune as the Chaney books took off. The reporter even quoted from some reviews that she remembered and considered glowing at the time, but now seemed eerily foreboding.

"Schiftmann's Chaney makes murder fun," one reviewer wrote. "Who would have ever guessed that something so completely evil could be so charming?"

She leaned back in her chair, trying to take all this in. The initial shock was slowly beginning to wear off. She'd read the story, and the essence of the article was that Michael was going to be indicted for murder. But the case itself had not been laid out. There were few details, few specifics about the evidence against him. It was, of course, impossible to believe that any of the accusations were true. But what was undeniable was that Michael, and she, had a fight on their hands.

"Joan," she said out loud. "Call Joan."

She reached for her office phone, then held off. No, not Joan. Not first.

Michael.

She picked up her cell phone and punched 1. The cell phone's speed dial went to work, and a few seconds later, her home phone was ringing.

"Hey, you," Michael said. His voice was relaxed, normal. "How are you?"

"You're still there," she said.

"Yeah, I was just reading the Sunday paper. Waiting for you to get home. What's up?"

"Have there been any phone calls?" Taylor asked.

"Brett Silverman called, but that's—"

"I talked to her," Taylor interrupted. "Listen, we've got to talk. I want you to stay there, don't leave the apartment.

If anyone comes to the door, don't answer it. And for God's sakes, don't answer the phone. Don't even pick it up. I'm on my way."

"What's up?" he asked, concerned now.

"Not on the phone. Sit tight. I'm on my way."

Michael exploded after she told him. His face turned red, and it seemed as if the skin of his cheeks was stretched to the point of tearing.

"Those ignorant bastards!" he yelled. "What the hell do they think they're doing?"

"I know," Taylor said calmly, trying desperately to placate him. Michael had a terrible temper, she knew. She had gotten glimpses of it only a few times, but it was enough to let her know that beneath the surface, there was a reservoir of angry energy.

"I'll sue the shit out of them!" he shouted.

"Yes, once we prove them wrong, we're going to drag them through every court in the country. Malicious prosecution, prosecutorial misconduct, libel, slander, the whole gamut. But first we've got to prove them wrong."

Michael stopped, turned, and stared at her. "What are you thinking?"

"We've got to find you a lawyer, and a good one."

Michael reached up and rubbed his forehead. He suddenly looked tired. "I don't even know any lawyers here, let alone any lawyers there."

"I'll call Joan," Taylor said. "She knows everybody. She needs to know what's going on anyway. This is going to hit the media, Michael, and soon. The only reason they're not at our door now is my unlisted phone number."

"Thank God for that," he said. Then he looked up at her, and for a brief flash, Taylor thought she saw fear in his face. "We've got to make this go away here. If I have to go back to that redneck shit hole, then I'm screwed."

"We'll get you the best lawyer out there."

"Won't make any difference!" he snapped. "Taylor, I've spent years studying the court system, police procedure, all for these books. And I'll tell you what I've learned, baby, and that's that we have more to fear from the cops and the prosecutors than we do the criminals!"

"Michael, that's—"

"I'm serious!" he yelled. He began pacing back and forth in the cavernous living room, agitated, talking as much with his hands as with his mouth. "Let me tell you how this'll go, Taylor. They've concocted some screwball theory because they're too fucking incompetent to catch the real killer, and they've taken a bunch of coincidental, circumstantial things and twisted them to fit their theory. And they'll perp walk me down there in front of the cameras for the goddamn media attention, and then they'll book me and throw me in a cell with some little punk in an orange jumpsuit who's facing a long term as a chronic habitual petty offender, or some such shit like that. And when it goes to trial, lo and behold, that little punk will get up on the stand and raise his right hand and swear I told him I did it. And the lying sack of shit prosecutor will stand there and ask the punk if any kind of deal had been offered in return for his testimony. And the little punk jailhouse snitch will shake his head and swear there was no deal. And when my ass goes off to prison, that lying punk will be out on the streets mugging little old ladies again."

He stopped in the middle of the living room and stood there, eyes wild, hair mussed, his body still yet tense. Taylor stood still for a moment, numb.

"This is still America. You're innocent until proven guilty," she said softly.

His voice erupted, almost like a bark. "Bullshit!" he spewed. "In America, once the government decides to come after you, you may as well bend over, put your head between your knees, and kiss your ass good-bye."

"You're forgetting two things, Michael," she said firmly.

"What?"

"First of all, you're rich. I don't mean to sound cynical, but let's face it. You can afford the best attorney money can buy."

He smiled. "Yeah. Yeah, I forgot about that. So what's the other thing?"

"You have me," Taylor said. "We're in this together. We'll get through this together."

Joan Delaney was at her summer house in East Hampton when Taylor found her. For once, Joan remained calm in a crisis. "The first thing we have to do is to get the best criminal lawyer we can find," Joan said.

"Exactly what I was thinking."

"That means Abe Steinberg."

Taylor made a note on the pad next to the phone. "With an E, right?"

"Yes. His office is on the east side of Park Avenue, around Forty-seventh Street. I'm not sure. You can look it up."

"So you know this guy pretty well?" Taylor asked hopefully.

"Quite. We had a thing going once, but that was a long time ago. About twenty years ago, I sold the rights to the book he wrote about the Trenton Black Panther trial."

"I remember that," Taylor said. "He defended that boxer, right?"

"Muhammad Sharquand," Joan answered. "He was a member of the Black Panther Party back in the late seventies and then became a contender for the heavyweight championship, until the Trenton police set him up on a bogus drug charge."

"Steinberg got him off, if I remember."

"Yes, but only after he was in jail for almost three years. Cost him his shot at the title. But it worked out okay. Steinberg went after the Trenton cops and won a ten-million-dollar judgment."

"So this guy likes to go after crooked cops?" Taylor smiled.

"He pours warm milk on 'em and eats 'em out of a cereal bowl. Let me track him down. I still have his private number somewhere. I'll call you back."

Taylor hung up the phone and leaned back in her leather office chair. Down the hallway, she heard the shower running. Michael had ranted on for another fifteen or twenty minutes, then decided to take a long, hot shower, more to calm down than anything else. Taylor spun around in her chair and scanned the bookshelves in her home office. The room was large, almost as large as her bedroom, with floor-to-ceiling bookcases along one wall, with the exterior wall being exposed brick. She loved this room; it was her private sanctuary, her place to hide and think.

She would need this place a lot in the coming weeks and months, she thought.

Taylor sat, staring at the brick wall until the lines of ancient mortar started to tremble and vibrate. All thought seemed to leave her. She felt the air blowing gently over her skin.

When the phone went off next to her, it sounded like a firehouse alarm. She jumped and grabbed the handset before the first ring ended.

"Yes."

"I'm trying to reach Taylor Robinson," a gruff voice said. She leaned down and looked at the caller ID box. She didn't recognize the number.

"Who may I say is calling?"

"This is Abe Steinberg."

The release of air from her chest made a whooshing sound. "Oh, Mr. Steinberg. Thank you so much for calling."

"Do you know where my offices are?"

"Yes. I believe so."

"We're on the nineteenth floor. Be there at ten A.M. tomorrow. I'll be expecting you."

Then, having delivered his instructions, he hung up.

By seven that night, the media had gotten wind of the story in the Chattanooga paper and were descending on it like a pack of wild dogs on a lame deer. The CBS affiliate buried the story during the local newscast, but the Fox, ABC, and NBC stations led off with the story. By nine that night, the vultures had tracked down Taylor's home phone number and had called so much that she finally disconnected the phone and turned off the answering machine. The only people she wanted to hear from already had her cell number, so she wasn't worried about missing anything important.

By ten, all the local stations were leading off with the

story, and MSNBC, CNN, and Fox News had picked it up as well. After a few minutes of channel surfing, she and Michael gave up and turned the set off.

"One thing we've got going for us," Taylor said. "No one knows you're staying here."

"At least for now," he said. "Let's keep it that way as long as we can."

They went to bed, but neither could sleep. Taylor lay as still as possible, thinking that Michael might be asleep. Then he let out a long sigh and rolled over to face her.

"You awake?"

She nodded. "Yes."

"Baby, I'm sorry about all this."

"Me, too," she said.

He scooted over in bed closer to her, then turned to face her and settled his left arm across her torso. His arm felt heavy and limp. He pulled her closer to him, his face against her left cheek. He leaned in and nuzzled her neck, then scooted in closer, his whole body pressed against hers now. He laid his left leg across the tops of her thighs. She felt him growing hard against her.

She stiffened, almost unconsciously. "I'm sorry," she whispered.

He raised his head. "What?"

"I'm sorry," she repeated. "I guess I've got too much on my mind. Not really in the mood."

He bent his right elbow, then raised his head and propped it on the palm of his hand, looking down at her in the dim glow of the outside streetlights filtering through the curtains.

"Might take the edge off," he said quietly. "Maybe help you go to sleep."

She turned to her left, facing him. She thought she could see a glimmer in his eyes. "I'm sorry," she said again.

He rolled away from her, then sat up on the edge of the bed. "Me, too."

Then he turned and faced her. "You want me to go stay somewhere else?"

She sat up quickly, her hips scooting across the smooth

sheets. "No, of course not. It's quite a jump from 'I've got too much on my mind to make love' to 'I want you out of here.'"

"You sure?"

"Absolutely." She reached over and brushed his face with the tips of her fingers. "I'll make it up to you. Honest."

She saw the white of his teeth as he smiled. "Okay. But I still can't sleep. I think I'm going to go downstairs, have a drink, catch a late movie on TV. Want to come?"

"No. I can't sleep, but I am tired. I think I'll stay up here and try to rest."

He shrugged, then leaned down and kissed her lightly and quickly on the cheek. It was, she felt, almost a dismissive peck. Then he was gone.

Taylor settled her head into the pillow and tried to clear her thoughts. Sometime around sunup, she finally succeeded and drifted off into a restless, troubled, and altogether too short sleep.

CHAPTER 27

The offices of Steinberg, Tillman, Gordon, Jenkins & Associates took up the entire nineteenth floor of a twenty-six-story building with a clear view of the East River and beyond. Taylor and Michael stepped off the elevator in the middle of a crowd of busy, droning office workers and entered the main reception area through a pair of heavy glass doors. The receptionist looked up, recognized Michael immediately, and stared for a few seconds before rising and taking them directly into Abe Steinberg's office.

Steinberg's office alone was bigger than most Manhattan apartments. A long plate-glass window gave them a view eastward of the sprawling city. Steinberg's desk was easily six feet wide, made of a deep, rich brown polished wood. As Michael and Taylor were led into the office, he rose to meet them. He was short, balding, almost nondescript, and had to be pushing seventy. He didn't exactly present a fearsome image, Taylor thought.

He crossed the room from behind his desk and met them in the middle of the room. "You must be Mr. Schiftmann," he offered, extending his hand.

Michael nodded. "Pleased to meet you, Mr. Steinberg." Taylor thought he seemed quiet, subdued, even a little nervous. The two of them had left Taylor's building through the basement and the boiler room, and out onto the sidewalk at the freight entrance. They'd dodged smelly garbage cans and pallets of flattened recyclable cardboard boxes to avoid the news trucks and vans parked out front. Michael had said less then five words during the long cab ride uptown.

"And you're Taylor Robinson," Steinberg said, turning to Taylor and smiling. "Joan Delaney's told me so much about you. She sees you as the future of the agency, you know."

"That may be stretching it a bit," Taylor answered. "But thanks for the compliment."

Steinberg turned and motioned toward a shiny leather sofa that occupied the center of the office. Next to it, a matching brown leather chair sat next to a long glass coffee table.

"Please, sit down. We've got a lot to do and not much time. We're going to be here awhile, so would you like some coffee, tea, a soda, perhaps?"

"No, thank you," Taylor said. Michael shook his head.

Steinberg turned and dismissed his assistant with a wave of his hand. Michael and Taylor sat down on the sofa at opposite ends. Steinberg loosened his tie and settled himself into the chair.

"Well, Mr. Schiftmann, you must feel like a character in one of your own books."

Michael reached up and rubbed his forehead. "I don't think I could ever write anything like this. No one would believe it."

Steinberg laughed. "You're not the first person I've ever met who was accused of something and couldn't quite believe it."

Michael scooted forward on the seat and put his elbows on his knees, his arms extended forward. "First of all, Mr. Steinberg, I want you to know I'm absolutely inno—"

"Don't," Steinberg interrupted. "Don't tell me that now. For one thing, it doesn't matter at this point. For another, we have too much else to do."

Michael leaned back in the sofa, looking a bit, Taylor thought, like a scolded puppy. Steinberg crossed his legs in the chair and leaned his head back, relaxed and confident.

"The first thing we have to do here is make a couple of decisions. The first is how you're going to choose to fight this. There are several ways to contend with it. First, you can lay low, keep quiet, and let the best lawyers in the country fight it out for you. On the other extreme is total war, total commitment. Take your case to the public. Hire the best public relations firm in the country. Work the talk-show circuit, the tabloids, the whole thing. Build a case for Michael Schiftmann as the victim of an overzealous prosecutor and an incompetent police department. We can hire private investigators, our own forensic researchers, experts, and take the offensive. We challenge every point, concede nothing, and make them pay with blood, sweat, and tears for every step they take."

Michael and Taylor looked at each other briefly, then back to Steinberg.

"The advantage to the former course of action is that it's less stress and cost on your part. Good lawyers with lots of resources can often make these things go away. The downside is that you're putting your fate in someone else's hands, and that requires considerable trust."

"And what are the ramifications of taking the other course?" Michael asked.

"The advantage is that your own personal involvement in the case will often swing public sympathy to your side, and don't negate the power of that. The downside is when it backfires and the public turns against you. And there's one other downside."

"Yes?" Michael asked.

"If you write a check to the lawyers and let them take it from there, it's going to be expensive. But if you decide to commit to total war—and make no mistake, my friend, this is war—then it could cost you everything."

"But if I beat this . . ."

"Then you become a kind of folk hero," Steinberg said, smiling. "And there are many opportunities in our culture for heroes. You're a writer. Use your imagination."

"Yes," Michael said, smiling. "And I think that I want to take this fight to them. I'm innocent—I know you told me not to say that, but I am—and I'm not going to let them run over me. I don't want to go to war with them, but if I have to, I will. Total commitment."

Michael turned to Taylor and held out his hand. She smiled and took it. Then she turned to Steinberg.

"Okay, Mr. Steinberg," she said. "Total war. What's the first step?"

"The first step," Steinberg said, "is you write me a check for one hundred thousand dollars. That's just to get started. And when we get your attorney in Nashville on board, you should be prepared to write another one."

There was a long moment of increasingly uncomfortable silence. Taylor looked over at Michael as he sat there with a shocked look on his face. Then he slowly extracted a leather-bound checkbook from his inside suit coat pocket.

"How should I make out the check?" he asked, his voice subdued.

"Steinberg, Tillman will be fine."

Michael slipped his black Montblanc fountain pen out of his pocket and removed the cap. "I'm writing a one-hundred-thousand-dollar check with a fountain pen that five years ago, I couldn't afford."

Steinberg smiled. "Funny how things change over time."

Michael signed the check, ripped it out of the book, and handed it across the table to Steinberg, who folded the check and slipped it into his shirt pocket. "Now, let's move on to some other things."

Then Steinberg began talking, nonstop. Taylor sat there, off to the side, as the old attorney went on and on, with Michael occasionally nodding his head or answering a question with one or two words. Taylor found herself drifting in and out of the conversation; she still couldn't believe this was happening. There was something about it so far removed from reality, so surreal, that she kept thinking that sooner or later someone was going to burst into the room, shout, "Just kidding!" and then it would all be over. Steinberg would roar back laughing, stand up, and rip Michael's check into shreds. Then they could all go have a big lunch and a few drinks and a good laugh over all this.

Only it wasn't a joke.

Taylor looked down at her watch; they'd been in Steinberg's office nearly an hour. Suddenly the door opened and a middle-aged woman wearing a stern blue pin-striped power dress, her hair pulled back tightly, walked into the room. Steinberg, irritated, turned to her.

"What?"

"I'm sorry, Mr. Steinberg," the woman said, "but you're going to want to see this."

She walked over to a large, closed cabinet that dominated the middle of the built-in floor-to-ceiling bookcases. She opened the door, revealing a large flat-panel television. She picked up the remote off the top of the TV and pointed it at the screen. The television powered up in a few seconds. The woman raised the volume and pressed the buttons to go to Cable News Network.

The shot was a live one, from the steps of the Davidson County Courthouse in Nashville, Tennessee. A podium had been set up on the steps with a bank of microphones jammed on top. A crowd milled around, restlessly murmuring. It was a bright blue spring day in Nashville, Taylor noticed as she got up from the sofa and walked over to the television. A moment later, Michael was standing on one side of her, with Steinberg on the other.

As Steinberg's assistant raised the volume, the screen split, with the courthouse scene in a frame to the right of the screen and the clean-cut, blow-dried, rubber-stamped CNN anchor to the left.

"We take you now to Nashville, Tennessee, where the district attorney has scheduled a brief statement regarding the rumored indictments of best-selling novelist Michael Schiftmann on two counts of first-degree murder."

"Jesus," Taylor muttered. No one else spoke.

They all watched as a tall, gray-haired man in a nondescript gray suit approached the microphone. He carried in his right hand a sheaf of papers, which he jogged into a neat stack as he stood at the podium. He looked up into the cameras, cleared his throat, and began:

"Ladies and gentlemen, I am T. Robert Collier, the District Attorney General for Davidson County and Metropolitan

Nashville. As you all know, last February, on February fifth of this year, there was a double murder here in Nashville at a place of business on Church Street known as Exotica Tans. Two young women were killed in what the police have described as one of the most brutal and horrifying murder scenes in the history of our city. These two women were gainfully employed in a legal establishment, working their way through college, with families and friends who mourn their violent and premature passing, and who seek justice for them and their memory."

Collier paused here, looking down at the papers in his hand. Taylor felt her heart thumping in her chest and cold sweat breaking out around her chest, under her breasts, in her armpits. She squeezed her arms into her ribs as a thin trickle of perspiration ran down her side.

"I am here today to announce to you," Collier continued, "that as of nine o'clock this morning, the Davidson County Grand Jury has issued a series of criminal indictments in connection with the events of that horrible February night."

Collier paused again, clearing his throat. "A Mr. Michael Schiftmann, whom we believe is currently residing in New York City, has been indicted on the following charges relating to the murders of Sarah Denise Burnham of Murfreesboro, Tennessee and Allison May Matthews of Fairview, Tennessee.

"First, under Tennessee Code Annotated 39–13–305, Mr. Schiftmann is charged with two counts of especially aggravated kidnapping, a Class A felony. Second, Mr. Schiftmann is charged with two counts of violating Tennessee Code Annotated 39–13–540, aggravated sexual battery. Third, Mr. Schiftmann is charged with two counts of violating Tennessee Code Annotated 39–13–502, aggravated rape."

Collier paused for a moment and looked out over the crowd, letting them wait for a heartbeat or two. *This guy*, Taylor thought, *has good dramatic timing.*

"Finally, Mr. Schiftmann is charged with two counts of violating Tennessee Code Annotated 39–13–202, which is first-degree murder."

Taylor gasped involuntarily. Michael reached over, took her hand, and squeezed it. She turned quickly to her left. Michael was staring at the television, his body rigid, his jaw clenched.

"And because of the especially heinous and violent nature of these two senseless, brutal murders, my office wishes to announce that we will be seeking the death penalty in connection with the first-degree murder charges."

Taylor went numb all over. She stared at the television as time seemed to stop for a moment. Michael's hand in hers felt cold, stone-cold, and hard as a rock.

"These are the charges that the grand jury has issued today," the voice on the television droned on. "Other charges may follow. An arrest warrant has been issued for Mr. Schiftmann, and my office is preparing extradition papers as we speak. I also want to say that I'm aware of the implications of bringing these serious charges against a suspect who is a high-profile celebrity, with a great many resources, including the court of public opinion. But my responsibility is to Allison and Sarah and the people of the state of Tennessee. We have taken this course of action only after much thought, deliberation, even debate. We believe the evidence in this case will show that this was the only way we could bring justice to Allison and Sarah and closure to their families."

Taylor looked over at Abe Steinberg, who was staring intently at the television and nodding his head imperceptibly.

"We have time for a few questions," the voice said. Steinberg looked at his assistant and made a motion with his head. The assistant hit the power button on the remote, and the television instantly went dead.

Taylor turned to Michael, the color drained completely out of his face, as he stared at the dark television. "They're serious," he whispered after a few seconds.

Steinberg laughed out loud. "Oh yes, my friend, they're serious. They're very serious. And this guy is very good, very good indeed."

Steinberg walked slowly back to his chair, with a slight limp to his gait, and sat down. "You notice how he managed to call the two girls by their first names not once, but twice. He humanized them. And how he attempted to defuse the argument that they were after you for their own glory by saying that indicting you was almost a last resort."

"He made it sound like they had no choice," Taylor commented, almost matter-of-factly, as she crossed back over and sat down on the sofa. She reached up, touched her face, and realized she couldn't feel it anymore.

"I'll fight it!" Michael said, crossing around and standing in front of the two of them. "I'll fight the extradition. I won't even go down there!"

Steinberg waved his hand at him. "Don't be silly. You can't beat extradition. The only way you could get around it is if you can prove you're not Michael Schiftmann, or at least not the Michael Schiftmann they're looking for."

"You mean I should just let them take me?" Michael yelled.

Steinberg looked up at him with a completely calm, blank look on his face. "My friend, you're going to be extradited, you're going to be arrested, you're going to be booked, and then you're going to be arraigned. You're going to smile for the cameras, look professional and calm, and you're going to behave yourself and control your temper. And you're going to let me and Wesley Talmadge take it from there."

"Wesley Talmadge?" Michael asked. "Who the hell is Wesley Talmadge?"

"The best criminal defense lawyer in the state of Tennessee and one of the best in the country. He was a student of mine at NYU thirty years ago. I spoke with him this morning and he's agreed to take your case."

"So what's next?" Michael asked, deflated.

"You're going to go home and pack. In addition to the usual underwear and toothbrush, you're going to need to pack two other things."

"What?" Michael asked.

"First, carry that fancy checkbook with you. You're going to need it. Second, take your passport."

"My passport? Why my passport?"

"Because," Steinberg said, folding his hands in front of him, the fingers interlaced, "the judge is going to want you to surrender it if he grants you bail."

Taylor looked up, and for the first time, saw real fear in Michael's face.

"If?" he asked, his voice low.

Steinberg nodded. "If . . ."

CHAPTER 28

Thursday morning, Manhattan

Time seemed to accelerate after the Monday morning press conference. Taylor found herself withdrawing, still numb, the touch of her fingers on the skin of her cheek foreign and strange. It seemed as if in a matter of only a few short hours, she had looked around to discover that the world had gone into a spin. *So this*, she thought, *is what free fall feels like*.

In short order, Michael had a conference call with the law-yer in Nashville and overnighted a cashier's check to him. Then Abe Steinberg sent him to Macguire and Madison over on Fifth Avenue, which was the top public relations firm in Manhattan, which meant it was one of the top public rela-tions firms in the country.

Taylor went back to work and tried to focus as—within a seventy-two-hour period—the man she loved and was going to marry and to whom her whole future was attached wrote checks totaling a quarter-million dollars just to begin his defense against the insane notion that he was a murderer.

She felt as if the world were falling apart. She sat at the cluttered desk in her office staring at the manuscripts in front of her, the pink telephone message slips she couldn't bear to read, the growing roster of unread and unanswered e-mails.

Michael, she thought, had yet to really deal with this. He had yet to confide in her what was going on inside him, what this felt like. He was, instead, totally immersed in what became a series of tasks that lay in front of him, many of them having nothing to do with the charges against him. While Wesley Talmadge in Nashville negotiated the terms of Michael's surrender to the police, Michael was faxing instructions to the solicitor in London about the closing on the flat. Taylor had asked him, practically begged him, not to go ahead with the sale, but he had stubbornly told her that he wasn't going to let a bunch of ignorant fools stop him from moving ahead with his life.

He reviewed a series of foreign-rights contracts and signed them. He met with the PR firm by himself, a meeting that went on almost all afternoon Wednesday. For the time being, he avoided interviews, but he answered correspondence and returned calls. He stayed up until all hours of the night, unable to slow down, unable to relax, as Taylor, exhausted and drained, fell asleep upstairs, alone.

They ate meals together, but were mostly silent. They had even stopped touching each other. Michael seemed distracted, his mind on other things beside sex. And Taylor found herself not wanting to be touched, by Michael or anyone else.

This felt awful, every bit of it, every moment of it. She was adrift, in ways she had never been adrift before.

"Are you going to go with me?" Michael asked, out of the blue, that Thursday night.

"Where?" she asked, looking up from her plate of untouched food.

"I was just telling you," he said. "Weren't you listening?"

She shook her head. "I'm sorry, dear. I was—I was someplace else, I guess."

Michael sighed and looked away from her. "I'm going to be someplace else, too, and very soon. And my question was whether or not you were going to go with me."

"Okay, tell me again. What did Abe say?"

"I'm supposed to book a flight into Nashville for Monday morning and be at the police station by noon. The lawyer in Nashville negotiated an arrangement where I wouldn't have to report before then. If I'd gone tomorrow, I'd have had to spend the weekend in jail before a bond hearing. This way, I'll go before a judge maybe even Monday afternoon."

"And they'll let you make bail, right?"

"Talmadge seems to think it'll work out, that I'll only have to spend a few hours in booking."

"And then we can come home, right?"

Michael smiled, then leaned over and took her hand. "We'll be on the next plane out. Trust me. I'm not going to spend a minute longer there than we have to."

Taylor let Michael hold her limp hand. He squeezed it, then with the thumb of his hand he rubbed her palm. She stared down at the two hands together as if they were separate from their bodies, two detached objects on the table in front of them doing a strange and unreal dance.

She looked up at him. "How long will it be before the trial begins? How long will we have to wait this out, to get some sort of resolution?"

"Abe says it could take months. A lot depends on what happens during discovery. If their evidence is weak and circumstantial, which it will be because I'm innocent, then we'll push to go to trial quickly. They could stall, but for only so long."

She looked away. "This is going to cost a fortune, isn't it? All that money you made, that money you worked so hard for. It's all going to be gone."

He shrugged. "I've been broke before. Have most of my life, in fact. The thing about money is, you can always make more."

"Let's hope so," she said, her voice flat. "No one knows how your readers are going to react to this."

"Well," he said slowly, "one can always make the case that in my business, the kinds of books I write, a little notoriety never hurt anybody. Who knows? When this is over, the books may sell better than ever."

She looked down, suddenly feeling very tired and heavy. "That's assuming you're around to write them," she said, in a voice strained by the weight on her chest.

"Hey, hey, what's that?" He reached out, touched her chin, and raised her head to face him. "Let's not bring any negative energy in here, okay? This is going to work out. I promise. I'll beat this. *We'll* beat this. As long as we stay together."

Taylor felt the tips of his fingers on her chin like someone touching her with the handle of a wooden spoon. They didn't feel like flesh, like people touching. Nothing felt like people touching.

"Trust me, this will be fine. I promise."

Taylor slept all weekend, the phone unplugged, the television and computer off. Michael stayed in, reluctant to go out in case there were any other reporters still stalking the building. The initial rush of publicity had died down, like a storm surge that had broken over the banks, done its damage, and then receded back into the ocean.

And Taylor slept, slept like she'd never slept before. She turned the heat down to where her bedroom was practically frigid. She bundled up covers, quilts and comforters and blankets, so that she could feel the weight of the fabric on her, pressing her down, insulating her from the rest of the world. She came up for water or for bathroom breaks, or for a bite or two of food before her stomach roiled inside her and she could eat no more. Friday night melded into Saturday morning. The afternoon went by unnoticed and the night fell over her like a layer of mist. Michael periodically stuck his head into the bedroom, concerned. She tried to reassure him that she was all right.

Sunday afternoon, she dragged herself out of bed and took a long, hot shower. That seemed to wake her up, to get her blood flowing again, and she felt briefly reenergized. Michael had slept in the other bedroom, the bedroom where she'd caught him with the blond what seemed like ages ago, that Saturday night when she threw the party to celebrate his success. He had found success, found it in ways he never imagined. And now it had come to this.

She went downstairs. Michael was nowhere to be seen. She made herself a cup of soup and turned on the television. She turned to one of the cable stations that showed old movies without commercials. She watched an MGM black-

and-white movie from the forties, one with Mickey Rooney and Judy Garland. The images moved and gyrated in front of her with no logical connection or narrative that she could figure out.

Hours later, Michael returned. Taylor was about to go back to bed.

"Where've you been?" she asked. "I was starting to get worried."

He seemed quiet, subdued. "I had some last-minute business to take care of."

There was a long silence, before Taylor said: "Last-minute business on a Sunday?"

"I had a couple of things to take care of and I hit an ATM for some extra cash."

"Oh," she said blankly. "Okay."

"Have you packed?"

"No, I thought I'd go get started. How long will we be down there?"

"I made a reservation at the Crowne Plaza for two nights, with the option to extend. A couple of days, we should know which way this is going."

Taylor nodded. "Okay. Guess I'll go pack."

She hated herself for feeling this way, this tired, this passive. She realized as she climbed the steps that this was just the way she felt when Jack died. Then it had taken her months to feel awake and alive again. Maybe a year . . .

But this was different. Michael needed her; Joan needed her. She was an adult with responsibilities and obligations. She had to pull herself together. She had to find a way out of this, to become focused and useful and productive again.

She took a deep breath and began packing.

The flight to Nashville left LaGuardia at seven-twenty A.M. She and Michael got up at four—after neither of them having slept much—then hailed a cab and arrived at the airport around five forty-five. They got through security much faster than expected and sat in a crowded airport fast-food place and ate tasteless bagels washed down with tepid coffee. It didn't matter anyway; she hadn't really tasted anything in a week.

Taylor had never learned the elusive art of sleeping on airplanes. This flight was no exception. She was so tired, her eyes burned, her muscles ached as she sat there crammed into the tiny seat. To make matters worse, she'd gotten the middle seat, squeezed in between Michael on the window and some guy in a black cowboy hat, tight jeans, and T-shirt, who was badly in need of a shave and shower. Michael shifted in the seat and curled toward the window and drifted off. The cowboy tried to chat her up, but had sense enough to realize after a few cold looks that she wasn't in the mood.

She lost track of time, her mind a blank, until the plane started to descend. Michael awoke abruptly, as if he couldn't remember where he was, then opened the shade over the window just as the plane banked steeply. Taylor leaned over and looked out the window. Below them, the rolling Tennessee hills seemed like blots of color, alternating between browns and greens and strange colors she didn't recognize. Then the jet passed over a sprawling lake, a dirty kind of murky mixture of brown and green that looked like it had been sprayed across the landscape palette in a completely haphazard fashion.

Taylor had never been to Nashville before, had never spent much time in the South. She felt her stomach knotting at the thought that this strange and foreign place held her life in its hands.

The jet leveled out and descended rapidly. Taylor felt queasy as the plane approached the runway, then lifted its nose in the flare and settled down onto the concrete with a thump. Then it seemed to taxi forever before finally pulling to a stop at the gate. Taylor left the plane first, with Michael a few people behind her. He wore a pair of dark sunglasses and kept his head down.

The Nashville airport was bigger than she expected, was newer and more modern, and not very crowded. Taylor looked around, caught Michael's eye, and then began walking down the concourse to the baggage claim area by herself. Taylor looked around nervously and was relieved to find there were no reporters to be seen anywhere. They'd booked this flight at the last minute, and as part of the negotiation with the district attorney for Michael's surrender, no word had been leaked of their arrival.

Taylor walked between a row of uniformed guards out of the secure area. In the waiting area just in front of the security checkpoint, a young woman in black trousers and a white dress shirt held a small sign with the words "Ms. Robinson" scrawled on it.

Taylor walked up to the young woman. "I'm Taylor Robinson," she said quietly.

The woman smiled at her. "Hi, I'm Carey. I work for Mr. Talmadge."

Michael walked up to them, and the three of them stepped out of the way of the disembarking passengers, off in a corner behind a bank of newspaper vending machines.

"Looks like we made it," Michael observed.

"I've kept my eyes open," the young woman said. "I haven't seen anyone. And there aren't even any news vans in the parking lot."

"Let's get out of here as quick as we can," Michael said. "What's the plan?"

The three began walking down the concourse as casually as possible, with Carey between the two of them.

"We head downtown," she said. "I drop you off at Mr. Talmadge's office and you'll go straight up to him. Then I'll take Ms. Robinson to your hotel and check the two of you in. Mr. Talmadge reserved the room in his own name and put it on his credit card. You're booked in as Mr. and Mrs. Jackson of Seattle, Washington."

Michael smiled. "You ever think we'd get married in Nashville, Tennessee?"

Taylor turned to him. "Not funny."

"Then I'll bring Ms. Robinson back to the office, pick you and Mr. Talmadge up, and we'll head for the police station."

"Will there be lots of news people there?" Taylor asked.

The young woman turned and looked at her. "Yes, ma'am,"

she said politely. "Lots of them. You might want to prepare yourself."

The black Lincoln Town Car sped out of the airport and onto the dense traffic of Interstate 40 West into downtown Nashville. As Carey maneuvered the big car in and out of the herd of cars, rarely dropping below seventy miles an hour, sometimes inches off the bumper of the car in front of her, Taylor found herself growing increasingly nervous.

The traffic slowed as they neared a construction zone. Cars that had been racing along at breakneck speed slammed brakes and were suddenly inching through at barely walking speed. Taylor's stomach lurched. She turned to Michael, saw him blanch as well, then smiled and reached across the backseat and took his hand.

"This all feels so strange," she said.

Michael turned back to her. "It *is* so strange."

Minutes later, they got through the construction and were back up to eighty. Then Carey raced across three lanes of traffic, worked her way into a long line of cars, then slammed on her brakes as they hit the exit ramp.

"Excuse me," Michael asked from the backseat.

"Yes, sir?"

"Does *everybody* drive like a bat out of hell here?"

Carey turned and smiled. "Yes, sir," she said. "State law requires it."

The Lincoln worked its way into the downtown area, through a maze of streets and what seemed to Taylor like traffic at least as thick as Manhattan's. Carey pulled the car up to a building on Third Avenue at the top of a long hill and double-parked.

"This is where Mr. Talmadge's offices are," she said. "Go up to the tenth floor. Roberta, the receptionist, knows you're coming. She'll take you straight back."

"Okay," Michael said. He turned to Taylor. "You'll be back soon?"

Taylor nodded. "Yes, as quick as we can."

Michael hesitated for a moment, as if unsure of what to say next. "I'll miss you," he said.

Taylor smiled, leaned over, and kissed him lightly on the cheek. "I'll miss you, too. But we'll be back in a few minutes. As soon as I check in."

Michael squeezed her hand, then pushed the car door open and stepped out onto the sidewalk.

As the Lincoln pulled away from the curb, the young woman turned and faced Taylor. "Ma'am, while we're taking care of this, is there anything else I can do for you? Anything else you need?"

"Make this all go away," Taylor answered.

Carey smiled and faced forward. "If I could, I'd be glad to. I can't. But if there's anyone that can make this go away, it's Wes Talmadge. He's the best."

Taylor eyed her. "Really? Tell me, how do you know?"

"Because," Carey replied, "he's my father."

Just under two hours later, Taylor and Carey in the front seat, with Wesley Talmadge and Michael in the backseat, drove around Capitol Hill and approached the Metropolitan Nashville Criminal Justice Center from the back way, through side streets. While the area around James Robertson Parkway was new and well-groomed, home to government buildings and high-rises, the area behind the hill and the parkway seemed considerably more run-down. Every other building sign, Taylor thought, seemed to be for a bail bonding agency.

As they turned a corner, Taylor saw the road ahead was blocked with a mob of reporters, cameramen, news vans, and trucks of every type, with microwave towers jutting into the sky for live feeds.

"Jesus," she muttered. "Look at that."

Wesley Talmadge, a thin, graying man in a dark suit, spoke up from the backseat. "You two know the drill, right? Neither of you says a word."

"Don't worry," Michael said. "I wouldn't know what the hell to say anyway. I've never seen anything like that."

Carey expertly slowed the car to a crawl and worked her way as close to the police station as possible, then pulled the car to the curb and stopped it. Immediately, the throng descended on them. Taylor watched as a blur of bodies, microphones, video cameras, cables, all piled in around the car. Michael got out of the right-hand side of the car, next to the curb, while Talmadge got out of the left and quickly worked his way behind the car and back around to stand next to Michael.

Taylor pushed out the passenger's side door as well, and edged up to Michael.

"Mr. Schiftmann!" a voice cried. "Mr. Schiftmann, how do you—"

"Mr. Schiftmann!" another voice yelled. "Are you guilty?"

"How do you plan to plead?"

Taylor felt like they'd been descended upon by a pack of wolves. Someone shoved her back against the car and her shoe buckled under her, twisting her ankle. Michael shifted to help her, then he got pushed back. Talmadge held up his arms and motioned the crowd away.

"Please," he said loudly, firmly. "Please step back."

"Can you give us a statement?" a voice in the back of the herd yelled.

"My client," Talmadge said forcefully, pausing to give the reporters time to point their microphones in his direction, "will have no statement at this time. However, he proclaims his innocence and looks forward to getting his day in court at the earliest possible time so he can prove these scurrilous and unfounded accusations false. That's all for now, folks. We've got an appointment to keep."

The crowd seemed to part as Talmadge stepped forward into them. Michael reached back, took Taylor's hand, and pulled her along behind him. Taylor kept her head down, trying not to make eye contact with anyone, struggling to stay connected to Michael. As they approached the entrance to the building, the crowd seemed to divide even further. Suddenly Michael stopped, and Taylor almost bumped into him.

She raised her head and saw a man standing in front of them wearing a gray suit and white shirt, with a blue-striped tie. His hair was cut short and his face was deeply lined. Taylor thought he looked tired as he stepped forward and faced them. Behind him, four uniformed police officers stood close by, watching, along with a young Hispanic woman who seemed to be staring especially hard at them.

"Mr. Schiftmann?" the man asked as he approached. Everything around them seemed to quiet. Taylor heard traffic noise in the distance and thought she heard the whirring of video cameras.

Michael nodded. "Yes."

"Are you Mr. Michael Schiftmann?"

Again, Michael's head went up and down. "Yes, that's me."

"I'm Detective Gilley of the Metro Nashville Police Department's Murder Squad. I have a warrant for your arrest."

Gilley turned and motioned to one of the uniforms, who approached Michael with a pair of open handcuffs. The officer stepped up to Michael, gently took him by the elbow, and pulled one hand behind his back. Michael let go of Taylor's hand with his left and held it behind him.

"Are the handcuffs necessary?" Michael asked.

"Yes, sir, it's standard procedure," Gilley answered. "Mr. Schiftmann, you have the right to remain silent. Anything you say can and will be used against you in a court of law. You have the right to an attorney . . ."

As the detective droned on, Taylor felt the world start to spin. She fought to hold on. She looked over at Talmadge, who stood next to his client, stone-faced, serious. He looked over at her, nodded his head almost imperceptibly, and winked.

"Do you understand these rights as I have explained them to you?" Gilley asked.

"Yes."

"Then come with me, sir."

Michael turned and faced Taylor. "You okay?"

Taylor took a deep breath and held it for just a moment, trying to clear her head, to get oxygen to her brain. "Yes, I'm fine. You take care, and I'll see you in a few hours."

Michael leaned over, kissed her quickly. As if he were going off to work or a dentist's appointment or to run a casual errand . . .

"We'll call on the mobile when we know the time for the

arraignment," Talmadge said as he got in step behind Michael and the officers.

Taylor was left alone in the middle of the pack. She suddenly felt frightened, isolated.

"May I ask you a question, please?" someone shouted. A microphone on a long boom pole suddenly appeared in front of her face. She felt someone grab her elbow and jerked around, startled.

It was Carey. She had a firm grip on Taylor's arm. "C'mon," she said. "Let's get you out of here."

CHAPTER 29

Thursday morning, six weeks later, Manhattan

The war began in earnest the afternoon of Michael's arrest.

The DA's press conference and the arrest warrant had been the first skirmish. They fired a few shots, just to test the enemy's resolve. Talmadge fired back with just enough force to show that he wasn't going to be pushed around when he openly announced Michael Schiftmann was looking forward to his day in court.

The arraignment was the first big battle. District Attorney Collier demanded no bail. Talmadge countered with a demand for release-on-recognizance. Collier countered again with an eight-figure bail request. Talmadge fired back with a demand for minimal bail.

In the end, Criminal Court Judge Harry Forsythe settled on a million-and-a-half bail. Michael put up one hundred thousand dollars and the deed to his Palm Beach condo. Forsythe also, as Steinberg predicted, confiscated Michael's passport.

Then they went home.

Two days later, the New York City police executed a search warrant requiring Michael to provide DNA samples for forensic purposes. An enraged Michael wanted to fight the search warrant, but Abe Steinberg convinced him there was no point. In Steinberg's office, a medical technician pulled a dozen hairs from Michael's head, swabbed the inside of his mouth with a cotton swab, and did a blood draw. The evidence was collected and secured, then shipped off to the lab at the Tennessee Bureau of Investigation in Nashville.

Meanwhile, in Nashville, Talmadge filed a motion for discovery. Thirty days later, a large file was delivered to his office. He went through the file sheet by sheet, paragraph by paragraph, then caught the next plane to New York.

Abe Steinberg met him in the lobby and shook hands with his old friend and protégé. "How are you, Wes?" he asked, laying his left hand on Talmadge's shoulder.

"Good, Abe, good."

"How was the flight?"

Talmadge smiled. "Food's pretty good on first-class, even these days."

Steinberg smiled back at him. "C'mon, our boy's back in my office already."

Talmadge followed as Steinberg led the way down the hall. "How's he holding up?" he asked.

Steinberg shrugged. "Hard to tell. I've seen better, but then again, I've seen worse."

The two walked down a long hallway to a suite of offices occupied by the most senior partners in the firm. Steinberg stopped as they entered the suite and faced Talmadge.

"Before we go in," he said, "I want to know. What's it look like?"

"Well, as Spencer Tracy once said of Katharine Hepburn, 'There ain't much meat on her, but what there is is *cherce*.'"

Steinberg stared for a moment. "Okay," he said. "Let's go."

The two entered Steinberg's office. Michael rose from the sofa as they walked in. Steinberg walked around and sat at his desk, with Talmadge taking one of the chairs as Michael sat back down.

"Good morning, Mr. Schiftmann," Talmadge said. "How are you?"

"I'm fine," Michael answered nervously, "and please, it's Michael."

Talmadge nodded. "Okay, Michael."

"Wes has the material the Davidson County district attorney's office returned to us in reply to the discovery motions," Steinberg said. "By law, the prosecution is obliged to provide a defendant with all the evidence against him or any exculpatory evidence prior to any trial or consideration. Our job at this point is to evaluate the evidence and to figure out how to best answer it in order to place in the minds of the jurors reasonable doubt."

"If we can do that, then there's every reason to expect a favorable verdict if this ever does, in fact, go to trial," Talmadge added.

"Is there a chance we can head this off before trial?" Michael asked. "Can we make this go away without a trial?"

Talmadge leaned back on the sofa. "Well, that's problematic. Of course, we'll try. The list of motions that we'll file during this phase of the process reads almost twenty typed pages. We'll challenge everything from the jurisdiction of the court to the makeup of the grand jury. We'll move to suppress everything they throw at us. But in the real world, unless there's been some incredible screwup on the part of the DA, you don't get very far most of the time.

"And in one sense, the district attorney has taken an incredible chance by announcing that he's going to seek the death penalty. He's essentially bet the rent money on the outcome of this. Now, I know Bob Collier pretty well, and he's not a blowhard and he's not a grandstander. The fact that he's even going for the death penalty means he thinks he's got a good case. And as a rule, if you're defending a capital case and it actually goes to trial, you're in trouble before it even starts."

Michael stared at the floor for a moment, then looked back up quickly. "That's as a rule. But let's talk specifics."

"Okay," Talmadge said, opening his briefcase. "Let's look at what they've got. I've taken the liberty of summarizing it for the purposes of our conversation so we don't have to spend hours going over it in detail."

He pulled out a stack of papers and thumbed through them, then pulled out a single sheet. "First, they've got the evidence of the crime scene. This was reported in the media as one of the bloodiest, goriest murder scenes to come down the pike in a long time, and from the photos I saw, they were right."

"Any chance we can get those photos suppressed?" Steinberg asked.

Talmadge nodded. "A chance we'll get at least the worst ones suppressed," he said. "They're clearly prejudicial. But all of them? I doubt it."

"Then what?" Michael asked.

"The photos in and of themselves only prove there was a crime committed. They don't prove you did it."

Michael nodded quickly. "Okay. Good."

"Then we've got the usual. The autopsy reports, the forensic evidence. The good news, to get to the bottom line, is this: They've got nothing that explicitly places you at the crime scene, at least not yet."

"Not yet?" Steinberg demanded.

Talmadge returned. "The results of the DNA swabs they took won't be in from the lab for at least another week or two."

"And the bad news?" Michael asked.

"They've also got nothing that explicitly proves you weren't there."

A tense silence followed as Michael sat there, trying to take everything in.

"Yes," Talmadge said after a few moments. "And then we move on. They've got credit card receipts, rental car and hotel receipts, restaurant receipts, all of which place you in Nashville the night of the murders. But so what? We concede that. You were doing a book signing. It was in the newspaper. But then we go on from there. The police have questioned witnesses at the hotel who say you left the hotel about ten that Friday night and didn't return until almost two in the morning. Which places you outside the hotel during the time the murders were committed."

"I couldn't sleep," Michael said. "I never can after a book signing. I went out, hit a couple of bars, had a few drinks."

"Fair enough," Talmadge said. "You try and remember what bars you hit and we'll try to find people who can place you there."

Michael nodded. "I'll start working on it."

"But then we come to the one thing they've got that might be problematic. Several days after the murder, a bum found a bunch of bloody clothes, a pair of latex gloves, couple other things in a Dumpster about three miles or so from the murder scene. The blood on the stuff was traced to the murder scene, and they've positively typed it to the two victims."

Michael shrugged. "So?"

"So," Talmadge continued, "they found the rental car you had the night you were in Nashville. They tracked it down to New Orleans, and when they examined it, they found traces of blood in the trunk. When they ran tests on the samples, they matched the blood on both the bloody garbage stuff and the murder scene."

"But that's impossible!" Michael said loudly. "That's crazy. No wait, it's not impossible, it's bloody fucking convenient. How much trouble does it take to dab a blood sample on a piece of carpet that you already know matches the victims into a car?"

"Maybe," Talmadge said. "It's certainly something we can look into."

"And how many people," Steinberg broke in, "had rented that car in the time between when Michael had it and how long it took them to find it?"

"Yeah, how long did it take them to find it?"

Talmadge shuffled through some papers. "Just a few days shy of two months."

"Two months," Michael spewed. "How many people rent a car in two months? It's crazy. They can't tie me to it."

"It's weak. And we can find out how many other people had rented that car. If we can break the causal link they're trying to establish in that fashion, then we've made a big dent in their case."

"What else have they got?" Steinberg asked.

"Of substance? Not much. Some pretty wild theories." Talmadge faced Michael and looked directly at him. "They're going to produce a witness who says that the plots to your books are pretty similar to some other murders that have occurred around the country. I think they're going to try and convince the jury that you're some kind of serial killer or something like that."

"That's insane," Michael said. "I've already explained those similarities. I've been researching a series of murders for years and using the material in my books."

"In any case," Steinberg offered, "that's the sort of testimony that we're never going to let them bring into court. No judge with half a brain is going to allow that kind of material in and run the risk of being overturned on appeal. We'll get that suppressed easily."

Talmadge nodded. "I don't think it's much of a threat. But the blood evidence is another matter. And, of course, the results of the DNA tests are absolutely crucial."

"I can tell you right now, there's nothing there for them to find," Michael said.

"Then we'll proceed on that premise," Steinberg said. "But let's also assume, for the sake of argument, that the worst-case scenario will prevail and we'll go to trial. What's the next step?"

Talmadge sighed. "We have to be prepared for that, although I hope we can cut them off at that pass. But we have to start putting the team together."

"Team?" Michael asked.

Talmadge nodded. "We'll need to hire a jury consultant. I know the best one in the business. She's been on *60 Minutes*, Court TV, the whole package. She'll start putting together what we need from a jury. And keep in mind, there's every good reason to think that while we probably won't get a change of venue, and maybe don't even want one, that we'll wind up going out of county to get a jury. Which means Jackson, Memphis, maybe Knoxville. And what we look for will change depending on where we go. Getting a death-qualified jury is a challenge. We want a good one."

"I don't know exactly what that means, but I'll go along," Michael said wearily.

"And then we'll need a good private investigator on scene in Nashville to go over everything the police have done and then some. I've worked with a guy in Nashville before, name's Denton, who's very good and very discreet.

He knows the cops, has connections inside the department, and is very thorough. And one other good thing: For some reason or other, he's willing to work cheap."

Michael smiled. "Well, so far he's the only son of a bitch who is."

"And then we'll want a forensic pathologist to go over the autopsy, from one end to the other. And also a crime-scene expert. Police often, more often than you'd think, mishandle evidence in ways that would shock you. If we can catch them breaking the rules, then we can swat them down like a housefly. After all, police screwups are basically how O. J. was acquitted."

Michael moaned. "Please don't mention his case in the same breath with mine."

"Why not?" Steinberg asked, smiling. "He's walking around swinging a nine iron. Nothing wrong with that."

"And then we'll have to go after the DNA analysis as well. We need to have the best people we can find to challenge the results if they turn against us. Obviously, if they come out in our favor, we'll punt on that. But I want them ready."

"I know Barry Scheck," Steinberg said. "I'll call him today and get a referral."

"Good. And we might even think about bringing in a psych guy."

"Psych guy?" Michael asked.

"Yeah, a psychiatrist who's an expert in this sort of crime and in profiling these sorts of murderers. If we can put him up on the stand and he testifies there's no way you are even psychologically equipped to do this kind of violence, that will carry some weight."

Michael sighed. "Okay, if you think we need it."

"We'll hold off on that decision, but keep it on the back burner. Now the next step," Talmadge explained, "is the settlement date. The judge has scheduled a hearing not quite ninety days out. Now depending on what happens with the DNA tests, we'll try to have the charges against you dismissed. The DA may try to broker a lesser charge, but I doubt it."

"I wouldn't take the deal anyway," Michael said. "I won't plead out on this."

"Then another sixty days or so later, we'll have a pretrial conference. At that point, the judge will ask if everybody's good to go. If everything's prepared, that's when we'll set a trial date. That's going to be complicated, though, since a capital trial like this is going to be long and involved. Everybody will have to clear a huge hole in their calendar."

"How long will the trial itself take?"

Talmadge considered for a moment before speaking. "A good month, six weeks," he said.

"Jesus," Michael said. "So we're looking at a good six months or so before we go to trial, and then six weeks or so after that before we know."

"That's about it."

"And the meter will be running the whole time," Michael said.

Talmadge shrugged. "Cases like this are expensive to defend. I'm sorry."

"I guess I need to get back to my laptop and start typing," Michael said. "I've got a lot of books to write if I'm going to keep you guys in the style you've become accustomed to."

"There's one other duck we need to get in order," Talmadge said. He looked over at Steinberg, who nodded at him.

"What?" Michael asked.

Talmadge looked back at Michael. "The state of Tennessee employs what's called a bifurcated trial system. In other words, a two-phase trial. The first phase is the guilt or innocence stage. We have every reason to believe you'll be acquitted of this if it gets that far, but we can't assume it. To protect you, we need a mitigator for the penalty phase."

"A what?" Michael asked.

"A mitigator, an attorney who specializes in convincing a jury that there are reasons why even if you've been found guilty, you don't deserve to die."

This time the silence between them was painfully leaden. Finally, Michael spoke in a voice so soft Steinberg could barely hear him.

"You know, if I'm found guilty of this, I'd almost rather be put to death. I don't think I can stand prison. I just don't think I could stand it."

"Everybody says that at first," Talmadge offered. "But when the reality hits, you realize that even a life in prison is still life."

Michael shook his head. "Not for me," he said. "Not for me."

PART III

THE TRIAL

CHAPTER 30

Monday morning, eight months later, Nashville

Taylor Robinson rolled over in the oversize hotel bed and turned to the windows. The covers were bunched around her, knotted up, her legs cramped under them. She opened her eyes and tried to focus on the window.

Is the sun even up yet?

She rolled back over and kicked the covers off, then stood up shakily beside the bed. Her head hurt, her eyes burning from lack of sleep. If she'd slept at all, it had been only in the last couple of hours. She pulled the heavy drapery aside and squinted at the light filtering through the gauzy thin sheer that covered the window. She looked over at the clock.

Six-fifteen. She groaned and pulled the curtain aside, then stared out over downtown Nashville. The city was just beginning to awaken on a cold but clear late-January morning, the sun looming large and vibrant in the east. From the eighteenth floor, she felt detached from the city, as if somehow she wasn't really here.

Sleep. All she wanted was sleep.

She walked into the bathroom and splashed some water on her face, then brushed her teeth to get the stale taste out of her mouth. She pulled her robe around her, then sat on the edge of the bed. She typed in a toll-free number from memory, then the twelve numbers of her calling card. Then she dialed Brett Silverman's home phone.

Brett answered on the fifth ring, barely ahead of the answering machine, her voice thick and groggy.

"Yeah?" she grumbled.

"Oh, God, you're still asleep. I'm so sorry. I figured with the time difference—"

"Don't worry about it," Brett mumbled. "The clock was going off in a few anyway."

"I'm sorry," Taylor said again.

Brett cleared her throat, then spoke again. "How are you?"

"Tired. I don't think I slept at all last night."

"Where's Michael?"

"I guess he's still in his room," Taylor answered.

"*His* room?" Brett asked.

Taylor felt her shoulders knotting up. "We took separate rooms. I know, it's kind of weird. But he stays up all night anyway. And the way I'm sleeping these days, it would have been impossible for me to get any rest."

"Darling," Brett said, drawing out the word, "why did you even go down there? This can't be good for you."

"What am I supposed to do?" Taylor asked. "We're engaged. He's my client and my fiancé. I have to support him."

"Even though it's cost you twenty pounds that you really didn't have to lose?" Brett said. "You're skin and bones, girl. God, I wish I could give you twenty of mine."

"They'll come back. When this is all over."

Taylor sat there for a moment, silently. The silence stretched into awkwardness, and she felt silly for calling her best friend so early.

"At this point, I'm more worried about you than I am Michael," Brett said. "Whatever's going to happen to him is going to happen. I don't want you to go down in the process."

"I'm okay," she said. "I just wish this was all over."

"When do you have to be in court?"

"Nine. A little less than three hours."

"You're going to eat something?" Brett scolded. "You're going to take care of yourself?"

Taylor nodded. "Yes. I'll be all right. I think I just wanted to hear your voice. You've really been a big help these last few months."

Taylor heard Brett let loose a long sigh. "It's been the weirdest fucking eight months I've ever been through. I've always wanted to have a real, for-true *New York Times* best-selling author. I just never imagined him going on *Larry King Live* to announce that he wasn't a serial killer."

"This is crazy," Taylor said. "Surely a jury's going to see how crazy this is."

"Yeah, for sure. Will you call me later?"

"I'll have my cell phone. I'll call you every break I can."

"Good, use my mobile number, too. Keep me apprised. Part of me wishes I could watch it on TV. Part of me is glad I can't."

"Me, too," Taylor agreed. "I was actually relieved when the judge banned TV cameras."

"Taylor," Brett said. "This is going to be okay. Whichever way it goes, you're going to survive this. Okay? Promise me?"

Taylor smiled. "Okay," she said. "Promise."

Carey picked up Taylor and Michael at the hotel and drove them silently to the Davidson County Courthouse. They avoided the news vans and the waiting reporters at the main entrance by using an entrance on the river side of the building.

Carey escorted them up to the third floor of the Davidson County Courthouse, where Talmadge and two other men in suits, carrying heavy briefcases, waited for them.

"There's a small conference room down here we can use," Talmadge said. "We've got about ten minutes before we kick off."

Michael and Taylor followed them to a narrow doorway off the main hallway. One of Talmadge's assistants held the door open.

"Should I wait out here?" Taylor asked.

"No," Michael said. "I want you with me, if that's okay."

Talmadge nodded solemnly. Inside the room, he turned and faced Michael. "You know my assistants, Jim McCain and Mark Hoffman, right?"

Michael nodded. "Yes, we met a couple of months ago."

"Jim, Mark, this is Taylor Robinson, Michael's fiancée and literary agent."

The two men nodded quickly. "Pleased to meet you," Taylor said quietly.

"We don't have a lot of time, Michael," Talmadge said. "I just want to go over a few last things with you. First, do your best not to react to anything the prosecutor or anyone else says. If you need to say something to me, whisper it very quietly or scribble it down on a legal pad. You don't have to say anything out loud, and I don't want you to. Just stay calm, look professional, and let us handle this. You good with that?"

Michael smiled, a look of confidence on his face. "I'm fine, Wes. I'm ready to go."

"Good. So are we. Now when we get in there, the judge will ask if there are any last-minute motions or questions. We won't have anything and the DA probably won't, either. Then the judge will seat the jury and we're on our way. The DA will start with an opening statement. As we've already agreed, we're going to hold off on our opening statement until the prosecution rests. We know what we're up against and we're ready for it. Let's just get our heads in the right places, okay? Everybody with me on that?"

Talmadge looked around the room. Both his assistants nodded, then Michael turned to Taylor. "You okay?"

"Yes. Yes, I'm okay. A little nervous, but I'll be fine."

"Outstanding," Talmadge said. "We're good to go."

They exited the room and walked down the long, cavernous marble-floored hall of the Davidson County Courthouse. Taylor expected to have to walk through a throng, but surprisingly, there were few other people in the hallway. As they approached the security checkpoint that barred access to the two massive wooden doors of the courtroom, Taylor saw a line of perhaps ten people waiting to be screened. She looked nervously at her watch. It was two minutes until nine.

Time seemed to drag. She fought the sense that this was

unreal, a dream that wasn't really happening. Her stomach knotted, and she felt, briefly, the urge to scream.

And then she was at the security checkpoint, handing her bag to a female officer and stepping gingerly through the large frame of the metal detector. She waited at the heavy wooden doors for Michael and the rest to get through, then grabbed the handle of the door and pulled.

The courtroom was packed. A murmur went up as she walked in, followed by Michael and the team of lawyers. She stopped, and a court officer nodded to her, then motioned toward the far side of the courtroom. She stepped aside as Michael entered the courtroom, then followed him around the edge of the audience and over to the defense table near the large windows. The courtroom seemed smaller than she expected. Cramped, in fact. But the ceiling was easily twenty feet above their heads, giving the room a cavernous feel. The air inside was still, almost stale, and the temperature was already rising from the dozens of bodies packed onto the hard wooden seats.

Michael, Wesley Talmadge, and the two assistant lawyers stepped through a wooden gate and entered the area in front of the bench. They started unloading their briefcases as Wesley pointed to an empty space on the bench right behind their table. Taylor eased in past four people and sat in the middle, placing her purse on the floor next to her foot.

She looked over to her right, where a tall, graying man and a younger woman assistant already sat with files and notepads piled in front of them. The man looked tired and a little rumpled, Taylor thought. The young woman seemed well-scrubbed and bright, almost eager.

Suddenly the door to the right of the elevated judge's bench opened and an elderly man in a court officer's uniform stepped through. "All rise," he said loudly.

A rustle echoed through the courtroom as everyone shuffled to his feet. "Davidson County Criminal Court Division Four," the court officer continued, "of the Twentieth Judicial District of the State of Tennessee is now in session, the Honorable Judge Harry Forsythe presiding. God save this honorable court, the State of Tennessee, and these United States of America."

A large man with a massive head, a long shock of graying hair down over a broad forehead, and large rheumy eyes stepped quickly through the doorway and took the three steps up to the bench quickly. He placed a bound portfolio on the bench, then arranged his robes and sat down in a large leather chair.

"Good morning, ladies and gentlemen," he announced in a sonorous voice that clearly was used to command. "We have quite a crowd in here this morning. I want to remind you all that I expect proper courtroom decorum as we get this trial under way. I also want to remind you that there are no cameras or recording devices of any kind allowed in this courtroom.

"And," he added, smiling out over the crowd, "if I hear a cell phone go off in this room, it belongs to me. Believe me, I have quite a little collection of them. Couple of shoeboxes full, in fact. And for those of you with the fancy vibrate feature, if I see a cell phone answered in this room, the same rule applies."

Taylor leaned down, stuck her hand in her purse, and pulled out her phone. She flipped it open, powered it down, then sat back up.

"Madame Clerk, do we have the proper forms completed for all pleadings and counsel of record?"

"Yes, Your Honor," a slim woman said from a desk in front of the bench.

"Is counsel present?" Forsythe asked, his voice booming.

The lawyers rose. "Yes, Your Honor," the tall man at the prosecutor's table said. "District Attorney General T. Robert Collier for the state, with Assistant General Jane Sparks in assistance."

"Wesley Talmadge for the defense, Your Honor, with Jim McCain and Mark Hoffman in assistance."

"Very good," Forsythe announced. "Are there any last-minute motions or pleadings before we get going?"

"Nothing for the state, Your Honor."

"Nothing for the defense, Your Honor."

"Then we're ready to go. Bailiff, seat the jury." The lawyers all sat back down.

Taylor took a deep breath, held it for a moment, then let it out slowly, trying to lessen the tension in her abdomen. She'd forced herself to eat a bagel earlier, just to have something in her stomach. It tasted like cardboard. Her stomach rumbled. She hoped no one heard it.

The jury filed in from a door to the judge's left. Taylor watched as the mixture of people, fourteen in all—twelve jurors and two alternates—took seats behind the jury box. She scanned the faces: eight men, six women. Ten whites and four blacks. Three clearly older, four in their twenties or perhaps early thirties, the rest somewhere in the middle.

How odd, she thought. *These are the people who can kill my fiancé.*

"Please be seated, ladies and gentlemen," the judge announced. "We're going to get started here in a few moments, but first I want to remind you of a couple of things. First, you are not to discuss this case among yourselves or with anyone else. You are not to form an opinion until all the evidence has been presented and I have instructed you in the law and given you your charge. You will be sequestered for the length of this trial, and during that time, you will read nothing of this case in the media, either in newspapers or magazines or on television. As you know, this trial has drawn a great deal of media attention. It is your responsibility as jurors and citizens to neither expose yourself to all this attention nor take any of it into any consideration. Does everyone understand this?"

The jurors shook their heads, almost in time with one another.

"During these proceedings," the judge continued, "you will be given an adequate number of breaks for meals and the necessities of nature. But if for any reason you need an extra or unscheduled break, simply make a motion to get the attention of the court officer and he will help you. You are not to talk among yourselves during the trial itself, although you may make notes as you see fit. You are also not to speak to any of the counsel, the defendant, or the witnesses during the course of these proceedings. If you have any questions or need any assistance with anything, just write a note and pass it along to the court officer, who will then give it to me. Does everyone understand this?"

Again the jurors nodded. Taylor tried hard not to stare at them. She looked over at the defense table. Michael sat stoically, not moving, his face revealing nothing, his black, pin-striped suit pressed and professional. A very expensive consultant had advised him on the clothes to wear during the trial, how to cut his hair, how to look in front of the jury.

"Finally, to briefly go over the procedure again, we will begin with the state making an opening statement. During this statement, the district attorney general will outline the case that the state intends to present before you. An opening statement is just that, ladies and gentlemen, a statement. It is not evidence. It is not to be taken by you as fact or construed as evidence. It is simply outlining the case the state intends to make. Then the defense can make an opening statement, although they are not required to. They can also defer their opening statement until the state has completed making its case before you. If they choose not to make a statement or to defer their statement, you are to draw no inferences or conclusions about that as to the defendant's innocence or guilt. You are to make those conclusions based solely on the evidence presented in this courtroom and on the charge I will give you as to the law."

Forsythe looked from the jury over to the defense table. "Does the defense wish to have a formal reading of the charges at this time?"

Talmadge rose quickly. "The defense waives formal reading of the charges, Your Honor."

"Very well. General Collier, you may proceed with your opening statement."

The tall man rose slowly and walked to a wooden podium in the center of the room. Taylor thought it odd that he had no notes, that he was apparently going to speak off the cuff. He walked with a slight stoop and seemed less imposing than when she had seen him on television.

But when he spoke, there was a firmness and an authority to his voice that was in sharp contrast to his tired demeanor. "Ladies and gentlemen of the jury," he began. "I'm Robert Collier, the district attorney general here in Nashville, and I'm not going to take up a lot of our time right now with an opening statement because I believe the facts of this case will speak for themselves. But before I do anything else, I want to thank you for your service as jurors. Jury service is one of our prime responsibilities as citizens of this great republic. We ask a lot of you as jurors. The fate of the defendant is in your hands. The victim's cry for justice is in your hands. And the state's responsibility to seek justice is in your hands as well.

"And that's a great responsibility. That's a heavy burden you bear. But it is one of the foundations of our society, as a civilized society, that when a crime is committed, justice must be sought. Some wrongs can never be righted, but a just and proper recompense to the victims and to society can only be found when those who commit great wrongs suffer a fair and just punishment for that wrong. Which is why we are here.

"Because on a cold and snowy—in fact, a freezing—Friday night last February, almost a year ago, two young, innocent women suffered a great wrong. Their lives were taken from them brutally, violently, and altogether too soon. They had their whole lives ahead of them. They were bright, beautiful young women just beginning their lives. They were working their way through college. They had parents and families who loved them. They had friends who loved them and have mourned their passing as a wound that can never be really healed.

"Their names were Sarah and Allison. Sarah Denise Burnham was nineteen years old. She was a sophomore down at Middle Tennessee State University where she was studying mass communications. Allison May Matthews was twenty-two. She was about to graduate from MTSU as well, with a degree in art history. Neither one of them had ever been in trouble before. They had good grades. They were close to their families. Allison attended a Baptist church close to the campus down there. Sarah hadn't been to church in a while, but she was raised by God-fearing parents."

Collier stepped out from behind the podium and paced back and forth slowly as he continued speaking. "But I don't want you to get the idea that Sarah and Allison were perfect. They were young and reckless and foolish, as many of us were when we were that age. Sarah and Allison had done something I wouldn't have wanted them to do, something that I would never have wanted my own daughter to do. Something their parents never knew about . . .

"They had gotten jobs working at a place down on Church Street here in Nashville, a place called Exotica Tans. This, ladies and gentlemen, is what is euphemistically referred to as an exotic tanning parlor, but what is, in fact, more commonly known as a massage parlor."

Collier paused to let this sink in. "Yes, a massage parlor. You may find that shocking. I certainly did, given the background of these two young girls. But as witnesses will testify before you very soon, Allison and Sarah were not the kinds of girls who typically worked in places like these. They were good girls who had foolishly gone astray in this one instance. Perhaps they could make more money this way than they could selling shoes in the mall. Perhaps they thought it was naughty and funny. Who knows?

"But one thing I do know, ladies and gentlemen, is that the place they were working was completely legal in the city of Nashville and the state of Tennessee. The owner of that business, as distasteful as we might think it, paid his taxes and his license fees and his rent. We may not like it, folks, but it's legal. And Sarah and Allison had a perfect right to be working there, as much as you and I might wish that they hadn't."

Collier paused here, as if studying the jury. Taylor could see he was trying to make eye contact with them, trying to reach them. She had thought initially that he seemed to be winging it.

Now she knew he wasn't. He knew exactly what he was doing.

"You're going to see some things here, ladies and gentlemen, and very soon, that are going to be hard for you to take in. For on that cold Friday night in February, someone—who we believe the evidence will show was the defendant, Michael Edward Schiftmann—entered Exotica Tans and murdered these two young girls. You're going to see pictures of what the murderer did to these two young girls, and they're going to be hard to look at. You're going to hear experts testify as to the extent of their wounds and how much they suffered before death mercifully took them out of their pain."

Collier turned and looked directly at the defense table, his stare hard and cold. Like stone, Taylor thought. A chill went through her as she watched the pallid man hold out a hand and point in Michael's direction, then turn back to the jury as his voice rose:

"And you're going to hear from a chain of witnesses, police officers, homicide investigators, forensic experts, and others who will trace the trail of Sarah's and Allison's blood from the place where they were brutally, mercilessly murdered to this man's front door. We will present to you a chain of events and evidence that will establish beyond any reasonable doubt or exception that the man sitting here before you now took the lives of these two young, intelligent, beautiful women."

Collier paused and took a breath, then lowered his voice and spoke calmly. "Now ladies and gentlemen, there are two kinds of evidence that you're going to see here. The first is direct evidence. That's the evidence given by eyewitnesses, experts, and others as to what they saw, what they did, what they personally can testify to from firsthand experience. The second kind of evidence is circumstantial evidence. This is evidence that requires us to examine it, and then deduce from what we see that something must have happened a certain way in order for what we just saw to be the way it is. This is evidence that requires us to make conclusions, draw inferences. This is evidence that forces us to think, to rely on our common sense, in order to discern the truth of something. If we come home from work and our spouse isn't there and the car isn't in the garage and the grocery list has been taken off the refrigerator door, then we deduce, or figure out, that our spouse has probably gone to the supermarket.

"Now in almost every criminal trial I've ever been involved in, the preponderance of evidence has been circumstantial, and this case is no exception. I'm going to tell you up front that we do not have a witness that places the defendant at the scene. No one saw the defendant kill Sarah and Allison. But we have other kinds of evidence that we will ask you to look at, and we believe and maintain that if you examine this evidence with a fair and open mind, you will conclude—as did we—that only one man could have committed these horrible deeds. Now I can't put words in my esteemed colleague's mouth as to what he's going to say to you when he gets up here, but defense attorneys often try and convince you that circumstantial evidence is somehow less valid than direct evidence. That you should discount what you see because there's no eyewitness to verify the results you conclude.

"Don't let them, ladies and gentlemen. Don't let them turn your eyes away from what you see and what you, with your intelligence and your common sense, have concluded must be the truth. You're good people, you're smart people, and you've taken on a tremendous responsibility. All the state can ask of you is that you use that common sense to give justice to Sarah and Allison, and to bring some peace and closure to their families and those who loved them."

Collier gazed at the jury for a few last moments. "Thank you," he said quietly, then turned and sat down at the prosecutor's table.

"Mr. Talmadge, are you prepared to deliver your opening statement at this time?" Forsythe asked.

Talmadge stood. "Your Honor, we're going to defer our opening statement until the state has concluded its case."

"Very well," Forsythe intoned. "General Collier, call your first witness."

CHAPTER 31

Monday afternoon, Nashville

Of all the things that had amazed her over the past year—from falling in love with Michael to seeing him become a major literary celebrity to watching the world explode around them as these insane charges went on and on—perhaps the most astonishing of all was the clinical detachment with which the morning had gone by.

For three hours nonstop, from the district attorney's opening statement until the judge declared a lunch break at twelve-thirty, witness after witness took the stand and related a series of events that should have horrified and repulsed everyone beyond description. Instead, the professional voices spoke quietly; the lawyers intoned with leaden heaviness; the jury watched attentively throughout most of the morning, with only a few eyes glazing over.

It was all Taylor could do to keep still. She wanted to scream, to jump up and yell: "Have you all lost your minds? *Look at him! He's normal, like you and me! You and me . . ."*

Her eyes burned from lack of sleep. She felt frustrated, desperate. Her skin crawled with invisible insects under her clothes, in her hair. She fought to keep still.

And the voices went on and on. The first police officer on the scene described the grisly scene in the detached, unemotional way he'd been taught in his report-writing classes at the academy. The first investigators on scene described how they cordoned everything off and began following accepted standard procedure—always accepted standard procedure—in their evidence collection, the samples, the bags, the labels, the sign-offs from one person to the next. The forensic examiner described the procedures for making a preliminary determination of cause of death, the estimates of time of death.

Explanations of algor mortis, rigor mortis, livor mortis . . . the singsong litany of death's sweet terms and verses. The clinical analysis and deconstruction of life gone from a mass of rotting tissue, the light gone, energy dissipated into the universe.

Taylor wanted to scream.

The hardest parts were the photographs. Somehow, detachment was easier to maintain when it was all just words. But the pictures, the blowups of the mutilated bodies, paraded in front of the jury—then and then alone did Taylor see a visceral reaction from the jury. Heads turned away, faces screwed up in winces . . .

A woman sobbed.

They took lunch at the City Club on Fourth Avenue, an exclusive, members-only club where Talmadge had a standing reservation five days a week. The two younger attorneys had rushed back to the office to research a couple of issues and to report back to the consultants who would soon be testifying for the defense. If they were lucky, they would grab a quick sandwich and a soda somewhere as Talmadge, his daughter Carey, Michael, and Taylor sat around a corner table with a gorgeous view of the city from twenty floors up. White-coated waiters brought them tall glasses of iced tea and expensive gourmet food Taylor couldn't bear to touch.

They talked little, the silence between them awkward, heavy. Talmadge described a little of the history of Nashville, of its incredible growth over the last twenty-five years from what had even in the seventies still felt like a small town to the churning, multicultural megalopolis it had become. Nashville had become a mini-Atlanta, Talmadge complained, as his daughter grinned at him, patronizing the old man.

Taylor stared at Michael, who seemed to be taking this all in stoically. Taylor estimated he'd said barely ten words all day. As they left the courthouse, through a gauntlet of television cameras, he'd not even taken her hand. He seemed off in his own world, shut down and removed from anyone or anything else.

Finally, Taylor couldn't take it any longer. "Wes," she said, interrupting a monologue about his long involvement in the movement to bring professional football to Nashville. "Where are we?"

"What?" Talmadge asked, confused.

"I mean," Taylor said, leaning forward over her plate, "where are we in this whole process? How did this morning go? I'm not an attorney. I've never done this before. How is it going? How bad does this all look?"

Michael turned to her, his face a blank mask.

Talmadge cleared his throat, then settled back in his chair. "Okay, this is how I read it. The initial part of a trial like this is always difficult. You see the crime scene, how awful it is. The evidence is gruesome, the pictures even more so. But this is the time when you have to keep your emotions in check. Yes, we're human. Yes, we can't help but react to this kind of horror. But we also have to keep our wits about us, our intellect intact. And looking at this from a legal point of view, an intellectual point of view, all they've done so far is prove that a crime was committed. They have presented no evidence that can tie Michael directly to any of this."

Taylor felt the tightness in her chest loosen just a bit, and she let out a long breath. "Okay, then it's not as bad as it looks."

"Of course not," Talmadge replied. Carey reached out and took Taylor's hand in hers.

"It's going to be fine," she said. "You're doing great. Just hang in there."

Taylor squeezed Carey's hand back, grateful for the touch, then turned to Michael. "You're so quiet," she said. "Isn't there anything you want to say?"

Michael's eyelids seemed heavy as he stared at her. "What can I say?" he asked after a moment. "Whatever's going to happen is going to happen. There's nothing we can do about it now except endure it."

He looked back down at his plate, staring at it as if it were some object from another planet that had landed on the table in front of him.

"Michael, are you okay?" Taylor asked quietly. "Do we need to get you something?"

"Like what?" he answered, not taking his eyes off his plate.

"Like I've been on antidepressants for six months. Maybe it's time you thought about it."

He jerked his head up and glared at her. "No," he said firmly. "Never."

Taylor shrugged, looked away.

Talmadge and his daughter looked on, uncomfortable.

A hotel desk clerk testified that Michael had checked into a Hampton Inn the afternoon of his book signing. Around five, he left the hotel and returned by nine, then had gone back out around ten-thirty. No one saw him return.

A clerk at the airport branch of a rental car agency testified Michael rented a car on Friday afternoon and returned it by eleven-thirty A.M. Saturday. He'd put forty-three miles on the odometer.

The manager from the Davis-Kidd bookstore established that Michael had indeed been in Nashville that Friday night in February and had signed books before a large and enthusiastic crowd.

Two more witnesses followed, all establishing facts of the case that were essentially self-evident. By three-thirty that afternoon, Taylor was struggling to keep her eyes open. She looked over and scanned the jury. Their eyes were beginning to wander as well. One man was scribbling something on a notepad. Another woman's head bobbed up and down on her shoulders as she fought to stay awake.

"You have to understand," Talmadge had said to them weeks earlier when they were in town for a conference, "a criminal trial is basically an eye-glazer. It's like being a life-guard; long stretches of tedium and boredom punctuated by moments of complete terror."

This, Taylor thought, as the afternoon wore on, *this is the tedious, boring part. Enjoy it.*

Hank Powell sat in the back of the courtroom as the testimony droned on all afternoon. Trying a homicide case was anything, he knew, but drama. It was tedious, dreary work, almost as dreary and tedious as investigating a homicide case.

But Hank wasn't bored. He was worried. He was worried because he knew the case against Michael Schiftmann was essentially circumstantial and weak. The DNA tests had come back from the lab inconclusive. Michael's DNA matched none of the samples left behind at the crime scene or on the bloodied clothes, or even in the trunk of the rental car.

The case was made even weaker by the fact that the jury would never hear the truth about Michael Schiftmann, the truth that the two girls murdered in Nashville were only the latest in a long string of murders that had taken place over the last five years. Collier had fought like hell to get the testimony of the old lady, the retired schoolteacher who'd figured all this out in the first place, admitted. But of course, he hadn't. Then when Collier tried to get the judge to allow Maria Chavez on the stand to testify how she'd tied all this together, Schiftmann's lawyers had thrown a conniption.

It had been a long shot, Powell knew. No judge would let a homicide investigator or anyone else on the stand offer as proof to one crime a supposition that others similar to it had been committed by the same person. He'd have to be convicted of the other crimes before that could be brought in, and even then, only in the sentencing phase.

But without that supposition, the evidence against Schiftmann—what there was of it—somehow looked weaker.

Not that it was hopeless, Hank thought. When the jury saw the chain of evidence that conclusively and inextricably linked Michael Schiftmann's rental car to the Exotica Tans murder scene, then the defense would have to do some serious shucking and jiving to get out of that.

Hank was relieved when Judge Forsythe called a halt to the trial at five-thirty that afternoon, with the prosecution's case probably half complete. The trial moved more quickly than anyone expected because the defense offered, in most cases, only a perfunctory cross-examination. Since nothing that detrimental to the defense had been presented yet, there seemed little point.

Hank had taken a room in the Doubletree Hotel on Fourth Avenue, just a few blocks from the courthouse. He'd decided that morning to leave his rental car and walk rather than struggle for parking. As he walked out of the courtroom, through the crowd of spectators and news crews, he felt like he was walking through a madhouse. The January sun had almost completely set, throwing a sulfurous orange glow over the western horizon that melded into the low-lying scud that filled the rest of the sky.

The air was cold, with a bite to it. Powell ducked his head, pulled his overcoat tightly around him, and worked his way through the crowd toward the sidewalk, grateful that no one would ever recognize him.

Back at the hotel, he loosened his tie, threw his jacket across the back of the sofa, and went down the hall to the ice machine. He came back and turned on the local news as he scooped up a glassful of ice. The NBC affiliate station was doing a live remote from the steps of the courthouse, with the young woman reporter with the long black hair and the fashionable red glasses speaking directly into the camera. Hank remembered her sitting in the courtroom a few rows up from him. He raised the volume on the television, then opened the hotel minibar, and pulled out a tiny bottle of vodka.

"The prosecution opened today," the young woman began, "with a series of witnesses who described in graphic and often hard-to-watch detail the murder scene at Exotica Tans on Church Street last February."

The station cut to the news film of that night as the reporter continued in voice-over. "Nineteen-year-old Sarah Denise

Burnham and twenty-two-year old Allison May Matthews were working that Friday night . . ."

Hank found himself not wanting to hear it all again. He muted the television, then opened the three-inch-high mini-bottle and poured the vodka over a tumbler of ice. He sat down in an overstuffed chair, took a long sip of the drink, and glanced at his watch—six-fifteen in Nashville, an hour later in upstate Vermont. Dinner should be over by now at the Butler School.

He picked up the phone, dialed a 1–800 number, then his calling card number, then a series of ten more numbers. *God*, he thought, *how do I remember all of it?*

Then his daughter, Jackie, answered, and he knew how he could keep all those numbers in his head. They were the numbers that got him to this voice.

"Hello?"

"Hi, baby."

"Daddy!" she said, excited. "How are you?"

"Fine, I'm in Nashville. Got in last night."

"Oh," she said, her voice becoming more serious, "you're at that trial. That murder trial. We saw a report today on CNN."

"Yeah, it's kind of a zoo."

"So how is it?"

"It's interesting. Sort of getting off to a slow start, but I think it'll speed up."

"Dads," Jackie said, "I thought you weren't going to go. I thought the guys in the front office didn't want you to."

"What gave you that idea?" Hank caught his image in the mirror across the room. He looked tired, he thought. And he missed Jackie. She'd only been back in school a week after Christmas vacation, and already he missed the hell out of her. It was going to be a long semester.

"I heard you talking in your office that day. You were talking to somebody on the phone. You sounded upset, like the guys upstairs were really giving you a hard time on this."

"Okay, pumpkin," he said after a moment. "You caught me. They didn't want me to go. I'm not testifying. I'm not an active investigator in this case. I've just acted in an advisory capacity on this, so my supervisor didn't think there was any point in my being here."

"So how'd you get there?" Jackie demanded.

"I took some personal time, vacation. I had it coming. And I'm footing the bill myself, although the hotel did give me the government discount."

"Daddy!" she said, exasperated. "I worry about you. Over the holidays, you looked exhausted the whole time."

"I did not," Hank shot back. "We had a great time. We had a wonderful Christmas."

"That's not what I meant. I meant you're overdoing it. You're working too hard and you've got too much crap to deal with."

"Hey, hey, watch the mouth there," Hank said, smiling. "Besides, I'm fine."

There was a long moment of silence, then Jackie spoke again. "Dads, be honest with me. How much trouble are you in at work?"

"Hmm," Hank said, wondering how candid to be. "Truth is, I'm dealing with a lot of crap right now. But not any more than I can handle."

"I hope not," Jackie said. "Oh, wait, Daddy, I've got to run. We've got a hall meeting at seven-fifteen."

"Okay, dear, I'll call you the next couple of days, okay? You stay warm up there."

"I love you," she said.

Hank grinned. "I love you, too. Take care."

There was a click on the other end of the line as Jackie hung up. Hank held the phone a moment, then placed it back on the cradle and took a long sip of the vodka.

"Not any more than I can handle," he whispered. "Hope I wasn't lying to her."

CHAPTER 32

Thursday afternoon, Nashville

"General Collier, anything on redirect?" Judge Forsythe asked.

Collier stood and faced the judge. "Nothing at this time, Your Honor, but we reserve the option to recall."

"So noted. The witness is excused," Forsythe instructed as Master Patrol Officer Deborah Greenwood stood up from the witness chair after describing how she had come to find the bloody clothes in a Dumpster on Charlotte Avenue. "General Collier, call your next witness."

"Your Honor, the state calls Detective Gary Gilley."

Taylor raised her hand to her forehead, then lowered her head a bit and rubbed her temples. She'd hoped the judge would call a recess, but he seemed relentless. He pressed the attorneys to move ahead with each witness, and if he thought they were dawdling, he jumped right in and got them refocused. If they rephrased a question or tried to ask the same question more than once, Forsythe was on them like a guard dog. He kept rigid control of his courtroom and the proceedings in it, and as a result, the trial had moved forward much faster than anyone had expected.

But it was still exhausting. Taylor felt more drained than she ever had before.

Detective Gilley, wearing a blue suit and a red power tie, his white shirt starched and his hair combed back neatly, took the witness stand and was sworn in. After the preliminaries, Jane Sparks stood and walked to the podium. Her voice was high and clear, with only a trace of the aristocratic accent commonly seen in educated Southern women of means.

"Detective Gilley, would you tell us your current assignment with the Metro Police Department, please."

"Yes, ma'am, I hold the rank of detective with the department and I'm currently assigned as a senior investigator with the Murder Squad."

"How long have you been with the police department?"

"Sixteen years."

"And how long with the Murder Squad?"

"Seven years. Before that I worked Vice for two years, was in Burglary for a year or so, and before that worked patrol."

"Were you called to Exotica Tans on Church Street the night of February fifth of last year?"

"Yes, ma'am, I was."

"And what function did you serve in the ensuing investigation of the two homicides?"

"I was the lead investigator."

"So you were in charge of the investigation."

"Yes, ma'am, reporting directly to Lieutenant Bransford."

"Detective Gilley," Sparks continued, "I want to draw your attention to a specific component of the investigation that occurred in the aftermath of the murders of Sarah and Allison. Did you at some point in this investigation endeavor to find the rental car that was—"

Talmadge shot up. "Objection, Your Honor, leading."

Forsythe nodded. "Sustained. Rephrase your question, General Sparks."

"Yes, Your Honor. Detective Gilley, in the investigation of the defendant's whereabouts while he was in Nashville during the times established by previous testimony, were you able to ascertain what mode of transportation the defendant employed?"

Gilley cracked a faint smile on the stand. "Yes, ma'am, we were."

"And what did you discover?"

"The defendant rented a car."

"Were you able to determine where he rented that car?"

"Yes ma'am, he rented the car from Hertz and he picked it up at the airport rental counter."

"And what kind of car did he rent?"

"A Lincoln Town Car."

Sparks nodded. "Okay, Detective Gilley. In the course of your investigation, were you able to determine the whereabouts of the Lincoln Town Car rented by the defendant."

"Yes, ma'am, we were. We requested that the Hertz people track the car down."

"And they found it?"

"Yes, ma'am."

"And where was it located, Detective?"

"It was located in the rental lot at the New Orleans International Airport."

"And what did you do then?"

"We requested that the Jefferson Parish Sheriff's Department impound the vehicle, which they did, and then they turned it over to the New Orleans Police Department, who held it for us until we could go down there and retrieve it."

"Did you ask the New Orleans Police Department to examine the car?"

"Well," Gilley hesitated. "We didn't exactly ask them to, but they gave the car a cursory examination anyway."

"And what were their findings?"

"Objection, Your Honor," Talmadge said, standing up. "Hearsay and calls for a conclusion."

Forsythe thought for a moment. "I'm going to allow some latitude on this one, Counselor. Overruled."

Talmadge sat back down.

"Answer the question," Forsythe ordered.

"In the trunk of the car, forensic examiners found what they believed to be a stain of some kind. They took a Hemident swab, which showed positive."

"And tell us, please, what a Hemident swab is."

"A Hemident swab is a simple test. It's a preliminary test for the presence of blood."

"In your expert opinion as a senior homicide investigator, is this a reliable test?"

Gilley nodded. "Yes, ma'am, for its limited purposes. It's a test designed to be used in the field in an on-site initial investigation. But it only detects the presence of blood. It doesn't tell you anything else. It doesn't even differentiate between human and animal blood."

"So the Hemident test doesn't type or identify blood."

"That's correct. But it did establish that blood of some kind was present in the trunk of the car."

"Subsequent to this test, what did you do?"

Gilley shifted his weight from one side of the chair to the other. "We requested that the New Orleans Police Department seal and impound the car, and the next day I went down to New Orleans and took it into my possession."

"You drove the car back?"

"Oh no, ma'am," Gilley said. "Not at all. I had it trailered back."

"And what happened after you got the car back to Nashville?"

"We turned it over to our forensic examiners, who performed a standard, routine investigation of the car. They found no other evidence other than the stain in the trunk, which again proved conclusively to be blood. We turned the sample over to the Tennessee Bureau of Investigation for further testing."

"And how did you do that, Detective Gilley?"

"We literally cut the piece of carpet with the stain on it out of the car, sealed it in an evidence bag, and forwarded it to TBI."

"Thank you, Detective Gilley. No further questions at this time."

Taylor watched as Talmadge stood quickly and walked to the podium, with his pressed Armani suit, his hundred-dollar haircut, and his crisp silk shirt, the very picture of a rich, successful lawyer. Everything within her was still, but in the back of her mind, a bubble was forming. Michael must have known that this testimony would be coming, but he hadn't told her, hadn't said a word to her about it. But Taylor knew, and she recognized this for exactly what it was—the first real evidence that could tie Michael to the murder scene.

"Detective Gilley, how much time elapsed between the time the defendant rented that car and the time it was discovered in the lot of the New Orleans airport?"

"Just a day or two short of seven weeks," Gilley replied.

"And how many people had rented that car in the seven weeks that elapsed before the car was discovered."

"According to the rental car company's records," Gilley answered, "forty-two people."

Talmadge shifted at the podium and turned toward the jury. "So forty-two people rented this car between the time Mr. Schiftmann drove it in Nashville and the time you found it."

Gilley nodded. "That's correct."

"How many people drove the car, Detective Gilley?"

Gilley's brow wrinkled. "I don't know the answer to that. There's no way to tell."

"And how many people actually rode in the car?"

"Again," Gilley answered, his voice tightening, "We have no way of knowing that."

"How many people who rented, drove, or rode in this car opened the trunk?"

"What?"

"How many people opened the trunk and used it?" Talmadge demanded.

"How should I—" Gilley stopped, frustrated. He took a breath and paused for a moment. "I don't know the answer to that question."

Talmadge smiled. "Did you obtain a list of the forty-two people who rented this particular Lincoln Town Car over the seven-week period."

"Yes, we did."

"And did you question each of these forty-two people?"

"No, we didn't."

"Did you do background checks on these forty-two people?"

"We did run their names through the NCIC computers," Gilley answered.

"And?"

"Six of the forty-two had prior arrest records. Two others had outstanding warrants."

"So eight of the forty-two people who rented this car over a seven-week period had previous scrapes with the law. Did you interview those eight people? Did you question them?"

"None of them were from Nashville."

"I didn't ask where they were from, Detective Gilley. I asked if you tracked them down and questioned them."

"No, sir, we did not."

"So eight people out of the forty-two people who rented that car over a period of seven weeks had arrest records or outstanding warrants, and you decide somehow that the defendant, who has never had a run-in with the law in his life, was the person responsible for the bloodstain in the trunk of that—"

Collier jumped to his feet. "Objection, Your Honor! This is totally inappropriate!"

Forsythe cleared his throat, angry. "I agree, General Collier. Objection sustained."

Talmadge turned back to the defense table. "Question withdrawn, Your Honor. Nothing further for this witness."

Collier walked to the podium. "One question on redirect, Your Honor. Detective Gilley, of the forty-three people, counting the defendant, who rented that Lincoln Town Car during this seven-week period, who rented it on the night of the murders at Exotica Tans?"

Gilley turned toward the defense table and nodded in their direction. "The defendant, sir. Michael Schiftmann."

In the gallery, in the row directly behind the defense table, Taylor felt her blood turn cold.

Thankfully, Forsythe declared the afternoon recess. Taylor got up and walked straight out of the courtroom without waiting for Michael and the lawyers. She walked quickly down the hallway, her heels clicking loudly on the marble floor. She went into the ladies' room and locked herself inside a stall. She held her hand up in front of her and noticed it was shaking. She stared at it a moment, as if it were some-one else's.

Her mind went blank as she stared at the scratched paint covering the metal door in front of her. Then, almost un-consciously, her brain kicked back into gear and she began thinking. There had to be some explanation besides the ob-vious. This was too easy for the police, too convenient.

She walked out the stall, past a couple of women from the courtroom who looked up in surprise when they saw her. She rinsed off her hands and wanted to throw water in her face, but then she'd have to repair her makeup. She didn't want to go back out there looking like she'd been crying.

She ran a brush through her hair, then squared her shoul-ders and walked back out into the hallway. Michael was a few feet farther down the hall, leaning against the wall, talk-ing to Mark Hoffman, the youngest of the three lawyers.

"Where were you?" Michael asked, his voice low. "You disappeared. I was worried about you."

"Sorry," Taylor said, forcing herself to smile. "Call of nature. I sure wish the judge wouldn't go so long between breaks."

Hoffman smiled back at her. She hadn't talked to him much over the course of the trial, but he seemed a little more relaxed, laid-back, than the other two attorneys. "Yeah, he's intense. A real slave driver."

"This seems to be moving forward a lot more quickly than everyone thought," Taylor said, wanting to make small talk about anything so she wouldn't have to discuss the testimony they'd just heard.

"It'll start slowing down from here on out," Hoffman said. "We're getting into the really contentious stuff."

"I gathered," Taylor said.

"Are you okay?" Michael asked.

Taylor looked up at him and smiled again. "Of course, I'm fine."

Hoffman looked at his watch. "We better go," he said. "When Forsythe says ten minutes, he generally means ten minutes."

Inside the courtroom, the gallery was rustling with spectators trying to get settled into seats before Forsythe entered. The court officer had just begun his announcement when Forsythe swept past him, took his seat at the bench, and rapped his gavel twice.

"General Collier, let's go. Call your next witness."

Collier stood quickly. "The state calls Ms. Patricia Hooper."

Taylor watched as a woman about thirty, if that, walked into the courtroom and took the witness stand. She was thin and pale, as if she rarely got outside. She wore narrow wire-rimmed glasses and little makeup. She seemed nervous as the court officer swore her in.

"Ms. Hooper, tell us please your place of employment," Collier instructed.

"I'm employed at the Nashville Crime Laboratory of the Tennessee Bureau of Investigation."

"And what is your job description there?"

"My job title is special agent, forensic science supervisor. Basically, I'm a biotechnician attached to the Serology/DNA Unit."

"And what does the Serology/DNA Unit of the TBI do?"

"Our job is to perform identification and characterization of blood and other bodily fluids like semen or saliva. We also perform DNA profiling to determine if the DNA of a person suspected of committing a crime is present at a crime scene."

"And, Ms. Hooper, what are your educational qualifications as a forensic science supervisor?"

"I hold a bachelor of arts degree from Vanderbilt University with honors in chemistry, and a master's degree in biochemistry from the University of Tennessee in Knoxville."

"How long have you been employed with the TBI?"

"Four years."

Taylor felt her backside going numb as she sat there listening to this dry testimony. The woman's voice was monotone, professional, and profoundly boring. The courtroom was quiet, still, almost stifling. She took a deep breath and let it out slowly and wished that this was all over.

"Ms. Hooper," Collier continued, "can you explain to us, in layperson's terms, what forensic DNA analysis is, how it works, and what it means in the process of investigating a homicide."

"Certainly. In its simplest terms, DNA is material in our bodies that governs inheritance of eye color, hair color, stature, bone density, and a long list of other human traits. DNA is a long but narrow stringlike object so tiny that a one-foot-long string of DNA is packed into a space roughly equal to a cube that measures one-millionth of an inch on its side . . ."

Taylor listened as the woman droned on for another ten minutes. She described the way DNA strands were named and characterized in strange combinations of letters and terms that seemed complicated beyond comprehension.

". . . the locus on chromosome four, GYPA, is particularly useful for forensic DNA testing because it's polymorphic, which means it takes different forms in different chromosomes. Each of the forms is called an allele . . ."

Even the jury was starting to glaze over. Taylor looked over at the defense table. Michael sat there, expressionless, staring. Not much color in his face, Taylor thought.

How long can this go on? She felt her head swim. She looked down at her watch: barely three-thirty. Two more hours of this.

The young woman on the witness stand droned on, monotonously, tediously. Taylor found it incomprehensible that something so dry could be so crucial, yet she knew it was.

"Now, Ms. Hooper," Collier said after the primer on DNA was complete, "tell us what kind of tests you use to identify and characterize the samples you receive."

"We use the latest technology to profile DNA samples, which is the PCR/STR process. PCR is an acronym for polymerase chain reaction, and STR is an acronym standing for short tandem repeat."

"Ms. Hooper, without going into too much technical detail here, what does the PCR/STR process allow a forensic investigator to do?"

"The technological advances of PCR/STR give us the ability to identify and profile a sample based on much less material and material that might not be analyzable under older tests because of degradation issues."

"So it takes much less of a sample to provide an identification."

"That's correct. In that sense, it's much more reliable. And it's much more discriminating. The FBI has established its accuracy down to one in two hundred and sixty billion."

"In other words, a match using this test is pretty well absolute."

Talmadge shot up. "Objection, Your Honor. Calls for a conclusion."

Collier turned and glared at Talmadge. "Your Honor, the court has already accepted Ms. Hooper as an expert witness. She's qualified and entitled to draw these kinds of conclusions."

"Objection overruled. Continue, Ms. Hooper."

Patricia Hooper nodded. "Yes, I would characterize a positive identification as absolute."

"Very well. In February of last year, did you receive a series of forensic evidence packets from the scene of a double homicide at an establishment here in Nashville called Exotica Tans?"

"Yes, I did."

"In your expert opinion, were proper procedures followed in the protection of this evidence, to avoid contamination and degradation?"

"Well, I wasn't at the crime scene, but when the evidence was presented to me, it appeared to have been properly preserved."

"And what did the evidence primarily consist of?"

"There were approximately eighty separate packets of evidence, the bulk of which were blood and tissue samples. There were also some hair samples found as well. And some skin tissue."

"Were you able to type these samples, to determine from whom they came?"

"Yes, we were."

"And what were your conclusions?"

"Virtually all the samples contained DNA resident in

the bodies of the two victims, Ms. Burnham and Ms. Matthews."

"Were you able to identify any other DNA that was excluded from that belonging to the two victims?"

"Well," she said, hesitating, "you have to consider the circumstances of the crime scene. The homicides were committed at an establishment where, to put it delicately, one was likely to find traces of other bodily fluids. We were provided with hair samples and semen samples that we were able to profile, but not to match with anyone else."

"On or about April thirtieth of last year," Collier asked, "were you provided a sample of hair and saliva that were obtained from the defendant as a result of a search warrant?"

"Yes, I was."

"Were you able to type and identify those samples?"

"I was."

"And were you able to match any of the samples at the Exotica Tans crime scene with the sample derived from the defendant?"

"No, sir, none of the samples matched."

"So you have no samples from the Exotica Tans homicide scene that positively place the defendant there?"

"That's correct," Ms. Hooper said.

Taylor thought it odd that Collier would bring up a point in favor of the defense. Then, after a moment, she was hit with how smart that was. Of course, when you've got a weakness and you admit to it, somehow it's less weak than when someone else points it out.

"With your permission, Your Honor," Collier said, turning to the judge, "we'd like to bring into the courtroom a portable bulletin board with a series of photographs and graphs that we'll be introducing into evidence."

Forsythe turned. "Any objections, Mr. Talmadge?"

"None at this time, Your Honor." Talmadge's voice sounded firm, unshaken.

Jane Sparks stood up as the door in the back of the courtroom opened and a large portable bulletin board was wheeled into the room. She took the board, wheeled it past the prosecution table and into the center of the courtroom in front of the judge and jury. The logistics were a little tough to negotiate, but she managed to get the board where everyone who had to be able to see it could.

Taylor craned her neck. There was a line of blown-up photographs that seemed filled with dark, blurry vertical lines and several charts.

"Ms. Hooper," Collier instructed, "if you need to leave the stand in order to indicate which of these exhibits you're referring to, I think that'll be okay."

Forsythe nodded.

"Now first, Ms. Hooper, tell us in its simplest terms how PCR works."

"As I said earlier, PCR is an acronym for polymerase chain reaction. And in and of itself, it's not really an actual identification. PCR is a method by which we can take a sample of DNA too small to profile and cause it to reproduce itself. This gives us a much larger sample. Now when we have enough DNA material to type, we can create a profile. Every DNA strand contains both constant and variable elements. The constant elements are areas that all human beings share. Interspersed with these areas are the variable elements, or the elements which are unique to each individual."

"Very good, Ms. Hooper. Now, in February last year, you were given, as you said, some eighty packets of evidence from the Exotica Tans crime scene. Can you give us the results of this examination of the evidence?"

"Yes, sir," she said, getting up from the witness stand and walking over to the bulletin board. She pulled a wooden pointer up off the rail and pointed to a photograph on the far left of the board. "As this label indicates, this is the DNA imprint of Allison May Matthews. And this second photograph is a blowup of the microscopic sample of Sarah Burnham. As you can see here, here, and here, on these loci, the samples are different."

"All right, Ms. Hooper. Now, on or about February tenth of last year, were you provided with evidence that had been obtained by Metro Police from a Dumpster behind a convenience market on Charlotte Avenue?"

"Yes, I was. And we obtained numerous samples from the material and were able to type them."

"Could you explain your results to us, please."

Ms. Hooper raised her pointer and tapped several photographs in a row on the board. "These photographs are representative samples of the material we obtained from the Dumpster. As you can see, here, here, and here, the loci match the target sample definitely identified as belonging to Ms. Matthews. And over here, at these six loci, we established that this sample definitely matched the sample derived from Ms. Burnham."

Taylor stared hard at the board, craning her neck to see the photographs as well as possible. She felt a tightening in her chest, as if she needed to loosen her clothes. Her face felt flushed. Patricia Hooper had been on the stand for well over an hour now.

"So in your expert opinion," Collier said, his voice rising just a bit. "The blood found on the clothing in the Dumpster on Charlotte Avenue definitely came from Allison May Matthews and Sarah Denise Burnham."

Ms. Hooper nodded. "Yes, that's correct."

"And on or about March twenty-fourth of last year, were you provided with a sample of carpet removed from the trunk of a 2004 Lincoln Town Car?"

"Yes, it was delivered to me directly at the Nashville Crime Lab."

"And were you able to perform a PCR/STR analysis of this sample?"

"Yes, sir, I was."

"Would you tell us the results, please?"

Ms. Hooper stepped to the side of the board and pointed to a series of photographs and charts. "As this graph explains, we look for certain pointers, or loci, which are areas on the actual DNA string that are unique to each individual. As you can see here, the material we obtained from the carpet matches both the samples discovered at the Charlotte Avenue Dumpster site and at the crime scene itself. The pointers match here—"

She tapped on the board.

"—and here—"

Again. The tapping echoed throughout the silent courtroom.

"—here and here and here."

"So," Collier said, his voice rising even higher, "in your expert opinion, the samples obtained at the crime scene, at the Dumpster, and on the defendant's rental car all share the same DNA and therefore could only have come from Sarah Denise Burnham and Allison May Matthews!"

"Yes," Ms. Hooper said, nodding her head. "That's correct."

My God, Taylor thought. *Merciful God in heaven! He did it!*

CHAPTER 33

Thursday afternoon, Nashville

The bubble that had been slowly growing somewhere deep in Taylor's subconscious had suddenly burst through to the surface. It was no longer something she could hide from or run away from. It was, she knew, inescapable. The defense lawyers would throw up every argument imaginable to convince the jury that the police had framed Michael, had set him up to vindicate their own incompetence.

Taylor knew better, though. He had done it.

Michael Schiftmann was a murderer.

How she knew this, beyond the evidence she'd seen earlier in the courtroom, she wasn't sure. But over the past eight or nine months, ever since the first rumors of the indictment had leaked out of the DA's office, she had begun to look at him in a different way. There had always been something in Michael's makeup of artifice, or if not exactly artifice, at least masking. She had known him for years, had slipped into being in love with him almost without knowing it, had been swept along by her own loneliness and the passion within her that he had tapped into and found in a way no one else ever had.

But all along, Taylor realized that she never really knew him. Never really knew him deep inside, in his core.

In his heart.

And now she knew why.

Judge Forsythe had recessed court for the evening after

the TBI crime lab agent had testified for more than two hours. Tomorrow morning, Wes Talmadge would go after her, tooth and nail. Taylor felt sorry for the young woman.

Michael looked ashen, almost gray as they all waded out of the courthouse through the crowd, past the cameras, and to Talmadge's car. For the first time, Taylor saw what almost looked like fear on his face. The shouted questions from the reporters echoed in her ears like the background noise in a riot.

As they walked out of the courthouse and down the steps in the fading twilight, the January wind sharp and bitter around them, Taylor tried to keep her head down, to avoid eye contact with any of them. But someone jammed a microphone out of the mass of bodies directly in front of her, almost hitting her in the face. She jerked her head up, dodged to her right, and through a break in the crowd, saw him.

The FBI agent . . . Powell, that was his name. He was staring right through her. She had seen him several times before at the trial, had noticed him sitting in the back of the courtroom spectator gallery, but she had avoided really seeing him.

Now she couldn't help it. They stared directly at each other for what seemed like several moments, then the crowd shifted and Taylor was shoved forward.

Everyone was silent in the car as they maneuvered through the thick, nearly impenetrable Nashville rush-hour traffic. Carey Talmadge, grim-faced and tired, drove, with Taylor in the front seat next to her. Talmadge and Michael sat in the back. Finally, Talmadge spoke up.

"Don't worry," he said out of nowhere, "we knew this was coming. We get our turn tomorrow."

Taylor turned, suddenly angry. "I didn't know it was coming! Why didn't you tell me?"

"I told you that they'd be throwing some things at us that looked bad," Michael said defensively. "We can counter everything they've got."

Taylor shifted back in her seat and stared out the front of the car. She clenched her jaw, regretting her outburst.

"Look, folks," Talmadge said. "We've got to stay calm

and keep cool here. This ain't over by a long shot. Not by a helluva long shot."

"Great," Michael mumbled, "I've got an attorney that says 'ain't.'"

Talmadge turned and glared at Michael, his eyes narrowing. "You've got an attorney that speaks the same language as your jury, hotshot. If I were you, I'd try not to forget that."

At the hotel, Taylor and Michael got out of the car quickly and slipped into the hotel, unnoticed, through a side door. They walked quickly across the cavernous lobby, their footsteps silent on the thick carpet. They hurried to the bank of elevators and were lucky enough to get one alone.

"Can we have dinner together?" Michael asked quietly as the elevator door slid shut.

Taylor stared at the front of the elevator, her hands at her side. "Michael, I'm not hungry. I don't think I could eat a thing."

"Well," he said, as the floor buttons above them lighted one after the other. "Would you spend the night in my room tonight? We could really use some time alone together. It's been a while."

Taylor felt her stomach convulse, then tensed, trying to hide it. "I'm exhausted. It's been an awful day. I think I'll just take a bath and read for a while, then go to bed early."

Michael turned and faced the front of the elevator next to her. "This isn't working very well, is it?"

"I'm just tired, Michael. Having your fiancé on trial for murder tends to take a lot out of you."

The buttons above them clicked from 9 to 10.

"You're not starting to believe them, are you?" Michael asked.

"Can we not do this now?" Taylor whispered.

The elevator door opened on their floor and they stepped out into the hallway. Michael's room was two doors down from hers. They stopped as he pulled out his key card. "I'll just get room service, I guess. I can't exactly go walking around downtown, seeing the sights. I'll just watch a movie and go to bed, I guess."

Taylor nodded. "I hope you get some sleep."

Michael pushed the door open. "Listen, you change your mind, all you've got to do is knock on the door."

Taylor nodded. "Good night," she said.

Then he was gone.

Taylor walked down to her room and ran her credit card-size electronic room key through the reader, then walked in. The room was cold, the air dry and stale. She tossed her bag down on a chair, took off her overcoat and hung it in the closet, then sat on the edge of the bed and took off her shoes. Her feet hurt; her head pounded.

She still couldn't believe it.

But she had to believe it.

The pounding in her head quickened. She realized she was hungry, that the headache was probably the result of a blood-sugar crash. She needed to eat, but she couldn't imagine putting food in her mouth.

She wandered into the bathroom and stared at herself in the mirror. Deep dark purple pockets nestled under her eyes, visible even through the makeup. Her eyes were bloodshot. They'd never been this bloodshot this often before. This had only been happening in the last couple of months.

Her neck ached. She rolled her head around on her shoulders, trying to loosen it. She was exhausted, so tired and sleepy she couldn't think straight. But, she knew, there was no way she would sleep tonight. Even the Ambien and the Paxil didn't work anymore. Even with the sleeping pills and the antianxiety medication, she rarely slept more than a couple of hours at a time.

She took off her watch and looked at it—seven-fifteen. It was going to be a long night. She couldn't concentrate on her reading. Television and movies held no interest for her. She was too tired to think of anything.

Then she stood there a moment, glaring at her own image in the mirror. *Funny thing about having your world crash down around you*, she thought. *Now at least you know what you're up against and what you have to deal with.*

Taylor set her jaw and walked quickly back out of the bathroom and over to the bed. She opened the nightstand drawer and pulled out the telephone directory. She opened to the blue pages, the government listings, and flipped to the heading labeled "U.S. Government." She squinted to bring the tiny type into focus and scanned down the listings until she found what she was looking for. She picked up the hotel phone, punched 9 to get an outside line, then dialed.

"You've reached the Nashville office of the Federal Bureau of Investigation," a recorded voice said. "There's no one available to take your call. At the tone, please leave a message."

The phone beeped. "Yes, my name is Taylor Robinson. You have an FBI agent named Henry Powell in town sitting in on the Michael Schiftmann murder trial. It's vitally important that I speak to him as soon as possible. Can you please get in touch with him and have him call me on my cell phone at 212–555–5645. It's urgent that I speak to him as quickly as possible. Please have him call me."

Taylor hung up the phone and sat there in the cold silence of her room. She pulled the covers back from the oversize bed and lay out flat on her back, her head sinking into the pillow. She turned the ringer up all the way on her mobile phone and set it on the nightstand next to her. She tried to will herself to relax, to concentrate on the hissing of the heating-unit fan as it moved the musty air around.

In time, she began to drift off. Not sleep really, just a gentle sliding under the radar screen of consciousness that was barely enough for her body to let go of the worst of it.

Then, what seemed like seconds later, the electronic chiming of the cell phone blasted her into consciousness. She shot upright, unsure of where she was, the bright yellow numbers of the alarm clock shimmering in the darkened room.

It was nine-thirty, she noticed out of the corner of her eye. She'd been out almost two hours. She picked up the phone and hit the talk button.

"Hello," she said, trying to sound awake.

"Ms. Robinson?"

"Yes, this is Taylor Robinson."

"This is Agent Powell, returning your call. How may I help you?"

Taylor rubbed her eyes. "Oh, thank you for calling. I—Could you hold on for a second?" She shook her head. Why had she called him?

"I'm sorry," she said. "I had drifted off, Agent Powell, and I guess I was—"

"I didn't mean to wake you up, Ms. Robinson," Powell said. "Should I call back later?"

"No," she said quickly. "No, not at all. I'm okay. I just, well . . . Agent Powell, I need to see you."

"What?" the voice answered.

"I need to see you. Tonight. Is there somewhere where we can meet?"

"Well, I don't know. This is a little unusual."

"I need to see you, Agent Powell. Please. Where are you staying? I'll come to your hotel."

"Well," Powell said, hesitating. "All right. I'm staying at the Doubletree Hotel, over on Fourth Avenue a few blocks down from the courthouse. There's a small bar in the lobby. It's usually not very crowded. We can get a table and talk."

"Fine," Taylor said, "I'll be there in ten minutes."

Taylor climbed out of the taxi, handed the driver a twenty, and walked quickly into the Doubletree Hotel. She stood there, scanning the lobby, and spotted a small, open-air lounge. At a table for two in the farthest corner, she recognized Powell sitting alone, in a pair of khakis and a white, button-down collar Oxford cloth shirt. He looked more relaxed than in the courtroom, she thought, almost preppie.

She walked past the half dozen or so others in the bar and over to his table. He stood up as she approached.

"Good evening," he said. "How are you, Ms. Robinson?"

Taylor pulled her coat off and folded it over the back of the chair at the empty table next to them, then rearranged a chair so her back would be to the lobby and sat down.

"I'm terrible, Agent Powell, if you must know. I'm terrible." She said it matter-of-factly, as if it ought to be obvious to him.

"I understand," Powell said. "I think anyone would be."

Taylor shifted in her seat, trying to get comfortable. She

found herself avoiding eye contact with him, looking around the room, at the heavy red draperies, the red carpet, all the usual upscale hotel decor.

A cocktail waitress in a short skirt and a blouse with puffy sleeves approached. "May I get you something?" she asked.

Taylor looked over at Powell. "It's been a long day," he said. "I'm having a vodka martini."

"That sounds wonderful," Taylor said. "Sign me up."

Powell held up two fingers. "Make it two."

The waitress walked away. Taylor watched her for a few seconds, then turned to Powell. "Now that I'm here," she said, "I don't exactly know what to say."

Powell eyed her coolly. "Does he know you're here?"

Taylor shook her head. "We're in separate rooms."

Powell lifted an eyebrow. "Really?"

"Have been for months. The stress, I think. Neither of us are sleeping well, or very much."

Powell nodded, understanding. "But he's still living in your co-op?"

Taylor looked at him. "For the time being."

The waitress brought their drinks over and set them on the small table. As soon as she walked away, Taylor picked hers up and took a long sip. Powell watched as she gulped.

"You did need that," he commented.

She set the drink down, her eyes watering. She lowered her head, almost hiding her face from him. A single tear ran along her cheek, and she brushed it away.

"Goddamn it," she muttered. Then she raised her head and looked Powell directly in the eye. "He did it, didn't he?" she said, her voice low, intense.

Powell studied her for a moment. "Yes," he said quietly. "He did it."

She put her left elbow on the table, her arm bent, and buried her face in her open palm. Her whole body seemed to shake for a second.

"I slept with him," she whispered, her voice breaking. "I had sex with him. My God, what he did to those poor girls."

"You didn't know," Powell said. "You didn't know."

"How can anybody do that?" she asked, raising her head. "How can anyone be two so completely different people?"

"That's the nature of what he is," Powell said. "I'm sure that when he was with you, he was completely normal and charming, in every way. That's the way this always works. They aren't raving lunatics running through a crowded theater swinging a hatchet at people."

"No," she said, her voice sharp. "They're much worse!"

"You're right," Powell said. "That's it. You're exactly right. I've spent most of my career trying to figure out what makes this kind of—person—work, and the truth is we can quantify some things. We can analyze some things and make some observations and draw some conclusions. But can we say definitely what makes Michael Schiftmann become the Alphabet Man?

"No, we can't."

Taylor Robinson's face clouded over, almost as if she had gone into a kind of shock. "What am I going to do?" she asked blankly.

Powell lifted his drink and took a small sip. The icy vodka felt good on his tongue, in his mouth, and when it hit the back of his throat, he felt a gentle burn radiate out from his center.

"I want you to know," he said, "that I don't believe, never believed, that you were any part of this. You were his victim, too. Maybe not in the same way as the other women, but you've been hurt by this. And the important thing for you to consider is how not to get hurt any worse."

"I'm leaving him," she said. "I'm going back to New York tomorrow."

"I don't know if I would do that," he said.

"I can't stay here," she hissed. "I can't have people thinking that I'm still—that I'm still, *with him*."

Powell raised his hands to his face and rubbed his jaw, the dry skin of his palm scraping across his now-past-five o'clock shadow. "You can't go," he said. "If you do, that may drive him over the edge."

"I don't care about that."

"This is a sensitive, delicate time in all this," Powell said.

"For one thing, the jury has seen you with him. They know who you are. If you disappear, especially after hearing the testimony that came out today, it could be construed as prejudicial."

Taylor glared at Powell for a second, then, almost angrily, picked up her drink and tossed back another gulp.

"And there are other things at play as well," Powell said.

"What? What else is going on?"

Powell hesitated. "I can't go into a lot of detail," he said slowly. "But as a result of what the police here have managed to put together, I think it's safe to say that this trial will not be the only one."

Taylor's jaw dropped, literally. "You mean, other . . . ?"

"Michael's DNA is currently being cross-typed with forensic evidence found at a number of other crime scenes. They're checking rental cars, hotel rooms, the evidence gathered at the scenes themselves."

Powell shook his head slowly, almost sadly. "This won't be the only trial. He's history, Taylor. He's finished. And if you leave now, and word gets out about the other places, then that's going to push him over the edge."

"What will he do?" she asked.

"He'll run. He'll run, and he knows he has nothing to lose. And he's not the type to let anything get in his way."

"Can't they lock him up?" she whispered again.

"No, he's out on bail. He's technically a free man. We're watching him, all the time. But he's smart. Real smart."

Her eyes wandered back and forth. "My God," she muttered.

Powell reached across the table and touched her hand. "Listen," he said, "I know you're a good person, a good person who's been hurt by this, and I know as a good person you want to see justice done. And you want to see that no one else ever gets hurt this way again, right? He's got to be stopped."

Taylor looked down at the table, to where his fingertips had just brushed the back of her hand. She looked back up at him. "What do you want me to do?"

"Stay close to him," Powell said. "Stay in his confidence.

If it looks to you like he's about to run, or anything else drastic for that matter, you call me. Here's my cell phone number. I've got it with me 24/7."

He pulled a card out of his pocket and slid it across the table to her.

"Can you do that for me, Taylor?" he asked softly. "Can you help me make sure that he's stopped?"

Taylor picked up the card and looked at it. It was glossy, shiny, with the FBI seal on it and embossed lettering. It was impressive, slick.

She looked up at Powell again, as weary as she'd ever been in her life.

"Yes," she said. "I can do that."

CHAPTER 34

Monday morning, three weeks later, Nashville

Like a political campaign, the trial seemed to go on forever. And like a political campaign as well, the constant ebb and flow of power from one side to the other left each opponent alternately elated and in despair. The prosecution rested its case after a week, and for a moment, the defense was off-balance. Then Talmadge began his attack.

Experts—expensive experts—challenged every component of the state's case. The evidence collection procedures, forensic procedures, protection of the crime scene: All were criticized and disputed. The defense tried to portray the police department and the Murder Squad as incompetent cowboys bent on hanging these horrific murders on anyone they could find because of political and public pressure.

The credentials of the TBI lab specialists were questioned. Expert witnesses hired by the defense cast doubt on every aspect of the lab's handling of the evidence and the conclusions that were reached. The testimony went on day after day, until the jury, the lawyers, and even the judge reached a point of exhaustion. Even the pool of reporters had dwindled; only the hard-core regulars showed up every day now.

As the trial neared its end, Forsythe pushed the attorneys to keep moving. The jury had been sequestered for almost a month. Two of the jurors became ill and were excused, their places taken by the alternates. If one more juror dropped off, Forsythe would have to declare a mistrial.

To wrap up the last of the prosecution's rebuttal testimony, Forsythe held court on Saturday. Everyone had Sunday off, with closing arguments scheduled for Monday.

A dozen times, Taylor almost left. One night, she even packed her bags and made a reservation on the last flight out of Nashville. At the very last moment, she changed her mind and unpacked.

Most days, she and Michael barely spoke. As soon as court was over, she retreated to her room and ordered room service. She hid from the world and tried to sleep. Sleep had come easier the past few days; in fact, something in her sleep patterns had shifted and now it was not only easy to sleep, it was all she seemed to want to do.

She woke up Monday morning, the day of closing arguments, perhaps the last day of the trial, thickheaded and tired. The bags under her eyes had grown larger, she thought, as she stared into the mirror and tried to bring herself to consciousness. She had a standing order with the hotel room service staff to send up a pot of coffee, a croissant, and some fruit at seven-thirty. That would help. In the meantime, she had just enough time to get a shower.

Carey Talmadge picked them up every day at eight-fifteen in the morning and chauffeured them to court. She was on time and upbeat, as usual, despite the cold, gray day that awaited them outside.

"Where's your father?" Michael asked as he slid into the backseat.

Carey turned, smiling. "He's already at the courtroom. He wanted to go over some last-minute things with Jim and Mark."

At the front of the courthouse, the news crews with their trucks and portable microwave antennas were back in force. One young, slim black woman was even doing a live remote. It seemed to Taylor that there were even more news vans now than at the beginning of the trial.

Carey dropped them off at the side entrance to the courthouse, and they walked in quickly. As they stepped through the doors and approached the security screeners, Taylor heard voices outside yelling.

"What's going on?" she asked.

Michael shrugged. "Bottom feeders," he muttered.

They took the elevator up to the fourth floor of the court-house, where Mark Hoffman was pacing around in front of the elevator banks waiting for them. His face was tense, his brow furrowed like a bulldog's. He looked around nervously.

"Wes wants to see you," he said. "C'mon, we don't have a lot of time."

He turned, his heels clicking loudly on the marble floor, and stepped quickly down the hallway. Taylor and Michael strained to keep up with him. He came to a heavy wooden door and opened it, then walked down a short hallway to a conference room.

Wes Talmadge and Jim McCain sat at a long table. They rose as Mark, Taylor, and Michael walked in.

"Shut the door," Wes ordered.

"What the hell's going on?" Michael asked, looking around the room. Taylor stood off to the side, her shoulders aching from tension.

Wes Talmadge took a step toward them. "Sit down, Michael. We need to talk."

"What?" Michael demanded, his voice strained and tense. "Will you please tell me what the hell is going on?"

"Sit down," Talmadge said quietly.

"No! Stop telling me to sit down and tell me what's going on. Now."

Talmadge sighed, and his head seemed to droop. "Okay, if that's the way you want it. Mind if I sit down?"

Michael nodded as Talmadge stepped back to his chair and sat down. "Michael," he said, looking up at them, "I had a phone call from a colleague last night. Hell, he's more a friend than a colleague, I guess. Lives in Scottsdale, Arizona."

Talmadge stared up at Michael for a moment. "Scottsdale?" Michael asked, his voice barely a whisper.

Talmadge nodded. "We've known each other a long time and he's been following this trial through the news media. Obviously, he knows I represent you."

"Okay, so what's the big—"

"Michael, he told me there's a rumor going around out there that the grand jury in Scottsdale is preparing to indict you on a charge of first-degree murder in connection with the death of a young woman that occurred almost seven years ago."

Taylor's hand went to her mouth. She looked over at Michael. He stood there, swaying slightly, as the blood seemed to drain from his face.

"I made a few phone calls this morning, got a couple of people out of bed early. And while I haven't been able to get anyone to come out and tell me point-blank that an indictment will be forthcoming, I think you should be prepared."

"Madness," Michael whispered. "It's insane. How can they do this to me?"

"I'm afraid that's not all," Talmadge said, looking down at the floor. "The police department in Macon, Georgia is going to issue an arrest warrant for you later today. And I think we can expect some action soon from Chattanooga as well."

Taylor felt dizzy, nauseated. The room seemed to swirl around her. She reached out and grabbed on to the back of a chair for support. Mark Hoffman stepped over, took her by the elbow and steadied her.

"Here," he whispered. "Sit down." He pulled out a chair, and Taylor settled into it.

Michael stood there, his eyes transfixed on a point somewhere in the middle of the opposite wall. "What does this mean?" he asked softly after a few moments. The silence that followed was onerous, oppressive.

"It means, my friend," Talmadge said, "that we're in a lot of trouble."

"What do we do?"

"I don't know whether Judge Forsythe knows about this. I haven't said anything to him. I think word must be filtering through the news media. That would explain the feeding frenzy going on downstairs. Clearly, if the jury finds out, if the news should leak out and they hear of it, he'll have to declare a mistrial. On the short term, that would help us. But long term, it doesn't solve anything."

Talmadge stood back up and pushed the chair behind him. He walked over to where Michael stood and faced him squarely.

"We should consider what's involved here. This is a capital case. The prosecution's case isn't open and shut, but they've done a better job of putting it together than we thought they would. If you're found guilty, you could be sentenced to die. And the other charges against you could go that way as well. Long term, we could be facing a very bad situation."

Talmadge stopped for a second, as if carefully considering his words. "On the other hand, if we were to go to the district attorney and see what kind of deal we could get—"

"What?" Michael snapped. "Are you—"

"Let me finish," Talmadge said forcefully. "I think we should consider an Alford plea, which is where you admit no guilt, but recognize the state may have enough evidence to convict to you. I think if we submit an Alford, we could definitely beat the death penalty and, given a few breaks, might even get you life with possibility of parole. Worst case scenario, life without possibility of parole. But at least you'd still be here with us. You could still write, still work, still have a life of some kind. And chances are, if you're locked up by the state of Tennessee for a long time, these other charges might go away. Under the circumstances, why waste the taxpayers' money?"

Michael grabbed the back of a wooden chair with both hands and squeezed until Taylor thought his knuckles were going to burst through the skin.

"If you think that I—" he started to say.

"It's my job to protect my client's welfare and my client's rights," Talmadge interrupted. "It's not my job to make sure you go free no matter what! If the best I can do for you is beat the death penalty, then that's what I'm going to do."

"No," Michael said coldly. "I won't hear of it."

"Michael," Taylor said, "maybe you ought to think about it. Maybe Wes is right. It's time to look at—"

"Damn it!" he yelled, turning to her. "You, too? That it, Taylor? You, too? You turning on me now?"

"I'm not turning on you, Michael. I just don't want to see you have to face the—" Taylor's voice broke.

"Death penalty?" Michael snapped, turning to Taylor and leaning down in her face. "Let me tell you, I'd rather be put to death than spend the rest of my life locked up like an animal. Even if I did commit these murders, which I didn't, so what? They were just sluts and whores, worthless trash! Of no value to society or anything else!"

He glared at her, his eyes wild and bulging. Taylor looked up at him, and for the first time, she was afraid of him. Around him, the three attorneys stared, shocked. Talmadge stepped over and put his hand on Michael's shoulder, pulling him away from Taylor. Michael whirled around, and for a second it looked as if he were going to hit him. The other two lawyers stepped toward them.

"If you can't go in there and defend me," Michael said, "then you're fired. All right? Is that what you want, off this case?"

"Forsythe won't let you fire me," Talmadge said, his eyes narrowing. "He'll go apeshit on you."

"Then get in there and do your job," Michael said, his jaw clenched. "And do it right."

She expected drama, but in the end it was all surprisingly muted. Perhaps it was fatigue, weariness at the relentless stress. Taylor realized as she sat in her usual seat a row behind the defense table that it had been a year since the two girls in Nashville had been murdered.

A year since she'd thrown that huge party for Michael to celebrate his first appearance on the *New York Times* bestseller list. The longest year of her life . . . A year that had held such promise, so many breakthroughs.

And it had led to this.

District Attorney General Robert Collier's closing argument lasted just over a half hour, and was strangely calm. He summarized the prosecution's case, faced its weaknesses squarely, countered the defense's arguments and challenges as spin control and disseminating, and then, in the end, appealed to the jury's basic common sense and humanity. He spoke of Sarah Denise Burnham and Allison May Matthews as if they were his own daughters, as if their loss had somehow become personal to him and should be just as personal to the twelve men and women who sat listening to him.

Then he thanked them for their service and sat down.

Talmadge stood up slowly and walked to the podium. He gazed at the jury a few moments, then began speaking. Taylor listened as he reminded the jury that it was the state's case to prove the defendant guilty, and that in a case like this—a case where a man's life as well as his liberty was at stake—the state had the highest obligation possible to prove beyond even the slightest shadow of a doubt that the defendant and the defendant alone could be the only person responsible for the crimes.

"And when you get right down to it," Talmadge intoned soberly, "what does the state have? You can argue procedures and processes, hypotheses and theories, but in the end, what is there? A spot of blood in the trunk of a car that has been used by literally dozens of people, most of whom the police didn't even question. Now I ask you, ladies and gentlemen, with a man's life at stake, is that enough? I don't think so. You have a great responsibility here, and a great deal of pressure has been put upon you by the state to accept their theories without question. But I put before you, as citizens in a free society, that your real responsibility is to protect the rights of any individual who finds himself in the state's sights. You are the one thing that stands between our democratic republic and a police state. As tragic as the deaths of these two young women are, the state has got the wrong person. It's up to you to not compound a tragedy by doing further injustice. It's up to you to say to the state: 'No. You haven't done your job. You can't do this. It's not right and we won't let you.' My client's fate and life is in your hands. Treat it as you would your own. And I, too, thank you for your service."

As Talmadge sat down, a silence as heavy and as thick as fog descended on the room.

"General Collier," Forsythe said after a moment, "do you have any rebuttal?"

"Just one quick comment, Your Honor," Collier said, rising. He walked to the podium. "Ladies and gentlemen, I only want to emphasize one last point, and that is that the bloodstains in the car are directly linked to Sarah and Allison, and the night they were murdered, as the evidence has clearly indicated, that car was in the sole possession of the defendant."

Collier sat down. "Any motions before I begin the charge to the jury?" Forsythe asked.

Talmadge rose. "Your Honor, the defense moves for a directed verdict of acquittal."

"Motion denied. Anything else?"

Talmadge shook his head. "No, Your Honor. Nothing at this time."

He sat down as the words were coming out of his mouth, as if the last thing he expected was for the motion to be granted. Taylor sat there, watching, as the judge swiveled in his chair and faced the jury.

"Ladies and gentlemen of the jury," he began, "at this point in the trial, the evidence has been presented, and both the state and the defense have had the opportunity to summarize the points in their cases. It is now my responsibility to instruct you in the law and how you are to apply it in your deliberations . . ."

Taylor settled back as the judge droned on. She took a deep breath and let it out slowly, silently. It was out of their hands now.

The judge's charge lasted almost an hour, and then court was dismissed right before noon. The jury went straight into the deliberations room, their midday meal delivered by court officers.

Michael and Wes Talmadge, with the two younger lawyers, remained behind in the courtroom. Taylor walked over and stood next to them as they spoke in lowered, hushed voices.

"—just a waiting game now," she heard Talmadge say.

Michael turned to Taylor, his eyes meeting hers, and cracked a slight smile. She found herself suddenly feeling sorry for him, despite everything, despite the scenes her imagination had created over the past weeks, the scenes that were even more horrible than the actual crime-scene photographs. If he had done the things they said he had done, and she was almost certain that he had, then hidden beneath the surface of this intelligent, driven, gifted, and even beautiful man was a monster.

And yet he seemed at that moment supremely human.

"Are you hungry?" he asked.

She had to think a moment on that. "I'm not sure. But we probably need to try and eat."

Michael turned, faced Talmadge. "What are our options?"

"The court clerk has my mobile number, so as soon as the jury is ready, she'll call. We ought to try and go someplace quiet, someplace where we can be left alone."

"Do you want to get a bite together?" Michael asked. "I mean, after this morning I'd understand—"

"We should stay close by each other," Talmadge interrupted. Then he smiled, reached out and touched Michael's arm. "And don't worry about this morning. People say and do things in the heat and stress of a trial they sometimes don't mean."

"I appreciate that, Wes," he said. "I really do."

Carey walked down the hall toward them. "I've got the car out front in a loading zone. If we hurry, we can get out of here without drawing too much attention."

Outside, they waded their way through the herd of media, dodging microphones and questions, and hurried away in the car. Carey drove like an expert, weaving in and out of traffic, skating across two lanes of oncoming traffic and disappearing down a side street. They drove a few blocks into North Nashville into an area called Germantown, an older section of the city that had become trendy and fashionable over the past decade. Nestled in an old building across from a Catholic church was a small restaurant, dark and intimate inside, with exposed brick walls and an open fireplace in the middle of the room. Talmadge had arranged a table at the back of the restaurant, tucked away in a corner where they could eat unnoticed.

Taylor ordered a glass of wine and a bowl of French onion soup. The men all ordered drinks and steaks, as if celebrating the victory they had yet to win. Or perhaps it was the liberating sense of it all being over, out of their hands. Taylor didn't know, but she found her own spirits buoyed by the conversation and the wine. She ate the soup, marveling at the fact that her sense of taste had come back.

Only rarely did anyone make reference to the trial. "How long will the jury take?" Michael asked at one point.

"It's impossible to tell," Talmadge said.

"The usual expectation," Mark Hoffman said, jumping into the conversation probably as a result of his second bourbon on the rocks, "is that if they come back quick in a criminal trial, that's often bad news for the defendant. If deliberations take a long time, that means it's up in the air, anybody's game."

Talmadge looked down at his watch. "They've already been in over an hour. That probably means they've had time to eat lunch and take a preliminary poll. If we don't hear anything in the next half hour, then we know they weren't unanimous."

Taylor, on the back side of the table, next to Michael, her back to the exposed brick, picked up her wineglass, finished the last of the Merlot, and signaled for another. Taylor almost never drank during the day, but this was one day when it simply felt right.

Two hours later, they were all full and buzzing slightly from the alcohol. There had been no word from the court. Carey, who had indulged in nothing stronger than iced tea, drove them back to the courthouse, dropped them off, then headed for the parking garage.

Inside the courthouse, their footsteps echoing off the floor, their voices muted by the cavernous hallways, the group went back up to the third-floor courtroom. Inside the courtroom, a lone court officer was sitting at a table reading a newspaper. Talmadge looked at him, questioning. The officer shook his head and turned back to the paper.

"Holding pattern," he said to Michael and Taylor. "No word yet."

Taylor sat down on the hard wooden bench, the place where she'd spent more time than she ever imagined or intended the past few weeks.

"I'm so tired," she said absentmindedly.

"Me too," Michael offered. He sat down next to her. "When this is all over," he said, "when this is behind us, let's go back to Bonaire. Back to where we started. We can make a fresh start."

Taylor looked at him. "Does life give you that kind of do-over? Ever?"

"It can if we make it," he said. He reached over and brushed his fingertips across her cheek. "I want you very much. As much as I always have. And I've missed you."

She instinctively drew back. "Don't," she said. "Please don't."

He nodded, then turned away from her. A few seconds later, he stood up and walked back over to Talmadge and the other lawyers, who were huddled around the defense table.

Taylor felt as if she were dragging time behind her like a ball and chain. She looked at her watch—two twenty-five. An hour later, she looked at it again and only ten minutes had passed. The soup and the wine in her belly washed around like waves pounding sand in a hurricane. She thought for a moment that she might be sick, but then took a few deep breaths and steadied herself. She realized her hips and legs were going numb; she couldn't sit on this damn wooden bench any longer.

She walked out of the courtroom, pacing up and down the hallway, stopping and looking out the tall windows at the traffic and the milling crowds below. The news vans were parked bumper-to-bumper, all awaiting the verdict.

Michael and Talmadge walked out into the hallway and stood next to her. "How long will this go on today?" she asked.

Talmadge shrugged. "Forsythe's a slave driver," he said. "He'll make them go at it until dinnertime, anyway. My guess is he'll keep 'em here until they're too tired to work anymore, then he'll send them back to the hotel."

Suddenly, a group of people hurried past them. Reporters, hangers-on, spectators. Talmadge, Michael, and Taylor turned.

"What's going on?" Michael asked.

Talmadge shook his head. "I don't know—"

Then his cell phone went off. Talmadge jerked it open. "Yeah? When? Yeah, okay. We're on our way."

He snapped the cell phone shut. "Let's go."

"They're done? The jury's back?" Taylor felt her gut tighten.

Talmadge nodded. "Yeah."

Michael suddenly looked flushed, his face tense, his breathing rapid.

"You okay?" Taylor asked.

"Look," Michael said, "I've got to go to the bathroom. No matter what happens in there, I don't want to embarrass myself."

"Okay," Talmadge offered. "I'll go with you."

"No," Michael said. "This'll only take a minute. You go with Taylor."

"Are you all right?" Taylor asked again.

"I'll be fine. Just give me a minute."

Talmadge turned and started down the hallway. "Don't dawdle," he said over his shoulder. "We don't want to do anything to piss Forsythe off."

Taylor hurried to follow him. At the courthouse doors, Taylor pulled up behind him as they stood in the crowd trying to get in. She reached out and touched his arm. He turned, a serious look on his face.

"I'm scared," she said.

Talmadge looked directly into her eyes. "Me, too."

Once inside the courtroom, she fought her way to her seat and jammed herself in between two other people. The room seemed stifling. Talmadge and the other two attorneys sat at the defense table as Collier and his assistant, Jane Sparks, paced around the prosecution table. Court officers buzzed around, the clerk taking her seat at the table in front of the judge's bench. There was a din of background chatter and the shuffling of bodies vying for seats.

A court officer came over to Talmadge and said something. Taylor read his lips as he answered, "In the men's room."

Minutes passed, the energy in the room seeming to build by the second. Talmadge looked around nervously. A court officer came in through the doors to the judge's chambers. He looked over at the defense table, his face stern, almost angry, and crossed quickly over to Talmadge.

"Where's your client, Counselor?" he demanded. "The judge is waiting."

"He's in the men's room, damn it, the man had an attack," Talmadge said, his voice tense.

"Get somebody down there to check on him. Quick, or you'll have some explaining to do to the judge."

Talmadge turned and nodded to Hoffman. "Go get him," he said, his voice low.

Hoffman wove his way through the crowd quickly and disappeared through the doors. Taylor felt a lump growing inside her. She swiveled her head around, scanning the crowded courtroom. In the back of the room, standing against the wall, stood Agent Powell. Their eyes met and locked for a few moments, then Powell raised his left arm to his waist, pulled back his coat sleeve, and checked his watch.

Hoffman pushed through the crowd back to the defense table. He leaned down and whispered something in Talmadge's ear. The lawyer sat up straight, his body almost stiff, as he glared at Hoffman. Taylor stood up, leaned over the rail, and motioned to the defense table. Hoffman saw her and stepped over to the rail.

"What's going on?" she whispered into his ear.

He turned to her and cupped his mouth around her ear. "We can't find him," he said over the courtroom din.

"Oh my God," she said out loud. Hoffman shushed her, turned back to the table as the court officer came in once again from the judge's chambers. He bent down into a huddle at the defense table, his face darkening. Collier and Sparks, watching from the other table, suddenly stood and walked over to the group. Taylor watched as Jane Sparks brought her hand to her mouth in shock. Collier turned and walked away from the group.

The court officer backed away, pulled a Handie-Talkie from his belt, and spoke into it. A second court officer stepped over from the other side of the room and whispered something to the first officer, then turned and disappeared.

By now, the noise in the courtroom was rising as the press and spectators got wind of what was going on. People pushed and shoved, voices were raised. The court officer motioned for people to quiet down. The radio on his belt crackled loudly, and he held it to his ear for a moment, then spoke into it. A second later, he turned and strode quickly through the doors into the judge's chambers.

Taylor stood at the rail, staring. Talmadge turned to her, his eyes dark and serious, and shrugged his shoulders.

Moments later, the court officer reentered, his voice loud: "All rise!" he began.

Judge Forsythe came in behind him, his robes in a flurry, and immediately took his seat and began banging his gavel before the officer could even finish his spiel.

"Be seated!" he yelled. "Everyone take a seat, or I'm going to have this courtroom cleared immediately! Those of you in the back, stand against the wall and be silent. This is my last warning. I *will* have this courtroom cleared."

It took a few seconds, but order was quickly restored. Forsythe looked out over the bench and glared at the defense table.

"Counselor, produce your client," he ordered.

Talmadge stood quickly. "Your Honor," he said, his voice breaking. Taylor had never heard him sound like he was losing it before. "Your Honor, I—I can't. He was here a few minutes ago. He was in the bathroom. I—"

"Mr. Talmadge, I just gave you a direct order to produce your client. I'm going to hold you in contempt if he's not delivered to this court immediately."

"Y-Your Honor," Talmadge stammered. "I'm sorry, but I can't make somebody just appear if they're not here."

Forsythe turned to one of his court officers. "I want this building locked down immediately. Search the entire courthouse. Find him."

The court officer fumbled for his radio, then bolted from the courtroom through the judge's door.

"General Collier," Forsythe said, "do you have any suggestion as to how to deal with this most unusual circumstance?"

Collier jumped to attention. "Your Honor, has the jury communicated to you that they've reached a verdict?"

"They have."

Collier turned to the defense table, stared at Talmadge for a moment, then turned back to the bench. "Well, then, Your Honor, the state moves that the jury be brought into the courtroom to deliver its verdict!"

A murmur arose throughout the room. "Objection, Your Honor," Talmadge shouted. "The defendant is not here. You can't deliver a verdict without the defendant."

"Objection overruled," Forsythe snapped. "If the defendant's not here, it's his own damn fault, and if it's not his own damn fault, I intend to find out whose fault it is. Bailiff, bring in the jury."

Seconds later, the jury filed in, looking lost and weary. Immediately, they spotted the defense table. The looks on their faces became even more questioning.

"Ladies and gentlemen, we have an unusual circumstance here," Forsythe said. "We seem to have lost our defendant. However, this does not mean that the verdict cannot be delivered *in absentia*. So, Mr. Foreman, have you reached a verdict?"

The foreman, a thin man with gray hair and wire-rimmed glasses, stood. Before he could open his mouth, Talmadge was on his feet again.

"Your Honor, move for a mistrial, as the defendant's absence is highly prejudicial."

"The jury has already reached a verdict, Mr. Talmadge, before the defendant went missing. So how could it be prejudicial?"

"Move for a mistrial, Your Honor," Talmadge answered weakly.

"Motion denied. Answer the question, Mr. Foreman."

The thin man looked frightened as his glance jumped

around the courtroom. "Yes, Your Honor. We have."

"Would you hand your verdict to the clerk, please?"

The man held out his hand as the clerk approached and took the forms from him. She walked over, reached above her, and handed the papers to Forsythe. He scanned them quickly, his face expressionless, then handed them back to the clerk.

"Since the defendant is unable to stand and face the jury, his representatives will. Gentlemen, on your feet."

Talmadge and his two underlings stood.

"Clerk, read the verdicts."

"On count one of the indictment, a violation of TCA 39–13–202, first-degree murder of Allison May Matthews, we find the defendant guilty as charged . . ."

A muffled buzz filled the courtroom. Forsythe slammed his gavel down twice as the clerk continued.

Guilty as charged. Guilty as charged. Guilty as charged . . .

How many times, Taylor wondered, would she say that? A roar grew in her ears. She looked to her right and saw all the people around her staring at her. She looked up and watched as Forsythe banged his gavel over and over, almost in slow motion, his voice a roar now, too.

She felt herself swaying back and forth, as if the room were swirling around her.

Forsythe turned to the jury. "Ladies and gentlemen, as I explained at the beginning of this trial, this is a two-part process. Ordinarily, we would begin the sentencing phase of this trial now. But that's not possible. The constitution requires that a defendant be present to speak to the jury about any mitigating factors in his favor, and as we can plainly see, that is not possible. There are constitutional grounds for delivering a verdict *in absentia*, but that's as far as we can go right now. Therefore, I have no choice but to thank you for your long and difficult service to the court and to dismiss you at this time."

The jurors looked at each other, almost in shock, as if to ask, "Can we really go now?"

Forsythe slammed his gavel down again. "General Collier, I will issue an immediate warrant for the arrest of the defendant on any charges you draw up. Just do it quickly. And I assume the police are already in the loop on this, correct?"

"We're on it, Your Honor. As we speak . . ."

"Fabulous." Forsythe turned to the defense table. "And I'm going to hold you, Mr. Talmadge, in contempt of court. You're going to be spending the next forty-eight hours as my guest. Bailiff, take him into custody."

Wes Talmadge, in his eight-hundred-dollar Armani suit, looked up at the judge in shock. His mouth opened, but nothing came out. His hands were shaking and he held them out, palms forward, as if to ward off the court officer walking up to him. Then his hands fell to his side in defeat.

"Court's dismissed," Forsythe announced, banging his gavel as he stood up. "All rise," the court officer shouted, his right hand holding Wes Talmadge's arm.

Taylor stood up, her mind blank, her vision blurring. People around her were jumping, scrambling to get out of the courtroom, yanking out their cell phones, shouting at each other. A half-dozen people jostled her, almost knocking her over as she stood there gazing out at the courtroom pandemonium.

He's gone, she thought. *He really did it.*

Then she looked down at her own hands, held out in front of her, shaking slightly.

What do I do now? she wondered.

Then there was a hand on her elbow. She turned. A young, attractive Hispanic woman, dark-skinned, coal-black straight hair, stood next to her.

"Ms. Robinson?" she asked.

Taylor nodded blankly. "Yes?"

"Ms. Robinson, I'm Detective Maria Chavez of the Metro Nashville Police Department. You'll have to come along with me now."

"I will?" Taylor asked. "Why?"

"Because," the young woman answered. "We have a few questions for you. I'm taking you into custody as a material witness."

CHAPTER 35

Monday evening, Nashville

The room was cold, the fluorescent light above her harsh. An immense framed mirror dominated the opposite wall, but Taylor assumed it was a one-way mirror and that they were watching her from the other side.

Just like TV, she thought. *Now I know what it feels like . . .*

The room smelled stale, with the faint scent of body odor and cigarettes lingering in the air. She sat in a metal chair that was bolted to the floor. She'd been there almost half an hour and no one had entered the room. She hadn't been allowed to call anyone or talk to anyone.

Suddenly the metal door burst open, and a man in a gray suit walked in with a clipboard in his hand, followed by the young Hispanic woman and Agent Powell. She recognized the detective from the trial, but couldn't remember his name.

"Sorry to keep you waiting, Ms. Robinson," the detective said. "As you can imagine, this is a somewhat delicate situation for us."

Taylor watched as the detective slid into the chair across from her and slapped the clipboard down on the table. "Now, we've got a few questions for you, as I'm sure—"

Taylor cleared her throat loudly, then said: "And you are?"

The detective stopped. "What?"

"Your name?" Taylor demanded. "Who are you?"

The detective glared at her for a moment, then she could see him stuffing the anger away. "I'm Detective Gilley, ma'am. I'm the lead investigator in this case."

"I see. Then tell me, Detective Gilley, am I under arrest?"

"No, ma'am, you're not under arrest. Not yet anyway."

"Not yet," Taylor said. "Hmm, that means I might be before this is over. In that case, I want a lawyer."

"Ms. Robinson, you're only being questioned as a material witness. At this point, you're not entitled to a lawyer."

Taylor glared back at him. "*Everyone* is entitled to a lawyer."

The woman, Detective Chavez, spoke up. "Ms. Robinson, we're really just asking for your cooperation. Do you have any idea where Michael is? Right now, he's an escaped fugitive who's been convicted of a capital offense, and that's a very dangerous place for him to be. Anything could happen right now, most of it bad."

"Yeah," Gilley said, "believe it or not, it's in your boyfriend's best interest to come in and let us take care of him."

"He's not my boyfriend," Taylor said.

"According to our information, the two of you are engaged."

"Your information is out-of-date, Detective Gilley," Taylor said. "We used to be engaged. We're not anymore. In fact, we were through."

Gilley and Chavez looked at each other for a moment. "When did this happen?" Chavez asked.

"At the moment during the trial when I became convinced he was guilty," Taylor said. "At the point where I knew he'd done it."

"But why did you stay?" Chavez asked. "You stayed for the rest of the trial, stayed in the same hotel . . ."

"But not in the same room," Taylor snapped. "Never in the same room."

"But why didn't you leave?" Gilley asked.

Taylor looked up at Hank Powell as he stood next to the

closed door across the room. Their eyes met for a few seconds as Gilley and Chavez looked around, confused.

"Because I asked her not to," Powell said.

"What?" Gilley said. "Hank, you could've given us a heads-up on this, buddy."

Powell stepped over to the table and looked down at Taylor, never taking his eyes off her. "She came to me about three weeks ago, after the DNA testimony convinced her Schiftmann was guilty. She was upset, distraught really. She was going to leave immediately. I asked her not to. I was afraid that would be enough to push him over the edge, to make him run."

"Which he just did, goddamn it," Gilley said, exasperated.

"Thank you, Agent Powell," Taylor said softly.

Chavez turned back to her. "So you had no idea he was going to escape?"

"None, Detective. Part of what I agreed to do for Agent Powell was let you all know if I thought he was going to run."

"And he never gave you any hint?" Gilley asked.

"Never."

Chavez shook her head. "And you have no idea where he could be? What his plans are? Where he's going?"

"No to all of those," Taylor said. "He never even hinted to me that this was an option. If he had, I'd have called Agent Powell immediately."

Powell sat on the edge of the table, his hip resting on the edge, and leaned over toward Taylor. "Where do you think he'll go?"

Taylor rubbed her forehead. "I don't know," she said, sighing. "He may have some friends left in Cleveland, although with all this publicity, how anyone would actually help him is beyond me. And—oh my God—he's still got the keys to my co-op."

Taylor looked up, fear etched across her face. Powell held up a hand. "Don't worry, we'll have a team of officers watching your apartment and your office within the hour."

"And I'm having all the locks changed as soon as I get home."

Chavez smiled. "Yeah, good idea. But let me ask you, you think he might have been planning this all along? Or did he just get a sudden impulse?"

Taylor leaned back and studied the three officers for a moment. She took a deep breath, held it for a second, and then let it out slowly.

"Michael's a lot of things," Taylor said. "He's sick, maybe he's evil. I don't know. But he's not stupid. If I were placing bets, I'd say he had a plan in place weeks ago. He's put everything he needs, including a lot of cash, in some safe place where he can get to it quick. And I'll bet he already knows where he's going, and I'll bet he's already on his way."

"What kinds of resources has he got?" Chavez asked. "How much money does he really have?"

Taylor bent her head and once again wearily rubbed her forehead. "Well, Detective Chavez, thanks to me, a lot."

A cold, depressing sleet had been falling long enough to freeze on the sidewalks as Taylor and Agent Powell walked out the front doors of the Metro Nashville Criminal Justice Center. Taylor pulled her coat around her tightly. The wind had picked up, driving the icy mix into her face. Strangely, though, it felt good to her after the overheated stuffiness of the interview room where she'd been the past three hours. As they walked down the steps, Taylor realized she felt strangely hungry, and took this as welcome evidence she was still alive.

"C'mon," Powell said. "I'll take you to your hotel."

"I can take a cab," Taylor said.

"This is Nashville, not Manhattan. You can't just hold up a finger here and flag one down, especially on a lousy night like this. Besides, what if he's still around? What if he's hiding in the hotel, waiting for you?"

Taylor raised her face to the streetlights and let the frigid drizzle rake across her face. "Then he'd be a damn fool," she said.

"All the same, I've got a car. Let's go."

He took her elbow and guided her toward the street, then into the parking garage across from the police department.

Two rows down, a government-issued Ford Crown Victoria sat waiting. Powell held the door for her as she slid into the front seat.

"You're at the Stouffer, right?" he asked.

Taylor turned to him. "Yes, but to tell you the truth, Agent Powell, I'm getting hungry. And I could use a drink. Maybe another of those Stoly martinis we had that night."

Powell turned to her and smiled. "So are you saying you'd like some company?"

"You did say, didn't you, that he might still be out there?"

"All right," Powell said. "On one condition."

"Yes?"

"It's been a long day and my shift is over," he said. "It's not Agent Powell. It's Hank."

Taylor turned to him as he started the car. She had absolutely no idea why she had asked him to spend time with her. Maybe it was that he seemed kind, and right now, she could use some kindness. Maybe it was that she didn't feel like being alone.

Maybe she was afraid.

"All right, Hank," she said. "Call me Taylor. Glad to meet you."

Thirty minutes later, the waitress set two vodka martinis—olives for him, pearl onions for her—on the table in front of them. They'd found a quiet table, beyond a row of potted palms, in a corner of the hotel restaurant that was out of view of the main lobby. They'd taken their coats off; he'd loosened his tie. It had been the longest day in a wearying series of the longest days she'd ever had.

The vodka felt delicious burning down her throat.

"So what's next for you?" Hank asked, fingering his martini glass in an almost contemplative way. "Where do you go from here?"

Taylor took another sip of the drink before answering. "I don't know," she admitted. "I guess I'll go home, go back to work. Try to figure out some way to live with myself."

"Don't do that," he said. "Don't punish yourself for this. You were a victim."

"I could write a book," she said brightly. "*My Fiancé Was a Serial Killer!*"

"Oh, please," he said, grinning. "Please don't."

"You know, I always thought it would be fun to be a celebrity. Now I've found out in the worst way possible. I don't know how I can ever hold my head up again. My career is probably over. I can't stand the thought of people I meet whispering behind my back. Imagine the kinds of clients I'll get; every wacko with five hundred pages' worth of sadistic, violent, misogynist crap will want me to get him a million-dollar book deal."

She stared across the table at him, wondering why in hell she was willing to talk to him this way.

"And then," she said sadly, "I'll probably need to undergo every medical test for every disease ever discovered. There's no telling what I've picked up—"

Her voice broke. "—sleeping with him."

"Hey," Hank said, reaching across the table, taking her hand. "Stop it. C'mon."

He held her hand for a second, then pulled back. "Listen," he said, hesitating. "I don't know how much detail you want to know about all this. But I can tell you that if it will ease your mind, go ahead and see your doctor, but I don't think you have anything to worry about."

"What?" Taylor asked, studying him. "What do you mean?"

"It's like this. He's a smart guy. He's completely up-to-date on modern homicide techniques, DNA and forensic testing, the whole schmear. He knew the only way he could get away with this was to leave absolutely nothing behind."

Taylor held her hands out, questioning. "And that's supposed to mean what?"

"What that means," Hank said, "is that when he had . . . sex, with his victims—"

"You mean *raped* his victims," Taylor interrupted.

"Okay, raped his victims, that he used, well, protection."

"You mean he wore a condom not to protect them, but to keep from getting caught?"

Hank nodded. "Yeah."

Taylor picked up her drink and slammed the rest of it down in one gulp. "My God," she muttered, "just when I thought nothing else could surprise me. That son of a bitch!"

She looked up at Hank. "How many were there? How many total?"

"Thirteen we know of," Hank answered. "There may be more. We'll never know unless he decides to tell us someday."

Taylor's eyes went dark and she felt a murderous fury of her own welling up inside her.

"Catch the bastard," she said. "Catch the bastard and send him to hell."

CHAPTER 36

Tuesday evening, Manhattan

God, it felt good to be home.

At first, Taylor was nervous, anxious. She'd been gone for over a month. The housekeeper had been in once a week to water the plants and check on things, but the place still felt stale, musty, in need of a good airing out.

It was cold as well, the heat turned down to sixty-five degrees so long that the apartment was frigid to its bones. She got the maintenance man to come up with her, to go into her apartment alongside her just in case. But no one was there; the place was deserted. The maintenance man set her bags down in the living room, walked through once with her, turning on every light in the house, then left. The moment he closed the door behind him, Taylor felt a chill.

And then, without warning, it went away. She was home, finally, and she was blissfully, sweetly alone behind locked doors. Suddenly the stress of the past month or so melted away and she wanted nothing more than a hot bath and a glass of wine. She turned up the thermostat to seventy-five, then walked into the kitchen and opened the refrigerator. There were two unopened bottles of Chardonnay on the top shelf.

As she was twisting the corkscrew into the top of the bottle, she glanced over at the answering machine and was surprised the message light wasn't blinking. Then she remembered: She'd turned the machine off and muted the ringer on the phone. Anyone she wanted to talk to knew to call her cell phone; to hell with the rest.

As she was pouring a glass of wine, she heard the faint chirping of her cell phone buried deep inside her purse. She walked quickly back into the living room and dug through her bag. She flipped the phone open, didn't recognize the number, but decided to answer anyway.

"Yes?" she said.

"Taylor?"

Taylor smiled. "Oh, hi. How are you?"

"I'm fine. The question is, how are you?"

"I made it in just fine, Hank. No problems. The place was well-tended, although a bit stuffy and cold. There was no sign of anyone having been here but the cleaning lady."

"Good. I meant to ask you last night, what are you going to do with all his things?"

"God," she said, sighing. "I haven't gotten that far. What should I do?"

"I'd like to have one of my guys from the New York Field Office go through them. NYPD Homicide might want a shot as well. After that, it really doesn't matter. You can trash it all, give it to the Salvation Army."

Taylor walked back into the kitchen and picked up the wineglass. She held it up, staring through the buttery, almost golden liquid into the kitchen. The kitchen light diffused into a series of brilliant yellow circular halos.

"I guess he won't have any need for it, will he?" Taylor asked.

"Was he working out of your apartment?" Powell asked.

"Yes, he was working on another book," Taylor said off-handedly. Then her voice caught in her throat. "I guess that means he was reliving another—"

There was a long moment of silence broken only by the static on the cell phone. "Yeah," Hank said, breaking the quiet. "I guess he was."

"You know, I can't think about that right now," Taylor said brightly. "I'm sorry, but I just can't. I've got too much else on my mind."

"I understand," Hank answered. "But I want you to do

something for me. Seal off the room he worked in and hold it for my guys. I want to go through his computer hard drive, any archived material, all his papers and correspondence, bills and bank statements. Anything that might give us a clue as to what he's up to."

Taylor nodded. "Sure, I can do that. I don't want to touch any of it, anyway."

"Great, thanks. I can have my team at your place tomorrow morning."

"Not too early. If I can sleep, I'm going to as long as I can."

"You need it. So how was the flight?"

Taylor took a sip of the wine. It tasted like heaven in her mouth. "Good," she said after a second or two. "Any flight that got me out of there would be good. How was yours?"

"We were an hour and a half late into Reagan, but all that meant was that I missed rush hour."

"So," Taylor said cheerily, "you got home in time to have a late dinner with Mrs. Powell."

Hank cleared his throat. "There, uh, there isn't a Mrs. Powell," he said.

"Oh, divorced or never married?"

"I'm a widower."

Taylor felt like an idiot. "I'm sorry," she said. "I didn't know."

"How could you? Besides, it was a while ago. Life goes on."

"Kids?"

"Yeah," Hank said. She could feel his voice brighten over the phone. "Daughter. She's seventeen, goes to the same boarding school her mother went to."

"I'll bet she's beautiful," Taylor offered.

"Gorgeous. Looks just like her mother."

"Wow," Taylor said softly.

"Look, Taylor, there's something else. I debated whether or not to tell you, but for all I know it's already on the evening news."

Taylor felt her throat tighten. "What? What now?"

"We know he's got a car," Hank said.

She could tell he was choosing his words carefully. "How? How do you know that?"

"There was a homicide in Nashville last night," Hank said. When the words came across the phone, Taylor felt her head swim. "This time it was a guy, mid-thirties, dark hair. Height and weight about the same as Michael's. Dressed in a nice suit. They found him stuffed in a dark corner of the top floor of a multistory parking lot. When they found him, he had Michael's driver's license on him and no other ID."

Taylor leaned against the counter, trying to keep her balance. "Which means Michael's got his driver's license and his ID," she said.

"And his registration and his car."

"So go after the guy's car," Taylor said.

"We will," Hank said. "Just as soon as we get a positive ID on the victim. Right now, we still don't know who he is."

"God," Taylor said, her voice breaking. "That means some poor woman is sitting home with her kids wondering why her husband hasn't come home from work yet. Is he out messing around? Has he disappeared? Has he—"

"Taylor, stop," Hank interrupted. "Don't. It won't help anything."

She slammed the wineglass down on the counter. The stem snapped in two; the glass fell and shattered, splattering wine everywhere.

"I can't stand this, Hank! Damn it, I can't take any more!"

"We'll stop him," Hank insisted. "I promise you. We'll get him."

"Please," she said. "Before he does any more."

"You've got my number?" Hank said.

"Yes."

"I don't think you'll hear from him, but if you do, let me know. And don't get into it with him. Play along, then let me handle it from then on. Okay?"

"Yes," Taylor said, looking down at the mess she'd just made. "I will."

"And call me if you need anything else, or if you just need

to talk. And in the meantime, get some sleep," Hank said. "You need it. It'll be the best thing for you."

"All right," she said. "I will. And Hank?"

"Yes?"

"Thank you. Thank you for calling. Thank you for the dinner and drinks last night. Thank you for giving a damn."

"No problem, lady," he said. "S'why I get the big bucks."

Taylor Robinson went back to work the next day. She was in her office by nine, after a fitful night's sleep, determined to get her life back. She waded into the mountain of e-mail, contracts, phone messages, manuscripts, and paper that was piled neck-high on her desk. She met with Joan Delaney for an hour and a half, trying to figure out how to handle the detritus of Michael Schiftmann's career. Taylor was surprised—and then realized that she shouldn't be—that Michael Schiftmann's murder trial had sent his sales into the stratosphere. The publisher had never seen anything like it. They couldn't go back to press fast enough.

Web sites sprang up all over the world commenting on Michael's murder case, his books, the details of the Alphabet Man's crimes. One Web site was running a contest: Match the novel with the murder. Society's sick fascination with violence, cruelty, evil had never been more exploited.

But in her quiet moments, alone in her office, facing the stacks of work, Taylor wondered if she wasn't part of the process as well. When she was honest with herself, even she admitted that she couldn't read Michael's books; they were too cruel, too twisted. Early in their association, she had even let herself wonder what kind of man could write such things. Like everyone else, though, she was charmed with his looks, his manner, and his style.

Then the money started rolling in. *God, the money*, she thought. There had never been so much of it. Her family was well-off, she'd grown up well taken care of, even entitled. But she had never seen anything like it. She had to admit that she was as seduced by the money and the fame and the attention as she was by Michael himself; maybe even more so.

She wondered if she would have allowed herself to become so enamored of him if his books had flopped.

No, she decided. No way. But money and fame are seductive and arousing and thrilling, like a drug, like a blinding orgasm.

Blinding orgasms. She blushed. It embarrassed her to go there even in the solitude of her tiny office, but she had never in her life had sex like that. With Michael, her orgasms were not only literally blinding, but blinding as well to a great many other things.

Thank God, she thought, the blindness was temporary. She forced her mind to go elsewhere. There was work to do. It would be a long, long time before she felt like getting involved with anyone again, if ever. And she never expected—wasn't even sure if she wanted—sex to be like that again. Sex that good makes you stupid.

She buried herself in her work, opened up the piles of paper and dived in headfirst. At eight that first night, her assistant, Anne, stuck her head into Taylor's office and asked if she was ever going home. Taylor looked up, distracted. She hadn't realized it was so late and apologized to Anne for keeping her.

Days went by like that. After a week, the NYPD stakeout of her building went down to one uniformed officer. After the third day, she began to relax and return to her old routines. She bought food and cooked for herself again. She ignored the news, stopped following anything about Michael's case. After a while, she could even find herself going a few minutes at a time without thinking of him.

She still refused all calls from the news media, and after about three days, word got around and the calls slowed to one or two a day. There was a famous writer doing a long piece on Michael for *Vanity Fair*, and another equally famous one for the *New Yorker*.

"They'll just have to get along without me," Taylor told Joan over lunch one day. "I've got nothing to say to anyone about anything."

"Good," Joan agreed. "Let's just get back to selling books."

One big concern was what to do with Michael's next book.

The Friday afternoon after returning to Manhattan, Taylor cleared enough of the pile away to meet Brett Silverman for lunch. She caught a cab over to Central Park, where Brett was holding a corner table at Tavern on the Green for them.

Brett was already nursing a glass of wine when the maître d' led her over to the table. Brett stood quickly and opened her arms, then wrapped them around Taylor hard enough to draw stares from the surrounding tables.

"I have missed you so much," she whispered.

"Me, too," Taylor said.

The two sat down as the waiter came over. "May I bring you something to drink?" he asked. Brett pointed at her glass of wine.

"I don't usually drink during the day," Taylor said, then added, smiling: "Oh, what the hell."

"That a girl," Brett said. The waiter disappeared as Brett leaned in. "Okay, look, let's get right to it. I have no idea how much you want to talk about this, but I have to ask. How are you? Really?"

Taylor shrugged. "I've had some bad nights," she admitted. "A couple of times when I wasn't sure if I was going to make it. But you know the old saw, that which doesn't kill you—"

"Beats the crap out of you and nearly kills you," Brett interrupted.

Taylor found herself laughing in a way she hadn't in a long time. It felt good, as if a weight had been lifted from her.

"You know," she said. "You're right. It feels like this nearly killed me. But it didn't. I survived. And it feels great to be back at work and back here, and it's wonderful to see you again."

Brett smiled back at her, then turned serious. "Have they made any progress toward finding him?"

"You get the same news channels I do, honey. I haven't heard a word. There's an FBI agent that's been really nice to me. We've talked a couple of times since I got back. Last I heard, they had nothing."

"Amazing," Brett said, then she lowered her voice. "Where the hell do you think he is?"

Taylor shrugged again. "Who knows? He could be any-where."

"What was it like when he disappeared? Did they just go nuts down there?"

Taylor nodded. "It was pandemonium. The first thing the judge did was throw Michael's attorney in the slammer for contempt, then they hauled me in for questioning."

"*You?* What the hell did they think, that you helped him?"

"I think they were just more embarrassed than anything else. They should have been watching him a little better."

"God, I feel like for the rest of our lives, he's going to be the eight-hundred-pound white elephant sitting in the mid-dle of the living room that no one wants to talk about."

"I'm okay with it," Taylor said as the waiter brought her wine. "Really. This is all going to work out. It's going to be okay."

The two ordered lunch and made small talk for a while. Then the conversation turned to business.

"Jack decided to move up the pub date," Brett said.

"That's interesting. How come, as if I didn't know?"

"He'd be crazy not to," Brett answered. "Look, darling, advance orders for *The Sixth Letter* have broken all company records. We've never had a book come out of the blocks like this one."

"You know," Taylor said, a sadness settling over her face, "when I really think about it, I hate that so much money is being made off human suffering. It's evil what he did. We ought to give the money to the families."

"Let 'em sue him if they want to," Brett said. "But this is the publishing business, and it's a business fueled by this kind of media attention. We'd be crazy not to take advantage of it. You gotta make hay while the sun shines."

"I know," Taylor admitted. "Doesn't mean we have to like it."

"So that brings up another subject," Brett said. "All this money, the royalties, the sub rights income. Where's it going to go? If the author is an escaped fugitive on the run, where do we send the checks?"

"Joan and I met with the lawyers on Wednesday," Taylor said. "We've set up an escrow account to hold the money until he's caught—or whatever. At some point, I would assume the courts will have some input into where the money goes. I know they've frozen all his bank accounts. He couldn't get to the money even if we did write him a check. He's already had his passport confiscated. His options are really limited."

"Then what's he using for money?" Brett asked.

"Who knows? My guess is he had some stashed away somewhere."

Brett and Taylor lingered over lunch for two hours, with two more glasses of wine each, then coffee afterward. Taylor enjoyed the company, the chance to get away from the office and to simply get lost in a crowd of people where if anyone recognized her, they had the good manners to not acknowledge it.

Just after two-thirty, the two left and hailed separate cabs. They made plans for dinner the following Friday night and agreed to talk before then. Taylor was relaxed and drowsy as she settled into the back of the cab. The driver headed across town back to the office on East Fifty-third.

As he pulled to a stop in front of Joan Delaney's brownstone, Taylor's cell phone went off. She stuffed a ten-dollar bill through the tray in the clear plastic shield between the front and back seats, then scrambled out onto the sidewalk. She fumbled in her purse for the cell phone, then pulled it out and flipped the cover open.

"Hello," she said.

"Taylor," a voice said.

Taylor froze. Everything around her seemed to go quiet and still, the people around her shifting into slow motion, the traffic noise hushed.

"Michael?" she gasped.

CHAPTER 37

Thursday afternoon, Manhattan

"What're you— My God, where are—?" Taylor stammered. She felt like she'd been body slammed. It was all she could do to remain upright.

"It's good to hear your voice," he said, as if he'd been away on holiday.

"Michael, where are you?" she asked.

"I'm in the city. You'll pardon me if I can't be more specific."

Taylor's mind raced. How to handle this? What to say? What had Hank told her?

Don't get into it with him, he'd said. But what did that mean?

"How did you get here?"

"It's a long story, but let's just say I had to take a very circuitous route."

Yes, Taylor thought, *and how many dead bodies did you leave behind on the way?*

"Look, Michael," she said, trying to keep herself and her words calm, "why are you calling me?"

"Because I missed you," the disembodied voice said with a thin layer of cell-phone static over it. "And because I hoped you'd be glad to hear from me."

Taylor stood there. The wind picked up off the East River, funneled down through the city streets by the rows of buildings. She shivered, wondered if she should just walk on to the office, but she knew from experience that her cell phone wouldn't work inside the building.

The silence was broken by a low hiss and crackle. She wondered if she'd lost the signal.

"And because I need your help," he said.

"My help? Are you crazy? I can't help you, Michael. You need to turn yourself in. Get this over with. They're coming after you and they'll eventually get you."

"Turn myself in so they can kill me? Is that what you want?"

"They haven't passed sentence yet, Michael. You don't know that that's what's going to happen."

"C'mon, Taylor. You and I both know that if the state of Tennessee doesn't do it, somebody else will. They've got it in for me."

"Michael, what do you want from me?" Her voice stiffened, sounded cold even to her.

"I know things are over between us," he answered. "I've accepted that. But surely you can't want them to kill me. I have to get out of the country."

"They've got your passport!" she said. "You can't leave!"

"I can sneak into Mexico," he said. "And if I can get there, then I can go anywhere else. Someplace where they won't extradite capital cases. France, maybe. I don't know. I haven't gotten that far."

"That's crazy, Michael. How are you—"

"I need money," he interrupted. "Cash is the only thing that's going to get me out of here. They've frozen all my accounts. I can't even use an ATM machine. But I've got money hidden, Taylor. Overseas. Lots of it. Enough to disappear forever. All I have to do is get to it."

"And what about the girls, Michael? What about all those girls, and God knows who else?"

There was a long beat of silence before Michael spoke again. "I know what you must think, Taylor. But I really am not guilty of everything they say I'm guilty of. Besides, I've lost my taste for it. It was something that got out of control because of the writing, because I was so far into the writing. I've got it under control now, for good."

"You make it sound like a drug problem, Michael. But it wasn't a drug problem. You were killing people!"

"You don't understand, Taylor. You don't understand what it's like."

"Of course I don't. I hope I never do! There is no understanding, Michael. You were *killing* people."

"Look, I can't stay on this phone forever. They're probably listening now. So I've just got to come out and say it: Are you going to help me or what?"

"I don't know," she said softly.

"Taylor, how much money have I made for you and the agency and that damn publisher? You owe me. Just call it an advance on royalties. And besides, they'll kill me if you don't. And while I know you don't anymore, remember, you once loved me."

Taylor felt her head swim yet again. Would this ever go away, ever be over with? "Look, I don't know. I need time to think, Michael. I just need a little time to think."

"How much time?" he asked, his voice just on the edge of desperation.

"Call me tonight," she answered. "I'll be home after seven. Call me on my cell tonight."

"I'm trusting you, Taylor. My life's in your hands."

She cringed. "Don't say that, Michael. Please don't say that."

He clicked off, and the phone went silent. She stood there a moment, staring as the steady stream of pedestrians shifted to avoid bumping into her. Taylor held the phone out in front of her and squinted to read the screen in the harsh sunlight. She pulled the number up and didn't recognize the area code.

He could've gotten it anywhere, she thought. Could've taken it from anyone. . .

She hurried down the block to the agency, then up the stairs to her office. She pulled off her coat, locked her office door, then sat down at her desk. She stared out the window for a moment, thinking.

Then she knew what she had to do.

* * *

Four hours later, Hank Powell pulled up in front of Taylor Robinson's apartment in a nondescript sedan driven by Special Agent in Charge Joyce Parelli. At strategic points in the block surrounding Taylor's building, NYPD plainclothes detectives and dressed-down FBI agents kept watch over the neighborhood.

Taylor met them at the door in a white blouse and pair of jeans. She looked pale, Hank thought, tired and shaken. Her handshake was firm, though, as she took his hand.

"It's good to see you again," she said, shutting the door behind them.

"I'm sorry it's under these circumstances," Hank said. "Taylor, this is Joyce Parelli. She runs the New York Field Office."

Taylor nodded. "Hi. Pleased to meet you."

"Me, too," Joyce said. "So how're you holding up?"

Taylor led them into the living room, where her cell phone lay on the coffee table like a time bomb waiting to go off.

"I'm hanging in there," she said, "but frankly, just barely."

She turned to Hank. "I thought you said he wouldn't call me."

Hank shook his head. "I didn't think he would. I thought he'd be smarter than that."

"He's desperate," Taylor said. "He needs cash. He's got money out of the country, but he can't get to it."

"Did he tell you how much he needs?" Joyce asked.

Taylor shook her head. "No. I assume that'll come when he calls me tonight."

"If he calls," Hank said.

Taylor turned to the kitchen. "Oh, he'll call. Don't worry. I could tell it in his voice. I need a glass of wine. Are you guys off duty?"

Hank and Joyce glanced at each other. "I'm good," she said. "Don't need a thing."

"If you've got a can of soda," Hank said.

"Diet Coke okay?" she called from the kitchen.

"Sure."

Taylor came back in few moments later with a glass of

white wine and a tall glass full of soda and handed it to Hank.

"What am I going to do?" Taylor asked. "When he calls, what's the game plan?"

"A lot of that's up to him," Parelli said. "What he wants you to do and how he wants you to do it."

"Can't you just tap the cell phone and find out where he is, then go pick him up?" Taylor demanded.

"We can monitor the calls," Hank explained, "and we will. But especially if he's on a cell and moving around, which he will be, then it gets really tough. Unless he stands still and talks to you a very long time, then by the time we figure out where he is, he's not there anymore."

"Shouldn't you go ahead and move whatever equipment you need up here now?"

"We don't need anything up here now. We've got a van outside now that's got everything in it we need."

Taylor paced back and forth in the living room. "This is driving me crazy," she said, exasperated. "We've got to get this over with."

Hank, concerned, looked over at Joyce for a moment. Joyce made a slight motion of her head toward Taylor.

"Taylor," Hank said, his voice reassuring, "we need you to hang in there with us just a little while longer. When he calls, I want you to listen to him, be calm, and I want you to agree to anything he says."

He crossed the living room and stopped in front of Taylor. He reached out and touched her forearm. She stopped pacing and looked up at him.

"Can you do that for me? Can you help me with this?"

Taylor gave him a look that was half smile, half sneer. "Men . . . You're all just looking to get something for free."

Hank smiled back at her. "I knew I could count on you. Now, we wait."

Ten minutes later, the cell phone rang. Hank nodded at her. She hit the connect button and turned the volume up as loud as it would go. Hank stood next to her, straining to listen.

"Hello."

"Taylor?"

"Yes, Michael. I'm here."

"Have you had a chance to think about this?"

"Yes, Michael. I'll help you, on one condition."

"Yeah?"

"You use the money to get as far away from here as you can. Don't ever come back. Don't ever let me see you again."

"Don't worry," he said, his voice brightening. "I'm out of here."

"Now," Taylor said, "how much do you need?"

"I need at least a hundred thousand," he said. "In small bills."

Taylor looked up, her face tense. Hank nodded at her. "Keep going," he mouthed.

"That's a lot of money. I'll need some time to get it together. I can't just run out to a cash machine."

"How much time will you need?"

"The banks open at ten. I'll have to move a little money around between accounts. Maybe a couple of hours."

"That's fine. Noon, then."

"Where are we going to meet?" Taylor asked.

A few moments of scratchy silence followed. "I've always thought the easiest way to get lost was to wade into the middle of a crowd. Grand Central Station at lunchtime."

"Grand Central's a big place," she said. "How will I find you?"

"Go to the kiosk, that place in the middle of the main concourse."

"You mean the information booth? Under the big clock?"

"Yeah, that's it. Put the money in a bag and go to the center of the main level there. Keep your cell phone close by. I'll call you."

"And then what, Michael?"

"There's a million places to hide in there. We'll meet somewhere out of the way. You'll give me the bag. If I'm lucky, you'll kiss me good-bye. And that'll be it. You'll never see me again."

"It'll be over," she said softly.

"Yeah, over."

"Michael, where are you?"

"I'm in the city."

"But where in the city? Have you got a place to sleep? Have you eaten? Are you taking care of yourself?"

"Yeah, Taylor. I am. I'm fine. Thanks for asking."

"I'll see you tomorrow," she said.

Then she clicked off. Joyce Parelli smiled. "Nice touch."

"What?" Taylor asked.

"That 'Have you got a place to sleep?' 'Have you eaten?' 'Are you taking care of yourself?' Nice touch, make him think you still care."

Taylor glared at her. "What makes you think I don't?"

Hank Powell hoisted the handle of his heavy, industrial broom and maneuvered it around a series of metal wire wastebaskets that were in his way. The green coveralls he wore were thick and scratchy, much more uncomfortable than his usual work uniform of suit and tie. But the overalls were loose and rumpled, covering up the outline of the Glock 19 that was holstered under his left armpit.

Around him, the lunchtime crowd at Grand Central Terminal ebbed and flowed like a human river, the bodies moving in dozens of directions at once and, miraculously, somehow managing not to trip over one another.

The tiny earpiece wedged uncomfortably into his right ear crackled. "Six-Able," a voice said. "In position. Nothing."

"Roger," Hank said, bending his head down as he spoke, as if to focus on his sweeping.

He looked over, across the main concourse at Grand Central Station, to the center kiosk. A herd of people milled around, the massive information booth with the famous four-sided clock almost a magnet for the crowd.

Hank had lost sight of her, but he knew that somewhere close around the information booth, Taylor Robinson was standing nervously, trying not to seem too obvious, holding a zippered canvas bag containing a small fortune.

"Three-Charlie," the earpiece crackled again. "In position. Nothing."

Around him, in civilian clothes, disguises, custodial

uniforms—anything they could come up with—were two dozen NYPD detectives and FBI agents. Joyce Parelli was walking around with an armload of shopping bags, looking like a tired suburban housewife, frustrated because her train was late.

Suddenly the earpiece snapped again and he heard Taylor's voice as she answered her cell phone. They'd wired her so at least they could hear her side of any phone conversations. Outside the building, a crew manning scanners tied into the cell phone repeaters would tape the whole phone call.

"Yes," Taylor said into the cell phone.

Hank continued slowly sweeping, resisting the urge to look up. He scrunched his shoulder to press the earpiece into his ear harder.

"Where? Track 42? And then—?"

There was a long pause. "Okay, the escalator up to the Forty-seventh and Madison exit. Right before the escalator . . . You'll be there . . . Yes, yes. I understand . . . Yes, this concourse. Okay, I'm on my way."

Then there was a popping sound and everything went silent. Hank leaned down and spoke into the tiny microphone concealed behind the lapel of the coveralls. "It's Track 42, main concourse, the escalator out to Madison. Beta Team, converge. Alpha Team, cover the outside entrance. Charlie Team, you're backup. Let's do it."

Hank stood up straight and leaned the broom against a wall, then began walking toward the train tracks. As he wove his way through the crowd, he spotted Taylor off to his right, walking quickly, just ahead of him. He maneuvered his way across the concourse to a position directly behind her, perhaps twenty feet away. She walked quickly up the short flight of stairs to the long hallway with the track entrances on either side. Up ahead of them, Hank recognized two NYPD undercover cops standing against a wall, chatting like two old friends. They looked up and watched Taylor as she walked by, then moments later made eye contact with Hank. As Hank passed them, they casually split apart and began meandering down the hallway toward the escalators.

Hank's pulse quickened as he felt the net tightening around Michael Schiftmann. The one thing he was afraid of was that something would go wrong and people—especially Taylor—might get hurt. But he also knew that his agents and the New York City police officers were as well-trained as they could be. They were ready.

Hank watched as Taylor's pace accelerated. "Don't run," he whispered out loud. "Slow down."

The numbers above him grew. The track numbers were in the forties now. Ahead of them, the bank of escalators up to Madison Avenue were crowded but not packed.

Hank watched as a figure dressed in black crossed in front of Taylor. He strained to get a look. The figure stopped, reached out, said something to her, then grabbed the zippered bag and exploded away from her.

She screamed. Around her, a burst of noise erupted as a panic spread.

Hank ran, shoving people out of the way. "He's got the bag!" Hank shouted into his lapel mike. "Go!"

He got to Taylor inside of three seconds. "You okay?" he shouted.

"Yes," she gasped. "But—"

Another officer in jeans and a T-shirt ran up. "Stay with her," Hank ordered. Hank turned from her and ran toward the escalator.

"Hank, wait!" Taylor shouted.

Hank hit the escalator and started up just as he saw a trio of undercover officers with a man jammed between them at the top of the down escalator. Hank rode up the escalator until he was almost even with them, then jumped to the other side. The man they held wore a satin black running suit, his head held down close to his chest. Hank grabbed him by the hair and yanked his head up.

It wasn't him.

He looked up at the other officers. "Did you get the right guy?" he demanded.

"Yeah, who the fuck'd you think we got?" a voice shot out.

"It's not him, damn it!" Hank yelled.

Hank turned. Taylor was at the bottom of the escalator. As they approached, Taylor stood there, her arms by her side, her fists balled.

"That's what I was trying to tell you," she yelled over the din around them. "It wasn't him."

They piled off the escalator, the scrum of bodies jamming into one another in the confusion and pandemonium. The cops and agents, with the guy in the running suit held tightly between them, pushed themselves off to one side. Hank grabbed the guy and pulled him toward him. He was about Schiftmann's size, with black hair about as long as his. From a distance, it could have been him.

"All right," Hank ordered, leaning down in the guy's face. "What the hell were you doing?"

Hank suddenly realized the guy was terrified. "Jesus," he squealed in a high-pitched, nasally voice. "The guy didn't say nothing about no cops."

"What guy?" Hank yelled.

"I met a guy down in Union Square Park," he piped. "He offered me five bills to get the bag from this lady and bring it to him. He said it was some shit he needed from his old lady but he was under a restraining order and couldn't go near her. He didn't say nothing about no cops."

"Where is he?"

"He said we'd meet outside, on Madison." Sweat poured down the guy's face, his eyes wide in fright. "Honest, I didn't know I was doing nothing wrong!"

"Five hundred bucks to pick up a bag and you thought this was a stand-up deal," Hank spat. "What do you take me for?"

"Should we go after him?" one of the cops asked.

"Save your breath," Hank said. "He's gone."

He keyed the lapel mike. "All teams, stand down. We missed him."

The crowd around them was moving on now, life in Grand Central as back to normal as it ever gets.

"What's next?" Joyce Parelli asked.

Hank shrugged. Suddenly Taylor's cell phone went off. Taylor almost jumped, then turned to Hank, imploring.

Hank, startled, nodded. "Go ahead," he said softly.

Taylor punched the button to take the call and held the phone to her ear. Even over the ambient noise of the terminal, he heard a muffled voice coming over the phone sharp and hard. Hank leaned in as Taylor went gray, the color visibly draining from her face. She looked up at Hank, her eyes giving away a level of fear deeper than anything he'd ever seen. Then, dazed, she lowered her arm in front of her and flipped the phone shut.

"What?" Hank snapped. "Was it—"

Taylor Robinson swayed. For a moment, Hank thought she might faint. He stepped to her, put his hands on her arms to steady her.

"He said he's going to kill me," Taylor said, her voice so low he had to lean in to hear it. "He said I've betrayed him, and now he's going to kill me. Just like the others."

CHAPTER 38

Monday morning, Manhattan

Esmerelda Cardenas stepped off the bus at Twenty-third and Ninth Avenue and started up the block toward Twenty-fourth Street. The Monday morning Chelsea traffic was lighter than usual, she thought, as she adjusted the large tote bag on her shoulder so it wouldn't pinch her weathered brown skin.

She turned left on Twenty-fourth and continued on down the half block to Señora Silverman's house. Every Monday for the last nine years, she had taken a two-hour-long combination of subways and buses in from her apartment in Queens to clean the Señora's brownstone. The commute was long, but compared to some of her other houses, the work wasn't that hard. The Señora lived alone and had few visitors. She kept her house neat. It wasn't a hard house to clean.

Esmerelda had let herself grow fonder of the Señora than she was of many of her customers. Five years earlier, Señora Silverman had given Esmerelda a key to the house so she wouldn't have to come in so early. Now Esmerelda could sleep in until almost eight. The Señora was always at work by the time she got there. Esmerelda could take her time cleaning the house. The Señora had cable TV and let her make lunch. The Señora trusted her.

Esmerelda worried about her, though. She saw the enormous number of liquor and wine bottles that were thrown into the recycling bins. If the Señora lived alone and drank that much, she must be *borracha* every night.

Perhaps, Esmerelda often wondered, the Señora was lonely. Every woman, Esmerelda knew, needed a man.

She climbed the stairs to the front door and pulled a set of keys out of her tote bag. She unlocked the door and walked into the Señora's house. To the right of the front door was a keypad for the burglar alarm. Esmerelda started to enter the code when she noticed the alarm wasn't on.

Muy extraño, she thought. She hoped the Señora wasn't ill.

She locked the front door behind her, then walked through the living room and into the kitchen. She set her tote bag on the floor and looked around. The sink was full of dirty dishes, with dried, crusty food left out on both the counter and the kitchen table.

Esmerelda's brow furrowed. "Señora?" she called out. "Señora Silverman?"

Esmerelda heard only silence. She left the kitchen and walked back down the hall into the living room. At the foot of the staircase, she stopped and looked upstairs.

"Señora Silverman?" she called out again.

Worried, Esmerelda slowly walked upstairs, the creaking of the wooden staircase the only break in the silence. She got to the top of the stairs and looked around.

Nothing.

"Señora," she said, her voice softer. Esmerelda flicked the hall light switch and continued on, her footsteps muffled by the carpeted runner that ran the length of the hallway. The Señora's bedroom door was closed at the end of the hall. She stopped, put her ear close to the doorway and listened.

She knocked gently on the door. "Señora?" she asked again. "Señora Silverman?"

Then she reached out, took the doorknob in hand and twisted it. The door was unlocked. She pushed the door open. The first thing she saw was a large letter—N—smeared in red on the wall above the Señora's bed. Then she saw what was below.

Esmerelda Cardenas started screaming. She didn't stop for a long time.

"I can't stay here much longer," Taylor Robinson complained as Hank Powell held up the coffeepot, offering her another cup. "And I sure as hell can't drink any more coffee."

"You have to stay," Hank said. "It's too dangerous for you."

Then he smiled. "But you don't have to drink any more coffee."

Taylor paced around the small center room in the hotel suite she'd been in since the debacle at Grand Central Station Friday afternoon. Hank had spirited her away to a midtown hotel right after Michael's threatening phone call, where she'd been under constant guard ever since. A team of NYPD officers had been with her around the clock, with frequent check-ins by Joyce Parelli's team from the FBI Field Office.

"It's been seventy-two hours," Taylor said. "I can't live the rest of my life like this. I've got work to do."

"All we're trying to do is make sure you're around to do it," Hank said defensively. He shook a small packet of powdered creamer into his own coffee and stirred. "Look, Taylor, we can't take any chances. NYPD's front-burnered this big time. He can't hide forever. Sooner or later, he'll slip up. And this time, he won't get away. Why don't we just order some lunch? I can hang around until two o'clock or so, then I have to catch the Metroliner back to D.C."

Taylor stopped pacing and slid into a leather easy chair in the corner of the room. "I feel so damn helpless," she said. "As though my whole life is out of control. Everything I do, everything I think, everything period, is controlled by this, this *horrible* thing that's come into my life. I can't even think of him as a person anymore."

Hank sat down at the small table across from her and cradled the plastic cup of coffee between his hands. "I know this is hard, Taylor. For what very little it's worth, I think you're being incredibly courageous in dealing with this."

Taylor laughed bittersweetly. "Me, brave? I'm scared to death. I've never been so scared in my life."

Hank Powell's cell phone went off. He pulled it out of his jacket pocket and flipped it open.

"Powell," he said.

His eyes darkened and his jaw muscles tightened. "When?" he asked. He reached into his jacket and yanked out a small notebook. Cradling the cell phone in the crook of his neck, he took out a pen and opened the notebook.

"Give me that again," he instructed. "Okay, Twenty-fourth Street. Got it. Now where is that? Between Ninth and Tenth, right? Okay, I'm on my way."

Hank closed the phone and slipped it into his pocket. He studied the page he'd just written on for a moment, then closed the notebook. He looked up. Taylor was staring at him, hard.

"Twenty-fourth between Ninth and Tenth," she whispered, her eyes questioning.

Hank reached over, picked up the television remote, and pushed the power button. The screen flicked on instantly and he punched in the channel number for the local CBS affiliate.

The midday news was on. The attractive, young, blond, anchorperson appeared on the screen just as the artwork behind her changed from a large bus with a red line drawn through it to the outline of a body on a sidewalk, with the headline below reading: BRUTAL CHELSEA SLAYING.

Hank raised the volume. "Police are at this moment on the scene of a brutally vicious murder in a quiet Chelsea neighborhood," she said. "The body of a woman whose name is being withheld pending notification of kin was discovered just this morning by a cleaning woman, as WCBS's Katie Jackson reports live from the scene."

The station cut away from the studio to a live remote. Taylor and Hank watched as the screen pictured the block of Twenty-fourth Street between Ninth and Tenth Avenues. The street was jammed with squad cars, EMT vans, even a fire engine.

A young woman with short black hair stood in front of the

camera. "The quiet Monday routine of this sedate Chelsea neighborhood was shattered this morning by the discovery of a murder that even the most hardened investigators are describing as the worst they've ever seen. Police are refusing to confirm or deny reports that the gruesome slaying here on Twenty-fourth Street is the work of the Alphabet Man," she said.

"Oh my God," Taylor snapped. "Oh my God."

Hank turned to face her.

"It's Brett," she squeaked.

"Who?"

"Brett. Brett Silverman. Michael's editor. My friend . . ."

Hank turned back to the screen and stared hard for a moment. "Are you sure?"

Taylor nodded. "I've been to her house," she whispered. And then she began to crumple. Hank muted the TV and ran to her as she seemed to fold over in the chair. He helped her to her feet, her whole body shaking, loud wet sobs bursting from her throat.

"Why?" she gasped. "Why did he have to do that?"

Hank pulled her to him, his arms around her, her face pressed against his jacket. He held her tightly, afraid for not just her physical safety now, but for her mental state as well. *How much can one person take?* he wondered.

Then she seemed to go still for a moment, the shaking stopped, the breathing quieted. He held her still, his left arm around her shoulders, his right hand at the back of her neck, stroking her hair, trying to calm her.

She pulled away slightly and looked up at him. "I want to see her. I want to go to her."

"No," he said firmly. "You can't. Believe me, you don't want to."

"I have to," she insisted. "She was my friend."

He stepped back and put his hands on her shoulders, holding her still. "Listen to me. You don't want to do this. I can't let you. It's a crime scene. The police won't let you past, even if I agree."

"She was my friend," Taylor repeated blankly. "She didn't deserve this."

"No one did," Hank said. "None of them did."

They stood there a moment in silence. Then Hank glanced at his watch. "Where is that guy?" he asked, annoyed. "I'm sorry, Taylor, but I do have to go down there. NYPD Homicide is waiting for me."

"What?" Taylor asked. "The officer?"

Hank nodded. "The one who was outside."

"You said he could get a sandwich."

"Damn it," Hank muttered. "I didn't say he could take the afternoon off."

Taylor turned and walked across the room. She stopped at the window, staring outside for a moment. Hank watched her. She seemed okay now, as if something had settled down on her and calmed her. Maybe it was shock, he thought.

She turned. "Go," she said. "The officer will be back in a few minutes. I'll keep the door locked. Won't let anyone in."

"No," Hank said. "I can't do that."

"Go on," Taylor answered. "I'll be fine. You don't think I'd be stupid enough to open that door to anyone who isn't wearing a uniform?"

Hank watched her for a few seconds, thinking. "All right," he said. "But you'll keep this door locked and chained, right?"

Taylor nodded. "Don't worry."

"You'll call me later?"

Taylor nodded again. "Okay," Hank said, turning for the door. "I'll check in, too. And I'll let you know if anything happens."

"Yes," Taylor said. "Thanks."

Hank opened the door to her room and stood outside. "I want to hear that lock click and the chain hooked before I leave."

Taylor closed the door, locked it, and hooked the chain. She looked out the peephole as Hank stood there for a few moments, then turned and walked toward the elevator.

A minute later, Taylor put on her coat, threw her purse over her shoulder, picked up the zippered canvas bag that still held the hundred thousand dollars, and left.

* * *

Taylor pulled her coat tightly around her as she exited the hotel out onto the side street. A cab sped down the street with its dome light on. She held up a hand and flagged it down. Once inside, she gave the driver her address, then hunched down low in the seat and settled back for the long ride downtown.

She was still trying to get her mind around this. Brett, gone. How much had she suffered? How unimaginably awful had it been?

She thought she would die herself. She felt her heart clutch in her chest and feared, for a moment, that it would stop beating altogether.

Then it hit her. The cops would never stop him. Michael Schiftmann was too smart, too determined . . .

Too evil.

No one would stop him. No one could ever stop him. They couldn't stop him because they didn't know him. When he was first accused of the murders, when she first believed he was guilty, she had thought that she didn't know him.

But she did. She knew him better than anyone. She had lain in bed next to him in the middle of the night and listened to his heart beat. She had whispered her secrets to him in the darkness. He had whispered his secrets to her.

Apparently not all of them . . .

Despite that, she knew him better than anyone else. And she knew what that meant.

That if anyone was ever going to stop him, that someone would have to be her.

CHAPTER 39

"Pull over here," Taylor called from the backseat of the cab as the driver turned onto Crosby Street. The taxi pulled over to the curb between a delivery van and a battered pickup truck. The driver reached over to stop the meter.

"Wait," she said. The driver turned and gave her a questioning look. "Just sit here a second."

She leaned forward and stared out the windshield, scanning the block in front of her building. There were no uniformed officers to be seen, and no obvious plainclothes officers. She looked as far to the left and right as she could without seeing anyone who looked like a cop.

"Okay, thanks," she said after a couple of minutes, folding a twenty in half and handing it up to the driver.

She climbed out of the taxi into a biting wind and walked quickly down the block. She checked behind her nervously as she walked, trying to stay calm.

Once inside her loft apartment, she slipped around quietly from one room to the next to make sure she was alone. She'd had the locks changed, but she had to make sure.

Then she went to her bedroom, to the large closet that had been built into the room during the loft conversion. The closet was huge by New York standards, a real luxury and one of the reasons she bought the place. Lining the back wall of the closet was a series of shelves piled high with boxes and clothes.

She went to the far right-hand corner of the closet, to the top shelf, and felt around a stack of boxes. Behind the stack, pressed up against the wall, completely hidden from view, was a black plastic case. She pulled the case out from behind the boxes, her hands shaking, and carried it over to the bed. She set the case down and stared at it.

She hadn't seen it in years, not since she'd unpacked it after buying the loft and quickly hiding it in the closet.

Taylor reached down and unsnapped the two latches and opened the case. She heard herself suck in a sharp intake of breath as the lid came up.

Inside the case, lying in custom-fitted foam mold, was a world-class, competition .22-caliber Hammerli-Walther Model 203. It was the pistol Jack would have taken to the 1988 Seoul Olympics.

If he'd lived . . .

Taylor stared at it for what felt like a long time. It was the only thing she had left of her brother's, and she couldn't remember exactly how she wound up with it. Probably, she dimly recalled, it was because no one else could bear to take it and she couldn't bear to throw it away.

Jack had loved the pistol, and he had taught her how to use it.

She carefully pulled the gun out of the case and examined it. The blueing was a little worn, the grip dull with a couple of minor scratches. She pried one of the magazines out of the foam and turned it upside down. The cartridges were still there. She wondered if they were still good, but then pushed that thought from her head. This was Manhattan; simply having a pistol was a felony. It's not like she could go down to the corner market and buy another box of bullets.

She slid the magazine into the gun, then opened her purse. If she dumped most of the junk out, she could just fit the pistol into her bag.

As she pulled out her cell phone, it went off. Startled, she fumbled to open it. On the screen was another number she didn't recognize. She hit the connect button and held the phone to her ear without saying anything.

She listened to the silence for a long time before it was broken.

"You should have heard her scream," a voice said. Michael's voice. "It was exquisite."

Taylor felt dizzy again. She grabbed the headboard with her free hand to steady herself. She took a deep breath, let it out slowly, then spoke.

"I've been waiting for your call," she said softly, evenly.

"I sliced off her clit with an X-Acto knife," he whispered.

Taylor reached over and picked up the pistol. It felt solid, heavy in her hand.

"And I'm next," she said. "Right?"

He laughed. *My God*, she thought, *the son of a bitch is actually laughing at me*.

"Oh yes," he said. "You're next. We're going to have a lot of fun."

Taylor gritted her teeth, hard. "Listen to me, you disgusting fuck. You're not laying a finger on me. Remember? I'm the one with the bag. I'm the one with the hundred thousand in small bills. I'm your ticket out of here."

"You mean there was actually money in that bag?" He sounded almost incredulous.

She stood up, the cell phone in one hand, pistol in the other. "Hell, yes, you sick perverted pile of dog snot. And I'm through making deals with you. I'm the one calling the shots now. Here's how it's going to go down. If you want to get out of here alive, you'll take the money and disappear. I'm buying my life back for a hundred thousand dollars and I want you out of it. That's the deal. If you don't take it, I'm coming after you. I'm coming after you and I'm going to kill you, I'm going to cook you, and I'm going to fucking eat you. Understand?"

There was a long silence over the phone. "My, my," he said finally. "I've never heard you talk like this before. It's kind of arousing."

"Make a choice," Taylor said. "You got one shot to live. Take it or leave it."

"This is a side of you I've never seen before," he said.

"You're running out of time, Michael," she snapped. "Make up your mind. Yes or no."

"Okay," he said. "Cool your jets. It's a deal. But this time, I'm not running if you're not alone. I spot a cop or another of those FBI pricks, then I'm just going to kill you before they take me out. We both go down together."

"Where do we meet?" Taylor demanded. "Let's get this over with now."

"No," Michael said. "Not in the daytime. Tonight."

"All right," Taylor said. "You call me at nine o'clock tonight. Don't be late."

She hit the disconnect button and flipped the phone closed.

Taylor looked down at the pistol in her hand. She wasn't shaking anymore.

Hank Powell stripped off his booties, mask, and latex gloves, then stepped outside the front door of Brett Silverman's brownstone and walked quickly down the steps to the sidewalk. He needed air, fresh air, and he needed it badly.

He'd never seen anything like this. Horrible didn't even begin to describe what he'd seen upstairs. He didn't even want to begin to think about what the victim had gone through.

One of the plainclothes NYPD Homicide detectives walked up to him as he leaned against a cast-iron fence that ran the width of the property. "You okay?" he asked.

Hank looked up at him. "Yeah, just got a little light-headed. I'm okay."

The detective pulled out a cigarette pack and held it out to him. "No, thanks," Hank said. "Gave 'em up years ago."

The cop nodded toward the murder scene. "Be a good day to start again. You ever seen anything like that?"

Hank shook his head.

"We had a uniform actually throw up in there. Guy'd never seen a homicide scene before."

"Oh, Jesus." Hank winced. "Imagine that being your first one."

Hank's cell phone went off. He pulled it out of his coat pocket and flipped it open.

"Powell," he said. "What? What the hell are you talking about? Goddamn it, you were supposed to be watching her!"

The detective watched as Hank Powell's face grew red and—even in the cold, heavy wind coming off the Hudson River a few blocks away—his forehead broke out in a sweat.

"Well, when the hell did it—" Hank paced a few feet away. "All right, damn it, look, get out an APB or whatever the hell you can do. Send a squad car to her building. She'll probably go there first. We've got to find her, and quick."

Hank flipped the phone shut. "Everything okay?" the detective asked.

"I've got to go," Hank said. "It's hit the fan."

He spotted Joyce Parelli coming out of the brownstone and ran up the stairs to meet her. She, too, looked drawn and shaken.

"What's up?" she asked.

"Taylor Robinson's disappeared."

"Christ almighty!" she snapped, her eyes widening. "How the fuck did they lose her?"

"C'mon, let's head for her place."

Joyce followed as Hank started for the corner of Tenth Avenue and Twenty-fourth, where Joyce had left the car earlier. As they walked, Hank pulled out his cell phone and dialed a number.

"C'mon, damn it, answer! Taylor, pick up the phone."

Taylor Robinson stopped in the entranceway of her building and stared out through the dingy glass. It looked clear outside, as far as she could tell. She walked outside, past a building almost completely covered in a rainbow of graffiti, up to the corner. She flagged down a cab and climbed in. As she did, she looked out the back window of the taxi.

An NYPD blue-and-white squealed to a stop in front of her building. Two cops jumped out and ran to the front door.

The taxi pulled away. "Where to, lady?" an older, dark-haired driver asked.

"East Side. East Sixty-second."

"Which block?"

"All the way over. The Bentley Hotel."

"Oh, yeah. I know it."

Taylor tried to sink into the seat. As the taxi pulled to a stop at a light, her cell phone went off again. She flipped it open, recognized the number as Hank Powell's, and hit the button to send the call to voice mail.

Right now, she didn't want to talk to anyone.

Twenty-five minutes later, the cab pulled up in front of the Bentley, a small boutique hotel where Delaney & Associates had an account. Inside, she tracked down her contact in the sales department and arranged for a room to be held in Joan Delaney's name, hinting that some big celebrity author was coming into town and didn't want to be noticed. Taylor took the key and went upstairs.

They gave her a tenth-floor room looking east. She locked the door and opened the draperies. The room looked out on the Queensboro Bridge, the traffic streaming across it in a continuous line as the afternoon rush hour approached. Taylor lay down on the bed and tried to relax. She mentally calculated how much sleep she'd had since Michael called her Thursday afternoon. An hour here, a couple of hours there . . .

She felt numb all over, numb and brittle. She felt herself dozing in and out for a while, then suddenly realized she was getting chilled. She kicked off her shoes and pulled back the covers, then eased under the blanket, staring out at the city lights as the sun went slowly down.

Soon, she drifted off.

When her cell phone went off again, she awoke with a start. She felt a sharp spike of panic. Where was she? Outside the window, the brilliant scatter of lights off the bridge and the surrounding buildings looked like gun bursts. She fumbled for the phone, hit the connect button.

"Yes," she said, trying to sound awake.

"Am I late?" Michael's voice sounded relaxed, professional, far too calm for the circumstances.

Taylor looked at the clock. "No."

"So where are you?" he asked.

"Uh-uh," she said. "No dice. You just tell me where to meet you."

He sighed. "All right, but you don't have to be so paranoid. We have a deal in place. This will all be over within a couple of hours."

"Let's skip the small talk, Michael. Just tell me where I need to go."

Silence punctuated by static was all she heard for a few moments. "Okay," he finally said, "ever heard of Pier 57?"

Taylor squinted in the dim light. "Down on the West Side? That abandoned pier where they locked up the protesters?"

"That's it. Go to West Fifteenth and the West Side Highway. Get out directly in front of the building. Facing the front, you'll walk to your left. On the left side of the building, you'll find a place in the chain-link fence where you can peel the fence back. Go through there, then you'll see a door to your right that's been yanked off its hinges. It'll be dark, so be careful. Come through that door and onto the pier. It'll be like you're inside this massive garage. Just stand there. I'll be waiting."

"Isn't it kind of creepy down there at night? Aren't you afraid of running into security?"

Michael laughed. "What security? It's an abandoned bus garage on a pier. They check it a couple times a night. That's it."

"It'll take me a while."

"I'll wait. And remember, Taylor. Come alone. I see you with anybody else, then I'm taking out you and as many of them as I can before I go."

"I know that Michael. I know that."

"Just remember, and—"

Taylor closed her phone and went to the bathroom to rinse off her face. She needed to be completely awake for this.

* * *

Pier 57, Taylor thought with a twinge, was only about ten or twelve blocks away from Brett Silverman's brownstone. Obviously, Michael had become familiar with the area.

It had been years since Taylor had been down to this part of the city. Over a decade ago, about the time Taylor moved to Manhattan, developers moved in and began revitalizing an area that had been run-down for decades. Many of the old piers had been restored and were now restaurants, art galleries, even a golf course and bowling alleys. But there were still pockets of the Hudson River waterfront that were empty and desolate.

As the taxi pulled to a halt in front of the massive, multistory pier that had once been a depot for cruise liners from around the world, Taylor realized that Michael had found the perfect place to disappear. A few short blocks away, the sidewalks were filled with people enjoying a night out, even on a cold late-winter night like this. Eight or nine blocks to the north, literally thousands of people might be at the Chelsea Piers complex.

But not here. "Hey, lady," the driver said, turning around. "You sure you want out here?"

Taylor nervously stuffed some cash into the cab's money tray. "Yes," she answered. "I'm sure."

She held the canvas bag tightly in her left hand as she exited the taxi, then pulled her purse tighter around her right shoulder. She felt the weight of the pistol as it bumped against her side.

The cab pulled away, its taillights shrinking as it disappeared into the darkness. The streets weren't totally dark; an orange, sulfurous glow from the streetlights filled the air. She smelled the dank, organic odor of the river wafting in from a hundred feet or so way. A traffic light at the intersection of West Fifteenth and the West Side Highway blinked a piercing yellow.

She stood in front of a hulking, dilapidated building that had been an MTA bus depot when the cruise liners stopped coming, but had recently gained an infamous reputation as

"Little Guantánamo" during the Republican convention of 2004, when rumor had it that the Republican National Committee leased the structure and then loaned it to the police as a holding facility for arrested protesters. Jutting from the street out more than seven hundred feet into the Hudson River, it was filthy and decrepit, as well as full of toxic chemicals leaked from the buses and asbestos falling from the decayed structures. Pier 57 was no place anyone would want to go.

Which, Taylor surmised, was precisely why Michael had picked it.

She stood there a moment, mustering her will, and then walked to her left, under the broken letters on the building that spelled out DEPARTMENT OF MARINE & AVIATION, CITY OF NEW YORK. At the left front corner of the building, a chain-link fence topped by razor wire kept pedestrians from actually going out onto the pier. She stepped close to it, walking into the shadows, squinting hard to see where she was going.

She got to the fence and looked at it closely, then reached out and touched the metal. It was cold and wet, either from condensation or slime; she couldn't tell which. Her senses seemed heightened, as if she were suddenly aware of every sensation around her. The wind picked up off the river. Behind her, she heard a distant siren. From a window somewhere nearby, loud hip-hop blared.

She tugged at the fence, gently at first, then harder. Near one of the metal fence poles, the chain link peeled up like the edge of a tin of sardines. She felt her heart pounding in her chest. Ahead of her, she heard something splash in the river, then water lapping against the rotting poles jutting up from the river.

Taylor pulled the chain link up from the asphalt as hard as she could, then ducked under it. A few feet down the building, in the dim light she saw the outline of a metal door. She stepped over to it quickly and saw that it had been torn loose from its hinges, then propped loosely back in the doorway.

She reached out, touched the metal doorknob. It, too,

felt slimy and cold. She shuddered, wished that she'd worn gloves. Her hands were stiff and cold now, as well as filthy. She pulled the door away from the door frame with a loud, painful screech of rusty metal on rusty metal. The door clanged as it spun around on one edge and slammed into the edge of the frame.

Taylor froze, terrified. She could turn around, run for the street, head for the light, scream her head off and hope someone heard.

No, she thought. *No, this has to end.*

Taylor stepped through the metal doorway, her senses instantly assaulted by the dank smell of mold and dust mixed with the metallic chemical stink of grease, spilled fuel, decades of rust and rot. She took a few steps and paused, listening, giving her eyes a chance to adjust to the darkness. She still held the canvas bag in her left hand. It seemed to grow heavier now. She instinctively reached into her shoulder bag with her right hand and caressed the wooden grip of the pistol.

She stood there for what seemed like a long time. The only sounds were the lapping of the river against the sides of the pier and the distant din of traffic. She heard no sound inside the building.

But she knew he was there. She could feel him, sense him.

She debated calling out his name and chose to remain silent.

Her eyes were dilating; she could see the dark outline of shapes now—columns, windows, a wall to her right a few feet away, and farther down that wall, a hallway.

Something scraped against the concrete. She jerked toward the sound.

There was a snapping sound, then light. It was painfully bright, directly in her eyes. She turned her head away, squinting.

And there he was.

Michael stepped out from behind a column perhaps fifteen feet away, with an electric lantern in his right hand. He leaned over and set the lantern on the concrete floor. Taylor forced herself to look at him, to focus. He had dyed his hair blond and grown a scraggly beard. He wore a torn T-shirt and a ripped denim jacket, with a filthy pair of jeans and a scuffed pair of motorcycle boots. He looked dirty, thinner. The wealthy, famous New York Times best-selling author had disappeared into the anonymous sea of New York City's homeless.

"Hello, Taylor," he said, his voice even, calm.

"Michael," she answered.

"It's good to see you," he offered. "I've missed you."

Taylor watched him silently. He took a step toward her, then a couple of steps to the side, as if circling her. "I've got your money," she said. She swung the bag back and forth with her left arm like a pendulum, then let it go toward him. It hit the concrete with a scraping sound that echoed through the building.

She saw him smile in the dim light as he bent down to the bag. He unzipped it, pulled it open, and looked inside. "Wow," he said softly.

"It's over," Taylor said. "Go now."

He yanked the zipper, closing the bag with a jerking motion. He stood back up, his right arm behind him. "Well, there is one little bit of unfinished business," he said.

When his right hand came back around in front, he was holding something dark, oblong. He flicked his wrist and a snapping sound rang out.

Then Taylor saw it. The weak light from the lantern glinted off the blade in a spark. Taylor felt a lump in her chest, somewhere deep down inside her, at her core. The blade was long, as long as his hand. He smiled as he held it.

"I had so much fun with her the other night," Michael said. "She was the best of all. You'll be even better."

"Why did you have to pick her?"

His smile widened even further. "C'mon, it's every writer's fantasy, killing your editor." He stood there for a moment, motionless. Then he took a step toward her.

"You didn't really think I was going to let you leave here, did you? After the way you betrayed me? Left me? Surely you're not that stupid."

"No," Taylor answered. "I'm not that stupid. I never imagined you'd keep your word."

Taylor pulled her hand out of the purse, the Hammerli-Walther gripped tightly. She pointed it at Michael as his smile disappeared.

"Where did you get that?" he asked.

"This is over, Michael," she said. "I'm going to get my phone out of my pocket and call the police. And you're going to stand there while I do."

His smile came back. "Oh," he said, meanly, "your brother's pistol. What was his name? Jack? Yes, Jack. The brother you killed."

"Shut up, Michael. Just shut up." Taylor reached inside her coat pocket for her cell phone. Michael took a step toward her. "Stay there," she ordered.

He shook his head. "No, Taylor. I'm not going back to jail. You'll have to kill me."

He started walking toward her, the knife held out in front of him. "Stop, Michael!" she barked. "Get back over there!"

He kept coming. She raised the pistol. "Stop!"

Ten feet away now . . .

"Stop!"

Two more steps. She sighted down the barrel, drew in a breath, as Jack had taught her, then let it out slowly and squeezed the trigger.

A sharp metallic crack erupted as the hammer hit the dead cartridge. Misfire.

She screamed, turned to run. He grunted, lunged for her. She threw the pistol at him, missed, then swung her purse at him, hard. The leather strap caught his outstretched hand and got tangled in it. They both jerked away hard.

In the darkness, the knife fell, clattering on the concrete.

He was on her now. She held out her arms. He swung wide, caught the side of her head. Taylor went down on the concrete, her shoulders and back taking the brunt of the fall. She gasped as the breath was knocked partially out of her.

He jumped on her, furious, his eyes wide, grinning horribly. She threw up a leg, trying to kick between his legs, and missed. But it threw him off balance. He landed only partially on her.

She tried to roll away, but he was too fast, too strong. He grabbed her shoulders and slammed her into the hard floor, the back of her head snapping against the concrete. She heard a noise, a strange, ugly combination of a yelp and a moan, then realized the sound was coming from her.

He straddled her chest, his hands around her neck now, squeezing hard, like a vise on her throat. In the dim light, she saw him smile down at her, the light glinting off his teeth. She felt a rage inside her she'd never felt before, a rage so powerful that for a brief moment, it even overcame her fear. She fought and bucked and scratched at him, but he held on, smiling meanly down at her.

"Let go, baby," he whispered. "Just let go."

Taylor felt her vision dimming, sparkles tingling in her peripheral vision. A thought raced through her mind.

He's actually going to do this!

She kicked her legs in the air as he sat on her chest, strangling her. She was flailing now, helplessly, uselessly. Then she felt her right foot hit something loose on the floor and she kicked involuntarily again, dragging whatever it was closer to her.

Her arms were slapping at him. Still he stayed on top of her. She brought her right arm down beside his leg, flapping like a child making snow angels.

Then she felt it. Her right hand brushed against it, her fingertips retaining just enough feeling and control to realize what her legs had kicked toward her.

The knife.

The handle was hard, cold. She felt it with her fingertips, just out of reach.

But her vision . . . She couldn't breathe, her throat closed off, the sparkles. Couldn't think. *Can't think anymore.*

She squeezed her chest as hard as she could to raise him up just a hair, then kicked her legs, scraping her body just a little to the right.

Her fingers wrapped around the knife handle. In her hand now . . .

All going black.

She brought her arm up, then swung, wide and hard, the knife blade sparkling in the light as it slashed in slow motion across and in front of her, above her, at Michael.

He jumped back, loosening his grip on her throat. She sucked in a huge gulp of air as the thin line across the front of his neck widened into a pencil's width.

"You fucking bitch!" he screamed. He let go of her completely and brought his hands to his neck, just as a spurt of oily, syrupy thick blood erupted in a shower across the front of his chest and onto Taylor.

He tried to jump to his feet, but stumbled and fell backward, landing on his hips on the hard concrete. She jerked upright, rubbing her neck with her left hand, the knife held tightly in her right.

She saw his face in the yellow lantern light as he looked down on his chest, blood pouring out of his neck. He glared up at her. "Jesus," he squeaked. "Look what you did."

"I'm sorry," she gasped, her voice broken and choked. Her neck ached, the back of her head pounded. "But you were going to—"

His hands were clasped tightly around his own neck now, trying to staunch the rhythmic spurts. "Oh God," he said, his voice softer, staring down at his own blood.

She scrambled to her hands and knees, trying to stand up but too weak. She crawled toward him. The blood had soaked the front of the T-shirt, his pants, the concrete floor in front of him. She moved toward him, her hands sliding in the wetness.

"Do something," he said. "Do something."

"Jesus, I don't know what—"

Suddenly he rolled backward onto the concrete. Taylor crawled over to him, the knife still in her hand. She threw it as hard as she could away from them. It clattered on the floor somewhere behind the lantern.

She put her hands on his shoulders. "I'm sorry," she said.

The flow of blood had slowed, his body relaxing, as he stared up at her.

"I don't feel good," he said, almost childlike. His eyes drifted left and right, his eyelids fluttering.

His hands loosened from around his neck and slid to his side. Taylor Robinson took his hand in hers, on her knees next to him, as the light in his eyes dimmed.

"I just wanted them to remember me," he whispered.

Taylor squeezed his hands, blood all over her now as well.

"Don't worry," she said. "They will."

EPILOGUE

"My God, it's as beautiful as you said it was," Taylor Robinson said, laughing, as she gazed out the front windshield of the rented Chrysler.

Next to her, in the driver's seat, Hank Powell turned and smiled at her. It was wonderful to hear her laugh again, he thought. "See, I told you."

"I thought I'd never seen anything as beautiful as the trees on the drive up here, but now this . . ."

"Fall in upstate Vermont," he agreed. "There's nothing like it."

He pulled the sedan into a visitor's space in front of Blackhurst Hall, the largest dormitory on the campus of the Butler School. Completed in 1921, the building more closely resembled an eighteenth-century Georgian mansion than an antiseptic dormitory. Modeled after The Hall at St. Hilda's in Oxford, Blackhurst was home to one hundred and fifty female upperclassmen, including Hank's daughter. Taylor felt like she was back in England as she exited the car.

The air was crisp and fresh, saturated with the smells of autumn. There was a slight chill in the air. Taylor pulled her field jacket around her a bit tighter. She looked around admiringly.

"The campus is really beautiful," Taylor said.

"Jackie loves it here," he said.

"Where do we go?"

"Well, I called her a couple of hours ago, when we stopped for gas. I told her we wouldn't make it for lunch, but we'd be at the game." He glanced at his watch. "As it turns out, the team has a mandatory game-day lunch, so we wouldn't have seen her anyway. Game starts at two. We've got a few minutes. Want to walk around?"

"Sure, I'd love to see more."

Taylor hooked her arm inside Hank's as they began strolling down a long sidewalk that ran to the main part of campus. They passed other students, parents, groups of people walking around enjoying the day.

"I really am glad you called me," Hank said as they wandered among the trees, surrounded by the brilliant oranges, browns, reds of fall.

"I'm glad you were willing to talk to me after all this," she said. "I just had to do what I had to do."

"So how was—what was it, five? six?—months in Europe?"

"At first it was awful," Taylor admitted. "I was so crazy I couldn't stay in one place for more than a few days. Looking back on it now, I think I must have had some kind of post-traumatic stress thing going on. But after a while, it slowed down and I noticed that every day seemed to get a little easier. First I could only go a few minutes without reliving it all, then it was a few hours. And then one day, in France, I think it was, on the Côte d'Azur, I woke up one day and realized I hadn't thought about him or that awful night for days."

They walked on, Taylor holding his arm, the leaves rustling around them. "I think it was then that I started to feel alive again."

"So what are you going to do?"

Taylor shrugged. "I don't know. I'm still taking it a day at a time. Joan Delaney's been great. She's given me a leave of absence from the agency. I can stay gone as long as I need to."

"That helps," he said. "Having an understanding boss always makes life easier."

"Problem is," Taylor continued, "I'm not even sure I can go back there. With all the publicity—hell, the infamy—associated with this, I'm just not sure I can ever be effective anymore, let alone happy. It's too much pressure. I want something quieter."

"Can you afford to just walk away from it?"

Taylor nodded. "For now. I have an agreement with Joan that my compensation is based on a percentage of the money my clients bring in, even if I've left the agency. And Michael's books are selling better than ever, or at least they did for the first few months after he . . . he died. I feel a little guilty taking money that way, but there's no denying there's been a ton of it."

"I don't think you should feel guilty," Hank said. "You didn't do anything but your job. You're supposed to get paid for doing your job."

"I guess so," Taylor said. "Maybe in this case I did my job a little too well."

They walked on, through the center of campus, past the old gothic buildings, the new library. "I've even been thinking about putting my co-op on the market," Taylor said. "With Manhattan real estate prices going through the roof, I could make enough to live on for years."

"And now that you don't have to pay capital gains on a lot of it," Hank commented.

"Yeah, it makes a lot of sense."

They walked on a bit farther in silence. Then Hank spoke up.

"I'm going to be making some changes myself," he said.

"Yeah?" Taylor asked. "What's going on?"

"Well, my dear, I am going to retire."

Taylor laughed. "What? That's ridiculous. You're too young to retire."

"I've got my twenty years in," he said. "And I've had it. All the heat I took for pursuing this investigation really soured me. This whole business of the FBI now being all about 'counterterrorism,' the 'war on terrorism,' blah blah blah. It's a bunch of political horseshit, to tell you the truth. What happened on 9/11 was awful, nobody's doubting that. But those of us in the trenches know that it was a crime committed by a bunch of thugs who should be tracked down and blown away. The politicians have used this as an excuse to pursue their own agendas. And meanwhile, the rapists and the thieves and the extortionists and the blackmailers and the serial killers get a pass because we're too busy chasing Muhammad the Bomb Thrower."

Taylor looked at him, surprised. "My, my, I've never seen you on your high horse before."

Hank laughed. "Telling the suits in the front office to take this job and put it where the sun don't shine is tremendously liberating."

Taylor clasped his arm a little tighter. "So we're both kind of at loose ends, aren't we?"

Hank nodded. "Yeah. Life takes some funny turns sometimes."

He stopped beneath a towering maple tree heavy with desiccated leaves turning the most amazing rainbow of colors. He turned and faced her. "I'm really glad you were willing to come up here this weekend with me. I've missed you."

Taylor smiled. "I appreciate your understanding of the separate rooms thing," she said. "I wanted to see you and meet your daughter, but I'm just not sure I'm ready for anything else yet."

"I'm not trying to put any pressure on you," he said. "We'll just see where it goes."

"Yes," she said softly. "Let's just see where it all goes."

He took her arm again and pulled her along as he walked briskly. "We've got to hustle," he said. "The game starts in a few minutes."

They crossed the central part of campus, to a broad expanse of area that held the sports fields and the gymnasium. The gym was old, almost run-down, but behind it was a state-of-the-art track surrounding a well-groomed soccer field. They climbed a slight rise and there it was, the girls from Butler uniformed in green gathered at one end of the field, stretching and loosening up, and their opponents in red down by the other goal. A crowd of perhaps two hundred partially filled the bleachers.

"Jackie!" Hank called out, waving his arms.

Taylor watched as a tall, slim girl with long brown hair and an athletic frame turned, spotted Hank, and began running toward him. She ran with a finely tuned athletic ease, a loping, relaxed grace that suddenly made Taylor feel quite old.

"Daddy!" she squealed as Hank took her in his arms and lifted her off her feet. Taylor stood off to the side, smiling at the obvious joy the girl took in seeing her father.

Hank settled her back down on the ground and turned her to face Taylor. "Jackie, this is the friend I was telling you about, Taylor Robinson. And Taylor, this is my daughter and the captain of the Butler School's varsity soccer team, Jackie Powell."

Hank's daughter grinned shyly. "Don't, Daddy, I'm just co-captain."

"It's a pleasure to meet you," Taylor said, offering her hand. The girl took it, shook it warmly.

"She's pretty, Dads. You did well."

This time, Taylor blushed shyly. "Yes, she is," Hank said, "but we are just friends and I don't want you to make anything else out of it."

"Right, that's why you brought her up here on parents' weekend," Jackie said. Behind them, a whistle blew loudly. "Oops, gotta run! You're staying for the game?"

"Of course," Hank called as she trotted away. "And dinner afterward!"

The players gathered in the center of the field, lined up against each other. Another whistle blew and the game started. Hank's daughter was on the line, the right side, and she took a pass cleanly and expertly from the center and began moving it downfield.

As the game began, Taylor entwined her arm through his, holding on to him as they stood on the sidelines next to the bleachers.

"She's beautiful," Taylor said. "She looks like that picture you showed me of Anne."

"Yes," Hank said. "She's just like her mother. In a lot of ways . . ."

"You must be very proud of her."

Hank pulled his arm loose from hers, then draped it across her shoulder and pulled him to her. "Yeah," he said. "I am."

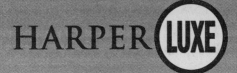